Sanctuary

Alan Janney

@alanjanney
ChaseTheOutlaw@gmail.com

First Edition
Printed in USA

Cover by MS Corley
Artwork by Anne Pierson
ISBN: 978-0-9962293-5-7

Sparkle Press

Dedicated to my sons

Jackson
and
Chase

Prologue

Teresa Triplett
Online Blog.
December 3rd, 2018.

First things first.

Mom, Dad, Justin, Anne - I'm alive. Alive and being treated well. I've begged them to return my phone, just for a few minutes, so I could contact you but it's no use. I'm sure the waiting and wondering has been torment. It has been for me, unable to hear your voices. I truly believe I'll be home in the near future. I love and miss you.

I am a prisoner of the Chemist here in Los Angeles. During the upheaval, intruders stormed the television studio and threw me into the back of a van. I remained there for thirty-six hours, expecting to die any moment. Eventually the violence quieted and I was brought to the Inner Sanctum (his words) to meet the Father (his words). He informed me I was chosen due to my previous interactions with the Man in the Mask.

The Chemist has been a gracious host, almost baffling in his politeness. He calls me his guest, and I'm afforded every luxury. Except freedom. I'm constantly followed, and kept inside a locked hotel room much of the time.

He also captured Elijah Floyd (the photojournalist) for visual documentation, and Elijah stays in the hotel room opposite mine. He's been a tremendous source of strength and determination through this time of despair.

On to business - The Chemist brought me here to be his chronicler, or memorialist. I'm recording everything he says and does into a running narrative, some of which will be released in real-time onto the internet. What you're reading now is the first real-time installment. Elijah took the photograph. (Don't judge my appearance. I haven't been to my stylist in a month. I miss you, Ross.)

Much of what I record is edited out each night. I'm not permitted to use names or places or anything too specific. So I don't know exactly what this report will look like in its final form.

In fact, I've just been ordered to delete my first significant observation. (It was Outlaw related, I can tell you that. I don't see how that poor man will survive much longer.)

Here is my second observation: if America doesn't take the Chemist seriously, the country will cease to exist as we know it...

Sanctuary
Among Monsters

Love is a madman
working his wild schemes
tearing off his clothes
drinking poison
and now quietly
choosing annihilation
-Rumi

Chapter One
Wednesday, July 1. 2018

"Here it comes." Samantha Gear set her jaw in simmering anger. She was glaring eastwards through a 15x50 tactical telescope.

"I see it."

She dropped the scope and asked, "You can see that?? Already your eyes are better than mine. I hate you."

An old C-160 churned through the Los Angeles haze, just ahead of coming dusk. The cargo plane was miles away, above Montebello, but I could see the oily smoke trail and hear the engine cough. It had been sitting at a Canadian airfield for several years until this final flight. In order to land, the plane would fly directly over our heads. We were hidden beside the Los Angeles River, on a Home Depot rooftop overlooking a police-barricaded bridge that lead to Compton, California.

A madman had captured the city of Compton. His forces took the world by utter surprise and effectively walled themselves in with destroyed automobiles, congesting a complete circle of interstate around their territory. He called himself the Chemist and no one had seen him in over three months, although he regularly communicated with authorities to discuss the release of prisoners in exchange for food. The military had attempted retaking the city three times. All three were highly criticized failures, resulting in massive death among the insurgents, the military, and the hostages.

The inbound C-160 was the second cargo plane this week. The Chemist had chosen his kingdom well; Compton had an airstrip. Gunmen loyal to him were commandeering cargo planes from all over the globe and landing them at the small Compton/Woodley Airport, bringing in fresh troops, hostages, ammunition, and ingredients for the mysterious and powerful drug the Chemist supplied his forces with. All the incoming cargo planes carried hostages so the government couldn't shoot them down.

"That's the biggest plane yet," Gear noted, watching the approach. "Too big for the little airstrip?"

"Too big to take off, but not too big to land," I said. "The Chemist doesn't care if it rumbles off the far side of the runway. They'll break it down into parts. Fortify their strongholds." Most of the smaller cargo planes had been unloaded and taken off again, quickly set on autopilot, and then abandoned via parachute.

"How are we going to stop these supply planes?" she growled behind her scope.

"I haven't figured that out yet." I turned my attention back to the city, towards the setting sun. "Puck, have you tried seizing control of the plane's autopilot?"

A male voice crackled in both our earpieces, "Of course, stupid. No such luck. Plane is too old. Even if I did, they'd start executing hostages until I released."

We stewed in silent frustration for several minutes while the big plane slowly banked and roared over our heads. The pilot was evidently not accustomed to the weight of the C-160; the plane's altitude dropped too rapidly on approach. The propellers sped up to compensate, but the landing gear touched down hard and the nose wheel collapsed. The metal screamed across the tarmac, sparks flying, while the pilot mashed the brakes and killed the engines.

"Damn," Samantha Gear grunted when the big airplane finally came to rest in a cloud of smoke at the far end of the runway, almost out of sight. "Wasn't pretty. But he got what he needed and that's all that matters. Every shipment makes it harder for us to remove him."

Life in Compton was surreal. From our vantage point we could see children playing in the fading sunset, parents chatting on street corners, and men walking home with groceries. Daily activities carried on largely undisturbed, despite the police barricades and enemy gunmen patrolling the streets and rooftops. What else were the people to do? They'd been hostages for over a hundred days.

PuckDaddy, the world's most feared and skilled computer hacker, blurted into our ears, "Heads up, here comes the jeep."

I squinted against the sun. Samantha Gear focused her scope on an intersection across the river in enemy territory. Usually PuckDaddy monitored everything from security cameras but the Chemist's henchmen had systematically disabled them all, so he was forced to watch from a top-down satellite feed. A brown jeep came rumbling down Caldwell and swung onto Atlantic without pausing at the stop sign.

"You're right, Puck," I said. Even at this distance I could tell the jeep's driver was a girl with tight cornrows, trendy sunglasses, and a serious scowl. She looked sinister and ready to fight. "That's our friend Carla. The girl Samantha shot. Definitely Infected."

Samantha grumbled behind the scope, one eye screwed up. "I refuse to acknowledge that you can see that far."

PuckDaddy crackled, "Stop being a stupid baby. Got a visual on target?"

"I confirm. That's her."

I asked, "Could you shoot her from this distance? Not saying we *should*."

She sniffed, "Of course I could."

"In the head? While she's in a moving jeep?"

"Probably."

I watched the brown jeep until it disappeared around a corner. "I don't condone shooting people. But for the Chemist, I could make an exception."

"Wouldn't matter," she said, stuffing the scope into her bag. "Carter says the Chemist can hear bullets. Whatever that means."

"Is Carter going in tonight?"

She shrugged and replied, "Who knows. He never tells me anything. You want to go?"

"No," I yawned. "I'm tired. Had to get up early for football. The last thing I want to do is crawl around Compton all night looking for that maniac's hideout."

PuckDaddy chuckled and said, "I can't believe you're tired just because you got up early. I haven't slept in almost three days, dummy. PuckDaddy rules." He was perpetually listening to the conversation through our bluetooth headsets.

Samantha said, "And I can't believe you're still playing football."

I frowned. "Hey both of you. Shut uuuuup. I still have a life."

"Yeah, but *football?*"

"I admit the game has lost some of its luster. But I want to beat the Patrick Henry Dragons this year. Besides, it's better than *shooting* people with wax bullets for *sport.*"

"No," she shook her head. "No it's not. And anyway, you have an unfair advantage on a football field. Playing football for you is more like...shooting fish in a barrel. With a shotgun."

I countered, "I don't cheat. I'm playing within normal high school parameters."

"Wait till the games start, quarterback," she said. "The disease won't let you play easy. It'll be craving action so badly you'll be consumed."

"What about you? You're on the football team too."

She scoffed and said, "I'm just the kicker. There's no chance I'll become nightly news. And if you quit the team then I will too."

"No deal. You shouldn't be playing anyway. You're, like, super crazy old."

She snarled and said, "I'm twenty-nine. I'm young and hot and you always check me out. And watch your mouth or I'll punch out your teeth."

PuckDaddy interrupted, "Hey dummies, you gotta move! Contact, coming out the stairwell!"

"What?!" Samantha hissed as we scrambled to our feet. The last thing we needed was for someone to see the two of us on top of Home Depot. "You said no one comes up to the roof."

"They usually don't. Don't yell at PuckDaddy! Just go over the side."

We were too late. An Army infantry man walked around a big silver air vent, whistling to himself, and stumbled to a stop. He was wearing urban fatigues, a sidearm clipped to his belt, and he'd been adjusting the lens on a powerful digital camera. The kid was clearly here for Compton recon photos. He stood completely still and stared, the blood draining from his face, and his mouth worked noiselessly.

I was dressed as the Outlaw: black pants, black and red vest, and a black and red mask. It might have been the most recognizable costume on the planet.

"What..." he said finally. We didn't move and we didn't respond. "But...but...but are you...?" He indicated my outfit. I nodded. "I...we...we thought...the whole world...the whole world thinks you're dead."

"And it's important we keep it that way," Samantha Gear told him.

"Are you really him?"

"I am," I confirmed. I always enjoy this part of the gig. He was just a kid, not much older than me.

"The Outlaw!" he stammered.

"I told you not to wear that," she shot at me. I shrugged.

"Wow...man, I...wow."

She glared at him and said, "Can you keep a secret?"

"This is..." He shook his head. "This is...I gotta..." He reached for his radio.

Samantha *Moved*. She was beside him in the blink of an eye. Her hand clamped onto his.

"Listen Corporal...Turner," she whispered into his ear. He turned very white. Samantha wasn't tall, but she acted tall. Tall and dangerous. She passed for a high school senior but she *felt* older. "Have you seen what happens when the Marines send their best teams into Compton?"

Corporal Turner nodded, peeking at her from the side of his eye. Samantha was pretty but she was also the most intimidating girl I'd ever met, like a hawk. I didn't blame the kid for being nervous. I glared at him to heighten the overall effect. "Yes ma'am."

"What happens, Corporal Turner?"

"We encounter enemy resistance. Sustain heavy casualties," he said.

"You *lose*."

"We lose," he confirmed.

"Do you know why?"

"Yes ma'am. The hostiles we encounter are, ah… they're…they're like you." His voice wavered.

"That's right. They have soldiers that aren't natural. Right?"

"Right. Yes, ma'am," he nodded. Beads of sweat were forming on his forehead.

"Just like the Outlaw. And just like me. Right?"

"Yes ma'am."

"Pretty soon the Outlaw and I are going in there. We're going to deal with those hostiles," she was hissing into his ear. It was theatrical and it was working. "It's going to be awful, Corporal Tuner. Bloody and awful and a lot of people are going to die. And our job will be a lot harder if you start blabbing about the Outlaw being alive. Right?"

"Yes ma'am."

"Right?"

"Yes ma'am!"

"So serve your country. And keep your mouth shut." He didn't respond so she started squeezing his hand. "Can you do that?"

"Yes ma'am. Yes ma'am, I can."

"What are you going to do?"

"I'm going to serve my country, ma'am, by keeping my mouth shut."

"God bless you, soldier," she said. She shot me a look and we went over the side before he could move.

Back in March, the planet had changed forever.

Monsters exist!

And the monsters live among us.

No one could view the helicopter footage of the showdown in Compton and reach any other conclusion; Hyper Humanity was real. Or aliens. Or both. And they'd fought each other to a terrible stalemate.

(Terms such as 'superhuman' and 'superhero' were quickly dismissed from the lexicon of serious discussion. Those phrases carried too much of a silly pop-culture connotation. The more prestigious news shows began calling the unexplained condition 'Hyper Humanity.' A clever writer altered the expression to Hyper Sapien and it stuck.)

The most infamous Hyper Sapien was the Outlaw. He had defeated dozens of masked gunmen within the close confines of a clogged interstate, leapt onto a streaking helicopter, faced down the Chemist, and engineered a massacre by jumping forty feet into the air. Plus a bunch of other stuff the grainy video couldn't confirm. However, the Outlaw had been vaporized in an explosion trying to save a teenage girl.

Or so it appeared.

I am the Outlaw. Very much alive.

But I wasn't about to tell the media this. The Outlaw would stay hidden in the shadows for as long as he could.

That left a host of unidentified shadowy characters that were more…reticent in their use of special abilities. One of the host, the most charismatic and vocal, planted his throne in Compton and daily held sway over the news channels. But where were the rest?

Earth wouldn't sleep soundly until that question was answered.

Fifteen minutes after jumping off Home Depot, I was zipping through downtown Los Angeles on my electric motorcycle, wearing a jacket and helmet over the Outlaw getup.

"What's Corporal Turner doing now?" Samantha asked through the headset. We were miles apart, traveling in different directions.

"Still on the roof," Puck answered.

I grinned. "Might be crying. Poor guy."

"Whatever. He's a big boy. In the Army. He can handle it. He better, or I'm going to hunt him down."

"Find me the Chemist, Puck," I said. "I have a promise to keep. Get me in there."

Puck sighed in frustration. I could hear him typing. "I know, I'm trying, I'm trying. One of these days."

"Good bye, weirdos," I yawned and I turned off the headset. PuckDaddy would track my phone and regularly report my position to Samantha. They'd grown increasingly paranoid and protective, which felt...nice, I guess. Most of the time.

My bike was running low on energy. It ran fast and silent, but it also murdered the battery. I charged it only two days ago. My house was too far away, so I pulled into a massive mid-city storage building and walked the bike to the large and lonely units in the back.

The Outlaw's hideout was an industrial storage unit. Classy!

I rolled up the large metal door and pushed the bike in.

Natalie North's voice pierced the darkness. "I *knew* it!" she cried. I almost fell over in surprise.

Natalie, America's Princess, one of the most sought-after celebrities on the planet, and also one of its highest paid movie stars, was sitting on the Outlaw's bed. She looked astonished. And furious.

"I knew it!" She swung off the bed and stormed towards me.

"Hi Natalie..." I offered, backpedaling.

"Don't even *Hi Natalie* me!" she seethed. She pushed me out of the unit and into the hallway. "I could *kill* you! I cried for weeks. Weeks! And all you had to do was text me. Just once!"

"You're right-"

"Shut up!" She hit me in the shoulder with a tiny fist, and she winced. "I watched you die. You and the pretty blond girl. We *all* watched you die. I cried on live television. You knew I was mourning for you!"

My whole body winced at the mention of the pretty blond girl. Hannah. I'd been so close to reaching her, but the fire got there first. Sometimes I still felt like I was falling. "I'm really sorry-"

"Shut up again! It's been months, and you didn't bother to message me?" Big tears were rolling over her cheekbones. "I wouldn't have told anyone!" She hit me again. "You know you can trust me."

"I know," I said lamely.

"I couldn't come down here. I tried. So many times, but I couldn't come say goodbye. I was still holding out hope. Like everyone." She jabbed me with a finger. "So today I decide to come down, and what do you know!?" she shouted. "It looks recently used!"

Her voice was echoing down the metal hallways. I dropped the helmet, scooped her up before she could protest, and carried her inside. She didn't fight me. I balanced her with one arm so I could haul down the rolling door, and then I sat on the bed. She looked up at me.

"I'm sorry," I said simply, quietly.

"I forgive you," she sniffed. "And you can kiss me if you want."

"I'm in love with someone else. If it's any consolation, you're even prettier than I remember."

"Does she love you back?"

"No," I sighed. "I really am sorry, Natalie. I wanted to tell you. But I thought the Outlaw might be gone for good. And his death would be a…natural goodbye. I've missed you very much."

"Liar."

"No, I really did. You were the Outlaw's only friend for a long time."

"The Outlaw has other friends now?" she asked. "The individuals in the videos? The Hyper Sapiens?"

"Yes. Some of them."

"I'm so glad you're back," she whispered. "I thought you died. I've been so scared."

We sat in silence for a long time. I was exhausted. The only light came from a table lamp. Eventually she said, "Los Angeles feels foreign now."

"Aren't you making a movie in Canada this summer?"

"Yes," she smiled. "You keep up with me, even though you're dead?"

"I follow you on Twitter."

"You're all we discuss on set. Well, you and the others. The whole

Compton debacle," she said.

I stifled a yawn. "Are you done filming?"

"No, I fly back in four days. The director gave me a week off. I'd been shooting for 35 days straight."

"Why'd you come back?"

"Actually," she said with an embarrassed smile. "Keep this a secret…"

"Okay."

"I'm dating someone here."

"Oh! That's great!"

"I think so!" she beamed. "But the press doesn't know. So hush."

"I guess I really shouldn't be feeling jealous," I mused.

"No, please do. I'm only dating him because I can't have you."

"Who is he?"

"That was a terrible thing for me to say," she said, chewing on her lip. "He's a good man, and I'm hopelessly fond of him."

"I probably don't know him, huh? I'm not very good with celebrities."

"You know him," she nodded.

"Is he in your movie now?"

"No," she grinned. "He's Isaac Anderson."

"Who? Isaac Anderson? …wait, the *FBI* guy??" I cried and stood up, almost tossing her onto the floor.

"Yes."

"The guy that's trying to *arrest* me??"

"No," she reminded me. "You're dead."

"Oh…yeah. Right."

"Silly."

"Anderson is a handsome guy, if I remember correctly."

She nodded and said, "The handsomest. And he's very nice. And kind. And sweet. And good. And he mourned the Outlaw's demise."

"Did he?"

"He did. He was a big fan."

I protested, "Still, I don't think you should be dating the FBI guy."

"You're in love with someone else, Outlaw," she glared at me. "I mooned over you for seven months, and then grieved for another two. You had your chance. And you were dead."

"How did you two end up together?"

She shrugged and said, "He called me and asked me."

"Just like that?" I asked. Dumbfounding! Impossible!

"Just like that."

"It's not that easy," I shook my head, and plugged in my bike. Night had fallen and I needed to get home.

"Have you tried? With the girl you love? Asking her?"

I took a long time replying. The truth was scalding. "No."

"Then you are a fool." She smiled.

"I know."

"You should ask her."

"I know."

"Tonight," she pressed.

"Okay. I will."

And I was.

Chapter Two
Wednesday, July 1. 2018. Later That Night.

Katie Lopez is changing, the way people do when they grow up. She's just doing it…better.

Unless something drastic intervenes, Katie will be one of our school's valedictorians. Her intelligence and superior work-ethic has been obvious to everyone except her for years. She's starting to realize it, though, and enjoy the reputation it provides. Instead of being the sweet, smart, cute, kind, timid girl that studies because she's terrified of failure, she's grown into the sweet, smart, hot, kind, confident girl that studies because she enjoys being the best at something.

Confidence. That's the main thing that's changed about her. And it's crazy sexy.

She's still faithful to a fault, and remains friends with her odd collection of boys despite transforming into a high school goddess (in my opinion). She's been in the news twice for getting caught in the crossfire of the Outlaw's many violent detractors, and she's still humble despite the accolades given to her by the media.

She brings chocolate to school because she knows I crave it. She also keeps her room stocked with Hersey Kisses. During football season she wears a jersey with my number on it. Before games she cooks dinner for me and our friends. She was at my mother's funeral and continues to pray for my father. She used to scratch my back before things grew too weird between us. When I'm sick she takes care of me. She tutors me in Spanish, but I can barely concentrate with her there. I have a disease that causes lethal headaches, but Katie holds my hand and protects me from the pain, though she doesn't fully understand this, and I'm not exactly sure how it works either.

Her hair is thick and long and brown and she's never dyed it. She has a wholesome, heart-shaped face. Her eyes are brown or hazel, depending on the light. Her smile is natural and easy, and her lips curl and her cute nose wrinkles. She was born to a beautiful Latina mother, and her skin is a light tan all year long. She is trim and athletic, light on her feet, and a natural dancer.

I love her beyond words. I'm drawn to her the way I'm drawn to oxygen.

At 10:30pm, I finally reached her apartment. Her bedroom has sliding glass doors that open onto the rear lawn of her building. I stood there until 10:36pm to calm my racing pulse, watching silhouettes of movements through her lacy curtains. From 10:37pm until 10:39pm I forgot to breathe. At 10:41pm I raised my trembling fist to knock on the door...

My phone buzzed. Or the Outlaw's phone buzzed. I almost had a heart attack. Puck messaged me.

>> OUTLAW!!! Y R U @ KATIES HOUSE?!?! R U GONNA TELL HER UR INTO HER?!?! THIS IS HUGE!!!!!!!!

Growling, I powered off the phone and tapped on her door with my finger.

The prettiest girl on earth cautiously peered through a slit in the curtains, and then slid the door aside. Her laptop was open on her bed and indie pop music filled the room. As usual, she smelled like flowers. She was wearing the shorts and nightshirt combination she used for pajamas, which bordered on being inappropriate attire for welcoming late-night male suitors. Two years ago the outfit looked harmless. Now, it was scandalous.

"Hi handsome! You're here late." She smiled and I stepped inside. "I think you've grown again, Chase. You're taller and broader. I'm working on my Stanford essay, and - Oh! You brought me Godetia!"

I held out the sprig of lavender and carmine flowers that I knew she loved. She took it, but I didn't let go.

"Katie I love you," I said. Her hand froze, our fingers touching, the petals near her chin. Her eyes were wide and shining like the sun. One song ended and another began while we watched each other. "I've been in love with you for a long time. At least a year. Maybe my whole life."

She took a deep breath and tried to speak but no words came out.

"I know this is a bad time," I continued.

"Why?"

"And I know you're dating someone else, and I know that he's very sick in the hospital. But there hasn't been a good time to tell you the past twelve months."

She was holding my hand with both of hers now, brushing the petals against her lips. Her eyes were far away. Our bodies had gotten closer somehow.

"You loved me while you were dating Hannah Walker?" she asked.

"Of course."

"You *can't* tell me this now," she said, suddenly sad. And maybe angry? "Not *now*."

"I know. But I had to. And I know this is the conversation girls dread," I grinned, "where the awkward friend confesses his love."

"You're Chase Jackson," she breathed, and she lowered her forehead to rest on my chest. "No girl would dread this conversation."

"But awkward or not, I had to say it out loud. To you. At least once."

"Why?" she groaned. "Why now?"

"You can't love me back. I know. But that doesn't change anything."

"I can't think," she said. The flowers dropped to rest on the tops of our feet. Her fingers were interlaced with mine and she was squeezing. "Stop talking so I can concentrate."

"I love you because you're perfect," I said, speaking into her soft brown hair. "And that doesn't change if you don't love me back. I love you unconditionally."

"Chase," she said and she pushed away from me. Misery and fury and tears were in her eyes. "I'm being interviewed again tomorrow, for the news, at the hospital. Half of Los Angeles is watching me, waiting for Tank to wake up."

"I know. I'm not asking you to break up with him. I just needed to say it."

"What am I supposed to do? I have no idea what to do." Her eyes were closed and her head was back and she was raking her nails through her hair. "Beautiful, sweet, perfect Chase. Oh my gosh. What a mess."

"You look super good when you play with your hair like that." I was trying not to ogle. "But this doesn't need to be a mess. You already kinda knew, right? A little bit?"

"You're so perfect and so stupid," she sighed and opened her eyes, a simple movement, yet so hot and steamy I nearly melted. "I will remember this moment the rest of my life."

"I wish I'd worn different clothes, then," I said, examining my jacket with distaste.

"It's July. What've you been doing? Why are you wearing a jacket?"

"Because of my...I mean, I was just talking with...err, I was in the...I...um...well..." I stammered, finding no suitable words.

"I need you to leave," she said, staring me down and taking a deep breath. "Before something...bad happens."

"Okay, yeah sure. I understand."

"No. You understand nothing, sweetie."

Ouch.

Then she said, "But I need you to do something. Just...because."

"For you Katie, anything."

She paused, a curious frown creasing her forehead, like she remembered something, and then said, "Write it down."

"Write it down?"

"I want to know why. Write down your reasons why."

"Why I love you?"

"Why you love me," she nodded. "I just need to know. To torture myself."

"That'll be easy to write."

"Good."

"How you look in those tiny pajamas," I said. "I'll be writing *that* down."

"Chase," she said, and she raised her finger and shook it at me. "I warned you. You're in dangerous territory."

"I'm going, I'm going."

But she was really close to me and we were touching… Then her mother burst into the room, the door crashing.

"Catalina!" she cried. Katie and I both jumped and stepped away from each other. "Su novio!"

"Mamá? Que? What?" she asked, throwing her hands up.

"Tank! The boy! He is awake!"

Chapter Three
Monday/Tuesday, July 13/14. 2018.

The next two weeks passed in a fog. I practiced football and hung out with my friends, Cory and Lee. That was it. That's all I did. Except for checking the news. I did that a lot too, to keep tabs on Compton and Tank. Stupid Tank.

"Shoulda killed him when we had the chance," Samantha Gear said. She showed up unannounced tonight. We were perched on the roof of my townhouse, a haunt we visited monthly. It was close to midnight. My neighborhood, in the suburbs of Glendale and close enough downtown that we could see the towers and lights, was hushed.

"Try not to be so morbid, Gear," I said.

"This is *Tank* we're talking about. I can be morbid."

"I don't blame the city for celebrating Tank," I said. "Completely understandable. Los Angeles has taken a lot of punches and him reviving is the first real *win* in a long time. Plus, he completely fooled…well, everyone. He suckered the entire planet, except for us. So the city thinks he's a great guy."

PuckDaddy said into our earpieces, "I still think I should blackout his press conference tomorrow."

"I concur."

I growled, "You two aren't thinking. That'll just make Tank mad, and it'll alert both him and the Chemist and everyone else that the infamous

21

PuckDaddy is working with us."

"I wish I knew what that dumb-ass was going to say," Puck said. I could hear keyboard clicks through his mic. "I searched his texts. No help. What the heck does he need a press conference for?"

Samantha shook her head and said, "What was Carter thinking, keeping Tank alive and comatose so long? His brain is probably past the danger zone now. He'll live forever."

Tank was sick, same as me, and our bodies were just emerging from an extremely sensitive and dangerous growth spurt, where aneurysms were a daily threat. My headaches had largely subsided, and Tank's probably had too.

"Tank's got the most wicked vitals you've ever seen," Puck commented. "I monitored them. He's like Adonis, even in his sleep."

"Carter usually hires new Infected immediately," Samantha said. "He plants them somewhere in the world, pays them, and gives them an identity. He does that for his benefit and for the benefit of the newbie. But that won't work with Tank. He's too powerful. And rich. And well-known."

Puck said, "Carter's planning on using Tank's strength against the Chemist."

"Didn't work last time," I said. "The Chemist just toyed with Tank."

Samantha said, "Because Tank was alone. He won't be, next time."

I shook my head. "That idiot will never work with me. Or Carter. No chance. He's too stubborn, too proud, too stupid."

"Yeah."

"And speaking of pride," I said, "You need to stop kicking record-setting field goals in practice, Gear."

"Uuuuuugh," she groaned, and she hit the roof with her fist, creating a slight indention. "Why are we still playing football with high school kids?? I'm so bored!"

"You don't have to play! Go do other stuff. This is my life, not yours."

"No," she snapped. "The Chemist is obsessed with the Outlaw. He knows you're still alive. I'm not leaving you alone until we deal with him."

"He doesn't know who the Outlaw is," I pointed out. "He can't identify

Chase Jackson."

Puck remarked, "But he's looking, stupid. I filter a lot of the data coming out of Compton. He's looking."

"Whatever," I sighed. "I'm going to bed."

"Katie still hasn't texted you," Puck observed.

"Thanks, Puck!" I shouted in annoyance. "Thanks for the reminder!"

"You shouldn't have told her how you feel."

"You *told* me to tell her! *Many* times!"

He said, "Don't shout at PuckDaddy."

"She's just busy. With the whole Tank circus. I'm still glad I told her. I'd do it again."

Samantha stood up and brushed herself off. I frowned and said, "Gear, out of curiosity, where do you live?"

"I'm not supposed to tell you, but whatever. I have a place in Atlanta and another in Germany."

"No, I mean around here. You've been in LA for seven months."

"Here and there," she said casually. Too casually.

"What does that mean? Puck, do you know where Samantha lives?"

He chirped, "PuckDaddy is forbidden to comment."

"What the heck?" I said. "Where do you freaking live?"

She glared at me. "I've already answered that question. Twice."

"Be more specific."

"No."

"Why not?? I won't come visit."

Puck shouted in our ears, "She lives in her truck!"

A long silence. In her truck?? She rolled her eyes. For the first time all night, I heard no keyboard clicks from Puck.

"*What?*" she said finally. "Who cares? I like it."

"You live out of your truck?" I asked.

"Sure."

"How?"

She scoffed. "What do you mean *how?* Don't be an idiot."

"All your clothes? Do you have a pillow? Where do you shower? Don't you get lonely?"

"Puck. I hate you."

"Why do you live out of your truck?" I persisted.

She shouted, "Why not??"

"Because that means you're homeless."

She snorted and said, "I'm not homeless, Chase. I just told you. I have *two* homes. And my truck. Which I love."

"Why don't you rent a place?"

She shrugged and said, "Cheaper this way. Plus, I want to be near you in case of an emergency."

"Then sleep in our guest bedroom," I suggested.

"Hah! No way."

"Why not?"

She said, exasperated, "Because of a thousand reasons."

"Name one."

"Chase. Just drop it."

"No," I said and I stood up too. "You're going to live with me and dad. None of my friends are homeless while I have a guest bedroom."

"Infected do not like living together," she said. "The virus makes us mean and suspicious."

"Are you suspicious of me?"

"….no. But still."

"Come on," I said, and I climbed back into my bedroom through the window. "Get your stuff from the truck. I'll show you your room."

"No."

"Fine," I said. "I'll go get your stuff."

PuckDaddy hooted, "This is so cool. Infected never live together."

"No, Chase, wait," she said, almost pleading. She came into the bedroom too. "This is too weird."

"No it's not."

"PuckDaddy is jealous," he said. "PuckDaddy wants to live there too."

"Puck, you should!" I cried. "How cool would that be??"

"PuckDaddy cannot," he said and the clicking resumed.

"Let's go, Gear," I said. "Get your stuff. You're living here now. We'll work on Puck after you've settled in."

"Chase."

"*What?*"

"I'm bad at this," she said. She hadn't moved. Her arms hung limply by her side.

"Bad at what?"

"I'm bad at people. My family didn't like me, and I don't blame them. I was kicked out for a reason. I'm grouchy and I don't like people, and this just won't work." She was staring at the floor, clenching and unclenching her fists.

"We'll hardly ever be here, anyway."

"Infected are loners. This is not how we do things," she said.

"It is now."

"It's not a good idea to care about people, Chase. This is making me like you. I don't want to like you. And I don't want to like your father either. We could have gotten the Chemist if Katie hadn't been in Compton that night. But we care about her. Emotional ties aren't good. They get us into trouble."

"Maybe PuckDaddy and I will get bunkbeds!" I cried. "And Cory and Lee can come sleepover!"

The clicking stopped. "PuckDaddy never had a sleepover."

"I'm so pumped!"

"Chase," Samantha Gear sighed and threw her hands up. "You're as bad as Carter."

I intercepted Dad at breakfast early the following morning. The sun wasn't up, and Samantha hadn't emerged from her room yet.

"Dad," I whispered urgently. "Just so you know, there's a girl upstairs."

Dad's blue mug of coffee paused at his mouth. He stared hard over the rim.

25

"Soooo…" I continued. "Just…act cool."

He said, "Repeat that?"

"Ugh. Dad, come on. There's this girl," I began.

"I got that part."

"And she doesn't have a place to stay."

"Uh huh," he said and he finally lowered the mug.

"So I told her she could spend the night."

"Uh huh."

"In the guest bedroom," I finished lamely.

My dad's a big guy. He has thick fingers, and eyes that can drill a hole through concrete. After a long stint off the police force due to a back injury, he had returned to his job in a part-time role. Soon he'd be a full-time detective again.

He took a deep breath and said, "Chase-"

"Dad. No. Just…shhh. She's coming down soon."

"I realize you're eighteen…"

"No, shush!"

"And we've never really talked about girls…"

"Oh my goooooooosh," I said and I collapsed into the wooden chair opposite him. "Dad, it's not like that. Please stop."

"But we should talk before you have…sleepovers. With girls."

I lowered my head and started banging it on the table. "Dad. Nothing. Happened. She. Is just. A friend. I. Want. To. Die."

Samantha Gear opened the front door and strode into the kitchen. Samantha is strong and striking. She was wearing jogging clothes and earbuds, and she was sweating freely. She'd been out running already?? Dad stood up.

"I'm Samantha," she panted and she stuck out her hand for Dad to shake. "I'm on the football team with Chase, and I slept in your guest bed. Thanks for having me. I'm going out for breakfast. Anyone want doughnuts?"

"Chocolate. With chocolate sprinkles. Many of them," I groaned, face down on the table. This wasn't going according to plan.

"I'm fine, thank you. Nice to meet you, Samantha," Dad said.

The door closed again, and I raised my head up from the table. Dad's eyes were boring holes into me.

"*That* girl was in the guest bed and you stayed in *yours?*" he asked.

"Yes," I groaned.

"The *football* team."

"I promise she's on the team." And then I clarified, "The kicker."

"That girl is not your age."

"She….she's in my grade," I said as truthfully as I could.

"If she's under twenty then I'm the Outlaw," he pronounced gruffly and walked out of the room.

Cory and Lee came over after morning's football practice ended. We played Call-of-Duty on my Xbox for several hours. The virus I'd been infected with had done something to my frontal cortex, or so Carter told me. The video game moved much slower than it once had. I was traditionally awful at first-person shooter games, but now I won more than I lost, which I pointed out often to my confused and frustrated compatriots.

Katie Lopez walked into my living room and said, "Hi boys!"

I dropped my controller and stood up. Cory and Lee said, "Hey" over their shoulders but otherwise didn't budge.

"Hi Katie," I said.

"You guys having fun?"

"I'm winning."

"Wow," she said sarcastically. "That's *so* great you're winning at video games."

"I think so."

She beckoned with her finger and said, "Can we talk? In the hall?"

"Absolutely," I said, my heart suddenly pounding like a drum. I had to be careful, because sometimes my body swelled when I was nervous and I wasn't wearing my loose shirt or shoes. "It's nice to see you. Finally. Are you on your way to the press conference?"

"Yes. How do I look?"

"Desirable."

"Chase," she said quietly and stepped closer. "You should know. I think about our conversation. Every minute."

I didn't know what to say so I nodded.

"Life has been crazy since he woke up, but…I've thought about you. A lot. You're everything to me."

"Thanks. I know."

"I haven't forgotten," she said. "And I won't forget. And we'll talk soon. About all this."

"You don't need to worry about me. I'm not going anywhere."

"I really want you to write me that letter," she smiled. "I check for it every day."

"I will," I grinned. "I'm just not sure how to phrase 'I love you for every reason.'"

She smiled wider. "Do Cory and Lee know that…that you love me?"

"They know. I think everyone knew but you."

The front door opened, spilling in sunlight, and Samantha walked in.

"Hi Katie," she said. "You look hot! Oh…you're going to Tank's press conference… Well, have fun with that." She slammed the door and stomped upstairs.

"Thanks," Katie called after her. "Nice to see you too, Samantha." She paused and then whispered, "Why is she going upstairs?"

I said, "Oh right, I didn't tell you. Samantha lives here now."

"*What?*"

"Yeah! Cool, huh?" I grinned.

"Why is…what's….why?"

"She's homeless! I had no idea. She's been living in her truck this whole time."

"*So?*" Katie said, peering up the staircase. "What's wrong with that?"

"What do you mean?"

"She's staying in the guest room," she said slowly.

"Right."

"The room beside your bedroom."

"Right," I said again. "Perfect, huh?"

"Yes," Katie said. "Perfect. For her. I'm so glad to hear she has a place to sleep now. Here, with you."

"Dad thinks it's weird," I admitted.

"How…closed-minded of him. Chase, I have a great idea," she said. "Samantha should come stay with me!"

"But you don't have a guest room," I frowned.

"Right, but I don't mind. It'd be fun! I like Samantha."

"Where would she sleep?"

"On the floor. I mean, I would sleep on the floor and she can have my bed," she said.

"Well…I can ask her…"

"No," she said, shaking her head. "That's…I can…I mean, I think I'm just…wow, I can't believe she's sleeping here."

"Are you okay?"

"I…I have to go, or…it's time for me to go," she laughed nervously. "Yeah. I'll call you later. Or text you. I'll text you."

She left in a rush, and I strolled back into the living room.

"Yo, she going to the interview now?" Lee asked. Lee is one of my closest friends. He's a stereotypical Asian math genius, and he also obsesses over the mysterious Outlaw, to the extent that he designed the Outlaw's vest.

"Yes," I said and I sat down with a big exhalation.

"She cold," Cory rumbled. Cory is my other best friend. He's a mountain of a man that will play offensive line in college football one day.

"No," I said. "She's conflicted."

"Dude, I wish Tank had just *died*, yo," Lee proclaimed, eyes glued to the screen. "Everything would be better."

"We can't start wishing death on people," I said. "We have to be bigger than that. Even if we don't want to be."

"*Start* wishing death? Tank plays for the Patrick Henry Dragons, dude. I've been wishing he was dead for months."

Cory grunted, "What's Tank gonna say, anyway? In the press conference."

"Someone once told me," I remembered, "that Tank is haunted with being the best. That's why he hates the Outlaw, because suddenly his sack total was no longer big news. The hero in the pajamas was getting the front page. Tank wasn't the best anymore, in the eyes of the public. And in March he got beat up on national television by the Chemist, so...maybe he's just trying to reassert his dominance. It's a vanity thing."

"Yeah," Cory nodded. "He a pretty boy. Prima donna."

"Dude. That ugly monster is no media darling," Lee scoffed. "Not to me."

Samantha came down and smeared us in Call-of-Duty, even when we played three versus one. The game seemed to provide some relief from the perpetual siren call of her disease, so we played for two more hours until the interview started.

Tank had lost weight during his three-month long coma, but none of it was muscle weight, apparently. His skin looked shrink-wrapped over his bulk. Katie, resplendent and beautiful, was sitting beside him with his parents. Katie and Tank both had Latin American ancestry, and I had to admit they made an attractive couple. Several local television crews set up microphones.

"I'd like to begin," he said, his voice a deep earthquake, "by thanking everyone for their concern. I appreciate all the cards and prayers. I'm going home tomorrow and I will be fully recovered soon. I know this has been a scary time for Los Angeles, but I'm okay now."

"Nobody cares!" Lee shouted at the television.

"I also want to thank my girlfriend, Katie," he continued, "for standing by my side through this. I just hope she stops getting kidnapped." Everyone laughed at the bad joke. "Saving her is hard work."

"Like you would know," I muttered. Samantha shot me a look.

"Thank you to the doctors and to my parents. And to my fans, I want you to know that I'll be ready for football season. And I'm going to lead our team to another championship. And I'm going to break every quarterback stupid enough to get on the field with me. Every. Quarterback."

Samantha chuckled, "Charming guy. I like his rage. Good looking, too."

"And lastly, to the stupid old man with the staff," he said, and Samantha and I leaned forward. He was referencing the big fight in Compton. Tank had been there, and the Chemist had badly beaten him. "The Chemist. If I ever see you again, I'm going to impale you with that staff." His parents fidgeted uncomfortably on their chairs. Katie managed to keep a straight face.

One of the reporters raised a hand and said, "Tank, glad to see you up and around. What were you doing in Compton that evening?"

"That's personal," he said.

"No one seems to know how you got from that intersection to the hospital. Do you know?"

"I don't care," he said.

"On the videos, it appears you spoke to the Outlaw. Do you remember what you said?"

"No. But if I see him again, I'mma beat his ass too."

Confusion among the reporters. "The Outlaw? Why? Weren't you two working together?"

"Just a joke," he grinned.

"The Outlaw died in the Compton explosion, unfortunately," one of the reporters told him.

Tank laughed darkly and quietly. "Oh no. The punk in pajamas fooled you suckers. He's still around."

Samantha sucked air in between her teeth. "That *moron*."

A pause in the interview and then several reporters started talking at once. Katie's eyes were wide with surprise.

"How do you know the Outlaw's not dead? Do you know the Outlaw's identity? Who is he? What about the explosion?"

"He's not dead," Tank repeated. "But he's a fool. He's a liar and a coward. And the world wouldn't like him if they knew who he really was. Maybe I'll tell you, one of these days. One day soon."

Chapter Four

Tuesday, August 4. 2018.

Samantha shook me awake at three in the morning.

"Get up. We gotta go."

"Mmmmmmmmrrgppfffffooooawaaay," I said, helpfully.

"Chase. Now," she hissed.

"'Manthalemmelone," I groaned. If I had a taser, I would've zapped her right in the neck.

"Carter needs us."

"This is your job," I moaned and I pulled a pillow over my head. "Not mine. I'm a kid. A child. An innocent youth that needs sleep."

"I'm going to screw on my silencer and shoot you with wax bullets until you get up.

"Oh my goooooooosh," I sat up with a huff in the dark room. The only light came from my red alarm clock. My eyes wouldn't fully open. "What could Carter possibly want?"

"Doctors at Hollywood Presbyterian Medical just revived an Infected kid," she said and she flipped my covers off. "Camera phones caught him throwing motorcycles before he passed out. Carter's out of town and the kid is unguarded."

"So?"

"*So?*" she snapped and she started throwing clothes at me. "Start thinking like an Infected. We need you. This is a war. A war of accumulation, and right now the Chemist is winning. He's going to come snatch that kid. We need to get there first."

Five minutes later I was howling down the interstate on my bike, peering through sleepy eyes at a blurry world. Samantha was nearby in her truck.

"How do we bust a kid out of a hospital without being seen?" I asked through my helmet mic. I was cold and tired and grouchy.

"Leave that to PuckDaddy," he said in my ear. "Breaking into their systems now."

"I'm getting sick of you two."

"Thanks!"

"What do we do with him? Isn't the kid insane? And freakishly strong?"

Samantha crackled, "I'm going to steal some tranquilizers. Keep him under until Carter gets back. We can stash the kid at your downtown hideout. Our main objective is to keep him away from the Chemist."

"Do either of you know how many Infected soldiers the Chemist has? I have no idea."

"PuckDaddy has a guess," he responded. "I've been scanning Compton with facial tracking software. Puck estimates six."

"Six dastardly Infected," I mused.

"Dastardly?"

"Yup."

"Only nerds say dastardly."

"Six plus the Chemist," Samantha said. "Plus the others he hasn't *hatched* yet. Remember, Carter said the Chemist has found a way to keep new Infected comatose for months while their brains heal."

"And we have…"

"You two," Puck said. "Plus me, kinda. And Carter."

"Seven verse four. Seems fair," I grunted.

"Carter called in reinforcements," Puck said. "Arriving soon."

"Good! I like reinforcements."

Samantha growled, "Not me."

"Puck, how many other Infected are there? Outside of Los Angles, I mean. What's our total number?"

"Outside of Los Angeles, there are five others. Used to be six, but she died on a mountain recently."

"Who are they?"

"Code names are Australia, Russia, Zealot, China and Pacific. That's all I can tell you."

"I hate them all," Samantha said. "I bet Carter called in Australia…didn't he."

"You know it, homie. Australia'll be here in a few days."

Samantha said a very bad word.

PuckDaddy directed us to a sprawling pink hospital on Vermont Avenue. We braked in the rear parking lot, near a loading bay. The silence of the place was deafening. I hated this; neither of us had ever been here and we had no plan, like walking into a skirmish blindfolded.

My body was thickening due to the stress. My cells carried a disease that interacted strongly with adrenaline, doing bizarre stuff like strengthening my heart, broadening shoulders, and hardening skin. Muscles bulged and the fibers began fast-twitch firing like pistons. The synapses in my brain revved up, like I could control time.

The overall effect was intoxicating, as if I'd never been alive until now. My senses were heightened and all the incoming stimuli was rich and potent. I could punch through walls, flip cars, leap houses, and I ached to do it all.

"Talk to me, Puck." Samantha looked awesome when she dressed for combat: thin neoprene gloves, tight black leggings, steel-toed boots, and her snug black shooting jacket. Night-vision goggles were perched on her head, and pistols were slung in two brown leather shoulder holsters.

"This place is disgusting. The building is so old," Puck whined. "I can't be very elegant in my assistance."

"Get us a room number." She double checked magazines and chambers on all weapons, including the pistol at the small of her back.

My weapon was my arm. I had purchased heavy, metal ballbearings a few months ago; I could throw steel faster and more accurately than a major league pitcher. Her weapons were cooler than mine, but mine wouldn't kill people. I hoped.

"The kid's in Neurology. Take the stairs located just inside the loading dock. Head to the third floor. Room 312."

"What about meds? I want him sedated."

"He's hooked up to a bag of ketamine, according to records. There might be another bag in his room or the nurses' station. I don't know how this works. I'm not a doctor, I'm a hacker."

"Outlaw, you're still wearing your motorcycle helmet," Samantha observed.

"You think I should ditch the helmet? Go with the mask?"

"No," she frowned. "Neither. Both are too recognizable."

"Gear, you don't care if people see your face. I do. I still have a life. I covet my anonymity."

"Then wear the Outlaw mask," she sighed.

"Puck agrees!" he shouted

"Yeah, it's sexier," she shrugged. "Plus everyone knows you're alive now. No sense hiding. And Puck can delete video if we need."

I left the helmet with my bike and we trotted up the concrete stairwell to the third floor. The hospital's administration wing was asleep and we slipped through like ghosts. I was twirling steel in my hand like Baoding relaxation balls, but it wasn't helping.

We pushed through double-doors to the Patient Care area. This part of the hospital was alive. Sleepy, but alive. The lights were on, machines beeped, and distant voices murmured down the pink and blue hallway. An elderly man in a hospital gown saw us and gasped. He stumbled back into his room.

We stuck out. Infected often do. It's hard to pinpoint exactly why. The abnormally erect posture? Powerful upper body? Hyper alertness? Less civilian, more warrior. The battle gear didn't help. We might as well be lions stalking the corridors.

"Hang a right. He's at the end of the adjoining hall," Puck said. His voice was hushed, which was silly, but I understood. Every sound we made felt amplified.

"Gear, you go," I said. "You're not wearing the ridiculous attention-getting mask."

"Roger."

She went, moving quick and graceful, like a ballet dancer packing heat. The elderly gentleman snuck a peek at me around his doorframe. I smiled. He couldn't see that. Duh. I was wearing a mask. But the Outlaw doesn't wave.

Thirty seconds later, on my bluetooth headset, "Empty. No one here."

"Patient is gone?"

"Affirmative."

"Puck," I said, "He's been transferred?"

"Not according to his medical records."

"Samantha, impersonate a police officer. You kinda look like one. Ask where the patient was moved to."

"Roger that."

Puck murmured, "Love when she talks like that. So hot."

I waited. Old guy peeked at me again. Puck was clicking. All was quiet.

"Something's wrong," Samantha warned. "The nurses are cowering. Won't even look at me. Acting like they've seen a ghost or something."

"Bingo," Puck shouted, so loud I jumped. "Contact! Walter and Carla, with two other Infected I don't recognize, wheeling a patient. They've got our boy!"

"Where??" I demanded. Walter and Carla. The Chemist's most trusted bullies. Those two were trouble. They nearly killed me in Compton.

"Ah jeez, I don't know. Which security camera am I looking at?"

"Puck, figure it out!" Samantha ordered, jogging back to me. She had a pistol in her fist, her face a mixture of excitement and rage. I recognized that visage. The madness was beginning to blaze in both of us.

"Got it! Opposite end of the hospital."

Samantha and I bolted in that direction. We'd cover the distance in seconds, bursting through security doors.

"They're moving slowly. Heading towards the western bank of elevators."

"How'd they get out of Compton?" I wondered. "And get here so quickly?" I had heavy steel in my hand, ready to remove someone's head if necessary.

The same virus burning in Samantha and me also burned in Walter and Carla, and presumably the other two with them. The virus interacted with our specific body compositions and affected us all differently. Samantha and Walter were both blessed (or cursed) with snap reflexes, crazy-good mental focus, and heightened hand-eye coordination, making them natural gunners. My body had grown quick and strong, even more so than Samantha's, but I'd be useless with a gun. I didn't know anything about Carla's abilities. Or the other two.

"Heads-up!" Puck called. His voice hurt my ears. "Ambush!"

Walter rose up behind a chest-high nurses' desk at an intersection and opened fire, aiming at me. The cluttered hallway erupted into a riot of shrapnel as the oncoming storm of bullets flung hospital equipment. I couldn't *see* the rounds, but some inner preternatural instinct *knew* how to dodge them. I was a blur, slipping through the storm, but Walter was lightning quick too, and POW! One lucky bullet caught me in the shoulder. I rolled behind a meal cart that shuddered with impacts.

Samantha returned fire. She emptied the clips of her two pistols so fast it sounded like a violent peal of thunder. Walter fell back as the Nurses' desk disintegrated.

Puck asked, "You okay?"

"*So* great!" I shouted, examining the smashed bullet-proof plate in my vest that saved me serious injury.

"Children!" Samantha screamed down the hall in delirious, sick joy. "You're just *children*!" She reloaded faster than my eyes could follow and aimed another volley at Carla, coming around the corner with a shotgun.

"Outlaw Outlaw Outlaw!" Puck repeated in my ear, barely audible over Samantha's gunshots.

"*What*?!"

"They're stalling! Some jerk is pushing our patient down the hallway!"

"Okay," I said, sneaking a peek. A kid (I'd never seen him before) was almost to the elevators with the bed. "I see him. I got him."

I gathered a fistful of metal and sent a heavy barrage after him. The steel ballbearings hummed like angry hornets and ripped through the rolling bed's legs. The patient spilled onto the floor.

"Nice shot!"

Carla came again, and this time she took us by surprise. She had an illegal eight-gauge semi-automatic shotgun whose concussive blasts shook the floor and rattled picture frames off their mountings. Samantha and I bailed into rooms on either side of the hallway as death whistled past, gouging the walls.

"Any ideas, Puck?"

"You're the Outlaw! Not me!"

"Then I'm going out the window."

Both Samantha and Puck said, "You're *what??*" but I had already broken through the third-story window. A billion slivers of glass went slicing off into the air. I snatched a hold on the outside wall before I fell. I put my fingers straight into the pink stucco-like material. It was quiet out here. I hadn't realized people inside were screaming in terror until I no longer heard them. I was above the parking lot, over a vacant ambulance. A nearby palm tree was almost touching me.

I glared across the sheer face of the hospital to the next window. It wasn't far. Easy. *Jump!*

"Outlaw, where'd you go? What are you doing?"

"Flanking maneuver," I said. "Just like Call-of-Duty!" Another Jump! I balanced myself on the window sill by pressing my fingertips firmly into the edges of the frame.

"Explain," Samantha demanded.

"Coming in behind them." Jump! "Get ready." Jump! "Else they'll shoot me a lot." Jump Jump!

I broke the glass and re-entered the mayhem from a new location.

The most beautiful girl I'd ever seen was hiding in the adjoining hallway. We were both startled, and for several seconds we only stared. She was perfect. So perfect it was hard to think. She had long blonde hair and an oval-shaped face and full lips and big blue eyes, and she was dressed in tight, trendy (and very unmilitary) blue clothes. The girl shook off her surprise and said, "Stop."

I stopped. Immediately. No questions asked. No movements. She was so attractive I had no choice. The lights dimmed. The sounds faded. There was only her.

"Go back out the window," she smiled. Her voice was as smooth as silk. Soothing and pleasant, with musical notes. My ears turned hot, like she'd said something indecent.

I obeyed. I went back to the window. The pretty girl told me. I had to…

"Wait." I closed my eyes and shook my head. Something was wrong. I was…where was I? My brain was full of fog. I was dizzy. "Wait. Why? What's…I'm confused."

"Go outside," she said again. "Please? Jump out the window."

"Okay," I nodded. That made sense. She asked nicely. I'd do anything for her. All I could think about was the beautiful girl; she was everywhere. She smelled so good I tripped and fell into the wall.

"Chase," a voice said loudly into my ear. "Chase, dummy. What are you doing?"

Puck. Puck's voice. His words blew away some of the mist in my brain. Where am I? My face was pressed against the blue wallpaper. I felt like a toy with two puppeteers. What's *wrong* with me?? My mouth wouldn't work. "Huh?"

"Stop being an idiot," he yelled. "She's Infected!"

I couldn't function. My mind was thick and slow. The gorgeous girl was *inside* my head. I stared suspiciously and said, "Who…you… who are you?" Behind her, the gunfight raged but it didn't seem to matter.

She planted fists onto her hips and said, "The Father predicted you might be able to resist me."

I didn't reply. I couldn't. Every move she made, every noise, was intoxicating.

She appeared caught between frustration and amusement. "You're a handsome specimen, and I wish I had more time to play with you."

"…what?"

She winked and then she intentionally changed her expression to one of fear, and she cried, "Help me! Please!"

Help me?! My first instinct was to obey her. Was she hurt?

A pack of hospital workers, hidden and cowering from the nearby gun battle, began pouring out of doorways. They leapt to obey her. Men, women, doctors, nurses and even patients all charged me, glaring and shouting. She was commanding them!

Puck said, "This is super weird."

"How is she controlling people?" I shouted, knocking hands away and shoving the mob backwards. There were about a dozen attackers.

"Who cares, stupid! Take her out!"

I *Moved*. I went through the crowd. Easily. They were slow and clumsy and I advanced like a nightmare. The startled girl turned to run. I tried not to notice her astonishing figure. She was Infected, that was obvious, but she didn't move well. She had locomotion issues, like her bones were brittle or her legs were injured. I grabbed and threw a cordless phone that connected solidly with her skull and she collapsed. The deranged crowd watched and wailed with grief, but at least they quit chasing me.

"That was trippy. Careful, here comes Walter."

Walter rushed into view, reloading his weapon. He was unprepared for me. I put the heel of my hand into his chest like a battering ram, driving with my shoulder. He landed nine feet away and slid across the thin carpet into the far wall.

"Chase! Move!" Puck cried, but it was too late.

Carla spun around the corner, and she fired. I caught the entire shotgun blast in my midsection. *Pain*! My consciousness flickered. The hospital whirled. I found myself on the carpet several feet away, unable to breathe, the heady smell of gunpowder thick in my nose. The mob of attackers were screaming and holding their ears. My chest roared and ached.

"Holy god, please don't be dead," Puck said, barely discernible from the ringing in my ears.

Carla. She glared and jacked another round into the chamber. I was dead. The body armor and my freakish skin absorbed the attack, and I'd heal from inner injuries. But she could take my head off with the next shot.

To my surprise, she snapped, "You don't use guns. Why not?" She wore a fierce scowl and her hair was tightly cornrowed around her skull. I sucked in lungfuls of air but got only a trickle. I tried and failed to say, *I don't kill people.* "We shouldn't be fighting, Outlaw. You and me. Us. You agree?" she asked. I nodded and winced. "You agree? This is stupid? This fighting?" Her words stunned me as much as the shotgun had. I nodded again. She was pleading, hoping I could reason with her. "You and I, we think alike. I can tell. We need each other. You hear me?"

Thunk. Carla's eyes rolled up and she fell, unconscious. Samantha Gear was behind her, holding a heavy leather blackjack. She'd hit Carla behind the ear; lights out. Samantha stuffed the blackjack into her side pocket and said, "You two have a nice conversation?"

I nodded and she pulled me to my feet. "Ooooooooouch." I couldn't raise upright completely.

"Did she shoot you? With her shotgun?"

"It was great," I wheezed in agony.

"Even with your skin hard as a rock, I bet that hurt." She indicated the gorgeous girl on the floor and said, "How'd you do with Blue Eyes?"

"Blue Eyes. Good name for her. She's like a witch or something," I said, partially unzipping my busted vest and inspecting the damage. The shot hadn't pierced.

"I should have told you," Gear nodded. "Leave her to me."

"How does she do that?"

"I'll explain later. Where is Walter?" she asked.

I pointed but Walter was gone. "Crud. Puck," I said. "Where'd they go? Walter and that kid and the patient?"

"I'm so glad you're not dead," he said in a heavy rush. "I'm trying not to cry."

"Aw. That's nice," I smiled.

Samantha stared incredulously at me. "Really? You two need a moment? Right *now*?"

"Thought she'd blown you in half," Puck sniffed. "I was praying so hard. Huh...I believe in God, apparently."

"*Puck!!*"

"Okay, okay. I'm scanning. You have no soul, Samantha."

"Hurry up."

"Shut it. Found them. Boarding the far elevator. If you hurry you can head them off at the pass."

We ran, no words. Well, she ran. I winced and shuffled. She jumped down the stairs to the first floor. I mostly fell.

We arrived at the lobby before the elevator did. Samantha pulled out two pistols and aimed them at the unopened silver doors. Young orderlies down the hall screamed.

"Puck, how much longer before police arrive?" I asked.

"Dunno, dude," he said, typing furiously. "Any minute. At least five calls to 911 have gone out from the hospital."

"Samantha, if possible..." I said carefully. "Try not to kill anyone."

"Shut up, Chase."

I sighed, which made my chest hurt. "I can't believe Puck said *head them off at the pass.*"

"Focus Outlaw."

"Like we ride horses or something."

"Oh...*crap!*" Puck cried. "The elevator went *up*, not down! My mistake. They're on the top floor!"

"Puck, kill the power," Samantha directed. We were moving, already at the second floor landing.

"Working on it."

"Puck..."

"This was a rush job!" he shouted. "Don't yell at Puck! This building sucks so much. There! ...jerks."

The hospital's power went out. All the lights in the stairway clicked off. Total darkness. More screaming throughout the building. I crashed into Samantha and we both sprawled across the stairs.

"Chase! Get off!"

"Why'd you stop??" I shouted.

"I'm putting on night-vision goggles!" At that instant the emergency lights flickered on, providing enough light to see. She snarled, "Come on."

The Patient Care area had been transformed into a spooky ward with only dim pools of light and far-off cries. We found the vacant elevator on the top floor. The doors were pried open.

"Where'd they go?"

"I killed the power," Puck remarked dryly. "Remember, dummy? No power, no security cameras, no idea. By the way, the back-up generators are about to kick in."

"Samantha you scan down here," I said. "I'll check the roof."

"Fine," she growled. She shoved a pistol into my belt. "Just in case."

I jogged up the final stairs to the penthouse, peering first around each turn in the stairwell. "The door isn't locked," I reported quietly. Neither Puck nor Samantha answered. I stepped onto the wind-swept tenth-story roof. This was the top of the hospital's new tower. Below, surrounding the tower, was the structure's older wings, each five stories tall. "Can't see much. No lights up here?" I whispered, squinting into the darkness. The only illumination came from the surrounding city. "How long before power comes back?"

No answer. I checked the phone. The call was disconnected.

"Great," I sighed.

"Yo Outlaw! Come out, come out, wherever you are," Walter's voice drifted across the rooftop. "Or I'm putting a bullet in this guy's ear."

Walter. That guy's the worst.

A loud pop and the outdoor lights snapped on. Walter was across the helipad, at the far corner of the roof with the other two. He stood between the Infected kid and the woozy patient. Walter and the Infected kid were harnessed in with ropes so they could rappel quickly down the face of the hospital. The patient was swaying next to them. Walter had a gun pointed at the patient's head.

"Oh my gosh," the Infected boy beside Walter said. "It *really is* the Outlaw."

I kept thinking of him as a *kid*, but he was my age, maybe a little younger. And he was Infected, which meant dangerous.

"How's your head, kid?" I asked him. A heavy steel ball was bouncing in my hand. "Still getting the headaches?"

"Yes sir," he squeaked.

"Awful, huh? Mine just stopped."

"Hurts right now," he nodded. He had short hair and a babyface. "A lot."

"Shut up. Don't talk to him," Walter growled. Walter was wearing a vest, like me. His arms were better than mine.

"Don't listen to Walter. I want you to come with me," I said. The boy's eyes got bigger. "I can show you how to survive. You don't need them."

Walter said, "Outlaw, the patient's either dying or coming with us." He thumbed the pistol's hammer back. "You pick."

"Walter, this is ridiculous. What are you doing?"

"Harvesting. And running short on patience."

"You can't have him," I said simply. "He's a human, he counts, his life matters. You'll have to kill me first, and I don't think you can."

"We'll see."

"You," I said, pointing at the Infected babyfaced kid. "You stay with me too. Walter and the Chemist, they think this a game, or, even worse, a war. But it's not. This is your life. You only get one, and they want to waste it."

"The Father gave me a home," the boy said.

"The *Father?*" I scoffed. I had closed half the distance between us. "Oh jeez. You have to call him *Father?*"

"He gave me a family."

"Kid, go," Walter growled, indicating the thick rope in his hands.

"He didn't *give* you anything," I said. "The Chemist is using you. He will use you up, and then he'll dispose of you."

"Go now," Walter barked and he shoved the boy. The kid tipped back over the ledge, tightened his grip on the rope, and rappelled out of sight. Gone.

"Walter," I sighed. "Put the gun away. Let me help the patient."

"You?? Chemist has the most success at keeping new Chosen alive," Walter chuckled. "He saves their brain. You can't do that."

"He might save their brain, but he throws their body into his fire," I said. "Why are you helping that madman?"

The patient, wearing a hospital gown, groaned. He was going to fall, any second. I was close.

"The Chemist is going to rule the world soon," Walter shouted. "Guaranteed. You're on the wrong side. And I can't let you have more soldiers. You going back downstairs?"

"I am not."

"I know you're fast. Fought you before. Saw you dodge bullets. You beat me in the Compton knife fight. So I got no reason to wanna fight tonight."

"Good."

"His blood is on your hands." He sniffed. He lowered the gun to the guy's chest and pulled the trigger. The gun went off, and the patient rocked backwards with a scream.

"NO!" I cried.

"See you soon, hero." He disappeared over the lip of the parapet.

The patient staggered sideways, clutching his chest. I got there in time to miss his sleeve. He fell over the adjoining edge, away from Walter. The parking lot was ten stories below, a dizzying distance. I jumped without thinking.

Not a great plan! I caught his flailing body after three stories. We plummeted, disoriented, and the wind scraped us painfully against the tower flying upwards. I reached for the parachute in the rear of the vest.

Can't find the clasp!

The Hollywood Presbyterian Medical tower has a wide base, beginning at the fourth floor. We smashed into the base at over forty miles per hour. I never had time to panic. The roof partially caved, bursting a pipe that spewed hot water over the edge. We came to rest in a small roof crater.

He was dead. I knew without checking. The virus makes our brains tender; plus he recently had an aneurysm, got shot in the chest, and just fell six stories. No chance. My body was healthier and harder, and my broken bones would heal within a few hours. But I doubted I had any, other than maybe a few ribs.

I stared at the sky, holding the kid in my arms. Walter shot him in the chest instead of the head, forcing me to attempt a rescue. Bought him time to escape. It worked. All four of the hostile Infected would return safely to Compton. Walter was good at his job. He was willing to sacrifice. I wasn't. He was a zealot for his cause. I didn't even know what his cause was. Nor mine. Nothing made sense. Everything hurt. The kid's body was still hot and I wanted to cry.

My headset rang.

I answered it and grunted. Sirens were getting closer.

"Outlaw! Where *are* you?" Puck asked.

"I'm sad, Puck. Really sad."

"What?"

"Walter shot the kid. And then got away," I reported.

Heavy silence.

"Samantha, you there?"

"Yes, Chase," she said.

"Get our vehicles out of the parking lot. Police are out front, I think. I'll meet you wherever. I need another minute."

Samantha and I returned home at 5:30am, before the sun came up. We each ate an entire box of cereal, and then split a bowl of fruit and three chocolate bars. We didn't speak for a long time. The house was silent, except for the distant noises of dad getting ready.

"Chase, I know this feels like we lost," she said eventually. "But we didn't. We kept the Chemist from getting another super soldier."

"He wasn't just a body to tip the scale in our favor or in the Chemist's favor," I said. My eyes were closed and my forehead was resting in the palm of my hand, elbow propped on the table. "That was a person."

"I know."

"He has parents. *Had* parents. Maybe siblings. He never got the chance to meet people like him, to have things explained to him."

"I know. But," she consoled me, "don't forget. The virus was going to kill him anyway, most likely. It almost always does. At least we tried."

"Walter said the Chemist would keep him alive," I said. I was numb, just thinking out loud. "Should we have let Walter take the guy? Walter gave me the choice, for the kid to live with them, or for the kid to die. What if the Chemist really can save all their minds from insanity?"

"The Chemist puts those kids in comas, wakes them up, brainwashes them, and then forces them to do terrible things," Samantha said. She stood from her chair, stretched, and laid down spread-eagle on the living room carpet near the couch. "That cannot be an option we consider acceptable."

"Do you get depressed after action?"

"Yes," she said, and she blew a mouthful of air at the ceiling. "An ocean of adrenaline is filtering out of our system. It's normal. Plus, I usually have to pee a lot."

"Tell me about the witch," I said.

"The what?"

"That girl. The hot one," I reminded her. "Blonde hair, blue eyes. She used magic on me, or something. Right?"

"No," she chuckled. "You're just a dumb boy who does whatever pretty girls tell him to do."

"That's not true! She...like...mind-controlled me."

"Carter warned me about the girl with blue eyes."

"What'd he say?"

"Said a few decades ago there was an Infected girl in Europe who could make people do whatever she wanted. Her charms mostly worked on men. Carter spotted the blue-eyed girl in Compton, and guessed she had similar abilities."

"What do you mean, her charms?"

"The disease heightens our natural assets. Right? For Puck, that's his mind. For you, it's your speed and strength. For her, it's her beauty. The disease blessed her with better hair, a better figure, seductive voice, you get the idea. But. I think her real secret is that she produces pheromones. Normal bodies don't do that."

"Pheromones. Like…mating pheromones?" That made a lot of sense. I felt like the girl had assaulted my entire sensorium by just saying 'Please.'

"Yes. Mating pheromones. That's Carter's theory. You *saw* her, you *heard* her, you *smelled* her, you *sensed* her, and so you wanted to mate with her."

"Stop smiling."

"I'm not!" But her face was contorted with suppressed laughter.

"You are too," I scowled. "It's not my fault."

"I didn't say it was! Science proves guys are idiots around a hot girl. And Blue Eyes is a hundred times more attractive than normal. You fell in love with her instantly." She was still smiling.

"Not just me. Everyone in that hallway did. So…shut up."

"Outlaw and Blue Eyes. Sitting in a tree. K-i-s-s-i-n-g," she sang.

"Mooooving on. I noticed she had locomotion trouble. She ran with a weird limp. Most Inflected move like the wind, but not her."

"Happens a lot. Infected have enlarged bones sometimes, like Carter's fingers. I bet Blue Eyes has a misshapen pelvis."

"Gross."

She shrugged.

I said, "I knocked her unconscious. Then you knocked Carla unconscious. It wasn't hard. Shouldn't the disease have given them reinforced skulls or something?"

She tapped her head and said, "Tender brains, remember? All newbies have them. Except maybe Tank."

Dad walked in. He was wearing work khakis and a dark blue polo. A pistol and badge were clipped to his belt. He looked fit and alert.

"You two are up early."

Samantha sat up and said, "Good morning, Richard."

I said, "Richard? Don't call him Richard."

"We went for a run. Chase is getting fat."

Dad frowned at me. "What happened to *you*, kiddo?"

"What? Oh," I said, looking down at my destroyed vest. I should have removed it. Hopefully Dad wouldn't notice it was a ruined version of the Outlaw's costume. "It was...I...fell."

"Looks like you got shot, ran over, and *then* fell," he grunted, his hands on his hips.

"Hah! Good one, Dad. But I'm *not* getting fat."

Samantha said, "You look sharp, Richard. First day back on the job?"

"Yep," he nodded and went into the kitchen for coffee. "Received the assignment yesterday."

"What assignment?" I asked.

"We call it the SAT assignment."

"Which means?"

"It's a nickname. Stands for Superhuman Apprehension Team. We can't use it officially, for obvious reasons. Supervisors hate it. It's the joint task force charged with investigating and apprehending the Chemist and Outlaw terror groups."

"*Hah!*" Samantha hooted from the living room. "You'll be great at that!" She started laughing hysterically.

"The Outlaw's not a terrorist!" I cried.

Dad looked curiously in her direction. "Since when do you defend the Outlaw?" he asked me, pouring his Keurig coffee into a to-go cup. "Thought you hated the guy."

Samantha's volume increased. "Chase *hates* the Outlaw??" I considered filling her open mouth with a couch cushion.

"I have to run," Dad said, grabbing his stuff. "Hollywood police just radioed. The Outlaw was sighted in a hospital shootout."

Samantha and I blinked innocently. ".........oh?"

"First sighting in months. Maybe he's not dead after all."

Samantha was leaning back on her hands and smiling, "Is there video?"

"Don't know. But it'll be all over the news soon."

"So your job is to catch the Outlaw?" I asked, my head about to explode.

"You could say that. I need to go. Have a good one." He threw me a casual salute, then said, "Samantha, I want your parents to call me. Soon. Got it?" he pointed at her. "Otherwise you and I are going to have a long conversation."

"Have a good day, Richard," she called as he marched out and slammed the door.

"Stop," I glared at her, "calling him Richard!"

"What?? That's his *name*! This is SO much fun."

I lay in bed that night, missing Katie. I hadn't heard from her in days. Earlier that day I wrote her a card, put it in an envelope, and dropped it in her mailbox. It said, *'I love you. For many reasons. One reason is you're the only girl I know who helps her mother garden. You two make your building look very pretty. And you look SUPER hot in your pink gardening tank top.'*

She hadn't replied. It wasn't a good letter. Maybe she was mad. I didn't know how to be romantic. I didn't know how to do anything well, it felt.

I picked up my phone and texted Puck.

Did you hear what Carla said to me last night? After she shot me?

>>**no what?**

I don't remember either. My head was ringing. But I remember she wanted peace between us.

>>**girl shot u and then asked 4 peace??**

Something like that.

>>**crazy b!tc#**

I think Carla doesn't enjoy violence. Just like me. She's rebelling against the Chemist.

>>**but didnt she try 2 stab u in compton?**

Yeah. She has issues. But there might be hope for her.

>>**if u say so**

I put the phone down.

My ruined vest lay at the foot of my bed. The ballistic plates were crunched, the zipper was jammed, and the fabric was torn beyond repair. I needed to contact Lee for a new vest.

I needed to stop getting shot.

I might be safer in jail. Maybe I'd get lucky and Dad would arrest me.

Chapter Five
Thursday, August 13. 2018

The hospital shootout was big news, primarily because of the Outlaw. Puck deleted all the security video, but two Hollywood traffic cameras took pictures of the Outlaw on his motorcycle; Puck didn't notice them until it was too late. The Return of the Outlaw led nightly newscasts for several days, and the Outlaw fan club (the Outlawyers) were whipped into a social media frenzy. Further fanning the flames was the second appearance of the mysterious girl. Helicopters had taken grainy video of Samantha Gear back in March, and now witnesses were describing her again. Was the Outlaw building a *team* of Hyper Sapiens??

"Ridiculous," Samantha sneered, scrolling through news on her tablet. "I'm referred to as the Outlaw's *Sidekick!*"

"Well, if the shoe fits…"

"The shoe doesn't fit, Chase," she growled. "I will stuff the shoe down your throat." Carter was back in town and he chewed Samantha out for letting the kid die. She'd been furious and devastated for two days afterwards.

But who had the Outlaw and his sidekick been fighting?? That was the question. Hospital workers and police sketch artists produced renderings of Blue Eyes, Walter, and Carla, none of which were very accurate. Nobody in the building remembered the babyfaced Infected kid. Nobody except me. An internet news article referred to the hostile Infected group as the 'Trio of

Terrorists' and everyone copied it.

Marshaling all available facts, the media constructed a possible narrative for the shootout; the Trio of Terrorists went to the hospital to bust out their comrade (the patient, who had been seen flipping vehicles earlier that night) but they were foiled by the Outlaw and his sidekick, and during the melee the patient had been shot and fallen off the roof. This narrative wasn't far from the truth, actually.

PuckDaddy entered the nation's collective conversation again. Police cyber-op teams blamed the lack of security footage on a powerful hacker, probably PuckDaddy. He'd been accused of helping the Outlaw previously.

All in all, we made a thorough mess. The only positive outcome of the hospital fiasco was that Dad seemed renewed and reengaged with the world. He spent hours questioning witnesses, examining photos from various cameras, talking with ballistic experts, and inspecting the scene of the gun battle. (Fortunately I'd changed the color of my bike and altered the license plate. Otherwise he would have already busted me.) He worked closely with the FBI, and once at the dinner table he even mentioned my old pal Special Agent Isaac Anderson.

School started in less than two weeks. Samantha and I had football practice each morning, during which we wrestled against the disease's urges to run faster, throw farther, kick higher, and hit harder than humanly possible. Football practices no longer presented any physical challenges, but they exhausted us mentally. After lunch I attended sessions at a quarterback camp. The camp was invitation only, and all the players were cocky alpha males, suspicious and judgmental, not wholly unlike Infected.

At night, Cory and I helped Lee experiment with parachute designs by jumping off his roof. The chutes were small and we landed hard in his pool. Sometimes they didn't even open at all. Lee was an inventor, so we were accustomed to his goofy trials. He never mentioned the fact he was designing the parachutes for the Outlaw's new vest. Samantha visited one night to jump in the pool but she refused the parachute.

Thursday was a gorgeous, clear blue Los Angeles day. Making it even better, Katie attended morning practice. She reclined in the stands, tanning, and alternated between reading *Pride and Prejudice* and watching boring football drills. More than one of my teammates openly stared at her.

Last year at this time, I was memorizing plays as fast as I could, trying to hit receivers in stride, and hoping none of the big guys stepped on me. This year, the football field belonged to me. My teammates hustled faster when I glared at them, and disappointing me was far worse than disappointing the coach. This hierarchal change had developed organically; I was the strongest and fastest guy on the team (even when the disease was dormant), and I was the quarterback, and I was the one being discussed in the sports articles and blogs. I didn't really like the changes and the responsibility, but I was growing numb to it.

After practice, we all huddled around Coach Garrett, a mustached Roman Praetorian Guard of a man. He chomped on his gum and smiled behind sunglasses.

"Good practice today, troops?" he asked and we groaned our answer. "The games are starting soon. We've got a good squad here, and we'll be competitive."

"No," Samantha glared. "We won't be competitive. We'll be *winning*."

"Gear, you've quickly become my favorite football player," he barked. "And a giant pain in my ass."

"Happy to help, Coach."

"Thought you'd all like to know," he continued, "that the Patrick Henry Dragons are favored to win the Division again this year, and also the state championship."

Groans. Jeers. I smiled grimly and spun the football in my hands. I was going to wreck the Dragons' plans.

"Another juicy tidbit," he grinned, "is that our old pal Tank Ware is playing offense now too."

"What?!" I shouted. Loudly. Everyone jumped.

Garrett nodded. "He told his coach he wants the ball. He's going to be the Dragons' starting running back."

"This is a joke."

"No joke, Jackson," he said.

"I hate that guy!" I threw the football in disgust. Judging by the faces of my teammates, I threw it *really* far. I didn't watch. "Freaking…ugh…stupid… stupid stupid Tank! What a self-absorbed glory hog. Jeez, I hate hate *hate* that big ugly cow."

"I like your fire, Jackson," Coach Garrett said. The team was staring at me with wide eyes.

"Coach," I said suddenly. "I want to play linebacker."

"Oh come on Jackson," he chuckled.

"I'm serious. Dead serious. I want to hit Tank when he has the ball. Knock him out of his cleats." I was grinding my teeth so hard the others might be able to hear it.

"Chase," Samantha warned, "Don't make this personal."

"Besides. You're the quarterback," Coach said. "Too valuable to play two positions. You could get hurt."

"I'm playing linebacker," I snarled. Garrett was no longer smiling. "Or I'm quitting as quarterback." The whole team stirred uneasily, except for Daniel Babington. He perked up. Daniel was the second-string quarterback.

"We'll talk about it later, Jackson." His voice had gained a stern edge. "But you don't set the roster. I do. And you don't threaten to quit on your teammates. Ever."

He was right. I was steaming and I couldn't think logically, but deep down I knew he was right. I just really really really hated Tank. I saw red when his name came up.

"Yes sir," I mumbled and I stalked off. Selfish arrogant thick-headed freakish ill-mannered ugly Tank. He was a troll. A goblin. Simpleminded selfish conceited weak dumb duplicitous conniving…

Katie Lopez descended the bleachers and joined me as I stormed off the field. She was wearing blue shorts, a white shirt, and sandals with raised heels. "My favorite quarterback appears…agitated?"

"Your imbecile of a boyfriend is agitating," I glowered.

"Oh?"

"He's going to play running back this year," I said. "Which means he'll play offense *and* defense, and bully kids smaller and weaker than he is."

"Isn't that what good football players are supposed to do?" Her voice held notes of sadness and frustration and defiance, all at once. We stopped walking. For a moment, I truly felt sorry for her. She had chosen the wrong guy, and she knew it, and her inborn loyalty was torturing her. I reached for her hand, and she didn't resist. She felt trapped, I could see it in her face, because she truly had feelings for Tank. Tank...

"He's a villain. Evil. And ugly. And thanks for holding my hand. And I love you." Her fingers sent tingles from my hand to my heart, which was pounding. Some of the football players were walking past us and openly admiring Katie.

She took a deep breath and beamed at me. "Say it again. I like it."

"Break up with him. And I will say it forever."

"How about," she said, squeezing my hand, "I come over tonight?"

"...Go on."

"And cook for you. And we can talk after."

"I accept."

"Count me in," Gear announced, strolling past us, cleats crunching on the gravel. She looked especially militant in her uniform. "I'd kill for Mexican food."

Katie blinked a few times. "Samantha, will you be joining us?"

"I live there now. Chase makes me. Did you notice how good his butt looks in his football uniform?"

"Kicker," I said. "Shut up. Or you'll be homeless again."

We were interrupted by a stranger. Some guy was coming our way, and laughing. Even I could tell he might be the most handsome man alive. He had longish blond hair combed back, a strong jaw, sharp cheekbones, piercing blue eyes, curvy lips, the whole thing. "There she is! There's my girl." He had an accent; he pronounced it *me gull*.

Katie gasped softly. I might have too. He was a beautiful human being.

Samantha groaned. "What are *you* doing here?" she demanded.

"What? You're not happy to see me?" the man grinned. He had dimples too. I wanted to hate him but he was too attractive. He wore jeans, cowboy boots, and a leather jacket. "I flew all the way from Down Under to find you."

"Your accent," Katie said. "It's Australian."

"Right you are, miss. Crikey, what a beauty you are."

"Go back," Samantha said, shoving her pointer finger into his chest. "Go back immediately."

He ignored the finger and wrapped her up in a hug. Samantha resisted, to no avail. "No way," he smiled. "You're even prettier than I remember." *Rememba!*

"Shut. Up," she growled.

"Besides," the guy continued. "Carter'd be cranky if I did."

"Carter?" I asked. The man noticed me for the first time, and nodded. "You know Carter? *The* Carter? Grumpy old man Carter?"

"I do," he said, and stuck out his hand. "I'm Mitch. Good onya!"

"I'm Chase," I said, shoving my hand into his. Another Infected!! "Wow, it's…wow, this is…It's great to meet you."

"Chase?" he laughed. "*The* Chase? Holy doley! This a real honor," he said, pronouncing it *reel onna*. "Finally get to meet the infamous Ou-"

Samantha threw her elbow hard into his stomach and said in a low voice, "Listen, Croc, go back to Australia. Right now. No one here is infamous."

"Ow, woman," he smiled, rubbing his side. "That hurt."

"Good."

Katie asked, "How do you two know each other?"

"Samantha here is my fiancé!" Mitch/Croc grinned.

"*What?*"

"*No* I am not," she bit off the words. "I said *No*, Croc. Twice." Football players trudging past were giving us curious looks.

"You said *No*??" Katie appeared unable to comprehend this. "Why…how…why?"

"Besides, I'm still in high school." Samantha spoke through clenched teeth. "Remember?"

Mitch said, "Of course I remember. I am too! I just enrolled here."

"Oh no," Samantha said. She looked unsteady on her feet. "Croc. Please no. Tell me you didn't."

"Ah yes, love. I'm about to be a senior!"

Katie protested, "No way. There is no way you're in high school. You're at least twenty-five."

I couldn't believe it. Another Infected! And he was nice!? Weren't all Infected supposed to be jerks?

"My birth certificate says I'm eighteen," Mitch said proudly. "I can show it to you; just got it in the mail. The receptionist couldn't believe it either. Suppose I just have one of those faces. And YOU!" he grinned and grabbed me by both ears. "You beautiful man, I'm glad to meet you."

"Not as glad as I am," I said. "We need the help."

"Help?" Katie asked. "With what? The football team?"

"The football team?" Mitch asked. He stepped back and looked Samantha and I up and down, inspecting our uniforms. "You two play American football."

"Croc," Samantha growled, "No."

"I'll play too! Sign me up."

"No no no!"

"Samantha girl," he smiled, and he brushed some of the hair out of her face. "Cheer up! It'll be aces. Where are you staying?"

"None of your business."

I said, "She's staying with me."

Samantha sighed and rolled her eyes. She was frustrated to the point of tears.

Croc grinned. "With you? But you're holding hands with the exotic sheila," he said and he indicated Katie.

"Croc," Samantha said, completely exasperated. "They aren't together. She's got a boyfriend. Some other guy."

"I could tell that immediately. But why is she holding his hand?"

"Because he loves her and she's conflicted. Stop asking questions."

He examined all of us curiously and said, "Wow. What a confusing scrum."

"Come with me," she said, grabbing him by the jacket and hauling him away. "We need to talk."

I watched them go and said, "This is so cool."

Katie beamed. "He called me exotic."

Katie was already in my kitchen when I returned home from quarterback camp. The house smelled like curry chicken and sizzling peppers. She handed me a sweet tea and said, "Change your shirt. You're disgusting."

"You look a lot better in that apron than my dad does," I observed.

"I'm glad you noticed."

"Are you wearing tighter clothes now? Or do you just fill them out better than you used to?"

"Hey!" she laughed. "You can *not* ask me that."

"You're still very trim," I said, and her face turned red as I examined her. "But now you've got these great curves…"

"Chase!" she cried and she flung a red pepper at me. I sat down and we talked.

Katie was lined up to be one of our valedictorians, and her schedule this coming semester was brutal. We didn't have any classes together, which would make the next few months less enjoyable, but once again our lunch periods matched, along with Cory and Lee.

Just for fun I asked her if the Outlaw had visited, and she glowered at me. The Outlaw *had* visited her (twice) at the beginning of the calendar year, a fact she revealed only after growing irritated with the man in the mask. She hadn't heard from the Outlaw since he rescued her in March and she was peeved.

I am the Outlaw. And I would tell her soon. I hadn't told her in the past because I didn't think she'd believe me and because Tank had threatened to hurt her if I blabbed.

Tank woke up from his coma a different man. He'd always been intense and prone to anger, but now he bordered on being unhinged. He was never violent towards Katie, and in fact seemed more deeply attached to her than ever, or so she told me. I pretended to vomit. And I almost did authentically. But now Tank would go through periods of rage and dementia, which the doctors said would eventually go away. But I knew otherwise; Tank was Infected, just like me, and the disease had permanently altered him.

"He hates you, Chase," she said at one point. She was cooking tortillas in the frying pan and she stopped momentarily. "I mean...really hates you."

"Do you know why?"

She shook her head and said, "No. Tank is very proud, though. He gets that from his parents. Everyone is beneath him. I think maybe it's because he's not threatened by anyone, except you."

"That makes sense."

"You offend his superiority."

I asked, "Do you enjoy this characteristic of his? You used to value kindness, not arrogance."

"Tank is very charismatic. He's engaging and fascinating, and his pride is part of that."

"How can you date someone that hates me?" I asked. "I'm so lovable."

Katie didn't answer but she didn't have to. I knew. She started dating him while I was dating Hannah, a colossal mistake on my part. She was with Tank because he had pursued her in a way that I hadn't. But I was determined to never make that mistake again.

"Do you ever think about Hannah?" she asked a moment later.

"I just was, actually."

"It's been five months since she died," she said, the frying pan forgotten. "And I'm still not over it. Even though we weren't great friends."

"Yeah but you were there," I said. "You saw it. That's one of those things that gets inside us and makes us who we are. Permanently."

"Sometimes I think it doesn't seem fair, that I made it out and she didn't. You know? I'm sure her parents feel that way."

"No they don't," I objected. In my mind's eye I could see the whole thing in startling clarity. During that awful night, Katie had been brave and tried to survive, while Hannah waited in her car and complained. A lot of people freeze in times of danger; not Katie. She'd been amazing. "I spoke with them several times. They know. Hannah chose to wait in a lake of gasoline. You didn't."

"It's not my fault," she said, wiping her eyes and offering me a half smile. "I know that. I tell myself that several times a day. It wasn't my fault. But still…"

Samantha returned from wherever it was Samantha always went. I wanted to ask her a million questions about Croc but I couldn't because Katie was with us. Then Dad came in and we all ate together. Dad and I usually eat at the television but this was better. We talked and laughed like a family is supposed to. Even Samantha enjoyed herself.

For dessert, Katie laid chocolate cake on the table. Samantha and I ate it all. Infected are drawn to chocolate. I don't know why.

Later that night, Katie and I were alone on the couch. We were under the same blanket and she was leaning against me. The lights were off and the Dodgers were beating the Braves on the television. I must have fallen asleep because I didn't remember Samantha and Dad leaving.

"We're alone," I observed quietly. She tilted her head back so she could look up at me. Her thick brown hair tickled my neck.

"Yes," she said. The light from the television was suspended in her eyes.

"As it should be."

She smiled. "Remember when we were just little kids?"

"That was a lifetime ago."

"Do you still love me?" she whispered.

"Always."

"Why? I'm dating your arch rival."

"I love you in spite of your glaring faults."

"Hey," she snickered and pinched me. "But. But what if everything changes?"

"What do you mean?"

"High school girls are lonely. Even me. We just are," she said. Her hand under the blanket was stroking my leg. "A lot of my world is built around you. What if…all this changes…and we aren't friends anymore? I would have nothing."

"As long as I live, I will be *at least* your friend."

"You don't know that."

"Think about it," I smiled. "You're dating someone that would honestly kill me if he had the chance. What other more terrible thing could you do? How *could* you drive me away?"

She smiled. Her lips were very close to mine.

"You shouldn't be with him," I said. "You have to know that."

"Chase Jackson. Are you going to pretend," she asked, "that you've never been conflicted romantically? About whom to date?"

Very clear memories surfaced. Of me. Being in love with Katie last fall. But dating Hannah. While sneaking off to Natalie North rendezvous. I was in no position to judge. "I will not pretend that."

"Good."

"Good."

"Want to know a secret?" she asked, a twinkle in her eyes.

"Please."

"I'm jealous of Samantha." Her cheeks colored a little. "She gets to sleep here and I don't."

"That's cute."

"I'm so jealous I can barely speak to her. Even though I really like Samantha."

"Would you like to sleep over too?" I winked.

"Yes. But. Mamá would kill me. And I have a boyfriend."

"What a confusing scrum we have."

Chapter Six
Tuesday, August 25. 2018

School began. I was a senior now and the pristine hallways were full of tiny people staring at me. Somehow, due to the mysterious forces at work in high schools, I'd become popular. People I never met were my friends, which was surreal but enjoyable. Excitement was already building for Friday's football game and even the principals wanted a high-five.

Both Samantha and Mitch were in my first period Science class. I stared them down suspiciously. Mitch (or Croc) was creating mayhem wherever he went, just by smiling. Two girls got into an actual fistfight over being his lab partner! Even the teacher shamelessly adored him. Samantha fumed.

Samantha had given me the intel on Mitch. He was the only known Infected in Australia, and long-time chums with Carter. During the 90's he'd been a championship rugby player, and now he raced dirt bikes. He never lost, she said, unless he crashed on purpose, which actually he enjoyed. His permanent home was deep in the outback, where he owned a colossal and prosperous cattle ranch.

"So he's handsome and fascinating and rich," I said.

"Yeah. So?"

"And he asked you to marry him?"

"Twice. So?" she asked, a dangerous glint in her eye. I dropped the subject quickly.

Next, second period. I walked into my new English classroom…and found Samantha and Mitch. Again. Already there. Waiting on me.

"You two," I hissed through clenched teeth. They smiled innocently from their desks. "Out. Get out. This is *my* English class."

"We're enrolled in this English class too," Samantha shrugged, palms up.

"Strange coincidence, mate," Mitch grinned and all the surrounding girls sighed loudly. I stormed out of the classroom and dialed my least favorite computer hacker.

He answered and I said, "I'm going to kill you, Puck."

"Don't be mad at PuckDaddy. Samantha made me. And then Croc made me. They're worried the Chemist will find you."

"Are they in *all* my classes?" I asked.

"......maybe."

"Find me another senior English class. This very second, Puck."

He sighed loudly and dramatically. "Fine, fine, hang on. No big deal, I'm just coding some bitching software that'll access cellphone cameras, but whatever."

"Get me another class, and transfer them out of my third and fourth periods. I'm not playing with you."

"You're worse than Carter," he grumbled under his breath. I waited impatiently while his keyboard clicked. Traffic flowed around me in a mad dash toward second-period classrooms. "Okay, here we go. Hmmmm, not a lot of options, your majesty. All the other low-level English classes are in the afternoon."

"Low-level??" I yelped. "I'm not *low-level!*"

"Well...you're not smart."

"Yes I am!"

"Chase, you're a badass. You kick butt. I've never seen someone move like you. But you're kinda dumb. Your GPA is pathetic."

I stared wide-eyed at the phone. "No it's not. It's like a 3.5!"

"Exactly. I graduated with a 4.5 when I was fifteen, stupid."

"Yeah, but...I'm very busy, and... Just put me in another English class!!"

"Fine. I'm force-adding you to the honors class down the hall."

"Thank you. And get those two goons out of my other classes."

"Hmm. Maybe. Maybe not. We'll see."

I hustled to the classroom, furious that everyone thought I needed a bodyguard, and tried to sneak in. I failed. The students buzzed when I entered, and the befuddled teacher asked if I'd completed the summer reading list.

Whoops. Hadn't expected this.

"The summer reading list," I repeated, thinking fast.

"Right," the teacher smiled, her hands tightly clasped together. "The list of novels?"

"The list of novels," I repeated again, turning red. Maybe I should just start running.

"Yes, he read them," someone chirped from the back. "We read the novels together."

Katie. She sat smoldering in the middle of her giggling friends, queen of the nerds, watching me with predatory eyes. With the teacher's permission, I took the seat behind her.

"What are you doing here??" she whispered. "Not that I'm complaining."

"Just a strange coincidence, mate," I grinned.

"This class is hard. You will fail."

"Worth it."

All her friends listened and smiled. I wanted to shoo them away.

"You might need a tutor…" she mused.

"I'm not *that* dumb."

"I wasn't insinuating you were dumb. I was hinting that I could help you study."

"Every night," I agreed. "For hours and hours. I'm deeply stupid."

"Obviously."

"I like to hold hands while I study with a tutor."

"I'm afraid my boyfriend is the jealous type," she winked.

The cute girl next to Katie said, "I'm available for tutoring!"

"You're hired." I stuck my tongue out at Katie.

"She can have you when I'm through with you," Katie whispered. Her eyes sparkled, and she turned back around.

Our lunch table experienced a population explosion. I walked into the cafeteria and found all the seats taken. A couple of young football players were sitting with Cory; Lee was presiding over a physics discussion with some fellow inventors; Katie had become a minor celebrity after both ESPN and Time magazine featured stories on her and Tank, and so she had a new retinue; finally, Samantha and Croc were new and they had groupies. In a school full of beautiful people who valued physical perfection, those two were royalty. They were athletic and lean and attractive (not to mention they looked like college students, at the very least) and currently a gaggle of girls were laughing at something Mitch said. Samantha had been noticed and admired last semester, but now she was being worshipped.

In the past, my friends and I had taken up four or five seats at a table for meant for twelve, near the door. Now, extra chairs were brought and there *still* wasn't a single vacant spot.

I was on the verge of demanding a share of someone's seat when a school administrators hustled in and handed Katie a vase of a dozen short-stemmed red roses. All of the girls ooh'ed and aah'ed and took pictures of Katie blushing.

"Tank," I grumbled, and I trudged outside to eat alone at one of the picnic tables in the courtyard.

Much to Samantha Gear's chagrin, Croc used his disease-enhanced body to walk onto the football team and earn a starting spot on defense. He was playing linebacker, and playing it so well Samantha and I kept reminding him to take it easy. He was *everywhere* on the field, as if he always knew where I was going to throw. On the bright side, he'd be able to hit Tank hard when we played the Dragons. Croc wasn't as big or as strong as Tank, but he was Infected, a Hyper Sapien, and he leveled the playing field.

During practice, while the special teams unit was kicking, Mitch came over and stood beside me. He made our uniform look super cool.

I asked, "Have you heard from Carter recently?"

"Best not to worry about that one, mate, always off on a dodgy walkabout. Could be on the North Pole," he grinned. "Haven't seen him in weeks."

"I'm surprised he doesn't stay in Los Angeles, considering what's going on in Compton," I said.

"Carter stirs a lot of pots. He's a deadly information broker, one of the most powerful men in the world. Hard to pin him down. That's why he asked me to come. Lend a hand."

"Where are you staying?"

"I don't sleep much, mate. But I rented a few rooms. One here, one in Compton, and another in Santa Monica."

"Compton?!" I yelped.

"Well, truth be told, I didn't exactly rent that one. Just broke into an empty room. Thought it might be suspicious, otherwise."

"You're staying inside the Chemist's territory?"

"I'll show ya, no worries. Keep yer voice down. We'll go soon. Maybe even Samantha-girl will tag along. It'll be bonza."

"What do you do in Compton?"

"I'm poaching," he winked. "Or at least, I will be soon. Still getting the lay of the land. But I'mma try to reduce Martin's *special* army."

"How?"

"Kidnap'em if I can. Else..." He drew a line across his neck. "That's usually Samy's job. But she's a bit busy these days."

Samy. He called her Samy. Hilarious. Her head would explode if she heard.

"Where else did you say you're staying? Santa Monica? That's over an hour away. Why'd you rent a room there?"

"Heard it's a great watering hole!"

I looked at him blankly.

He clapped me on the back. "You're a right grommet, you are. Surfing, mate!" he clarified. "I love to surf. Especially at night. Let's go this weekend, it'll be aces!"

Croc might be the coolest person in the world.

I stayed after practice to work on the game plan with Coach Garrett and Coach Keith, our offensive coordinator. Our veteran running back had graduated, and our hopes weren't very high for his replacement, a bruiser named Gavin.

When I arrived home, Samantha Gear and Dad were sitting across the kitchen table from each other, intently focused on bits of metal in their hands. Gleaming hardware littered the tabletop surface. They were using plastic oil bottles, cotton swabs, and copper wire brushes to clean and polish the already perfect metal. Neither looked up. Neither spoke.

"Are you two…cleaning pistols?" I asked, bewildered.

"And your father's shotgun," Samantha said. "An Ithaca 37. Unfortunately."

"Standard issue weapon," Dad noted, still bent over his brush. "It gets the job done."

"Not against the Chemist's super goons, it won't," Samantha shook her head. "You need more firepower."

I asked, "Sooooo…did anybody make dinner?"

Dad was amused and he asked, "What shotgun do you recommend?"

"You don't want a shotgun at all," Samantha said, and she blew the hair out of her eyes without breaking focus. "If you're close enough to use a shotgun, you're dead."

"Your friend Samantha is an impressive gun expert."

I nodded. I knew this. Dad, however, probably shouldn't.

Samantha shot me a discreet look and said, "My father taught me about guns."

"Yes," Dad mused, rubbing his chin and peering at her thoughtfully. "I spoke to him. Nice guy."

My head was spinning. "You…you spoke to Samantha's…*dad*?"

"Something wrong with that?"

"No," I said quickly. "Nothing. I guess…not. Did you guys already have dinner?"

Samantha ignored me and said, "I'll tell you what you need, Richard."

"Don't call him Richard."

"You need an assault rifle. And you need grenades." She started jamming metal parts together and the mess in front of her coalesced into a pistol. "A handgun is useless, unless you're a Hyper Sapien like them; his goons are too quick. A shotgun is better, but still not ideal because you'd be too close. Your best chance is to stun or injure them with grenades, and then fire long-range with the assault rifle."

Dad, to his credit, was not dismissing her opinions. "That's the theory we're operating under too. It sounds like you've seen the classified videos of our failed Compton operations."

"Everyone has, Richard."

"Stop calling him Richard."

Samantha continued, "There's no such thing as classified once it hits the internet. At least that's what a hacker told me. Your troops lost because they tried traditional tactics. But those tactics are based on being able to hit slow targets with short bursts. That'll never work."

Dad finished reassembling his gun, and rammed the clip home. "I'll keep that in mind."

"No. Listen." Her jaw was set. "Don't bother with crowd dispersal techniques. Don't bother with non-lethal munitions. They're worthless against the monsters. Trust me. Throw grenades in large numbers, Richard. Better yet, park attack helicopters a half-mile off your strike zone and unleash hell. *Then* send in the infantry with grenades."

Dad shook his head. "Too many civilian casualties."

"You can't outfight them," Samantha said, serious and grim. "You'll lose. But you can outgun them. That's your advantage. Better firepower."

"Your ideas are surprisingly sound, coming from a high school senior. But we do not risk civilian lives. Not even as a last resort."

"Then you only have one option left," Samantha shrugged.

"Which is?"

"Send in your own monsters."

I texted Katie that night.

Having a hard time with your letter. I have, "I love you because I want to love you."

She replied quickly, **>> =) =) =) I like that one a lot. It's probably deeper than you realize.**

I smiled. I'm deep.

>> Where did you eat lunch today?
Outside. Our table was full.
>> Silly. You're the reason we all sit there. You can always sit with me!

For reasons I couldn't explain, my heart filled to bursting and tears seeped out of my eyes.

Thanks. But it looked like you had your hands full with flowers.
>> Yeah

A long pause.

>> Chase, you're perfect. And you deserve someone who treats you that way. My situation is so complicated. I don't deserve your affection.
Katie, keep in mind, I don't love you because you deserve it (even though you do). I love you because I want to. It brings me joy and peace.
>> That cannot possibly be true. Just the thought of it makes me want to cry.
>> And make out. =P
That can be arranged.
>> But I feel like I'm hurting you. Daily.
Then break up with the bozo.
>> It's not that simple. I wish it was.
What did the card say? With the flowers he sent you?
>> You don't want to know stuff like that, Chase.
Sure I do.
>> It said, 'In a world of fool's gold, you're the only treasure that's genuine.'
Wow. That's not bad, actually.
>> I was surprised too.

Was Tank developing real feelings for Katie? How could he not be? She's perfect. For a long time he'd just faked it to hurt me, but now?

I sighed and I pulled out the Outlaw's phone on a whim. I texted Natalie North.

Hello Natalie. Are you back in Los Angeles?

She texted back after a minute. **>> Yes, last week. Filming was behind schedule.**

Still dating Captain FBI, Isaac Anderson?

>> He's here right now!!

Tell him the Outlaw says Hi.

>> I will NOT. He's trying to relax. He cannot know that we text like this.

I told her. The girl that I love, I told her.

>> Good! How'd it go?? (I'm a little jealous)

>> (Okay, a lot jealous. But I have a boyfriend, so it's okay.)

She's very conflicted. But I knew she would be.

>> She

>> Is

>> INSANE

Just then, Croc knocked on my window. I nearly had a heart attack, and my phone went clattering into the far corner. My bedroom was on third floor! I opened the window and he gracefully climbed in, like a gymnast.

"Sorry to scare you, mate," he laughed, looking at my stuff with interest. "I can't reach Samantha's room. She wouldn't let me in, anyhow."

"What are you *doing* here??" My heart was about to pound out of my chest.

"I brought her flowers and lollies." He held up a bouquet. "To surprise her."

"Okay," I said, although this made no sense. At all. "I'll take them to her."

"Ah, good on'ya, Chase, but I'll take them. It's a special day."

"A special day. Why?"

Samantha Gear burst into the room, wearing athletic shorts and a t-shirt, and nearly breathing fire. "Because it's my birthday," she growled.

"Too right!" Croc laughed. "There's my girl."

I cried, "It's your *birthday*?? How could you not tell us?"

"Croc," Samantha said, covering her eyes in obvious vexation. "You are exhausting me."

I asked, "How old are you?"

"Chase, I'm a senior in high school. That's what matters."

"It's the big one," Croc said, presenting the flowers, which she ignored. "She the dirty thirty. And isn't she a beauty in those shorts!"

Samantha glared at him. "You're like a gnat that I can't get rid of."

"Hey. Be nice. What's the matter with you?"

"Thanks mate," Croc said, although the harsh treatment didn't appear to affect his spirits.

"We should have a party!"

"Chase." She held up a finger in my face. "If you throw me a party, I swear I will move out."

"Aces! And move in with me!"

"Croc," she said, and she took a firm grip on his chin. "Mitch. Sweetie, listen to me. It's not going to happen. Ever. Please believe that."

I asked, confused, "Why not? Croc is great!"

"The lad's got a point, you ask me."

She said, "Because. Because of everything. Infected just don't work like that. At least not with each other."

"I brought you all your favorite chocolates," he smiled. The man had relentless optimism. "Happy birthday, love."

"Thank you, Croc. Now go. You're driving me insane."

Dad appeared at the doorway. We all froze, like guilty little kids. His piercing scowl had been strengthened by years on the job. It didn't help our resolve that he was wearing a badge on his belt. He stared hard at all of us, but mostly Mitch.

"G'day, sir," Mitch said. "Sorry 'bout barging in. I'm mates with Chase."

"Son," Dad said.

I responded, "Yes sir?"

"This is unusual."

"I know. Sorry."

"Can you understand why this late-night visit makes

me…apprehensive?" he asked.

"Yes, but it's no big deal-"

"You don't owe me an explanation. Even though it's after eleven. But I expect your conduct to be worthy of my trust. We clear?" His words might as well have been chiseled in stone. All of us nodded.

"Yes sir. Absolutely."

Samantha said, "Definitely."

"Good night," he said. "Keep it down."

"Good night, Richard," she smiled.

Dad arched his eyebrow at her and said, "Good night, Sam." He left.

"Out out out!" she hissed and shoved Croc towards the window.

I asked, "Sam? Why'd he call you Sam?"

"Get out, Croc. I mean it. You just embarrassed me in front of Chase's dad," she glowered.

"I'm going, I'm going," he smiled. "Want to invade Compton with me tonight? I need backup."

"I can't," she said.

"Why not?"

"I have homework."

"*Homework?*" he hooted.

"What??" she glared. "I don't want to fail. You have homework too."

"Chase? How about it? Compton could use an Outlaw sighting. Give'em some hope. Could be bonzo!"

"Sorry, Croc," I yawned. "I'm exhausted."

"Righto, mate, you look zonked. Okay, I'll rack off. But you two remember," he said. "I'm here for a reason. There's a dodgy man holding a lot of people hostage, a right dunny rat. And he needs to cark it."

That went straight over my head. For my benefit, Samantha explained, "That's slang for, it's time for the Chemist to die."

"Bingo, love."

I said, "I agree. Let's do this. Soon."

"Good. Aces. I'll ring Carter and we'll get a plan. Ta-ta," he grinned and he disappeared through the window.

"He's insufferable." Samantha slammed the window and stalked back to her room.

"He's so cool! And why does Dad call you Sam? ...hello?"

Chapter Seven
Thursday, August 27. 2018

Samantha Gear

Another cargo plane landed in Compton Thursday night. I watched the live feed on television with Richard and the Outlaw, all of us frustrated.

Beyond frustrated, actually. With each shipment, the Chemist grew stronger. Each shipment gave him more ingredients for his drugs, more troops, more ammunition, and more clout within the world of zealots. Maniacs from across the globe were arriving in Los Angeles with the intention of sneaking into Compton and joining the Chemist's cause. Some of them were apprehended by the police, and some of them were shot as they attempt to cross the restricted barriers. The rest were captured by the Chemist's forces and put through a rigorous screening process, according to Puck.

I've crawled all over Compton, and I still can't find that old man. I just want one clean shot.

On screen, the fat aircraft taxied to a stop, lights blinking red and white. Airport workers scurried out, pushing a ramp and staircase.

Richard and I stood up in disgust, as if on cue. He stormed up the stairs, answering his buzzing cellphone. The Outlaw stayed on the couch, yawning so big his jaw cracked. I stomped out of the house, cursing. The anger and the disease were rampaging through my body, threatening to overwhelm me.

I didn't go far. To release tension, I practiced jumping over my truck. Chase had forbidden me from shooting civilians with wax bullets, which used to be my stress reliever. So now I practiced jumping, because I was indignant he could jump so much higher than me. Ten times as high.

I never go far. I'm drawn to him. I worry about his safety. I obey him. I need him. Not for any romantic reason or any other reason I can explain. Puck feels the same way. Carter does too, to some extent. I KNOW the Chemist feels it. And I bet Croc will feel it soon. He's our gravity. He's the center of our world now, though I don't know why. He's important and powerful. And kind, which is impossible in our condition. Power corrupts, and we're the most powerful people on earth. We are heavily corrupted. But not him. The Outlaw shines like the sun. I would give my life to keep him alive, no questions asked.

Twenty minutes later, as I was leaning against my truck and panting, Mitch drove up. I groaned and hid; the last thing I needed right now was an overly eager Croc. He scaled Chase's house without a sound and went in through his bedroom window. I suppressed a chuckle; the Outlaw was going to quickly tire of Mitch's entrances, just as I did.

Mitch (I nicknamed him Croc years ago) is handy in a fight. He's irrepressibly energetic and optimistic. Obviously he's gorgeous. And rich, and charming and entertaining and fun, but none of these things matter to me. His affectionate loyalty is cloying and unprofessional, and I can't make him stop.

The Outlaw trudged out his front door, yawning. He and Mitch climbed into the truck and roared off. I mashed a button on my phone. Puck answered.

"What up girl."

"Puck, what the hell is Croc doing? Where's he taking Chase?" I climbed in my own truck, gunned it, reversed out the driveway and chased the distant taillights.

"Training. Croc told me you approved."

"No!" I switched the call from the phone to my bluetooth headset. Puck's noises started pumping straight into my ear. "Training? What kind of training?"

"I don't know," he grunted. "Infected training stuff."

"Damn it, Puck, we don't train each other."

"Never?"

"Never. Where is he going?"

"Some local construction warehouse. I'll push the address onto your phone."

Croc and Chase parked at the back of a dark supply yard and went over the chainlink fence. I parked farther away and entered from a different direction. The open warehouse had canyons of pavers, treated lumber, bags of concrete, hay-bales, rocks, and everything else local construction companies needed, including forklifts and mixers. The night was clear and warm, and I leapt quickly along the ridges of materials, twenty feet in the air, towards the security lights burning in the back. I sat down at a safe distance, on top of a plywood tower, wrapped arms around my knees, and watched in secret. The two guys were clearing a space to work.

Chase asked, "What if we get caught?"

"Crikey, Chase. You run away."

"Dad will kill me if I get caught."

I smiled. Despite being perhaps the most sought-after person on earth, Chase remained just a kid worried about disappointing his father.

"Why would you get caught?? You're Infected! You could outrun a German Shepherd, if you had to."

"*You're* Infected. I'm still a kid in high school."

Croc grabbed fistfuls of Chase's shirt and glared. I stiffened. "No, Chase. No you're not. You have the disease, mate. You must wake up. The story of your life has been entirely rewritten. You will never have a normal life again."

I shivered, partially because of the chilly night and partially because his words brushed against my soul, the way scary truth often does.

Chase took his time answering. "I can have the disease and still live a normal life."

"How many Infected do you know?" Croc hadn't relaxed his grip on the

76

Outlaw's shoulders.

"You. Samantha and Puck. And Carter, I guess."

"And the Chemist. And some of his baddies. Righto?"

Chase nodded.

"Do any of them lead normal lives? No. We don't. We're apples, Chase. Crackers. Crazy. And you will become increasingly so." He smiled suddenly. "And it's brilliant. Your headaches are gone, right? You survived. Now you must embrace the insanity. Admit you've gone apples."

"Apples?"

"You can do anything. And I'm here to lend a hand." Croc released Chase with a shove.

"What can you do?"

"You mean, what abilities has the virus given me?" Croc grinned.

"Yes."

"I'm not as strong as you. Or as fast. Or as coordinated. Or anything, really. But I can read minds."

"What??" Chase cried. "No you can't."

"Too right, I can't." He laughed and I rolled my eyes. Croc will never change. "That's bollocks. But I can *predict* what people will do. Minor prescience through observation. I naturally observe people, especially during periods of extreme stress, and I anticipate their movements and thoughts. I operate during the infinitesimally small period of time between instinct and action. Fast reflexes and all that rot. Martin can do this too, to a lesser extent."

"Martin? The Chemist?"

"Yep. I'll show you. Think of a word, and I'll tell you what it is."

"That's impossible. Or at least, it better be," Chase grumbled.

"Let's try. Ready? Go." He smiled and arched an eyebrow. "Wood. An elephant. Katie Lopez."

"Whoa who WHOA!" Chase cried, waving hands in front of his face and reeling. "What the HECK! How did you…?"

"I was right!"

"Yes, good gosh." Chase pressed his hands into his eyes. He was taking deep breaths. I stifled my laughter; I had a similar reaction the first time Croc used that trick on me. "That was insane! How did you do that?"

"Easy. I watched your eyes. Pretty standard. Plus it's always an elephant."

"Wow. I hated that." Chase was still shaking his head, probably trying to dislodge the feeling Croc was in there.

Then Croc beat him in rock/paper/scissors. They played three games to ten. Croc won ten to three, ten to one, and ten to zero. Chase was grinding his teeth by the end, and Croc was enjoying this far too much. I debated shooting him with one of the wax bullets I always kept in my pocket.

"Okay, I get it," Chase fumed. "You can predict what people will do. You should play poker."

"I make millions playing poker, mate."

"You *do*?! Cheater."

"Hah! When are you going to figure it out? We Infected are bastards. The virus makes us mean as cat's piss."

I nodded. He was right. I pulled out my phone and alternated between reading the news and watching the training.

"Now what?" Chase asked.

"I've seen you fight, Outlaw. Puck sent me all the videos. You're a right tartar. A real bruiser. No one your age should be able to fight like that. You're more than a match for any of the Chemist's beauties. But can you control it?"

Chase waffled his hand. "More than I used to."

"Your body responds strongly to fight-or-flight episodes. Do you follow? Like pouring gasoline on a fire. The more epinephrine you have pumping, the harder your skin, the faster you run...you know the drill, righto? But you can learn to *initiate* these physiological changes, instead of depending on external stimuli."

Croc was right, though I'd never given it much thought. Eleven years ago, when my freakish abilities were still new and foreign, I couldn't control them. I broke my mother's car door by accident. I was nervous on a date and broke the guy's hand. Mom almost called the priest when she saw me snatch four aces out of a deck I'd thrown into the air. I moved out soon after, and Carter found me. Somewhere along the way, I grew into my new body. But it took years, and the Outlaw didn't have that much time.

He put Chase through a series of impossible drills. Juggling bricks. Flicking quarters, sprinting twenty yards and back, and catching the spinning quarter in midair. Hoping around on one hand. Listening for noises a mile away. Throwing knives. Chase was really good at that. Lethal. At everything else, he struggled. He was tired and his adrenaline laid dormant and the minutes ticked by slowly.

Eventually Croc said, "Alright, well done. Keep at these, kid, on your own time. Now let's have a biffo."

"Biffo?"

"Biffo. Fight. A blue. I watched the tape of you in Compton. That night you moved faster than a possum going up a gum tree. You ran circles around those Chemist blokes, mate."

"That was out of desperation," Chase yawned.

"Which is why you practice, so you can do it on command. Do you have any combat training?"

"Absolutely not."

"Show me what you got," Croc grinned. "Hit me."

"Don't be weird."

"M'not. Hit me."

"No Infected has offered to teach me combat."

"Can't say I'm gobsmacked. We don't like to help each other. 'Sept me, I'm the cat's whiskers." He pointed at himself with his thumb.

"The what? You're the cat's...what?" Chase floundered with the Australian slang.

"So far you've only fought regulars, right? The un-Infected?" he asked. Chase confirmed. "Totally different story than fighting Infected, especially one that's been around a while. Now hit me."

"How many Infected do you know, Croc? Other than the Chemist, and Carter, and Gear, and Puck, I mean."

"Not many." Croc rolled his eyes up in thought, and scratched the back of his scalp absently. "I knew Europe, but she carked it last year. Real shame. She was a handy cobber, for a sheila. Who else? I met Retractor. Twice. But he's gone."

"What about Russia? Or China? Or Pacific? Or…I forgot the last one."

The Zealot, I thought. That was the one Chase missed. The weirdest one, currently living in an African prison. Voluntarily.

"Heard about Pacific," Croc nodded. "And I've met Russia once. Huge bloke, nasty Stand-Over Man, you know? Now hit me!"

Chase tried. He couldn't. Despite wearing cowboy boots, tight jeans, and a cumbersome jacket, Croc evaded him easily. Within a few minutes it became obvious that Chase was quicker than Croc, but that didn't help because Croc always vanished. Just like he stated, Croc knew exactly what Chase was going to do.

I grew irritated, quit watching, and went back to my phone. As usual, news about the Sanctuary dominated the headlines. Earlier today, Chemist forces shot down two military surveillance drones. Yesterday a jet raced over Compton and released ten thousand pamphlets about non-violent resistance, blanketing the small city in case any hostages weren't checking the internet. Soon the government would storm the city again, this time with more troops, heavier equipment, and from multiple insertion points. It might work, but the loss of life would be catastrophic and it would not solve the long-term problem. The real danger was the Chemist and his elite leadership team. A large-scale assault would never succeed in capturing him.

It drove reporters mad to have evidence of extraordinary people under their noses but be unable to locate them or learn about their remarkable gifts. Wild conspiracies abounded across website and news channels, and politicians ran entire platforms based on dealing with these 'unique individuals.' The world ached for fresh Outlaw reports, but there weren't any.

Little did anyone know he was just a furious kid in Glendale, stalking a grinning Australian around a lumberyard. Over the course of an hour, the frustrated masked vigilante grew angrier and bigger. Not only did his body swell with the virus's inflammation, his *presence* increased too. During times of stress, the impression Chase made on our senses was heightened, and none of us knew why. He actually *was* bigger, but he *felt* bigger than that.

Croc offered advice and pointed out mistakes. Don't lunge. Don't overextend. Keep your balance. Don't swing so hard. Small movements. You can overwhelm civilians with speed, but not Infected; you must be shrewd. Croc open-hand slapped Chase after mistakes to prove his point. Twice he grabbed him by the ear, like a child, to get his attention. Soon, however, as Chase grew angrier and more focused, Croc was having to block as well as dodge, and he could no longer launch counter-attacks. Croc, the wily veteran, had his hands full with the young quick-learning predator.

There's nothing natural about Chase when he's mad, I thought. He's frightening, even to his allies. It's the same way with Tank. Young Infected require years to learn their new bodies, but not those two. Carter thinks it's related to the superior nutrition modern-day American athletes have access to, and the years of training they both had before displaying Infected symptoms. Chase was a gymnast before playing football. I wasn't an athlete in my prior life, and neither was anyone else that I knew of.

"Okay," Chase said, holding up his hands and backing off. His chest was heaving with exertion for the first time I could remember. "I surrender tonight. I need some sleep before school."

Croc was out of breath too. "Good onya, Chase! This is a good start."

"Why are we doing this? Don't most of them use guns?" He rested his hands on his knees, and sucked wind.

"You need to get used to your body. You need to start thinking like an Infected, you know? You were stumbling around like a baby giraffe. But you still 'ave a long way to go."

Carter said, "I concur." Carter was sitting on top of a pile of lumber near the edge of the guys' practice area, wearing his customary black tactical fatigues. He had arrived twenty minutes ago, sat down, and watched silently. I had seen him but the others hadn't.

"Ah, there's the old slurry!" Croc laughed, and Carter cracked a fraction of a smile, which was a lot for him. "Back from destroying the world?"

"Mitch, my friend. Thank you for being here."

"No worries, old man. I can already tell this is going to be ripper!" He pronounced it *rippah*.

"You enrolled as a student, Mitch," Carter said. Chase, momentarily forgotten, opened and began devouring several chocolate granola bars.

"Yeah, I figured, since Samantha was-"

Carter interrupted. "That wasn't part of the plan."

"Too right, but it's been bonzer. I like it. Plus, since when do I ever follow your plans, mate?"

Croc's willingness to irritate Carter made me nervous. The old man was annoyed.

"I was forced to make unnecessary adjustments, Mitch. Stick to the plan in the future." A lighter flicked in his hands. He pulled the flame to his mouth, and a plume of blue cigarette smoke billowed out of his lips. "The hacker showed me the location of your room in Compton. I'll rendezvous with you there in one hour. I want to survey that area."

"Stella! I'mma rack off, change my clothes, and meet you there." He thumped Chase on the back and said, "Well done, Outlaw. Let's practice again, soon."

He left and in the distance we heard his truck growl to life. Chase jumped up and sat next to Carter, and finished his snack. Carter smoked in silence for several minutes.

"I don't understand it," Carter said eventually. To my surprise he removed his bluetooth earpiece and switched it off. Did he not want Puck eavesdropping? "I don't understand why they are drawn to you."

"What? Who?" Chase asked. I leaned forward to listen. Carter might shoot me if he knew I was eavesdropping.

"All of them. This is the first time I've witnessed one Infected training another. And the Shooter is living in your guest bedroom..." He chuckled in disbelief, staring into the distance. "Infected don't operate this way. We are alpha lions, so to speak, and we don't co-exist peacefully in a single pride."

"I hate to be a broken record, but that might be because you're a jerk."

My eyes widened. He called Carter a jerk. I knew for a fact Carter would kill most people for that. I'd seen it happen. There were many things Chase didn't know, and one of them was Carter's occupation. Yes, Carter was Infected but he was also one of the most powerful men in the shadowy underworlds of intelligence and the black market.

Infected are naturally drawn to chaos and action and danger. Carter provides this for us, along with a salary. We Infected have been his most important weapon for decades, securing his place in powerful circles, making him (and us, to a lesser extent) rich. That's why he always meets the new Infected - to evaluate and recruit. Now the Chemist was threatening to expose us, even more than Chase already had, which could destabilize his whole empire.

"Only one Infected in the last two hundred years was able to draw others to himself, like you can," he said, talking around the cigarette pinched between his lips. "Take a guess."

"The Chemist."

He nodded. "Martin. Martin always induced followers. He sees this trait in you, and that's why he searches for you. To live on through you, for you to be his heir."

"His heir? Pretty strange."

"Not all that strange, hero. He has no children, or at least none that I ever knew of. His wife died centuries ago. Don't we all want to live on, in some way?" He pointed at the city, cigarette in his fingers, towards the towers at which he'd been staring. "I think that's why he's here. To find a successor."

"Is he dying?" Chase asked.

Carter nodded and said, "He is."

Whoa! Didn't see that coming.

The two of them pondered this silently from within the thin blue clouds of cigarette smoke. Several minutes passed before Carter said, "My sources indicate he's on dialysis. His internal organs are finally surrendering." Carter was a tall, imposing figure of a man, usually full of fire and energy. Tonight, however, he seemed introspective and overly calm. "Must be terrifying to have lived for so long, through many decades, watched so many generations come and go, and to finally face the end. I wonder if the length of his life has heightened his fear of its termination."

"You promised you'd tell me about how the virus is spread. When the time is right. Tell me now."

Carter took a deep drag, flicked the cigarette away, and said, "Nineteen years ago, a powerful man named Alfio Alessandro died in an extravagant house near Milan. Alfio was Infected. And he was almost two hundred and fifty years old. I was there. So was Martin. He was a recluse, but he asked us to witness his final moments. Alfio never tolerated the company of other Infected, and so the request was a surprise. He was very weak, very emaciated. At this point in time, Martin and I weren't enemies but neither were we allies. We avoided entanglements, like two old professional poker players. Do you follow?"

"So far."

"We kept to our respective hemispheres, until Alfio called. We came out of respect and curiosity. He gave us each a large vial, full of blood, and told us the secret which had been passed down to him."

"Which is?"

He lit a fresh a cigarette and said, "The virus becomes communicable as the host body dies. It has to be a natural death. Dying of old age, in other words. Very few Infected live until their body gives out. We all die young because we're stupid."

"Like supernovas. Burn up fast and bright."

"Like supernovas. But not Alfio. As the human body begins to die, it releases a variety of opioids and cortisols in such specific combination that the virus begins germination, for lack of a better word. It wants to survive and it becomes contagious."

"So Alfio handed you and Martin vials of his own contaminated and contagious blood."

"Bingo."

"Why?"

"Why indeed," he said. "He didn't tell us. I have guesses. But one thing was certain; for the next few days Martin and I each had a bottle of magic elixir. Perhaps the most powerful force on the planet was in our hands."

"Why just a few days?"

"It's impossible to isolate and stabilize the virus. Or so Alfio told us. Like dynorphins and alkaloids, it has a very short half-life. We didn't want to risk freezing the blood, so we were rushed and, in retrospect, acted foolishly."

"So you came to Los Angeles and began infecting infants," Chase finished the story. The story of his origin. His history. Our future. My mind was reeling. "But you didn't track where the infants went, because you assumed it'd be obvious later on. Did you ever try infecting a teenager? Or an adult?"

"Yes. We tested on prisoners in Mordovia, Russia. It was a disaster. Their brains were already too developed and they went insane and died soon after injection."

With a shock of comprehension, I realized what Carter was saying. Like someone had thrown cold water on me. I understood with complete certainty the nightmare we were walking into. It was going to change the world...

"...on my god..." I breathed.

"Wait a sec," Chase was saying. He was making the connection seconds after me. "The virus is communicable as an Infected body begins to die of old age?"

"Yes," Carter said.

"The Chemist is dying."

"Yes."

"So his blood is about to be..."

"Very soon, Martin will be able to spread the virus. He's extremely old. He's dying. And he's about to start manufacturing blood worth millions. Maybe billions."

"Oh no," Chase groaned. "I'm really going to miss civilization."

"Exactly, kid." He pointed his cigarette at Chase to emphasize the words. "*Oh no* indeed. Given his penchant for chaos, I predict he'll use his blood to...further upset the balance of our planet."

"Infect infants all over the world?"

"Perhaps. He's an extremely intelligent man. Probably one of the more creative scientists alive, hence his nickname. I'm expending an enormous amount of money towards discovering his intentions. All my energy is focused on it. Thus far, I'm coming up empty."

"Why isn't he just dying peacefully? Like the other old guy. Alfio."

"Alfio lived a quieter life than most of us do. He was as peaceful as his condition would allow. Martin has never been that way. He's a showboat. A celebrity, in his own mind. And now he's in pain. He's grieving. Facing his own mortality."

"He wants to go out with a bang," Chase said.

"Basically. And he wants you, hero, to continue his work."

"Why me?"

"You and Martin have much in common. You're a bit of a showboat yourself, Outlaw. A rule breaker. A headline grabber. More advanced than your counterparts, like he was. Plus…and I think this is the clincher…he helped create you. Perhaps for the first time in his long life, he has developed paternal instincts? Maybe. Hell, I don't know. I'm still trying to figure all this out."

Another long silence. My pulse was throbbing all over my body. The Chemist was dying. The virus was going to be contagious soon. The maniac was after Chase.

My concentration was broken when I realized a man was sitting beside me. He was very close. I hadn't heard him arrive, and I only saw him now peripherally because I shook my head. It's impossible to sneak up on an Infected.

I was about to go for my knife when he smiled, revealing beautiful white teeth. "Freng."

He was black, thin, and his face was criss-crossed with old puffy scars. His outfit was similar to Carter's. He had to be the Shadow, Carter's mysterious bodyguard. I'd never met him, but it could be no one else. "Fhreng," he said again.

"Friend?"

"Freng," he nodded. We were speaking in whispers.

"You're the Shadow."

He smiled wider and said, "Yahh."

"You startled me, Shadow. I about cut your throat."

He laughed, a husky, raspy sound. "Car'ah wahngs you fohhow him Compong tanigh."

His words were heavy and thick, and decoding them took me a moment. "Carter wants me to follow him to Compton tonight."

The Shadow nodded.

"Carter knows I'm here? Watching?"

He nodded again.

Uh oh.

"Okay?"

"Okay."

The Shadow grinned and pulled out a Kindle and began reading. I risked a glance at the screen. Poetry. He was reading a poem. About love. There was no end to tonight's surprises.

"Shadow, why do you follow Carter around?" I asked.

He shrugged without looking up and said, "He hhav'g me wheng I wa'h young. From bag famayee."

"He saved you when you were young from a bad family."

"Hepp me. Give me goog 'ife."

"Carter gives you a good life. Why do you pronounce words differently from me?"

"I'm from Africa," he said and then he nearly fell over with silent laughter. His whole body shook. I didn't understand, but his joy was infectious and I couldn't resist the urge to join him. He laughed until tears rolled down his cheeks. "A jhoke, a jhoke." He opened his mouth wide. Behind his perfect white teeth, most of his tongue was missing. He was forming words without a tongue.

"Your evil family cut it out?"

He nodded and said, "'hink I wah a wich!" More laughter, more tears. His eyes screwed shut and he smothered his mouth with his palms, like a child. Was he mildly insane? I couldn't tell. He looked old, perhaps half as old as Carter, but gauging the age of Infected was tricky at best. Maybe seventy-five? Most civilians would guess he was forty.

I wanted to comment further but he became reabsorbed in his poetry. So instead I returned to the ongoing conversation between the grouchy old man and his young upstart protege, sitting on a pile of treated lumber beneath an outdoor security light.

"That's why we need to keep you safe, kid," Carter was saying. "He's not trying to kill you. He's trying to capture you, so he can brainwash you. Turn you. Try his drugs on you. Stay out of Compton unless absolutely necessary."

"What a mess," the Outlaw said. I silently agreed with him.

"Oh, it gets better. Look at these photographs our hacker collected." He passed Chase a tablet loaded with photos. I ground my teeth, unable to see.

"That's the Chemist," Chase said. "Who's he eating dinner with?"

"A California senator, named Joe Younger. The other guy is military, a three-star general at Fort Hunter. And you should know the last man."

"I do. That's...that's Mr. Walker. Hannah Walker's father. I met him once. Gave me my motorcycle."

"Mr. Walker was the driving force behind the new law that sparked the riots. And it appears Martin was the driving force behind Mr. Walker."

"So you're saying," Chase said slowly, his wheels turning, "the Chemist influenced politicians as a means to pass that law?"

"I believe so."

"The Chemist started the riots purposefully?"

"That's my guess."

"Why?"

"Possibly because he wanted a smokescreen to cover up his more sinister activities. And he thrives on chaos."

Chase asked, "When was this taken?"

"Two days ago."

"*What?*" he blurted. "How is that...what? I thought the Chemist was holed up in Compton's sewer system."

"Martin has many identities," Carter said, lighting his third cigarette. "The Chemist is just the most infamous one. He's also an advisor to

Californian politicians. The evidence suggests he's only spending half his time in Compton."

"How's he getting in and out?"

"He's Infected," Carter shrugged. "He's brilliant and powerful. He can do almost anything he wants and not get caught."

"Where does he go?"

"Christ, I forgot how many questions you ask. If I knew where he went, I'd meet him there and shove him through a wood-chipper. I'd pay half a billion dollars to know where he's going. Go to the next picture. Recognize her?"

"Yes. I know her. Samantha calls her Blue Eyes. She was in the hospital the night of the shootout."

"She's a handful, isn't she?" Carter chuckled.

"She messed with my head! Like she had an Outlaw voodoo doll. Samantha said the virus causes her to secrete pheromones."

"A nasty trait. Everyone around her falls helplessly in love with her. Or wants to mate, which is the same thing."

"No it's not. This picture was taken in Washington D.C. What's she doing there?"

"Controlling powerful men. Making them do things we're not going to be happy about."

"To summarize," Chase said, ticking things off on his fingers. "The Chemist captured Compton. He will soon release contagious blood into the world for some nefarious purpose. His army is growing larger. And he and his minions are controlling powerful political and military leaders. This sounds like a disaster."

"There's always a disaster, champ. I specialize in disasters. You just never knew they existed until now. The public doesn't know the full extent, and I like to keep it that way."

The Outlaw grinned. "I really rocked the foundations of your world when I warned the Times about the Chemist, huh?"

"In more ways than you know."

"I'm awesome."

"You're a pain in my ass," Carter said. "But this disaster will be a lot worse if Martin gets his hands on you."

"I'm tired," Chase yawned. "I've been tired for hours."

"I had your motorcycle brought. It's just beyond the fence. I'll leave you now. My night is just beginning."

Chapter Eight
Thursday/Friday, August 27/28. 2018

Samantha Gear

We crossed the Glenn Anderson Freeway into Compton later that night. Technically the Chemist had captured a fiefdom slightly larger than just Compton, but we called it that because using the term 'Sanctuary' was unacceptable. That's how the *Chemist* referred to it.

Sneaking in was simple. The boundary was too long for every inch to be monitored at all times by the military. I'm sure the motion sensors detected us, but we were deep inside enemy territory before the captain of the night shift even set his coffee down.

Like all cities, Compton never truly sleeps, even now in the middle of the night. Televisions winked behind curtains, dogs barked, couples fought, babies cried, and occasional cars thumped past. The only obvious oddity about Compton was the patrol of heavily armed gunmen stalking the perimeter of wrecked cars. My hands shook with the urge to pick them off. One shot from my pistol, no noise, simple, easy, clean, their brains would just turn off, pop, one less goon in the world. But Chase would disapprove. Damn it, why did I care what he thought?

Carter and I waited at a vacant storefront. He smoked and I scanned the rooftops, paranoid, until Shadow rolled up in a black SUV. We climbed into the back, the engine purred, and we began ghosting through the hostile streets.

"You heard everything?" Carter asked me. He was staring out the tinted window.

"Yes."

"And?"

"Illuminating," I said. Shadow darted a glance at me in the rearview mirror.

Carter sniffed and said, "That all?"

"Why don't I go to Washington? Unfetter Blue Eyes from her mortal coil?"

"*Could* you go? Even if I required you to? Could you leave the boy?"

I looked away in hot shame. He knew. I had hoped my attachment to the Outlaw was undetectable. Apparently not.

He continued, "I feel it too. There is something in Chase that…engages the virus within us. We're suspicious by nature, but we trust him. Martin also has this trait."

"I feel protective. That is all. I want him alive."

"Which is why you must stay. Keep Chase alive. Besides, Mary has a body guard. An effective one."

"Who is Mary?"

"You call her Blue Eyes. Mary is her real name. To borrow your term, she has a *shadow*. With her, in Washington. I sent a small team to dispatch her. None came back."

Carter had never been this forth-coming before. I was absorbing information as fast as I could.

"A small team? Certainly not Infected."

"No," he said, and he blew a blast of frustrated air at the vehicle's ceiling. "I wish. Infected are a very finite resource. I sent a team of my own mercenaries. Good men. Mary and her shadow eliminated them. I never received a final communication. You'd have a better chance but…I'd rather have you alive than Mary dead."

"I'm not so sure. Blue Eyes had instant control of Chase in the hospital. She's potent."

"Her sphere of influence will grow larger, too. In future combat, she's your number one priority."

Our vehicle braked to a stop near the intersection of Rosencrans and Alameda. Croc was waiting for us beside a brick residential building with darkened windows, and he opened my car door.

"Welcome, love, to my Shangri-La."

"Save it, Croc."

The apartment building didn't have a roof built for visitors, but we went up there anyway. Carter always took the higher ground. We sat under the stars on humming HVAC units, and we examined Compton as if it would surrender secrets once we stared hard enough. Carter periodically glanced at incoming text messages on his phone, but never responded; his thumbs were misshapen from the virus, and accurate texting was impossible. I surveyed the skyline through a high-powered scope, noting the location of sentries. Shadow was somewhere close and silent. Croc's head was swelling from the effort of not speaking.

"Cities are like rivers," Carter said at last. "Energy flows through them constantly, never at rest. They move. They swell and retreat, and rise and fall. Life grows naturally within. But not Compton. It's become a bog. A swamp. Nothing gets in, nothing escapes. The discontent, the hate, the anger is accumulating like pond scum."

"Right-o, Carter."

"What have you observed, Mitch?"

"The town is feral. Putrid," Croc said. "The people have lost their life. No spirit. They're bored. Bored and angry."

I said, "Bad combination."

"Too right, love."

Carter lit a cigarette and said, "There's a great story about George Harrison, one of the Beatles. Are you two old enough to remember the Beatles? I've always enjoyed them. Anyway, the Beatles helped usher in the drug culture of the Sixties. Did a lot of LSD. So George Harrison went to visit Haight-Ashbury, a hippie commune in San Francisco. It *should* have been a utopia, according to their beliefs. Just a bunch of free-thinkers, smoking dope, doing acid, listening to the Beatles, peace, love, harmony, all that. But it wasn't. Harrison was horrified. Called it ghastly. He finally saw the truth. It was a pile of unwashed drug addicts, hungry drop-outs in dirty laundry. Listless and covered in their own filth. Drug utopias are an illusion, a happy fantasy. Can't work. So here's the question, my Infected brethren. Martin is one of the most intelligent men alive. He knows this small drug-infested kingdom can't last. He knows this is a lie. What's he doing?"

I had no answer.

Croc grinned and said, "If you don't know either, Carter, we're up a creek."

Carter ticked a list off on his fingers. "Compton's hospitals are low on supplies. The Bloods and Crips are at each other's throats, and the body count is mounting. A big chunk of the population is either high or crashing, continuously. There's no law and order, other than what the gunmen enforce through homicide. Fresh produce is long gone. Everyone is getting tired of eating from cans. Parents are exhausted with their children. Tell me. What's he doing?"

I said, "He's stalling."

"Why."

"He needs something here."

"What."

"I don't know," I replied. "Maybe he's still collecting all the Infected he created at birth."

"I think that's over," Carter said. "The outbreak lasted for nine months. More or less. We'll see no new cases. That's my guess. The number of Infected in the world is once again set in stone. But I agree with you; he's stalling. Waiting on something."

"What?"

"I wish I knew," he laughed darkly, filling the air with smoke. "It's not just a territory grab. He knows he can't compete with the entire American government. They'll break in eventually. Soon. After the Outlaw exposed him in the newspaper, he should have retreated. He's collected a stable of new Infected; he should have taken them and gotten the hell out of dodge."

"He's dying, right?" Croc asked. "Kicking the bucket? Maybe he can't leave."

"That's not how Infected work. We keep our vitality and our energy until our organs quit. He's still active. I have evidence of him roaming the country."

I said, "Maybe he's staying until he can capture the Outlaw."

We were silent, considering the implications. It fit. He was obsessed with Chase. And nothing else made sense.

"I hope not," Carter said darkly. "If he gets the Outlaw, we've lost."

Chapter Nine
Friday, August 28. 2018

Friday. Game day! Our first one.

The hallways were festooned with red and black, and I was pounded on the back all the way to science class. The teacher had finger-painted my number onto her cheek. She even forgave my forgotten homework; I'd gone straight to bed last night after training with Croc. I was exhausted, but he looked fresh as always, because he was a beautiful punk.

To everyone's surprise, Lee landed the job of co-anchor on our school's morning newscast. He had so many credits that he technically graduated last May, so now he took media studies and a bunch of classes for college credit. Usually his news stories focused on current events and social media, but today he unveiled a video titled "The Genius's Game Plan." He used last year's game film (and newer practice footage) to illustrate how we should beat the Pasadena Panthers. It was witty and clever, and also demonstrated he knew absolutely nothing about football. He ended with, "That's how we'll win. And if we lose? Don't blame *this* genius, bro."

"Too right," Mitch crowed. "We'll all blame Chase!" Everyone laughed. Ha. Ha. Hilarious.

Next came my favorite time of the day: English class with Katie. We played a daily game of racing to the room for the right to sit behind the loser. The loser was harassed during class by the winner, who was hidden from the teacher's eyesight.

Katie won again today. Her brown hair was back in a ponytail, she had eyeblack on the tops of her cheeks, and she was wearing my jersey. She was so pretty and happy that even her friends openly admired her.

"Hi Chase!"

"I'm going to text Tank a photo of you wearing that jersey."

"Don't you dare!"

"Break up with him and I won't."

"You're a stinker." But she smiled. So big and beautiful it hurt to look at her. "I will never wear it again if you do."

"Yes you will. Because I'm soooooooo great."

The guy next to us said, "Ew."

"Hey you shut up, Cody. I saw your last quiz, smart-guy. It was a B. You need to focus on English. Not on Katie." He stared wide-eyed at me through his stylish glasses, his mouth working without sound. "Just kidding, Cody. I like your bowtie."

"Chase. Sit down." Katie tugged my shirt. "You're in an honors class. Not on a football field."

Class started. Before long, Katie passed me a note on pink paper.

She wrote, If you were a vegetable, you'd be a cute-cumber!!

I wrote back, **That's the worst thing I've ever heard.**

Maybe you're a banana. Because I find you a-peel-ing!

Hoooooooly cow.

= P Let's see you do better.

Marry me.

Chase!

Okay, fine. Come over later and let's make out.

Instead, let's go to Starbucks. Because I like you a latte!

So bad. Focus on English.

English?? I thought we had Chemistry!!

I drew a dirty picture of us. She gasped and balled up the paper.

I arrived late to lunch. Again. The table was packed. Again. This time with a *second* row of seats around the central table. No empty chairs in sight. Sigh.

Katie caught me by the hand as I was heading outside to eat in the courtyard. "Come on, handsome. Don't abandon us. We only sit there because of you."

"Going to share a seat with me?"

"I will share a seat with you the rest of my life." She blushed. I might have to. She drew me back to the cafeteria. "Even if I marry the King of England, I'll still share a seat with you. Besides, you're the most popular guy in school. You're nobility. You tell anyone to move and they will."

"Really?"

"Well. Anyone except Samantha."

"No, I mean, I'm the most popular guy in school?"

"Gosh you're clueless." She shook her head as we sat down at the table. "Somethings never change."

Lee asked, "What never changes, bro?"

"I liked your morning report."

Cory nodded. "Yeah. Yeah, that was fly."

I asked, "How long did that video take to make?"

"Not long. I'm a genius, dude."

"Right. I forgot."

"My next report will be on the Outlaw!" he announced triumphantly.

"What??" I sputtered. "Why? Don't do that."

Katie cheered. "Great idea, Lee! He's my favorite."

I risked a glance down the table. Mitch and Samantha were rolling their eyes. There were so many students, and so many conversations, they'd have to shout for us to hear them.

"Do you want to be interviewed, dude? I mean, Katie? You have a personal Outlaw video on your phone. And he *rescued* you. Twice!"

"No thanks," she wrinkled her nose. "I'm a little tired of interviews. I want to leave all that in the past."

Lee shrugged and said, "Whatever. I'm going to show everyone texts the Outlaw sent me."

I frowned. "Why?"

"To establish legitimacy, man. Prove I'm an authority on him."

"That's a breach of trust."

Cory, chewing a chicken patty sandwich, nodded and said, "For real. That's cold, Lee."

"Dude, no it's not! You all shut up!"

"Lee," Katie said softly. "What if word gets out in the media that you communicate with the Outlaw? You could become a target. And the Outlaw would eventually hear you betrayed him, and he'd quit texting you."

"Fine!" he huffed. "Whatever. But you can't spoil all my fun. I've figured out the Outlaw's real identity."

Samantha straightened in her chair. Katie cried, "Oooooooh, I want to know!"

I said, "He doesn't *really* know, Katie."

"Yes I do, dude! Or at least, I've narrowed it down."

"How?"

"I can't tell you!" he practically shouted, knocking over his bottle of water. Before it could spill, Croc caught it from across the table and sat it upright again. I'd seen him do that twice, both times in the blink of an eye. "I'll never ruin the surprise!"

"You don't know who the Outlaw is, little man," Samantha teased, raising her voice to be heard. Our conversation was extra weird because so many kids were eavesdropping. The little blonde girl next to me kept bumping me by accident (I think) and smiling. She was cute. No idea who she was.

"Okay fine I'll tell you. Dang you people are nosey," he complained. He didn't know. There was no way. But still, I got a little nervous. "Okay, here are the clues. He's big. He's athletic. He's got a cannon for a right arm; we all saw him throwing on the Compton videos. I've watched them dozens of times, and he can throw a hundred miles an hour. I guarantee it, dude. He only operates at night, which means he's a night-owl. Nocturnal. Crepuscular."

"Cre-what?" I asked.

"Shhhhush!!! And he's more active between the months of October and April. Those are our clues. Can anyone figure it out?" he asked. To his credit, we were all a captive audience. Katie's eyes screwed up in thought. Cory stared off into the distance. Samantha and Croc shared a concerned expression. My hip was pressed into Katie's, so that was cool.

The little blonde girl next to me whispered, "Do you know who it is?"

"Yes," I whispered back, conspiratorially.

"Who?"

"Me."

She dissolved into silent giggles. I'm so funny.

"Okay, dudes," Lee said, like a magician about to reveal his secret. "I'll tell you. The Outlaw is...a starting pitcher for the Los Angeles Dodgers!"

General approval hummed from the table. Katie loved the idea. Samantha snorted. Cory nodded and chewed thoughtfully.

I said, "Lee, I think that's brilliant."

"Yeah?"

"Makes total sense. Athletic. Puts on the mask after night games. More active in the offseason. Throws hard. Lives downtown. It's fantastic."

"Thanks bro."

The girl next to me piped up. "I think Chase is the Outlaw!"

Everyone laughed, but Samantha gave her such a withering stare I thought she might never return.

That night, as per tradition, Katie's mom made a pre-game dinner for Cory and me. This year Katie also invited Samantha Gear and Croc. Her small kitchen table was dangerously over capacity. Even dad stopped by! We ate so many shepherd-style tacos that Samantha raced to the store for extra groceries and Croc slipped a hundred-dollar bill into Ms. Lopez's purse. She kept referring to us as her *familia grande*.

After dinner we returned to school, took a dozen pictures with tailgaters in the parking lot, and marched into the glistening locker-room. The only thing more exciting than a Friday night football game is the almost certitude of victory. Expectations for the season were skyscraper-high. The face-painted fans were delirious with victories not yet earned.

Croc was nervous. I hadn't expected that. I wasn't nervous, just eager. Perhaps my butterflies had been ground into dust by the previous twelve months. He paced in front of my bench, spinning a football on each of his pointer fingers.

Cory said, "Croc. Chill, homie. You 'gon be good."

I grinned. "Yeah mate. This will be fun."

"Too right," he nodded, but he didn't stop pacing.

"What's got you worked up?"

"M'not."

I asked, "Didn't you race motorcycles? The chances of breaking your neck are much less on a football field."

"Yeah," he nodded. "Yeah. But if you wreck a ringdinger, the only person disappointed is yourself, mate. Jus' you and the bike. Don't you ever worry about that? Disappointing the mob?"

"Well...maybe..."

"Katie's mum will be watching, right? What if we play like buggers? What if we lose? She cooked dinner for nothing. And what about Katie? Your dad?"

"*Alright*, Croc!" The first hint of cold anxiety crept in. What if I *did* play bad? "Maybe you should shut up now."

"Yeah," Cory agreed, looking a little queasy. "That was messed up."

I felt better on the field. The Panthers didn't look nearly as monstrous as last season. They stomped the green grass, raced through warmups, and bellowed like animals, but they looked more like kittens than jungle cats.

"Did they get smaller?" I wondered out loud.

"No sir," Coach Garrett said, walking up with a clipboard clamped in his hand. "You've gotten better. And more experienced."

"I'm going to torch those poor guys."

"That's the plan." He smacked me on the butt, the way football players often do. However, my adrenalin was pumping and my skin and muscles were hardening, and he walked away with a grimace, shaking his hand.

The players were announced. The band played. The fans roared. The national anthem was sung. Cory and I had been selected as two of our team captains; we shook hands with the opposing captains at midfield, and lost the coin toss.

As we trotted back to our sidelines, above all the screaming and madness, I distinctly heard Katie laughing and cheering with her friends. Her soft voice pierced the cacophony, like a searchlight in the night. Infected often have heightened senses. Perhaps mine were tuned towards Katie in particular?

"I know!" she was saying, the sound intimate and warm in my ears despite the distance. "I knocked over my drink in less than thirty seconds. I'm clumsy." More laughter. Her friend brushed beads of water off her shorts. "At least I didn't get it on Chase's jersey." More discussion from friends. "Yeah, I sleep in this most nights. Please don't tell my boyfriend!"

Katie was fifty yards away, but I was watching and listening like we were at the same lunch table. The experience was dreamlike. She pulled strands of hair from her face, surveyed the field, and found me. Our eyes locked. Hers widened slightly with surprise and pleasure. Her heartbeat quickened, the pulse in her neck visible to my eyes. I felt like I'd been struck with electricity.

"Chase." Samantha Gear hit me with her helmet. "Focus. I don't want to lose my first football game."

I shook out of my trance. Samantha glowered at me like a drill sergeant inspecting her troops. The sounds of the stadium crashed back into my ears, filling the void left by Katie's absence.

"What's the matter, kicker? Nervous?"

She shot back, "Heck yes, I'm nervous."

"Why? This is a game. You've been in *combat.*"

"I never played school sports. I've never been cheered for. Or booed. This is intense. So get your act together," she called as she ran onto the field for kickoff.

"Yes ma'am."

Samantha was pumped. Her kickoff sailed across the field and out of the end zone, practically impossible for a high school student. That hadn't happened once last season, not even close. The other team watched it fly by in disbelief. She's a *girl*?? Our fans nearly hyperventilated in delight.

Back on the sidelines, she scowled at me defiantly, so I kept my mouth closed. I didn't need to tell her the kick was too far. She knew.

"Hell, Samantha," Coach Garrett said, chomping his gum with relish. "Never seen that before. School division is going to test you for steroids."

"Once in a life-time kick, coach," she explained. "Won't happen again."

"Better not," I mumbled under my breath.

"Shut. Up. I'm excited."

Croc intercepted the Panther's very first pass. He darted in front of the receiver, plucked the ball neatly out of the air, and ran out of bounds. Our players and coaches pounded him on the back. He released a primal roar, tore off his helmet and pumped his fist at the crowd. He was so happy and handsome I worried our fans might rush the field.

I grabbed both of them by the necks of their jerseys. "Nice game so far, high school *students*," I hissed. "You're playing well for *teenagers*. Keep up the good work, *normal kids*."

The message didn't penetrate. I could tell. The virus was a roaring inferno inside their bodies, filling their eyes with mania. They were volcanoes.

I couldn't stay mad at them, though. I ran onto the field with the offense, the crowd raged, and I was engulfed by the disease too. The virus floods our bodies with vitality and life, and I could have thrown the ball to the moon. The fight-or-flight response was consuming. My breath came in ragged heaves. I wanted to start a fight against the other team. The *entire* other team. I wanted to leap into their midst and start swinging, not from hate, but from urgency, to release pressure.

I rifled my first pass a thousand times harder than I should. It hit Josh Magee in the helmet and ricocheted thirty yards into the sky. All twenty thousand fans and players stared at the ball spinning upwards into the dusk, and then held their breath as it plunged. I jumped over them all, far too high, caught the ball, and was massacred at landing. Even from underneath the dog-pile of Panthers leaping onto of me, I heard Croc and Gear howling with laughter.

"Nice job, *teenager!*"

"Good on'ya, mate! You're a *normal student!*"

They were laughing so hard they couldn't stand.

After that debacle, the three of us bore down and played more like high school football players should. Really really *really* good football players, but still. I threw touchdown passes to Josh Magee and Brad Atkinson, both junior wide receivers, and another one to Gavin, our running back. He and I also rushed for one touchdown each. Samantha's kicks returned to the realm of normalcy, and Croc only intercepted one more pass. We won forty-one to ten, and our fanbase's thirst for blood was satiated.

Samantha, who wasn't allowed inside the boy's locker-room, was waiting for Croc, Cory and me outside. Croc spread his arms and smiled. "Which victory rager should we attend?"

Samantha scowled. "I'm sick of people, and I'm going home."

I didn't say anything. PuckDaddy was texting me.

> >Nice game i listened on the radio
>> dont want to crash ur party but...
>> the chemist just sent u a message
>> and thats not a typo

Chapter Ten

Saturday, August 29. 2018

When the sun came up Saturday morning, it found me staring at the message on my tablet.

From: napoleon
Date: August 28. 19:32
Subject: Los Angeles

Dearest Wart,
The future king,

Greetings. From your most ardent admirer.
All is on the hazard. Eh, scout? The fate of Rome rests on your shoulders. So perhaps its greatest generals should have parlay.
Good words are better than bad strokes, young man. You can trust me. Merlin was never treacherous.

Martin
* respond quickly, son. Soon your city will be no more and I will be elsewhere.
* if I were you, I'd leave Carter out of this. Old Baldie is using you.

What. The. *Heck.*

I called Puck last night, seeking answers. "He emailed me," Puck said. "Believe it or not, he and I used to communicate a lot, though it's been a while. Last night, bing, there it is in my in-box, with a polite note asking PuckDaddy to forward the message to the Outlaw."

"Did you tell Carter?"

"…no. It's addressed to you. And I think I agree with the Chemist's final line."

"What should I do?"

"Beats me, man. This is way above PuckDaddy's pay-grade. I'm just the messenger."

So I stared at the words until I feel asleep, and I was staring at them again in the morning. I knew he was referencing Shakespeare's *Julius Caesar*, because I studied it in English last year. The Chemist was comparing our situation to Anthony and Brutus battling for Rome, and he wanted to talk before he destroyed Los Angeles, like the generals did in Act V. And he thought I should leave Carter out of it.

Soon your city will be no more.

Old Baldie is using you.

I needed to talk with someone about this. Someone I could trust. Someone who cared about the city as much as me. Someone not tainted by Carter or the Chemist. Someone…without the virus.

I texted Natalie North.

I need to meet with your boyfriend. Pronto.

That night, just after dark, Croc and I went to our training grounds again. The spot he found was perfect: a secluded clearing in the back of a construction/lumber yard. Croc was quickly leap-frogging up my list of favorite people. Most Infected were grouchy and secretive, but not him. He was secretive alright, but also honest and happy and eager to be around others, like a stray golden retriever.

"Okay, mate," he said, holding up a quarter. He was wearing his usual jeans and cowboy boots. "Let's see how you do. I'll flip it, you get to the pile of wood and back, and then catch it. Ready?"

"Croc, I can't do that. Maybe in the heat of battle, during a fight-or-flight episode, but not right now."

"I'm sorry to hear that, Chase," he grinned. "Real sorry. Because my girl Samantha is going to shoot you with a wax bullet if you fail."

"What?!" I whirled around. Sure enough, Samantha Gear was sitting cross-legged on a stack of treated lumber, ten feet high, calmly screwing a silencer onto her pistol. Both the silencer and pistol caught the cold gleam from the overhead security light. "Samantha! You can't shoot me. I took you into my home! Shame on you."

"Sorry, Outlaw," she shrugged. "Better learn fast." She fired four shots, the bullets snapping and breaking on a nearby pallet of bricks and rocks. "First failure, I'll shoot you in your rear end. Second, your shoulder. Third, your skull. That one's gonna hurt."

"Guys," I half laughed, half groaned. This sucked. "I'm not good enough-"

"Ready Go!" Croc called, flicking the quarter upwards.

I bolted without thinking, cursing under my breath! Stupid friends…gravel, lumber! Back! The world was a blur. Made it! I snatched the quarter a foot off the ground and hurled it at Samantha. She yelped and ducked, just inches under the slicing coin. Had she been a tenth of a second slower, the coin would have scalped her like a small scythe. I'd thrown hard enough to bury the metal into concrete.

"Hey!" she shouted. "What's that for??"

"You were going to shoot me!" I yelled back, anger hot and gritty in my voice.

"But I didn't!"

"Well, I didn't hit you with the coin either."

"You tried!"

"No I didn't! I *hit* my target."

"Me too," she snarled, and she fired. Two shots.

Time slowed. I could see the projectiles distorting the air. I heard their hiss. Outraged, in the ocean of time during that half-instant, I twisted away from the first bullet and plucked the second bullet out of the air. Or rather, I redirected it, slinging the bullet around my body and releasing it back in her direction. The bullet caught her in the stomach. The wax melted from the hard impact against her jacket, sticking to the leather. She didn't react. She gaped at me, stunned.

"Crikey," Croc whistled.

"Jeez, Chase."

"What?!" I asked. I was still mad, determined not to be distracted by their shock. "What's the matter with you two jerks?"

"You just…"

"That was a pretty spiffy trick, mate." Croc laughed and shook his head. "Ripper, bonzo, you know? Good on'ya."

"You just caught a bullet, Chase." She was gingerly rubbing her stomach.

"No." I frowned and tried to remember what I'd done. It didn't seem impressive at the time. "I just…aimed it back at you. That's all."

"*That's all?*?"

"I don't…" I said. The details were fuzzy. It just…*happened*. "I don't know what that was. Yeah, that was weird."

"Didn't know we could move that fast. And, mate, you caught the quarter."

"Of course I caught the quarter! She was going to shoot me."

"No she wasn't," Croc said. I was getting sick of his mischievous smile. "We just told you that. Made you believe a whopper."

Samantha said, "We lied. There was no genuine external stimuli, Outlaw." Her jacket and shirt were pulled up, and she was examining the skin of her stomach. Her abs were impressive. She could be on an exercise magazine. "You just thought there would be."

"In other words, brother, yer brain tricked yer body. You controlled the ability."

"You two are the worst friends ever."

But he was right. I had launched myself into the virus's clutches simply out of fear. There was no real danger. It was a mental ruse, a device I could potentially use in the future. The rest of Croc's drills were simple, now that I was engorged with adrenalin. My muscles strained against hard skin; my emotions strained against will-power; the impossible became elementary. I was punchy and felt like fighting them both at the same time, or juggling blocks of concrete, or taking Compton by storm.

"Focus, Outlaw," Croc warned, noticing my impulses were becoming harder to control. "This is how Infected die. The virus is a rager. You give it control and yer toast. Up a creek. *Use* the energy, mate. Don't let it use you."

Controlling the storm inside was like flexing a muscle. It was exhausting and after an hour I was mentally and physically drained.

"Okay," I panted, laying on my back and staring upwards past the light at the nonexistent stars. "Done for the night. I've got another appointment."

"With who?" asked Samantha, casually, from her perch.

"With Katie."

"Liar."

"Say's who?"

"Puck. He told me you're going to meet that FBI agent."

"Ugh. Freaking Puck," I growled. "All up in my business. He still monitors all of my phones?"

"Always."

Croc noted, "Nosey bloke."

Samantha said, "I'm going with you."

"I told Captain FBI I was coming alone."

"Don't care. I'm coming. I can stay out of sight."

We scaled the chain fence and went to our vehicles. I pulled on the new black vest I'd picked up from Lee's backyard a week ago.

Croc said, "You trust this FBI fella?"

"A little. But I trust his girlfriend completely."

"Right-o. I'm gone surfing." He waved and roared away in his truck. Samantha sat in hers, lost in thought, as I camouflaged my bike and my helmet with red decals. I also altered the license plate. The Los Angeles night was quiet and thick around us.

"Puck told me about the letter. From the Chemist," she said.

"He tells you everything." I was reapplying a few misplaced stickers. Just like all crimefighters do.

"He came to the same conclusion I have."

"Which is?"

"This battle is not between the Chemist and Carter. It's between the Chemist and you."

"I bet Carter disagrees with you," I observed dryly.

"And we're not sure we trust Carter anymore."

"Did you ever? And does it even matter if you trust him?"

"Chase!" she snapped. "You're not listening. Carter is a way of life. Our leader. For years. Decades. And suddenly…we're questioning our allegiances. Our everything. This is not a small detail."

"I don't understand the significance."

"Our existence has always been about secrecy. Most Infected naturally want it that way, but also because Carter enforces the secrecy. We've lived in shadows for centuries, like scared animals, and the only unifying element was Carter. Do you know how much good we could have done over the years? But we didn't. We laid low, did Carter's bidding for money, and died spectacular deaths. Now…right and wrong have entered our world. Good and evil. Choices. Morality. And it's all because something inside of you resists the reptilian tendencies of the virus, and we see what we *could* be. Is any of this making sense to you?"

I stood and brushed the gravel off my pants. "I get it. At least, a little. But I'm just a kid trying to graduate high school. I realize I was born strange. I'm slowly coming to accept that. But I don't live in your world. At least not yet."

She threw her hands up in exasperation. "You know how hard these changes are for you to accept? That's how we feel too. Suddenly, I don't think I can go back to my cold, empty house in Germany."

"Cool. Stay with us."

"I wish," she growled, "that I could make you realize how unlike an

Infected you sound. No one says stuff like that. Especially not Carter. Which is one reason I think this fight is more about you, and less about him."

"I'm not crazy about Carter either. But I wouldn't make him an enemy yet, if I were you. The world is full of them already."

"He's not an enemy. I'm just reevaluating…blind loyalty."

I pulled on the black mask that covered my nose and mouth, and then I tied the red bandana around my forehead, Rambo style. "An excellent idea. But don't be blindly loyal to me, either. I'm not the leader."

She scrutinized me with pursed lips for a moment and said, "A hurricane is a hurricane. Whether he admits it or not."

I groaned, yanked on the helmet, and said, "Let's go."

Months had passed since I'd been on top of Natalie North's building. I decided to try a new route to the roof: Jumping.

"Gear, you in place?" I asked through the bluetooth earpiece. I was standing in the murky shadows of an alley, watching midnight cars roll by.

"Roger."

"Puck?"

"PuckDaddy is always ready, dummy."

"Okay," I took a deep breath and let it out through my mask in a sharp blast. "Here we go." Gonna jump up this wall. No big deal. I've done stuff like this before. Easy peasy. Won't even think about it. Just go straight up.

I ran. Fast.

I jumped.

And I hit the bricks hard, barely five feet off the ground. I dropped, stumbled and fell onto my backside.

"Oooowwwww," I whimpered. "That hurt."

A noise crackled in my earpiece. For a moment I assumed the impact had broken it, but then I recognized the noise: laughter.

"Oooooooowww," I said again, holding my shoulder and my head with different hands. I laid down in the filthy alley. "It's not funny."

"What? What happened? Tell PuckDaddy."

"He...he hit the...he hit the..." Samantha tried to articulate the words between hysterics. She sounded like she was crying.

"I jumped into the wall, Puck. Can you zap Gear with a satellite laser or something?"

"He hit...so hard...so hard!...ohmygosh...ohmygosh..."

"I wish I hadn't taken my helmet off. My head is ringing."

Gear laughed so loudly I heard her voice without the aid of the earpiece. She was behind me on a small tower a couple blocks away, but the sound wafted on the air currents over city noises. I stood up, shook off the cobwebs and glared at my enemy, the wall. The accumulation of embarrassment and anger was all the motivation I needed. I charged the wall again only this time I *Leapt* three stories high, snatched a purchase on the wall, and flung myself upwards. I sailed over the building's decorative soffit and landed on the green astroturf.

Natalie North and Isaac Anderson both started in surprise. As per my request, Natalie had turned off all the rooftop lights but enough ambient illumination from the city reached us to make out details. They were an attractive couple; she was one of the prettiest and wealthiest actresses in Hollywood and he looked like Captain America.

"That's quite an entrance," he noted. Due to my shocking and dramatic and theatrical and sudden and heroic and super cool arrival, his hand automatically went for the pistol at his belt, but he didn't draw it.

"Don't touch anything, Outlaw," Natalie said. "I know him. He's going to fingerprint everything later."

Special Agent Isaac Anderson didn't budge or blink.

"Thanks for meeting me," I said, keeping my voice to a low growl.

"Oooooh, I've missed that voice."

Isaac said, "I appreciate you arranging it. I think perhaps we can be of mutual assistance."

I glanced around. "You're not videotaping?"

"No. You have my word."

"No audio?"

"No. She made me promise."

"Your girlfriend is persuasive."

"Yes I am."

His hand finally released the butt of his gun, and he said, "I'd be a fool not to comply. For many reasons. Should we sit down?"

"No. Keep your distance," I said. "My companions might be jumpy. They don't trust you."

"You brought someone here?" he asked in surprise. He scanned the area, but Samantha could have been in a million windows or on hundreds of rooftops.

"Not here. But we're being watched."

"By who?"

"Doesn't matter. Let's talk business."

He ran his hands through his hair, his thick brown Captain America hair, and he said, "I have so many questions. I don't know where to begin."

"Tell me what you *do* know. I'll fill in some gaps. I think you and I are after the same thing, anyway."

"This is so cool," Natalie said. She smiled a ten-million-dollar smile and sat on the turf between us.

"Okay. Okay, yeah sure. Here's what I know. There are people in Los Angeles that seem to have enhanced bodies. According to an audio file we have of you, these enhancements are due to an illness that is often fatal. We've termed you guys Hyper Terrorists, or Hypers for short. One of the terrorists is named the Chemist and he's holding a large portion of Los Angeles hostage for unknown reasons. And finally, there appears to be division among the Hyper Terrorists. You guys aren't getting along."

"That's correct. Your overall impressions are accurate."

He nodded. "Here are a couple of things we don't know, but have assumed. First, the criminal computer hacker known as PuckDaddy is one of your accomplices. Right? That's how you can guarantee most, if not all, of any video taken tonight from a nearby window will be deleted."

My earpiece crackled. Puck said, "Tell him if he asks about me again I'm going to empty his bank account."

I hesitated... "Next question."

"Okay. Fair enough. The Los Angeles Sniper was terrorizing Los Angeles earlier this year and then abruptly stopped when Compton was seized. The Sniper, he's one of you guys, right?"

My earpiece crackled. Again. Samantha said, "Tell FBI that if he calls me a *guy* again I'm going to shoot him in the foot."

I hesitated. Again. "Um. Next question."

He sighed. "I have more questions than answers. Such as...how many of you are there? And, for lack of better phrasing, why aren't you all getting along? And how long have you been around? And what do I call you and your group?"

"What has Natalie told you?"

"Nothing. She's impossibly loyal to you."

I held out my fist. Natalie gave me a fist-bump and looked extremely pleased with herself.

I growled, "I'm not getting into details. But I'll clear up a few things, so you'll trust me. This information is for your ears only. Understood?"

"You can trust me."

In my ear, Puck said under his breath, "This is craaaaaaaaaazy. Can't believe we're doing this."

"There aren't many of us. In fact, I don't know the exact number. We call ourselves Infected, but it's just a meaningless term. We're all sick, and few of us get along."

"Do you mind if I write this down? You said there aren't many. Give me a ballpark. A dozen Infected?" he asked. "A hundred?"

"Twenty? Maybe? Maybe less. There was a sudden burst of new Infected recently, and most of them sided with the Chemist."

"The Chemist." His face hardened as he scribbled notes with a pen. "You two aren't friends, I take it?"

"No. The Chemist is an Infected madman. We're trying to stop him."

"Who is *we*?"

"Me and a handful of other Infected. I'm afraid he has us outnumbered."

"He hasn't announced his intentions with Compton. Could you shed some light on that?"

"I can't. I wish I could. But the Chemist is the reason I'm here tonight."

"How so?"

"Yesterday he sent me a message. He informed me he's going to destroy Los Angeles soon."

Isaac paused, staring hard, before putting his notepad away. He laced his fingers together and rested his hands on his head. He began pacing and staring off into the distance. Every few steps his eyes would flick towards Natalie, his girlfriend who happened to live downtown. He looked tired. "How soon?"

"Didn't say."

"How would he destroy an entire city?"

"Didn't say. I thought you might have intel that could help."

"We have informants in Compton. Constant surveillance from a thousand angles. Thermal imaging, night-vision, long-distance microphones, satellite feeds, drones, data taps…everything. We still don't know much about the guy. Not even a clear photograph. But there's no way he has an atomic bomb. We'd know. Leveling a city isn't easy."

"Your military is planning on going into Compton again?"

"Yes. We'll have to speed it up," he said.

"What's to keep you from getting wiped out?"

"Sheer force. We tried tactical incisions previously. This time we'll launch a full-scale Normandy-style invasion. Twenty insertion points. Aerial support. Paratroopers. Even the kitchen sink."

"Massive collateral damage," I said.

"That's why we haven't launched yet."

"I have a suggestion."

He spread his arms wide. "I'm all ears. Truly. Anything you say, I can pass along."

Natalie said, "This is amazing. When this comes out as a movie, I'm going to play myself."

"Fight monsters *with* monsters. Send in your own."

"Huh," he half laughed as he pulled out his notepad again. "That's funny. Guy at a meeting said the same thing the other day. Almost word for word. One of the LAPD."

Samantha said into my ear, "He's talking about Richard."

I know. Duh. And stop calling him Richard.

Isaac said, "The big-swingers didn't love the idea of sending in civilians."

"We go in all the time anyway. The perimeter security is child's-play for Infected."

"Really?

"And the Chemist leaves whenever he wants. I could show you recent photos of him outside of Compton.

"Wow. Well...okay, jeez. Good to know."

"Infected can dodge bullets. Or block them. Some of us can influence our enemy. Control their actions. Some of us are more accurate than highly trained military snipers. We're faster than sprinters. Each of the Chemist's Infected will kill dozens of your soldiers. Maybe more. And we don't know how many they have."

"...influence...enemy...accurate...snipers...faster than...sprinters," he repeated, scribbling furiously. "...dozens...or more...per...You understand that I'm small potatoes, right? Low man on the totem pole? We've got fifty different agencies butting heads over this thing. And we're not getting along. Even worse than usual."

"In the movie adaptation, I'll get to make out with both of you," Natalie said quietly to herself.

"Why is the government bickering even worse than usual?"

"Good question." He shrugged. "We have a bunch of chiefs in a small teepee. This ongoing act of terrorism within our homeland activates obscure laws, grants power to different agencies, and creates ego struggles among cynical old men. The military is involved, so are the police, and the FBI, and the CIA, and a dozen others. Worst are the lawyers and politicians."

"We know the Chemist is influencing politicians. And also military generals. Are any of them acting weird?"

"Yeah," he said, standing completely still and examining me with intensified interest. "Yeah, they are. Really off the wall stuff."

"Oooooh," Natalie cooed. "Conspiracies!"

Isaac said, "You're telling me the Chemist has high-ranking moles in our government." He looked like he needed to sit down; his face was white.

"Not just moles, Anderson. Saboteurs."

"My god," he said shakily. "Can you get their names?"

"Maybe." I tapped my earpiece and said, "Team. Does anyone remember those names?"

"...yes...but..."

Samantha said, "I agree with Puck. Not a good idea, Outlaw."

"Why not?" I glanced at Isaac. He and Natalie were watching this one-sided conversation with great interest.

"That information came directly from Carter's contacts," Puck said. "That's his intel. I'm a dead man if I share it without his consent."

"And he'd never agree to share with the FBI," Samantha continued. "He'd freak if he knew about this meeting."

Isaac asked, "There a problem?"

"Yeah, the source of our intelligence is...complicated. We need to get his permission to release the names. But we didn't even tell him about this meeting because...well, he's complicated."

Natalie gasped softly. "A rift in the ranks of heroes. Juicy. And terrible."

"This is a time of war," Isaac protested. "Surely he'd see reason."

"Do all of your co-workers see reason?"

"Point taken."

"Listen," I said. "I'm going to get those names. It'll piss off some powerful people, and that's okay. But I can't ask my co-workers to do it. It'll take time."

Puck sighed in my ear. "Great. Looking forward to a civil war."

"Okay," Isaac nodded. "Perfect. That will grease some wheels if we have concrete evidence of the Outlaw terror group helping American citizens."

"You need a new name for us."

"Agreed. If you're going to stick your neck out, then I will too. I've established solid contacts within all the law-enforcement agencies here, and most of the level-headed thinkers agree with me; we should be cooperating with the Outlaw group. With your permission I'd like to quietly spread the word that I established positive contact with the Outlaw, and that he wants to work with us. It'll have to be done under the radar, because the higher-ups are bound by policy and process."

"Outlaw, PuckDaddy doesn't hate this idea," Puck said. "I can monitor communications to make sure neither you nor Isaac Anderson are being double-crossed."

"And," Samantha said, "they provide resources. We just can't tell Carter."

"This is soooooo badass!"

"Just to be clear," Isaac said, holding up a hand. He could tell I was listening to cellular chatter. "I would only alert a small group of trusted individuals. Need-to-know basis."

"Okay, but understand that I'm not meeting with them. I'm willing to communicate with you only. And you will stop attempts at identifying me. I value my anonymity."

"That's going to be tricky," he chuckled. "I'm charged with apprehending you."

"Make it work. One more thing. Our only goal is to eliminate the Chemist. He's a worse man than you realize. If we get him, the whole evil structure will deteriorate rapidly. And you'll never hear from us again."

Natalie pouted, "Awww."

I continued, "You won't get him without our help. He's too good. You handle his military, and we'll get the maniac."

"You said the Chemist sent you a message," Natalie said. "Are you going to reply?"

"Yes."

"What will you say?"

"Good question."

Lee texted me later that night. **<< Dude. I'm going to an Outlawyer rally soon. THE Natalie North will be speaking!!!! You wanna go??**

I smiled and almost typed No. But I stopped. Why not? Could be fun. I wonder why Natalie hadn't told me.

Yeah sure. Sounds good.
>> Sweet!!!! I'll let you know.

My bluetooth earpiece buzzed. I activated it and Puck said, "You're going to your own fan club? Not a good idea, dummy."

"Jeez, Puck. How about some privacy?"

"Whatever. You want Puck to respond to the Chemist? Send him a message?"

"Yeah," I sighed.

"Good! I'm pumped! What do you want to say?"

"Tell him…"

"…yes?"

"Tell him…"

"…yes?"

"Shut up, I'm thinking. Tell him…I think a parlay is a good idea. I want to talk. And inform him we haven't told Carter about the message."

"Got it," he said. His keyboard was clicking.

"And Puck? Sign it *From Antony.*"

"Okay. From Antony. Why?"

"Because Antony is one of the generals from Julius Caesar. And Antony won."

Chapter Eleven
Sunday, August 30. 2018

Dad woke me up the next night at one in the morning. I came awake with a start to find him sitting on the edge of my bed. The hallway light was on. He was fully dressed.

"I have to go to work, son," he said.

"Mmmphf. Okay. Have fun."

"This is kind of a big one. So…in case I don't come back, I want you to know, that…you know, I'm proud of you. And…well, obviously everything I own is yours."

"What?" I sat up and rubbed the sleep out of my eyes as fast as I could. He moved back to give me space. "What's going on?"

"Trouble downtown. Sounds serious."

I grabbed my phone. No messages from PuckDaddy. Dad stood up and checked his phone too. How could there be trouble and I not know about it?

"I have to go," he said. He shoved the phone back into his cargo pants.

"No wait! Is it the Chemist?"

"We think so." He paused at the door. "Miles of jammed cars, just like last time. Gunmen broke through Compton security lines, streaming into Paramount."

"What are you going to do?"

"I'm part of SAT. So…"

"Dad, no." I swung out of bed and stood up, wearing boxers and a t-shirt. I couldn't think straight. Where was my vest? My mask? "Listen, Dad. You need to stay out of there. The Chemist is a monster."

"Exactly."

"Exactly?!"

"Monsters can't roam free," he said, and his lantern jaw was set. "We stand between them and the world."

"We?"

"Law enforcement. It's my job."

"No, it's not! Let someone else handle this. These guys…you don't know, Dad. They're too strong. They'll kill you."

He came back and put his hands on my shoulders. "Chase…"

"Dad, no," I shook my head. "No, Dad. Samantha was right. You need monsters to fight these monsters."

"This is what cops do, kiddo. We protect those in danger. And the Chemist has put everyone in danger. Even you, way out here in Glendale, even you are in danger." He squeezed my shoulders.

"Dad…"

"I would die to keep you safe, son."

I couldn't speak. I tried. But I couldn't.

"Go back to sleep," he said. "I'll be back tomorrow sometime. Safe and sound." And then he was gone.

I waited as he hurried down the stairs. I waited while he gathered his things. I waited while he got into his car. I stared through the blinds and waited as he made a phone call from the driver's seat. As he drove away, I finally flew into action.

I called Puck and put it on speaker. While it rang, I flung aside books and shirts and football stuff, hunting for Outlaw gear. Where was it?! I was in a panic, blinking away tears.

"Hey dummy," Puck answered. He sounded groggy. "I only sleep once every four days. What do you want? I'm tired."

"Puck, check the news!" I shouted. "The Chemist is moving! This is an awful time for a nap. Ah-hah! Found it!"

"Found what?" he asked.

"My mask."

Samantha walked in, yawning. "Why do you need your mask?"

"It's the Chemist," I said, hopping into the Outlaw's pants.

"Whoa!!" Puck cried through the speaker. "Lots of action! Crazy movement!"

"Details, Puck," Samantha shouted. She darted back into her room. "Talk loud!"

"Ah jeez, I don't know, this is a lot to digest…aaaahhhh…okay, okay…looks like the interstates surrounding the area to the east of Compton are all clogged. Another big chunk of the city. About as big as Compton? Roughly? Hang on, I need to alert Carter."

Oh man, oh man, oh man. Why does Dad have to be going too?! Now I'm going to worry about him the whole time. Where are my shoes? Stuff like this should be left to…other people. People wearing armor. People who aren't Dad. Ballbearings. I need ballbearings in the vest. Where'd I put them? My room is a hot mess. I really need a weapon, other than just throwing stuff. Kinda lame. Maybe borrow Lee's Hazer again, or whatever he called it.

I zipped the vest, grabbed my mask and jumped down the stairs. Samantha was on the phone with someone, probably Croc. "I'm gone!" I cried. She told me to wait, but I didn't. I slapped red decals on the bike, jumped on, and aimed it downtown.

What was my plan? Did I have a plan? Heck yes I had a plan. Leap into the middle and hunt down Infected before Dad could find them. I called Isaac Anderson. No answer. That guy sucks.

Seven minutes later my speedometer read 130 mph, and I was hurtling south on the 5. This part of the interstate was four-lanes wide, and I rocketed under green roadsigns faster than I could read them, weaving around red taillights. Puck called.

"Talk to me, Puck."

"Outlaw, I've got you and Shooter on the line. I'm also coordinating with Croc, Carter and Russia. They're inbound, southwest of Compton," he said, voice loud in my helmet.

"Russia? Who's Russia?"

"Reinforcement, from Russia. He's Infected. I'll fill you in later. Shooter is three miles behind you, playing catch-up. Recommend you stay on the 5 and avoid 710. But you won't get close, even on the 5."

Samantha spoke. "Traffic backed up?"

"For miles. But Puck has good news. The Chemist has finally shown his face."

"Finally," I said. "Change of plan. Let's go take him out. Where is he?"

"That's the bad news. He's in East Compton. I have multiple visuals on social media, but it'll take you over an hour. Too congested. Carter will get there before you."

"So," Samantha asked, "he's just posing for pictures?"

"No. Folks inside Compton are using Twitter and Instagram to document the chaos. The Chemist is in the background of a handful. Web analyzers picked it up."

I was skirting the edge of the city instead of driving straight through. The crowded downtown skyline looked peaceful compared to the mayhem ahead. I could see the glow of a thousand distant emergency lights. The cars around me had slowed.

"Puck, I have a weird favor to ask. Can you locate my dad?"

"Sure. First chance I get. I'll pull his number off your phone and find him that way. I don't usually monitor him."

"Keep us posted," Samantha said.

Just then, another call came through. I answered it blindly because I couldn't check the caller-ID. It was Isaac Anderson. Love that guy. We spoke for sixty seconds and I clicked back over to my call with Puck and Gear.

"Shooter, get off at the next exit. We're catching a ride."

Los Angeles was in pain. Millions were scared. Hundreds of thousands were angry, many of them armed and moving at the whim of a madman. The

American military was neither outmanned nor outgunned. But it's hard to win against zealots, especially zealots snorting drugs and fighting without pain or fear or reason.

Soto Elementary School is a flat pale building with a large parking lot. Gear and I waited there next to a chain fence, bouncing on our toes, as the beating of helicopter blades grew louder over the city noise. Gear had a black custom-made MSG90 semi-automatic sniper rifle slung across her back. I didn't know what the letters or numbers meant, but it looked like it could shoot down the moon.

A dark FBI Black Hawk came thundering over the school. The rotor wash whipped down onto the parking lot, flinging pebbles and litter in all directions. I was sick of helicopters, but this one looked super cool. And fast. And dangerous.

"Sexy ride," Samantha called.

"Only the best."

The landing gear touched down, the gunner-door slid back, and we leapt in. The deck under us lurched as the chopper took off again. There was barely room to stand in the crowded passenger bay. Six men in tactical gear stared at us. Their severity and black face paint was uniform.

"Head-set, gimme a head-set!" Gear shouted. Thick headphones with attached mics were pressed into our hands. Through the open gunner-doors I could see that our chopper was banking up and over neighborhoods; fires and emergency lights were visible in the distance. Our chopper fell into place behind another Black Hawk, flying in formation.

"Welcome aboard the FBI's eleven million dollar taxi service!" Isaac's voice came over the headsets, and from the cockpit he gave us a thumbs-up. "Gentlemen, meet the Outlaw!"

"Thanks for the lift! Get us as close to East Compton as you can," I called.

"You're positive about the Chemist sighting?"

I said, "Multiple confirmations."

"I will absolutely be court-martialed for breaking orders, but maybe they'll let me keep the Chemist's head for a wall-mount. New heading, south southwest!"

"Roger that! Tally-ho, and rock and roll!"

"You boys, you HRT?" Samantha yelled at the men through her mic. They all nodded with a jerk of their chin. These men were soldiers in the FBI's elite Hostage Rescue Team, the best of the best.

The guy directly in front of us smiled and said, "Yes ma'am."

"Listen up, HRT! Your weapons will only knock small chunks out of the Infected. If you can even hit them, which you can't." Her voice was rattling our eardrums, but at least she had their attention. "You want to drop an Infected? Take them on as a team, take cover, lob multiple grenades from multiple directions, and *then* use your assault rifles!"

"Three minutes out! Target is hot!" Isaac Anderson called. Additional radio traffic was bleeding through the headset. Authorities reported that the petrol plant in Paramount was a total loss. That didn't sound good. And the Bellflower police were screaming for reinforcements. Havoc had broken suddenly, and police, military and emergency responders were all reeling.

"No offense, pretty girl," one of the guys grinned, "but what the hell is an Infected? And who are you?"

"I'm your best chance at getting out alive!" she yelled back over the noise. Before he could move, she snatched his nose and held on. He bellowed in anger but couldn't push her off. His friends were caught between amusement and outrage. "And the Outlaw is *my* best chance! Stick with him. You want to know what an Infected is? It's a demon. Like me. Like the Chemist. And we're going demon hunting!"

"We've hunted worse."

"No, soldier. You haven't. The Middle East is nothing compared to what you're about to see. If two of you make it out, it'll be a miracle."

That gave them pause. We bounced in silence for several minutes, other than the radio chatter and engine roar. Something about Samantha's demeanor and electric confidence was arresting. We were all under her spell and we believed her implicitly.

"Incoming!" Anderson cried. The Black Hawk in front of us shattered, taking a direct hit from an unexpected surface-to-air missile. Our aircraft banked hard to avoid the bright ball of fire, and all eight of us in the passenger-bay were thrown to the side. The superheated air slammed into our rotors, thrusting us upwards. "Damn it! Hold on back there!"

"Where the hell they get SAMs?!"

"Get us out of the sky, Anderson!" I shouted. Through the wide doorway we saw the remains of the ruined Black Hawk crash between the Long Beach Freeway and the Los Angeles River. "He'll have more rockets!"

"Coming in hard! Prepare to jump!"

We banked again and the scene below unfolded. We were above Compton. In the distance, the bridges had been overrun by a sea of humanity heading east into Paramount, the section of Los Angeles directly adjacent. Houses were burning. Businesses were burning. Cars were burning. Sporadic gunfire sparkled, probably between Chemist gunmen and retreating law enforcement. This part of the city had transformed into a war zone, pure and simple.

Below us, lights began winking, short pops and flashes. It was gunfire.

"They're shooting at us," I observed, brilliantly.

"Mobs do stupid stuff when they're angry and scared." Samantha was beside me, holding on to the handle above the door. "Anderson, put us down!"

I squinted and focused on the group of muzzle flashes. A dozen gunmen firing wildly into the sky. Maybe it was my Infected eyes, but I could inspect the crowd easily despite the distance, and make out clear details. One of the gunners was reloading...something...a rocket! His last shot hadn't missed...

"We don't have time to land," I said, disentangling my wrist from the handhold. "See you down there."

"What?? No!"

I jumped into the night. The cord yanked the headphones off my ears immediately and I began plummeting. The helicopter was...a hundred feet in the air? Maybe less? The sky was loud and angry, threatening to rip off my mask, and the neighborhood below was expanding, enlarging. I became immediately disoriented and my eyes stung. I got my fingers around the parachute cord...but...wouldn't this be faster if I didn't use the chute?

Bullets were perforating my airspace, and I didn't want to be a floating duck. Maybe I should wait until…too late!!

I made a small crater on impact, the blacktop buckling slightly under my feet. But that's the only thing that broke. I experienced no pain. In fact, I felt otherworldly good. On fire.

The gunmen stared at the sky, laughing; they hadn't seen me land. I took them apart, attacking from behind. Their guns made handy clubs and projectiles. Thunk. Thunk. Thunk. Disabling them was cathartic, a release of steam. One by one they fell without sound until I stood alone. They wore red bandanas over their noses and mouths. Ugh. Hate that; makes me look bad. I stepped over the bodies, bending their weapons to render them useless, and I scanned the skies. The Black Hawk had passed out of my line-of-sight, but I could hear it nearby.

"Yo! That was crazy, man!"

I whirled around. A couple of kids were watching me from the sidewalk, recording me with their phones. They looked young, maybe nine years old.

"Yo, dooo! Yo, man! Yo, you the Outlaw, man?"

"Go home, kids! Get inside and stay there," I ordered. They didn't obey. They gaped at their phone screens, with cameras aimed at me. It was a little awkward. "Where is everyone?" I asked. I was in the middle of an empty street full of squat stucco houses with threadbare yards.

The bigger boy said, "Everyone gone, Outlaw."

"Yeah, or hiding."

"Or hiding, you know? In the shelters."

I nodded. "Those guys with guns and rockets weren't gone."

"The Father's got guards everywhere, man."

"The Father," I grunted under my breath. "He's got more guards? Around?"

The bigger boy grinned and said, "Yo, for real, are you the Outlaw?"

I jogged to them, primarily to get out of the street, out of sight. They cautiously backed away, the bigger boy shielding his friend. This brief lull in pandemonium, after the chaos I'd seen from the helicopter, felt dreamlike. The eye of the storm.

"I *am* the Outlaw. And I need your help."

"We get money if we see you."

"You get money?"

He nodded and said, "A reward. From the guards, you know? We get money to snitch." Neither of them wore shirts, but they had thin chains around their necks and new sneakers on their feet. The bigger boy was black and the smaller Latino. Their faces held no timidity, no fear, only the defiance of the oppressed.

I asked, "Gonna snitch on me?"

"Nah man," he smiled. "Bout tired of the Father. Bout tired of canned peaches."

I asked, "Are you two buddies?"

"Brothers from other mothers, Outlaw. Brothers stick together, brothers survive."

I held out my fist and they bumped it. "You two are awesome. I'm from Los Angeles too. That makes you *my* brothers."

"You just killed Javy, my real brother."

"Oh," I winced. "Was he one of those guys with a gun? He's not dead."

"S'okay," he smiled big. "Javy a jerk, most times."

"Can you tell me where the Chemist's guards are?"

"You in the Ways, Outlaw," he said and he pointed his finger at me like a gun. "The guards usually at Camino."

"The Ways?" I asked, making mental notes.

"You on 67th Way. One block over, 68th Way. We call it the Ways."

"Gotcha. What's Camino?"

"Camino about seven blocks down the street. We always steer clear, because of guards."

A loud burst of gunfire, fast like firecrackers, came echoing through the neighborhood. Then the hiss of another rocket, followed by an awful crash. The sky to the south flared red. The Black Hawk! Samantha…

"Back inside, guys, now! Go to the shelters!" I shouted, and I chased the sounds of gunfire south, darting between houses and leaping over iron fences. I was in a maze of stucco walls and barking dogs. Another hiss, another detonation, and I corrected my course. The sound faded from my eardrums, and I no longer heard the percussive chatter of helicopter blades.

Puck called. I answered, and we yelled at each other simultaneously.

"Puck, Shooter's chopper is down!"

"Outlaw, turn right on Artesia! Gear is surrounded!"

"What?" I shouted.

Samantha interrupted our incoherence and screamed in my ear, "Outlaw, get your ass over here NOW! Don't you EVER jump out of a helicopter again!"

"You're alive!"

"And pissed!" she snarled.

"Outlaw, dead ahead is Artesia, a main thoroughfare. Careful, it's crawling with gunmen. The FBI's helicopter emergency-landed on Starr King School, directly to the west. Errrr, to your...right."

"We're surrounded. And bombarded with rockets. These HRT guys won't last long. Move those feet!" Even as she spoke, I heard another explosion. I heard it with my naked ear *and* through the headset. I was close.

I exited the Ways, egressing directly onto Artesia Boulevard. The scene at the school could have been straight from a horror movie set. Power lines were down and sparking on the pavement. Traffic lights flashed yellow. Two cars were engulfed in flames, providing flickering, eerie, angry illumination for the nightmare. The helicopter smoldered from the roof of the two-story school, and embattled FBI agents returned fire from hidden prone positions. Dozens of masked gunmen hid behind cars and buildings, taking potshots in relative safety. Gear and Anderson were surrounded and outnumbered four-to-one, at least.

Puck wondered in my ear, "Where are all these guys coming from?"

"Rumor is they've got a hideout nearby. Someplace called Camino," I said. I found a guy peeking at the school from a discount storefront. I shoved his face hard into the bricks, and he dropped quietly. I bent his pistol.

"Camino? Camino...camino..." His keyboard clicked while I approached the battle.

"Gear!" I shouted in alarm. "Guy reloading a rocket behind the Honda, in the intersection. Cover me."

"Negative," she snapped. "That'll put you in the crossfire. I got him."

She fired her heavy rifle five times, loud booms that rattled windows. The five rounds smashed straight through the vehicle's fiberglass, turning the rocketeer into pulp. My stomach lurched.

"Bingo. Camino College," Puck said. "Three blocks west of your position. Must have been repurposed as a barracks? You are deep in enemy territory."

"Gear, here's what we're going to do." I was eyeballing the noose of gunmen slowly tightening around Samantha's position. Soon there'd be hostiles both inside and out of that school, with more rockets deteriorating the roof. "I'm going to sprint around that school as fast as I can. Let them see me. They'll shoot at me. They'll miss. You guys shoot them. It's basic, but it should work."

"Negative, hate that plan."

"Tough. I'm going. Just don't miss."

"I. Don't. Miss."

I ran down the street, towards the school, picking up speed. Time was relative, and it slowed as I accelerated. At top speed, I circled the school five times in less than a minute. Cries and gunfire followed me around the building, but I couldn't be caught. I altered my path as I went, the world a dizzy blur, hitting gunmen with a busted two-by-four when they were too slow to duck. I never broke stride.

"Don't shoot them in the head!"

"Shut up, Outlaw," she growled underneath the roar of her cannon. "Can't believe this is working."

Puck laughed. "This is hilarious."

I finished by doing something ill-advised. Gunfire was coming from inside a yellow school bus under a low hanging tree. On my last revolution, I grabbed a live power line and tossed it onto the bus. The electricity made contact with the bus's metal shell, and the connection was bright and violent and terrible. I felt the shock from five feet away, and the men inside screamed.

Stumbling, I fell and rolled twenty feet before slamming into the school. My head was spinning.

"What was that?!"

"A bad idea," I moaned.

"*Terrible* idea! Electricity can kill an Infected!"

I laid down, panting, my face in the mulch of a flower bed, the planet rotating around my head. "That was awful. I hope it didn't kill them."

"We're coming down," she crackled in my ear. "No visual on active hostiles."

"My plan worked," I said weakly.

"It wouldn't have if any Infected had been here. You're too valuable to be a decoy, or a target."

"Speaking of Infected," Puck interrupted, "I have updates."

"Go ahead."

"Walter and Carla have been sighted in Paramount, miles from your position."

"What are they doing?"

"Terrorizing the National Guard in a similar fashion to what you just did. And one more update. You are half a mile from the confirmed Chemist location."

That perked me up. I was hungry for that man's destruction, one way or another. "If we get him, the whole bad dream goes away."

"That's what Carter just said. Almost word for word."

I regained my feet as Gear appeared. Her rifle was slung over her shoulder, a pistol gripped in both fists, her eyes everywhere. Anderson trailed, walking with a limp, a phone to his ear.

"We're on our own," he said, covering the receiver with his free hand. "Every agency is over-taxed. No free resources. We're being overrun across the board."

"Good," Samantha growled. "No offense, FBI, but extra men only slow us down. I already feel like I'm babysitting."

Anderson was unnerved by her low opinion of his elite combat team.

ALAN JANNEY

That was obvious. Being belittled by a young woman wasn't an everyday occurrence. He addressed me, "I've got two wounded men up there."

"We're moving out," I said. "We'll draw the fire away from them. Trust me. They'll be safer than you are."

His eyes bored into me, and he said, "I'm a believer, Outlaw. That was some other-level stuff you just did."

"Night's not over. Let's move."

He took a deep breath and said, "We're with you." Anderson made an unspoken transfer of power to Samantha and me. He was in over his head and he knew it.

I put a hand to my ear. "Puck, where to?"

Anderson caught his breath. "PuckDaddy," he said softly. "I knew it."

Samantha and I both listened to Puck's instructions. "Keep going on Artesia. Three blocks away. I googled Camino. It's a big campus, multi-building. Too big to thoroughly investigate. But maybe you'll get lucky."

Our team proceeded down a side street, paralleling the bigger and more exposed Artesia Boulevard, carefully scouting and inch-worming forward. There were enemies ahead; we caught flashes of activity, only brief glimpses. Other than that, we could have been on the moon. All the remaining civilians inside Compton were hidden and silent.

"I won't be much help," Puck said. "I'm fighting hundreds of users for satellite data, and I'm the only one that wants Compton feed. The eyes of the world have shifted to Paramount tonight. Captain FBI is right; there's no help coming soon."

"What's Carter's location?"

"Carter's a maniac. He's barreling down Walnut Street from the west in a big dump truck. You'll hear him before you see him."

Samantha shook her head. "He's trying to goad the Chemist into showing himself."

Another block and the Camino Community College came into view. Our hearts sank. It was an enormous labyrinth of buildings plunged into darkness. A city within a city, a deathtrap with far too many black windows.

"Christ," Anderson said. We huddled a block away, staring at the

132

imposing fortress. "He's in *there?*"

Samantha snapped open her tactical scope and began scanning the campus. I could see movement with my naked eye. Behind the windows. On the roofs. Running through the quads and along the sidewalks. Everywhere.

"He's in there," I said. I was furious all of a sudden, angered at his close proximity and his cowardly defenses. "I can smell him."

"I think I can too," Samantha said. Her voice was hesitant and curious. Maybe even frightened. "It smells like…"

"Like blood."

She nodded. I'd never seen her confidence shaken before. That scared me more than the forbidding campus. "Yes. Blood. And something else.

"Yeah, I smell it too. Something…I don't know. It smells wrong. Evil."

"We can't go in," she sighed irritably. We fell back, further into the shadows, and squatted in a tight cluster.

Anderson nodded. "I agree. We have no support and no evacuation. Fortunately the Compton border isn't far. We can hoof it out." There were quiet murmurs of assent from his squad.

Samantha got behind her scope again, squinting and scanning, and said, "I see Infected. I've got a bad feeling we grossly underestimated his numbers."

I said, "It's a trap."

"Clearly a trap," she nodded. Puck remained silent. His neck wasn't on the line.

"He knows we're here." My own words gave me goosebumps. He knew. Somehow, he knew that we were here. That I was here.

She shifted uneasily. "I think you're right, but how the hell is that possible?"

"It'd be suicide to go in there," I said.

She glanced at me. I grinned.

"You're going in anyway," she glared. "Aren't you."

"Yes I am."

Chapter Twelve
Sunday, August 30. 2018

The sounds started softly, just one or two cries, and then swelled. The eerie hoots coming out of the college campus grew louder and louder until our skin crawled. I felt like I was in a jungle, surrounded by howler monkeys.

"The hell is that?!" Anderson asked.

"A challenge."

"Puck, can you light that place up? Turn on the power?"

"Negative. Power grid failed in that area. Even the mighty PuckDaddy is helpless. Your trek into hell will happen in total darkness."

I stared at Samantha in disbelief. She returned the look. "Jeez, Puck. Take it easy on the theatrics."

"Whatever, dummy. Shut up. I'm very anxious. You're a moron if you enter that hole of death."

The screams were fading, and I said, "The Chemist is in there, Puck. I can tell. This is the closest we've been in six months. We can't just let him go."

"This is absurd," Puck grumbled, keys clicking. "I'm going to push maps of the campus onto your phones, including Captain FBI's."

"Hey, Puck," I said, a thought occurring to me. "Did you find my dad?" Samantha glanced up.

"Lost the signal. Last I checked, he was someplace called Paramount Park."

Samantha asked, "Is that near Walter and Carla?"

"Well...kinda..." he said hesitantly. "Less than a mile. Those two are giving the police *fits*!"

"Okay," I said, squeezing the ball of metal in my hand so hard it might have left impressions. "Okay. We need to do this fast."

Anderson spoke up, "Outlaw, I've risked my career for this. I want to put a bullet in the Chemist's ear as much as anyone. But storming this place will be a tactical nightmare. None of us will come out."

"Shooter only needs one shot," I said, indicating Samantha, trying to protect her anonymity if I hadn't blown it yet. "And then we bail. And to be honest, I think you guys should wait here."

"This is America, Outlaw. We don't run. If you're going in, I'm going in. Seems like a good day to die." The hardened veterans behind him grunted agreement. Maniacs. "What are we up against? Any ideas?"

"Most of the hostiles will be standard thugs," Gear said. She was pushing thick bullets into magazines. Guns are awful; each of those bullets would result in a life taken messily. "But they're hopped up on the Chemist's super drug. No fear, no pain. Intimidation tactics won't work. Suppressing fire won't work. We need head shots. Or several in the torso. We go in, we go in shooting to kill."

"Or knock them out," I suggested.

"That works for you," Samantha snapped. "Not us."

Isaac Anderson asked me, "Where's your gun?"

"Don't have one. Couldn't hit anything anyway."

Samantha continued, "Anderson, if you boys encounter Infected, throw grenades and run. Do not engage. Retreat or hunker down and wait for us. You need monsters to fight these monsters."

"Roger." His hands were shaking, and he was sweating. He was about to speak when we heard distant gunfire. We scanned the campus but saw no flashes. It wasn't close.

Puck came through our earpieces. "That's Carter, with Russia and Croc. They've engaged hostiles. You're near the southeast corner of the campus, and they are at the northwest, exactly opposite."

"Perfect," I said, standing. "Time to go."

The FBI boys lowered night-vision goggles and switched safeties off their assault rifles. They looked cooler than me. I needed a weapon.

Puck crackled, "Tell Captain FBI I'm calling him. I want to be in his ear too."

Isaac Anderson's phone lit up with an incoming call. He glanced at the unknown number.

I said, "Answer it and put it through to your bluetooth headset. That's PuckDaddy. He wants to communicate with your squad."

"How does he have my number?"

"Don't ask questions. He's probably got nude photos of you too."

"What? Why would he have-"

I interrupted him. "Here's the plan. I'm going in and draw their fire. Anyone that shoots at me, you drop them."

"No. Hell no. You're awful at plans," Samantha snapped. She raised her voice. "Listen up. We're going straight in from Cummings Avenue. Make for that gymnasium. This campus runs north and south, so we'll regroup there and push north. We have friendlies that need help. Anderson, you got a sniper on your team? Put him on the gym roof. We have one goal, gentlemen. Extermination. This place is infested. Let's clean it out. And if we're lucky, we'll bag the most destructive person on earth in the process. Anderson, keep on the horn, try and get us air support and an evac. Outlaw, that building directly ahead? Get on top of it. You'll be building hopping, our eye in the sky, eliminating hostiles as you go. We run into any Infected, you and I handle them. Any questions? Good. Let's move."

The campus grass was long, and the blades hissed as I sprinted across. My blood was pumping adrenaline into muscles, and I leapt easily onto the roof of the Math/Science building. Behind me, somewhere in the darkness, gunfire erupted, shattering bricks near my feet. Samantha and the Hostage Rescue Team returned fire. There were two sentries on the roof with me, and neither could see me well. I dropped the first with a steel ball thrown over a hundred miles per hour. His skull fractured, but he'd survive. The next guy ducked.

He ducked?!

I breathed, "He's Infected."

"What? Who is?" in my ear.

He was big. Taller and broader than me. We met in the middle of the roof, near ventilation pipes.

"Listen to me," I hissed. He swung and missed. "Listen, I'm here to help!" He missed again. He was newly Infected, like a 16-year old driving a car too fast. He over corrected and stumbled and basically didn't know what to do with all his strength. "We're both Infected, listen to me!" I caught his fist and held it. His head was shaved and he glared at me, breathing so hard spittle came out of his mouth. "Listen, you big oaf. We were born the same, you and I. I know what you've been through. Let me help you."

"Wasn't born," he snarled, and he pushed me away so hard I stumbled. He was fierce and quick, I had to give him that. "I am Twice Chosen."

"Alright big guy, I'm out of time. And I don't know what Twice Chosen means anyway. Come with me, and I'll get you out."

"Outlaw, quit playing!" the voice in my ear rang. "No time!"

The bald kid advanced, rage making his muscles quake. It was like he couldn't even hear me. Or he'd been brainwashed. That was a scary thought. Time to quit goofing off. I planted my foot in his chest and kicked him hard enough to propel him off the roof. Samantha shot him three times before he hit the ground.

She was staying with Anderson and his squad. They'd been spotted and were taking heavy fire, ducked behind trucks in the parking lot. She rose, her gun shattered the night three times, and she dropped out of sight again. The glass below my feet exploded and someone fell out of it, already dead. But there were too many windows, too many hiding spots, too much gunfire.

She screamed, "This isn't working! I'm going mobile."

"Shooter, there's a squad pinning you down. They're underneath the trees, between my building and the gym," I said, risking a glance over the side. "I'm going to land on them, and you'll be free to roam. Understood?"

"Waiting on you, hotshot."

"On my way," I said, and I fell on the gunners from above. They'd been peering around a cluster of palm trees. I clunked their heads together. It was over so fast I had time to witness Shooter spin away from her shelter.

This was the first time I'd seen Samantha Gear *truly* use her terrifying gift. She spun away from the truck, both pistols out front, each roving independently and firing at targets in her peripheral vision. She dealt death, violent and efficient. As soon as the clips emptied she dropped the weapons, retrieved two more from her belt, and continued the murderous onslaught. She was a thunderstorm bursting with continual lightning. She didn't miss, demolishing targets I never saw. A shocking number of bodies rained from rooftops and windows, landing on the ground like drumbeats. This was her Infected curse in full-effect.

She came to a stop at my tree, ramming new clips into her smoking pistols.

"Ready?" she asked.

"I think I'm going to be sick." I took deep breaths to steady my stomach, and I refused to look at the piles of ruined people behind us.

To our north, two massive structures loomed, the Student Resource Center and the Theater. Between them, out of the gloom, came a blur. Two blurs, on second glance, moving like Olympic sprinters.

"Look out!" I cried. I shoved Samantha and fell back. The tree between us exploded from twin shotgun blasts, bark flying like confetti. One of the new attackers, a girl, got close enough to kick me. Hard. *Really* hard. I hit the ground and kept rolling, shotgun concussions churning up the ground between us.

Anderson and his team came swooping across the grass, guns blazing. The two blurs were too quick to be hit, but they were forced to fall back. They retreated into the murky night. They were fast. I never saw their faces.

"Okay," Anderson said, taking up a position behind a palm tree. His squad found positions at the gym. "I get it now. They move like ghosts. Too fast for us to aim. Were those two Infected?"

"Yes," Samantha said, shooting me a concerned look. "New ones. All speed, no aim."

"How many Infected are there?"

Puck said in our ears, "That's the million dollar question, dummy." The northern sounds of sporadic gunfire continued. Carter was evidently still alive and causing mayhem.

Anderson split his remaining four-person team. Two on top of the gym, two on top of the Resource Center.

"Shoot anything that moves," he ordered. "Stay alive. If either the Outlaw or the girl comes back, follow them out. I'll be dead by then."

We all laughed. But it was probably true.

The three of us pushed north silently through the campus. I hated it. I wanted to be on the roofs. But Isaac and Samantha couldn't jump or move like me. All the plants were overgrown. Samantha glared at every possible hiding spot but held her fire. Our opposition had mysteriously disappeared. We heard shots behind us, a brief volley from the FBI team. We moved forward until we came to an impassable barrier: a large, wide-open grassy quad. No cover, completely exposed.

I was losing heart. The Chemist could be hidden in any of these buildings. Or maybe he'd fled the scene by now. "We can't cross," I said. "Let's go around."

Anderson said, "Absolutely."

Samantha grabbed my vest as I was about to head westward. She put her finger to her lips and pulled me into the grass near the abandoned campus police department. Anderson followed silently. She holstered her pistols and unslung the assault rifle.

A silhouette was pacing the rooftop across the quad. I checked my map. The sentry was on top of the bookstore. Samantha took careful aim.

"Infected," she said.

Anderson whispered, "How can you tell?"

"I can always spot Infected. The posture, the swept shoulders, the arrogance. Prepare to move." She took a breath, held it, and squeezed the trigger. The muzzle flashed with a roar, and the silhouette dropped. We bolted.

As we did, a new sound caught our ears. Laughter.

The Chemist.

He was cackling.

The disease flared inside me like fever.

His voice floated towards us from everywhere. "Would that be the lovely Shooter I hear?"

"Damn damn damn," she hissed as we skirted backwards into some scrub bushes.

"Christ, that's him?" Anderson hissed. "Shouting at us?"

"You may have noticed that my Chosen have ceased their aggressions," the Chemist said, his voice amplified by the unnaturally quiet night. Where was he?! "You are granted safe passage. I give my word. It is time for Marc Antony and I to parlay."

"Marc Anthony?" She frowned. "Who is Marc Anthony?"

"A Roman general. Didn't you ever read Shakespeare? Right now he's referring to me."

"I don't get it."

"Can you smell him? I can. Blood and…and something else."

"Yes. He's pungent."

Captain FBI looked askance at us, and he sniffed the air unsuccessfully. He shrugged.

"Okay. Let's go," I said.

"Go where?"

I grinned. "Go meet him."

Anderson's eyes bulged. "Is that a joke?"

"No. He promised."

"*What??* He's a madman!"

"He's also polite. He wouldn't lie and kill us," I said. "Well, at least not immediately. He'll talk a lot first."

"This is insanity," Samantha snarled. "We walked into his trap. And now we're going to meet him, voluntarily. I hate hate hate this."

"This is our chance, Shooter. We waited months." She rubbed her eyes with her thumb and forefinger a long time and then said, "Okay, I'm going to the top of the bookstore. You distract him, I'll blow his head off, and then we can all three die."

"So I'm the bait?"

"Yes."

"Sounds good."

PuckDaddy groaned. So did Captain FBI.

Samantha said, "I hate this. Please don't die. Let's go."

"Hang on," I said. I pulled out my phone.

I love you, Katie Lopez.

I pressed Send, stowed the phone, and nodded to them. "Ready."

We jogged across the quad, ghosts in our own graveyard. Samantha and Anderson angled away, towards the bookstore. The Chemist had advanced hearing, so he probably heard my heart pounding as I approached.

I found him in the thin, grassy quad between the long writing and math buildings. The buildings were parallel and evenly spaced, and he sat between them on a mountain of…something. His chair was resting four feet off the ground, sunk into what looked like two tons of cocaine. A pair of torches was burning on either side of him.

"You need a weapon, my son." He was changed. During our previous encounter, the Chemist had been haughty and exuberant, full of both life and death. Now he appeared weak and emaciated. His voice lacked vigor. He still had long silver hair, and the heavy staff rested across his knees. "We all do. Even you."

I indicated the surrounding college. "This has been your home the past six months? Probably the only place we didn't look."

He smiled, good-naturedly. "I am flattered. But this is not my home. Think of it as my…" He waved his hand in the air as he searched for the right word. "…my office."

"Making your super drug?"

"Among other things."

"Are you sitting on top of a hill of that stuff?"

"Yes. There is no charge for my stimulant. Free to all."

"I'm here to kill you."

"I know that, young man. That's why you need a weapon. You won't be able to with your bare hands. Your heart is too good. Too pure. Taking a life is messy. You haven't the stomach."

"We'll see," I said, shifting uneasily. But he was right. I couldn't. I needed Samantha to do it. Where was she?

"Besides, even in my weakened state I'm still a match for you. Capable of brief violence." He chuckled. "But I have other plans for you, Antony. I'm so very glad you see me as Brutus, the noblest Roman of them all."

"Brutus lost that war."

"Yes. Well. We're in the business of re-writing history, aren't we."

"Your story has already been written. And you lose."

He arched an amused brow. "How did you find me tonight? To be perfectly honest, I wasn't ready yet."

"Ready for what?"

"I'm going to wound you. Grievously, I am afraid. And then I'm going to remake you."

The stirring air brought wafts of blood to my nostrils. I knew we temporarily stood in the center of a storm about to break. "Sounds like a party. But first, tell me. Why are you here? Why did you need Compton?"

"I told you before, dear boy. Because of you. When you revealed our existence to the newspaper, you accelerated everything. But I thrive on chaos. I couldn't leave yet, so I just…annexed what I needed."

"What do you need?"

"Time. Resources. You."

"Resources for what?"

"Them," he said, and he indicated the sky with his index finger. I glanced up. The rooftops of the surrounding buildings were lined with dark silhouettes blocking out the stars. There were dozens of silent and nearly invisible watchers. The hairs on the back of my neck stood up. So many.

"Infected?"

He replied, "Chosen. Twice Chosen, more accurately. There's more than one way to skin a cat, as the saying goes. Come with me and I'll introduce you to the wonders of gene therapy."

"Gene therapy?" I didn't understand. None of this made sense. He looked like an empty Capri Sun pouch, sucked dry.

"You are meant to *rule* them, Outlaw," he whispered, his voice abruptly feverish. He leaned forward in his chair, causing small avalanches in the narcotic powder. "We come along once a generation, you and I. We control our gift, instead of the other way round."

Puck whispered in my ear, startling me. "I can't see you. I can't hear him. I've lost contact with Carter. I don't know how to help."

"Perhaps," the Chemist smiled, reading my mind, "you are waiting for your friends? They won't be much help, I'm afraid."

I whirled, scanning the host above. Samantha and Anderson lay on their sides, balanced precariously on the edge of the two-story roof, hands bound behind their backs. Their mouths were gagged and blood flowed freely from head wounds. My eyes met Samantha's, and she started bucking so fiercely it took three Infected to quell her.

Captured.

Now what??

If the Chemist dies, this nightmare will too.

"I vouched for your safe passage," he said. It was more of a croak. He was tiring rapidly. "I will release them tomorrow, ultimately unharmed. But now that you and I have parlayed, I see you will not be swayed. You bear me ill will. There can be no peace between us."

I intentionally sprung this trap, and now I needed to make it pay off. One shot, straight for his throat. I gathered my feet under me, preparing to leap. I felt the host above tensing.

He continued, "So let us begin. My newest creations aren't exactly perfected, but they'll do."

Banks of windows either side of me exploded. A foul reek spilled out, and so did two enormous tigers.

Tigers?!

They met in the middle of the lawn, between the Chemist and I, barring their fangs and shoving one another with forepaws the size of car doors. I knew nothing about tigers but these seemed…massive. Their heavy heads were level with mine. The bigger one, with a slightly whiter pelage, was roaring in short angry coughs.

"Genetic engineering, dear Outlaw!" the Chemist cackled with delight. I backpedaled slowly, so terrified I couldn't speak. Couldn't think. Could barely hear. Their scent was overpowering. "Thanks to Nepal, and borrowed research from various tiger genome projects, and a flare of creativity on my part, these two young beautiful animals have been…Infected."

Puck was shouting, "What's going on?? I can't see! Why is Samantha not communicating?! Did he say something about tigers?"

I tried to reply but was unable to exhale. Samantha was screaming against the tape across her mouth.

Infected tigers…

Not possible…

"Join me."

"No," I managed.

"These beautiful beasts are sick. They have a disease that over-produces muscles and bones and adrenaline. Sound familiar? It will kill them before long, but until then… Can you not see the power? The possibilities? I've only begun changing the world. You'd be a fool to fight for the lesser side."

"You're more impressed with your fancy cats than I am." My breath was coming in ragged heaves.

"They are more than fancy cats. You see, Outlaw…" He learned forward again, torchlight reflecting in his eyes. "…they share my DNA."

I backed into a bush.

"Join me," he insisted. "I made you. At birth. Don't force me to undo it."

"Sorry about this," I heard myself say.

"Sorry? For what?"

"For killing your tigers."

He threw back his head and laughed richly, clapping his hands.

One of his Infected flicked on a powerful flashlight, throwing a cone of brilliant illumination around me. Quick flashes, on off, on off. The animals responded, curling away from the Chemist and padding towards me. Their powerful shoulders pulled the earth towards them, closing the distance.

"Killing tigers?" Puck shouted. "*What??*"

They didn't look mad. But they kept coming. My night vision had been destroyed by the flashlight. The animals moved like striped phantoms I couldn't quite see. His ring of Infected began chanting rhythmically between outburst of laughter.

"I really need a weapon…"

"What?! What's happening??"

Without warning, the smaller and darker tiger snarled and lunged. He was fast. He? Whatever. He was fast, and his claws extended and he caught me as I desperately tried to jump over him. He batted me out of the air, one razor claw snagging my belt. He dropped to all fours, slamming me into the turf. His fur was everywhere and his musk made me gag, and he lowered his open maw onto my head.

I put my fist into his teeth as hard as I could. His canines broke, and possibly so did the bone under his eye socket. He reared away, squealing in agony and surprise. Great gouges opened up along my hand and forearm as his broken teeth tugged and ripped.

"Tiger, tiger, burning bright," sang the Chemist, his voice shrill and caroming off the bricks. "In the cities of the night. What immortal hand or eye, could frame thy fearful symmetry?"

The larger animal swiped at me as I scrambled to my feet. Blood ran down my fingers, and blood poured from the wounded animal's mouth. The spectators laughed and screeched. The Chemist loved a good audience.

"And when the stars threw down their spears," he continued the poem, standing as his intensity increased. He used his infamous staff as a cane. "And watered heaven with their tears, did He smile His work to see? Did He who made the lamb make thee?"

His staff!

The big tiger lunged, but this time I was ready. I easily leapt over him, though I nearly landed on the smaller, wounded animal beyond. He gave chase, wincing and yowling in pain. The gathering screamed a chorus of madness. I leaped away to avoid terrible claws, momentarily running along the side of the wall, heading towards the Chemist. Closer, closer.

He laughed and clapped with delight, reveling in the audience's reaction. Too late did he realize I was coming for him. I reached. He ducked, so fast my eyes couldn't process it. But I hadn't swung at him. I swung at his staff. And I got it.

I sunk knee-deep into the powder. Off balance, he stumbled and sank too, on the other side of the mound. The staff was beyond heavy. It was impossibly heavy. How on earth did a metal rod weigh this much?? I turned in time to see the smaller tiger leave its feet, forepaws stretched towards me. I swung the staff with all my might and connected solidly with the animal's skull, just behind his ear. In that moment of slowed time, I saw the light go out of his eyes. His brain essentially exploded on contact. Instant death.

Momentum propelled him into my chest, knocking me down and scattering the powder in a plume of smoke. The animal landed on top of me, pinning the staff and my hands beneath a half ton of dead flesh.

I couldn't move!

Both the Chemist and the big tiger advanced.

"Very acrobatic. Have I mentioned recently how much I adore your mask?"

I heaved. Nothing happened. It was like wearing a straightjacket. The flashlight flicked on and off again, spotlighting me, marking me as a target.

The living tiger stepped onto my shoulder, his jaw's wispy mane tickling my ear.

"You will not be devoured," the Chemist said, like disciplining a child. "I will stop the tiger after you have suffered enough."

"Very thoughtful," I groaned, pushing and squirming.

The tiger calmly lowered his head and sunk five-inch teeth into my right shoulder. *Pain!!* Blinded by fur. No light, only darkness. My skin and muscles were thick and tough, but his jaws were powerful. All was strangely quiet, even his untamed Chosen. I could hear Samantha.

This isn't how I want to go…

Katie…

Suddenly, Puck pierced my eardrum. "There he is!! About *time*, Carter! Go go go!!"

146

The tiger heard it first. He released my rotator cuff and looked up in alarm. Then we all heard the noise. An engine roared. Headlights, coming through the *windows*.

A heavy, white and bright orange CalTrans dump truck burst through the wall of the math building. Bricks and glass erupted like a bomb going off.

Croc was driving. He laid on the horn, screaming, "Wooooohooooooo!!" He cut the wheel and plowed straight into the tiger's haunches. No time for the big cat to react. The animal's pelvis shattered against the truck's reinforced grill and the brick wall, and he howled in rage and pain.

Carter rode in the bed of the dump truck. Before contact with the tiger, he exited the vehicle, leaping into the night, straight over me. My eyes followed him, as if in slow motion, as he sailed headfirst into the stunned Chemist. Carter had a knife clamped *in his teeth*, which is still one the coolest things I've ever seen.

Before they hit the ground, the sky emptied of Infected. The Chemist's legion poured in, descended upon us like animals, rallying to their master's defense.

A man rose up from the wrecked truck, standing in the bed and hefting a truly enormous gun. It was a hand-held, belt-fed, .50 caliber machine gun, and he squeezed the trigger. The weapon bawled to life and he cut through lines of enemy Infected with molten lead. I couldn't see his face; he wore a full bomb-proof suit. The enemy Infected returned fire, ricocheting harmlessly off his armor.

Croc was a ghost. He saw everything before it happened and he slipped through attacking crowds, one step ahead, an invisible scourge armed with knives.

I pressed the dead animal far enough to squeeze free, and scrambled up to help my team.

The Chemist's Chosen came like a tribe of savages, brawny and fast. But also uncoordinated and clumsy, and for the first time I fully understood their disadvantage. They were newborns. I could dispatch handfuls easily, but there weren't handfuls. There were dozens. And dozens. They were black, white, Asian, Latino, men, women, a seething riot all about my age. I threw them off, absorbing punches and deflecting knives, twisting away from gun barrels. Their bodies were hard and strong and they were everywhere.

Carter didn't kill the Chemist. Carter was bodily hauled away by the madman's Chosen, but they were paying the price. Carter was the devil, an elemental force of nature, and he eviscerated the helpless horde unable to scramble away. He ripped out throats. I tried not to watch.

"Carter, my fusty old friend," the Chemist laughed and brushed himself off. "You're failing again. And tonight, you pay for it."

In one whip-like motion, he produced a pistol and fired.

His aim was true across the distance. Blood spurted from Samantha's shoulder and she buckled in pain. Her handler shoved her off the roof and she fell, helplessly.

"Sam!" Croc cried, and he got there before I could. He caught and cradled her.

All was madness. We were losing the fight. We fought an unending and overwhelming ocean. We'd be suffocated under the sheer weight. Carter had the right idea.

Get to the Chemist. Our only hope.

But we couldn't. Impossible. His fanatics were fearsome, and we were about to be overrun.

I was shot in the back. The vest absorbed it. Another one caught me in the stomach. My shoulder ached from the bite. Hands everywhere, weighing me down. My energy was spent. My body fought on autopilot with heavy limbs. We needed a miracle. And we got one.

"Grenades!!"

Grenades??

Explosions! Chaos. Screaming. Unbelievably, the HRT guys swarmed in, guns blazing, brave men with wills of steel. The FBI team was heroic and inspiring, but they died too quickly. As skilled as they were, they were slow compared to their targets. Their soft bodies weren't enhanced, and the soldiers were cut down by Chosen fighting despite ghastly wounds.

The lead FBI soldier kept absorbing gunshots until he reached me. For a moment, the world stilled and I heard only him. He was a bloody mess and he died in my arms, but not before delivering a message.

"…evacuation   coming…rendezvous   at   the   gym…go now…place…blown to hell…go…" he gurgled as he died.

"He's right, Outlaw," Puck shouted. "I'm scanning Anderson's phone! You've gotta go! Now! Everyone out!"

Croc and Samantha were gone. I bellowed at Carter and the new guy on the truck. Puck did the same, through headsets. This could still end well. We could get out, via advanced warning, and incoming attacks might destroy the Chemist.

We retreated through the path carved by FBI warriors. I collected Anderson, who was alive but unconscious. I roared for Croc over and over, but he never answered. Puck reported his phone was moving away from the college.

Two helicopters came prowling over the campus, stub-wings freighted with death. The smaller attack helicopter pushed forward, obviously acting on coordinates and instructions provided by the HRT team, and began destroying the world with Hellfire missiles and autocannons. The military was tired of playing it safe and decided to scorch this section of earth. The noise and heat was a volcano eruption.

The transport helicopter landed, flattening the long grass with rotor wash. I slid Anderson's body onto the deck. Carter and Russia pulled themselves in. I grabbed on as the chopper lifted off from hell and plunged back into the sky.

A medic secured Anderson and shouted into my ear, "This Special Agent Isaac Anderson? Was he shot?"

"I don't know." I collapsed near the open cabin door. My legs dangled freely above our landing gear and Compton.

"Puck," I said with as much volume I could muster. "Where's dad?"

"He's…hang on…looks like he's okay. Never made it to the heaviest fighting."

I nodded. Thank God. That would have been awful. I could still beat him home. Holy moly, did I have school in the morning??

Carter stood next to me, jaw set, glaring at distant explosions on Camino's campus. Tiny figures poured out of buildings, like ants escaping a burning colony. "You shouldn't have gone in."

"Think we got him?"

"No."

Chapter Thirteen
Monday, August 31. 2018

Croc pulled three bullets out of my body. One from my arm, one from my shoulder, and one from my butt. During the firefight my skin thickened and muscles hardened to a tough leather texture, and the jacketed-lead slugs hadn't deeply penetrated. They hurt coming OUT though. He removed Samantha's too, and treated us with antiseptics, disinfectants, antivirals, and narcotics; every bottle he had.

"Only thing I'm worried about is that shoulder, mate. It's a doozy. Can't believe you got bit by a *tiger!*"

Thanks, Croc.

I called in sick to school. Samantha too. We laid in our bedrooms and groaned. I phoned for pizza and subs when the sleeping pills wore off and requested food be delivered straight to our rooms.

Katie texted me during lunch.

>> Where are you??
Sick day. Had a rough night.
>> Poor baby! If you're lucky, I'll bring you soup!
>> Miss you!!

Then, a little later...

>> Samantha isn't at school either.
She's taking a sick day too, here with me. I didn't elaborate. Typing hurt.

>> Okay

>> Wow you're both sick
>> At the same time
>> What are you two doing?
>> Never mind I don't want to know
>> I'm so jealous I can't hear the teacher

I laughed. Hard. (It hurt) My texts were a little misleading, I now realized. I imagined her reading my messages and getting the wrong idea, her eyes widening, her friends wondering what's wrong...

Nothing going on. Promise.
Don't be jealous.

I considered typing, *We're both recovering from gunshot wounds*, but that might require a tricky followup explanation.

>> I'm not allowed to be jealous
>> I know I'm not
>> You can do whatever you want
>> With whoever you want
>> But
>> Ugh
>> I miss you

I took a screen-shot of those texts and stared at it within the foggy delirium of hydrocodone.

She misses me!

The attack was international news. The whole world watched the Chemist throw a larger net around his portion of Los Angeles. The uprising had been fast, brutal, and efficient. His forces struck unexpectedly, overwhelming the thin border patrol, and joined with waiting reinforcements in Paramount. Like last time, he used hundreds of stalled tankers to clog the interstate, very effectively preventing outside intervention. The police and military were wholly and unreservedly defeated. During the chaos, two cargo planes landed at his airstrip with fresh supplies, most likely weapons and drugs. The size of his territory and the number of his hostages had doubled in one night.

Samantha, Croc and I met Carter the next night at the lumber yard we used for practice. We parked at the rear security fence. The mood was somber; we had whiffed on our chance to fix the planet. The grumpy giant called Russia attended. Russia didn't speak. Russia glared behind a nose that appeared to have been broken dozens of times. His eyebrows were shockingly thick and his skin was pockmarked.

"Los Angeles got its ass kicked again," Carter said. "But *we* didn't."

Samantha asked, "What do you mean? I *feel* like I got my ass kicked."

Carter handed us each an iPad. I took it with my left hand.

"We're all still alive," he responded. "And we gained valuable intel. Hacker, you seeing these photos?"

A voice came buzzing out of a speaker temporarily set on the hood of Croc's truck. "PuckDaddy has the photos."

Carter lit a cigarette and pointed at our laptops. "Look through. The three of us wore small cameras. The photos were uploaded and I picked out the most significant. Tell me what you see."

The photos weren't high definition and the lighting was bad, but they were usable. Dozens of still-shots taken during the gunfight on Camino's campus. Cameras had been affixed to their shirts, and another positioned inside the truck. I flipped through, reliving the melee with a cold knot in my stomach. I paused at photos of the Outlaw.

Croc looked up from his tablet and grinned. "Samy looking as gorgeous as *evah*! Even with tape across her yapper."

She ignored him, and stated, "I see too many Infected."

Carter nodded. His bald scalp dully reflected the nearby street light. "I agree."

"He shouldn't have this many. Where'd they come from? We only heard about a handful."

"Keep looking, specifically at his Infected." His plosive syllables were punctuated with blue smoke puffs. "He has too many. What else about them?"

I said, "There's something wrong with his Infected. I noticed last night."

"What did you notice?"

"I'm not sure. Something was...*off*. I spoke with one of them, but he couldn't communicate well. Like he was too full of rage to process." I snapped my fingers, remembering a detail. "He referred to himself by a weird title. I forget what…"

Puck chimed in from his speaker. "Called himself Twice Chosen, or something like that."

"Right. That was it. The Chemist referenced it too."

"Twice Chosen," Carter echoed, hard eyes searching stars and memories for clues. "Twice Chosen. Twice Chosen. I don't know what that means."

I shrugged. "Neither did I."

The giant called Russia wasn't looking at the photos. He was staring at us with bored, baleful eyes. He needed a shave and a haircut. His thick arms were crossed over his barrel chest.

"Here's what I think." Carter tapped the screen of my iPad, scattering ash across it. "I think whatever process Martin uses to preserve his Chosen from aneurysms and insanity, I think it doesn't completely work. I think his enhanced army is full of unsound minds. Almost like rabid dogs, living only to please their master."

"Too right." Croc agreed. "They went after you like a mama bear protecting cubs. You got too close to their master."

"That's my opinion too, Mitchell."

"Insane or not, they're dangerous. They made quick work of the FBI team. And who's this guy?" I flipped back and forth through a sequence of photos showing Carter fighting off Chemist goons, and in each picture there was a man dressed all in black, attacking Chosen from behind. "I don't remember him."

Samantha Gear grinned. "Spooky, right? That's Carter's Shadow. I met him."

"Wow. So he *does* exist. I think I saw him during the Compton showdown in March. He's very good. I never even saw him last night."

Carter grunted. "He's essentially invisible when he wants to be."

Croc turned in a circle, scanning the lumber and construction materials. "Where's the bloke now? I wanna shake his hand."

"He never tells me."

Samantha held up her iPad, displaying a photo of a dozen Infected. "Carter, let's assume that his brain preservation process isn't perfect, and his Chosen are at least partially deranged. But that doesn't explain where he got them. He has...jeez, I don't know. Thirty? Forty?"

"I count around forty. A surprising number. The hacker is running facial recognition software, and comparing their faces against missing person reports. I want to know who they are. The photos aren't high quality, so it's difficult. He's trying."

The speaker buzzed. "I have a name, you know."

I paused at a picture of the Chemist. "Carter, why does the Chemist look like this? The last time I saw him, he was healthy and jumping around. Not last night. He looks like a corpse in these photos."

"I agree." Samantha peered over my shoulder at the photo. "Radical change in his body and energy level."

"I have a theory." Carter flicked his dead cigarette away and immediately lit a new one. Russia watched him without interest. "I think he's draining his body of blood, as often as he can, in hopes that he's already contagious."

We all fell silent. A contagious Chemist would be worst case scenario for peace in our future. We wouldn't feel the repercussions for two decades, but if he was injecting hundreds or even thousands of infants then there would be mass hysteria eighteen years from now as teenagers across the globe began throwing cars and dropping dead.

"You think he's storing the blood?"

"Doubt it. He's a brilliant neurobiologist. I imagine he's tinkering with the virus on a molecular level, and then injecting every infant he can get his hands on. Though after last night, I'm optimistic we've temporarily disrupted his machinations."

Croc said, "If he's contagious, then isn't the fella almost dead? Like, any day now?"

"Possibly, but I doubt it. He doesn't have long, but he's creative, as evidenced by his mutated tigers. He'll delay his death as long as possible, through any means necessary."

"What's this final video?" I asked. The photos ended with a silent video in slow-motion. The video was of me, fighting, as seen by the camera in the truck. The Outlaw was spellbinding, a madman shouldering aside the storm. My muscles pumped like engines, throwing destructive wrecking-ball fists and trampling others beneath my feet. I threw a guy *over* the math building. I couldn't remember half this stuff. Russia picked up the iPad and browsed to the file with his thick fingers.

Carter laughed without humor, pointy white teeth clamped on a filter. "That video is evidence of the reason Martin is after you, tiger."

"Because I'm awesome? And I do not love that nickname."

"No, although you certainly move faster than the rest of us. Watch it again."

I did. I was fighting my way towards Samantha, away from the dying tiger, and constantly battling several Chosen at once. There were always enemies ready to engage me, waiting their turn. Waiting and watching. Mostly watching…

I concluded, "His Chosen aren't attacking all at once, like they did with you."

Carter nodded.

I viewed it again, and said, "A handful of his Chosen are fighting, but most are just…staring. They could have overwhelmed me, but they didn't."

"*That* is what Martin is after. Most of his Chosen don't want to hurt you. Highly unnatural. Infected usually despise each other. Look at us. The Infected I've worked with over the past decades don't like living on the same *continent*. Our skin crawls being near each other."

Big Russia barked a deep laugh and said, "Yah." Samantha nodded.

"But not the Chemist. He's always had followers. And so do you, kid. You're the first in…two hundred years? His Chosen are staring at you, astonished, because they feel what we all feel. Instead of being repelled by you, we are drawn towards you. Something in the way the virus interacts with your body chemistry. And it's powerful. And Martin wants to control it." He flicked his cigarette at me. It bounced off my shirt, leaving a small ash stain. "You'd be an unstoppable weapon for him, a unifying force within his chaos. Which is why you should have stayed out of Compton."

"We almost had him," I protested.

"You walked straight into a trap."

"And it worked. We got within inches."

"The three of us had to save your ass."

"Took you long enough."

"You were tiger food, little boy. And Martin was going to use you as a pawn."

"I'm not his pawn, and I'm not yours either, old man."

"Every time you speak to him, every time you two interact, he learns more about you. He's tracking you, *mate*. Hunting you. If he discovers the Outlaw's identity, if he finds out who Chase Jackson really is, then he'll show up at your door and kill everyone you love."

Samantha interrupted us. "Okay, boys. Cool it. Is this a picture of me?" She held up her screen for us to see. "Is this a screenshot of a web article?"

Both Carter and Russia were still glaring at me. Carter's veins were visible in his neck and he was taking deep breaths.

"Hey." Samantha snapped her fingers twice. "Hey. What's this picture?"

"That's a picture the police are circulating," he growled. "Of you. A street camera got a clear picture. The hacker deleted copies as fast as he could, but people are beginning to store data on external hard drives so he can't get to them."

Samantha examined it from all angles, wrinkling her nose. "It's not *that* clear. I look good, though."

"Love, you look *gorgeous*."

"Thanks, Croc. Now hush."

Puck rattled, "There are digital photographs of all of you dummies. Though none that clear. And our good friend Captain FBI is facing significant discipline from the government."

"I still have a difficult time believing you went to the FBI," Carter sneered. His grip on the truck was so ferocious the hood was bending. "You have undermined *decades* of secrecy."

"Sorry to hear that. Guess you shouldn't have infected a bunch of infants, eh?"

He seethed and for a long moment I thought he might swing at me. He was furious and his blood boiled and the disease was a storm inside his body, turning his muscles and skin to steel while my disease lay dormant. I knew baiting him was a bad idea, but I couldn't stop. He shook his head and snorted, like a bull. "Your arrogance is going to kill us all."

"You think *I'm* the one who's arrogant?! I'm looking for help! I know we need it. You're the man with the Lone Ranger act."

Puck's voice came from the speaker. "This argument is stressing me out. Is it crazy tense there?"

Samantha quipped, "Yes. We're having a Who's Tougher contest. We're all losing."

I shrugged. "The Avengers don't get along either."

Russia scoffed, like an arctic blast.

Carter said, "What? Who?"

"Shouldn't we meet somewhere cooler than a lumber yard?" I asked. "We're, like…a secret group of…super secret soldiers. The entire planet is fascinated with us. We need a heli-carrier. Or at least an office. With a shiny table."

Puck shouted, "That would be crazy awesome!" The speaker vibrated so violently it almost slid off the hood.

Carter and Russia turned at the same time, storming back to their truck. "Children," he spat, "My patience with you is almost at an end."

He drove off with angry taillights and angry tires spitting gravel at us. Croc whistled. Puck said, "What? What happened?"

Samantha grabbed me by the arm. "Listen, Outlaw. Listen carefully. About five years ago, Carter killed a man. We called him the Extractor. Don't know his real name. He was Infected. Carter surprised him. Put a shotgun to the Extractor's eyeball and pulled the trigger. All because the Extractor had changed plans without consulting Carter. The Extractor disobeyed orders, but he thought he was doing the right thing. Didn't matter. Carter killed him."

"Oh yeah." Croc chuckled grimly, scratching his unshaven face. "Forgot about that mess. Extractor was a solid bloke, too."

"Chase. Carter will do the same to you. He will. I promise. I'm surprised he hasn't yet, to be honest."

I winked. "I'm tougher than the Extractor."

She hit me. Hard.

"Ow!" I yelped. "That was my bad shoulder. My *tiger* shoulder."

"Wuss."

Chapter Fourteen
September. 2018

September passed in a blur. Like my life was on fast-forward. My days were crammed with fluff that felt less and less relevant to the real world. Coach Garrett's rants were hollow and distant. Video games with Cory and Lee were a maddening waste of time. I had Bs and Cs in all my classes. Not a single A. But I didn't care; the school would be overrun soon if the Chemist wasn't captured. When Dad scolded me, he might as well have been complaining about the moon.

Sometimes I wonder if, after the story of my life has been told, all I will remember is Katie.

During September, my life was divided into two categories. When I was with Katie, and when I wasn't. English class was the best part of school. You know that scene in *The Hobbit* when Bilbo climbs the tree to escape the dark scary endless forest, and at the top of the tree he finds butterflies and brilliant sunlight and for that one shining moment all is well? That's what being with Katie was like. Whatever it is that happens to girls, propelling them out of late adolescence and fully into adulthood, that had happened to Katie. She was no longer a child. Katie Lopez belonged on a college campus. And she'd be the prettiest one there. And the smartest. And the nicest. I was so attracted to her it scared me. Sometimes I couldn't think of words when she smiled.

Katie's heart was torn in half, split between me and a monster. When she and I were together during English class and after-school tutoring, our chemistry was red hot. The air crackled. We alternated between being unable to look at each other, and long intense eye-contact. Some days she would sit across the kitchen table like I was a leper. Other days she sat so close our legs touched, and she found any excuse to touch me, setting my skin on fire. I ate extra granola bars after study sessions.

But she also had genuine affection for Tank. He was charismatic, rich, and handsome, and treating her better each passing day. They were a famous couple. People Magazine gave them an exclusive page in the 50 Most Beautiful edition, and rightly so. They were a scintillating redemption story in the midst of Los Angeles's tragedy.

I hated that guy.

Tank was churning out impossible football stats. He finished the first game of the season with six sacks, two forced fumbles, two rushing touchdowns, and he also injured the other team's starting quarterback, running back, and free safety. He kept up the absurd production for the whole month, vaulting himself even higher into our national football ethos. High school football magazines called him a Once-In-a-Generation Athletic Freak, possibly the most highly touted senior of all time.

My team, the Hidden Spring Eagles, also rolled through September. We won all four games by an average of twenty-four points. College scouts attended our games in droves. Our late season showdown with Tank's Patrick Henry Dragons loomed larger and larger with each game.

"It's not fair," I told Samantha Gear one day at practice, the first drizzly day in weeks. She held a magazine in her angry fists, glaring at the article about Tank. "I jumped out of a helicopter. Fought twenty guys. Faced down two tigers. And I can throw a football over a mile. It's not fair to the other teams. You know? To the kids on those teams."

She mumbled something unintelligible.

I sighed. "Maybe I should quit."

"No." She bunched up the magazine in a thick wad. "That wouldn't be fair to the kids on *this* team. You're playing well, but you're also playing within the limits of reason. Tank isn't. Just keep doing what you're doing.

Besides. I like playing. I don't want to quit."

The Shooter's face was splashed all over the news, and more than one person at our school commented on the resemblance to Samantha. She laughed and told everyone the photograph *was* of her. After that, the students just treated the likeness as a joke.

The media dubbed us the Fearsome Four. City employees and amateur photojournalists must have combed through thousands of pictures taken from scattered automated cameras, because authentic photographs of Carter, Russia, Samantha, and the Outlaw surfaced on the internet. (Puck didn't try erasing the data. The proof of our existence was now too substantial to fret over.) Somehow Croc had avoided exposure. So had Shadow.

Our evacuation was discovered and sensationalized. The helicopter pilots had reported the rescue of four men: two strangers, the Outlaw, and Special Agent Isaac Anderson. Speculation was rampant. Some media outlets called us The Outlaws, but Samantha nearly killed me the one time I mentioned it.

Isaac Anderson disobeyed direct orders that night, resulting in five deaths and two serious injuries. However, his court-martial was being commuted due to extraordinary circumstances. Evidence began pouring in from photographs, pilot testimony, radio reports, and eye-witness accounts suggesting Anderson made decisions based on the good of Los Angeles, and that his alliance with the Outlaw and the Fearsome Four was an unprecedented and bold war-time collaboration, resulting in the destruction of the Chemist's fortress. The press screamed for interviews with Anderson, demanding details of his clandestine involvement with Hyper Humanity.

The Outlaw was once again cast as a heroic public defender. Banners were hung near Natalie North's building, stating **The Outlaw Fights For Us.** Her relationship with Anderson wasn't public knowledge. Yet. She texted, thanking me for getting Anderson out safely. And asking me to come visit.

On the final Sunday of the month, Dad and I went to church. I love that place. As the world was thrown further into disarray and I increasingly realized we spent too much time worrying about vapid priorities, the church's message seemed more and more…true. Love. Honesty. Forgiveness. Denial of self. These words pierced my heart in ways that Nike commercials didn't.

I forgot all about them, however, as we returned home. Tank Ware stood in my driveway.

The Tank.

My driveway.

Gosh I hate that guy.

"Who is the giant?" Dad chuckled as we parked.

"Tank Ware," I grumbled. "Patrick Henry Dragon."

"Oh yeah." The muscles in Dad's jaw flexed. "Want me to run him over?"

"The only injury would be to our car." I shoved the door open and climbed out.

Tank smiled the sparkling, winsome smile he used to dupe the planet. Had to give him credit; he could act. He was dressed in his customary white button-up shirt and thin cotton gloves. "Jackson family!" he roared good-naturedly, like he wasn't Satan. "I'm sorry to barge in like this. I suppose my church lets out earlier than yours."

That stopped me. "You go to church??"

"First African Methodist Episcopal Church, my whole life."

"What the *heck* do they preach over there??" I was genuinely bewildered. Maybe I didn't understand church as much as I assumed. Was this a kidnapping and bullying church?

Tank shook Dad's hand and congratulated us on my fine football season. He also thanked Dad for his public service towards our troubled city. Dad, the biggest sucker in the world apparently, seemed genuinely grateful and he invited Tank inside. Inside *my* house.

"Mighty kind of you, sir, but I just came to get Chase's advice on a few football matters. I won't trouble you long, and I won't come inside."

"Very well. Nice to meet you, son." They shook hands again. "Chase, I'm going inside. Need anything?" He shot me a knowing and understanding look.

"I'm starving. Start making lunch?"

"You got it."

He threw a quick salute and strolled inside our townhouse. I stayed outside with the Dragon.

"Mighty kind of you, sir," I mimicked him. "Law'have mercy, sir, been going to church m'whole life!"

Tank threw his head back and laughed. He had gotten bigger. Must be close to seven feet now.

I said, "That's quite an act you have."

"Thank you, thank you." He nodded. "Gotsta keep up appearances. But you know all about *that*, pajamas."

"Do you actually attend a church service?"

"Sho' do. Lawd Jesus save my soul when I's just a wee child, sir."

"Okay. Enough. Why the heck are you here? We said No Families. I know where you live too."

He paused and the grin faded. A deep breath. He shoved his huge hands into his huge pockets. First he stared at the ground, then squinted at the city skyline, and then back at the ground. By all appearances, he appeared to be struggling with words. He had the audacity to kick a pebble during his deliberations.

Finally, "I'd like to call a truce."

"A *truce*? You cannot be serious. A truce."

"Entirely serious."

"You promised reporters you'd reveal my identity. You threatened me on national television."

He shrugged. "I won't."

"You told America you were going to beat me up."

Another shrug. "I won't do that either."

I sniffed. "Couldn't if you wanted."

"Listen, tiny hero," he grunted, a hint of his dangerous side, "I won't pretend I like you. But I think you and I have more in common than not. Especially at the moment."

"You been talking to Carter?"

"Carter? Don't know no Carter."

"Yes you do," I snapped, intensely annoyed at this bizarre conversation. "Bald guy? In Compton with us that night in March? Old chums with the Chemist?"

"*That* guy." He nodded, slow and deep, lost in angry thought. "He pretended to be my doctor."

"Yeah, that's him. He's everywhere."

"My last day at the hospital, he told me I was *like* him. Told me I'd see him again."

A car drove by. My neighbor. She slowed down and gawked at us as she passed. Tank nodded and waved. He *was* quite a sight. I would slow down and gawk too if I didn't know him already.

I said, "Don't plan on getting chummy with Carter. He's tried to kill you twice. Now he wants to use you. To help him defeat the Chemist."

"Can he explain what's wrong with me?"

"What do you mean?"

"You know." He shuffled uncomfortably. "The headaches? The nausea? I'm seven feet. I have to hide how strong I am. Since I woke up, I've been having hallucinations, and hearing voices. Sometimes, my skin feels..." He trailed off.

"Hallucinations? Voices? Huh..." I rubbed my lower lip in thought. "Maybe the disease made you crazy. Well, crazier."

"What disease?"

"...you don't know about the disease?"

"No. The hell should I? What disease?"

"Jeez Tank," I sighed. I laced my fingers behind my head and started pacing the driveway. I assumed he'd known the truth about the disease for months.

"Same stuff as you. Right?" he asked. "We're the same, right? You have a disease too?"

"You kidnapped my best friend. You tried to kill me. Multiple times. You burned down my homecoming dance. You're dating someone very important to me, just to cause me pain. And now you show up here and want help??"

He held his hands up in front of him like a shield. "I get it. I do. I get that. You don't have to tell me. I'm leaving. First, though, about the Latina…"

"Katie? If you want to call a truce then leave her alone. Break up with her, and *then* I'll trust you. A little. Maybe."

"See, that's the thing, pajamas. I like her."

"I don't care."

"I love her."

I groaned. "Oh my goooooooooosh. You can't love her! Don't be stupid! She's an angel and you're a dumpster fire. She's good, you're evil."

He chortled and shook his head. "Don't know what to tell you, hero. I'm in love."

"NO YOU'RE NOT! You do not possess the ability!" I saw red. It wasn't a figure of speech. The world was turning shades of red. "You don't deserve her. You're not worth one hair on her head."

"We agree on that."

"Shut up."

He laughed again. I hate when he did that. "Thought you'd be happy! I'm going to treat her right. The way she deserves to be treated."

"No no no no." I bumped my fist into my forehead with each word. "You don't get it! You can't treat her that way. You have no hope. The dirt cannot treat the sun the way the sun deserves to be treated."

"I'm sorry you feel that way." He seemed legitimately offended, the big ogre. He turned and walked to his brand new Hummer. "But anyway. She cares about you. So the truce is good on my end."

"Yeah," I chucked sarcastically, caustically. "I'll take *your word* for it. I'll take the murderer's word. I'll take the crime boss's word. I'll take the kidnapper's word that he'll keep his hostage safe."

"Cool it, little hero," he growled, halfway into his SUV. "I'm trying to do the right thing."

"I'll tell her." I couldn't see. Tears of anger and frustration welled in my eyes. My voice bordered on breaking. "I have to. I will tell her the truth about you, and who you are."

"Likewise, Outlaw. Truce."

Chapter Fifteen
Wednesday, September 30. 2018

"Jackson!" Coach Garrett called as I was trudging out the locker room, toting a laundry bag over my shoulder. Practice was over, and all I could think about was driving to Katie's apartment. "Stick around for a minute, champ."

I walked into the conference room with him. Coach Todd Keith was sitting at the glossy table, flipping through paraphernalia. The table was covered. The rest of the team was in the adjacent room, still showering and changing into clean clothes. I was first to leave because my tutor was the cutest.

"Yes sir?"

Garrett clapped me on the shoulder, and he grinned. "Time we start talking about this. Don't you think?"

"Talking about what?"

Coach Keith, our offensive coordinator and my intermittent spiritual advisor, held up a college brochure. "Your future."

"College," I realized.

"College."

Garrett sat down and indicated I should too. Instead I let my eyes wander the names of colleges. Every big program I'd ever heard of had a pamphlet on the table. I placed my knuckles on the surface and stared. College.

"I field about three calls a week from college coaches," Garrett raved. He was chomping gum and wearing sunglasses, even indoors. "And they all want to talk about you."

"And that's just the big-time universities," Coach Keith said. "USC. UNLV. San Diego State. Oregon. Arizona."

"What do they want to know?"

"Everything," Garrett grinned. "Everything about you. Most importantly, how soon can you visit their campus."

I heard Croc in the other room, joking with the guys. He'd quickly become a crowd favorite, and not just because he was good.

"These colleges want me to play ball for them?"

"They do."

"On a scholarship?" I asked.

"Everyone is offering you a full ride," Coach Keith said. "Though not every school can guarantee you playing time as a freshman. You'd be redshirted at programs with established quarterbacks."

"Never had this many calls before," said Garrett. "Our P.R. department has requests from over a hundred schools."

"A hundred," I echoed.

"Which is why," Garrett said, banging his hand on the table, "it's about dang time we figure this out. Tell us your favorites and we'll schedule visits."

"My favorites," I said. I was repeating a lot. I couldn't stop.

"Yep."

"I haven't even thought about college," I admitted, sheepishly. My face was hot. "I don't...I don't know a thing about any of them."

Their expressions were incredulous. I didn't blame them. This was every football player's dream, and I hadn't thought about it?

I continued, "You know, it's just...with all the, ah, the war in Los Angeles and...you know, college hasn't been on my mind." I paced and rubbed my eyes, talking into my palms. "That's...a little embarrassing, I know."

"Well hell, son. All right. Talk to your dad about this? He and I've spoke a few times."

"Um. No. No, I guess I haven't."

Coach Keith asked, "Everything okay at home?"

"Yeah, sure. No problems." I picked up a football pamphlet for the University of Southern California, and I tried to be interested in it. But I wasn't. Couldn't even fake it. Like chasing after wind. All was vanity.

Croc stuck his head in the door. "Hey mate! I'm takin' off. See you later at your place. I'm making suppa!"

"Okay," I replied without turning. "See you. Might be late."

"See you boys!"

The coaches nodded to him and he left. Garrett grinned and said, "Starting to get calls about him, too."

"About Croc?" I chuckled. "Playing college football?"

"Yes sir. A fine player."

"A fine player," I repeated. "Coaches are calling about *Croc* playing college." Impossible. Ludicrous. So much they didn't know. He couldn't...I couldn't...

I sank into the chair across from them and put my head into my hands. I couldn't believe this was happening. My normal life was slipping away, and I had to let it go. Colleges would test me for steroids and drugs and who knew what else. And I couldn't let it happen, not even once. My blood tests would come back off the charts, if they could even get the needle into my skin.

Your life has been rewritten, Croc told me.

You're Infected.

You will never have a normal life again.

He was correct. About football, at least. I couldn't play in college. No chance. It wouldn't be fair to the other players. I'd have to pretend every day, every practice, that I wasn't abnormal. Pretend I couldn't outrun them all. That I couldn't just jump over the pile.

"Something wrong, Chase?" Coach Keith asked.

"No," I said. But big tears were running down my face. "Well. Yes, I guess there is." Coach Garrett was frozen. Football players don't cry. "I won't play football in college."

Neither of them spoke. I'm not sure they were breathing either.

"I decided recently. It's just...not for me, you know?" I wiped my eyes and my cheeks. This was awful. Dad was going to be crushed.

"Why the hell not?"

"Just not." I couldn't stop crying.

Coach Keith asked, "You've spoken with your family about this?"

"Just me and my dad. And I haven't told him, no."

"Well, don't make up your mind yet."

"You're one of the top three quarterback recruits in the country, son," Garrett barked in disbelief. "I've seen how hard you work. You *love* this!"

"I know." I stood up, leaving teardrops on the table. "I'm sorry. We'll talk more later. After I speak with Dad. Okay? But, don't schedule any visits."

I told Katie about my decision to not play football in college. She didn't understand. I promised I'd tell her one day. One day soon. I cried. She cried. She kissed my cheek, and my shoes and shirt instantly felt tighter as my body responded.

After tutoring I found Samantha Gear sitting on the front steps of my home. Croc was inside singing and cooking.

I inquired, "What are you doing out here?"

"Keeping my distance."

"From Croc?"

She nodded and rubbed the palms of her hands up and down her thighs. "From a lot of things."

I dropped my bag and sat next to her. There were very few bad days in Los Angeles. The air was sunny and warm, even in the early evening, and the palm trees stood happy and still.

"I told Coach," I sighed. "About not playing college football."

"Ugh. I'm sorry, Chase. That's the worst."

I nodded.

She commiserated, "Being an Infected, it really is a debilitating disease. But it's not your body that's destroyed, it's your life."

"I am now fully realizing that."

"It gets worse, too," she said with a wry grimace. "I wish I had better news, but that's the truth."

"How so?"

She took a long time replying, staring at the grass and rubbing her legs like she was cold. "Because of Katie."

"What do you mean?" I asked, alarm tightening my stomach.

"Think about it, Chase. How old is the Chemist?"

"I don't know." I shrugged. "Over 200. Why?"

"And how long will Katie live?"

I didn't respond. I'd never thought about the math. Even if I could make her love me, which seemed doubtful, I would potentially outlive her by...well, who knew. But it might be a long time.

"Yeah," I said slowly. "But that's an issue I'll deal with in the future. I have too many problems on my plate as it is."

"Your love life isn't just a problem you can ignore." She lowered her forehead to her knees. I'd never seen Samantha pensive before. Pensive? Or depressed? "At the end of the day, you're a human. And humans want to be loved."

"Are you sad?"

"No. Sad sounds weak. More like...melancholy."

"I don't get you, Gear. You've got a great guy inside who loves you. A lot." I jerked a thumb over my shoulder towards Croc, who was belting lines from *Don't Stop Believing*, by Journey. Between verses he and my dad made small talk.

"He's Infected." She grumbled the words, clearly aggravated by my inability to grasp this. "Infected don't get along."

"He likes *you*."

"He likes me in short bursts," she explained, sitting up and running fingers through her hair. "He's affectionate once a year or so, and then he gets wary of me and leaves. Like all Infected. Well, except for you. But when he's around, I'm tense and I can't help it. I'm on high alert, like two alpha males in the same room."

"So your body won't let you be with him?"

"Right. We're like magnets that repel each other. All Infected are. Can't help it. Plus, he's not my type."

I grinned. "You have a type? What is it?"

"Shut up, Chase, or I'll punch you in the eye."

"No seriously. What's your type?"

"Croc is too pretty. He's too…goofy. I prefer *men*. Like, manly, dirty, hard-working, serious, strong men. Not silly boys like Croc." While she spoke, her fingers flexed in front of her, like she was trying to create the guy out of thin air.

"Dirty men. Gross."

"You know the guy that hosted Dirty Jobs? I forget his name. Tall guy, deep voice?"

I laughed. "Yeah, I know him. I think he looks a little like Dad."

"Whatever his name is," she grinned mischievously. "I'm into him. He's older, I know, but that's good too."

"Older men are good?"

"Very. This is weird, Chase. I haven't talked about my love life in…ten years? Maybe twelve?"

"But you have the same problem as me. You'll outlive everyone, right?"

"Yep." She nodded. "I know I can't be with the same man until I die. I've made my peace with that. And I'm not the type of person that fantasizes and daydreams about living with Prince Charming forever. But, it'd be nice. For a little while, to be with a big strong man."

"A big strong television-show host."

"Or a firefighter. Like the station chief. Big guy, can take a punch. A smart man that bosses other men around."

"You're weird."

"Or, you know…a cop. A police officer? Those are good too."

"I'll be on the look-out for you!"

"No thank you."

"This'll be fun. I'm looking for a guy older than you, big, tall, strong, serious, deep voice, bosses people around, like a firefighter or a cop and…" I was ticking her requirements off on my fingers, but I stopped. Somewhere in the recess of my brain, awareness dawned. The coin dropped into the slot. She was staring fixedly straight ahead. I could tell her heart was pounding because of the pulse in her neck. I said, "Samantha."

She didn't look at me. Her expression was wooden, eyes wide. We were both taking deep breaths.

"Samantha."

"Shut up."

"Samantha, it sounds suspiciously like you're describing my father."

She didn't respond. Her fingers were curled under her toes.

I continued. "My father. The man whom you call Richard."

"Chase…"

"My father Richard, who is old as heck."

"No he's not," she retorted. Her voice quavered. "He's like forty."

"Right. Super crazy old."

"I'm thirty."

"This…" I stared at the same point in the distance she was staring at. "This…this is a lot to absorb."

"It's not my fault." Her voice was small. Samantha was one of the most dangerous people on earth. Out of seven billion or whatever, she was certainly in the top ten. But the threat of romance completely cowed her. "You made me live here."

"So?!"

"So he's perfect. He's very handsome. And we live together. And it's…intense.'

"Okay, that's enough, stop talking, hooooooooooly moly be quiet, blah blah blah." I stuck fingers into my ears and shut my eyes. When she was silent for a moment, I peaked at her.

She smiled. "And his big calloused hands. Oooooooh…"

"Samantha. I'm serious. I'll set your hair on fire if you keep talking."

"It's simple. He's lonely. I'm lonely. I'm attractive to him. He's attracted to me."

"What do…wait. He's attracted to you?? How do you know?"

She shrugged. "I can tell."

"How?"

"I just can!"

I said, "He thinks you're *my* age."

"No he doesn't."

"What?!" I yelped.

"Richard is smarter than you give him credit for."

"What does that mean? And dooooooon't call him Richard."

"He just knows things aren't exactly as they seem." She stood up and brushed invisible dirt from her shorts. "I'm tired of talking about this."

"Have you two…?"

"No. We barely speak. Nothing is going on."

"Good," I sighed in relief.

"Yet."

"What?!" I yelped again.

"This stays between us. If you tell him then I'm telling Katie."

"That's not the same!"

"Keep my secret, I'll keep yours. Truce."

Chapter Sixteen
Friday, October 2. 2018

I received messages from both Lee and the Chemist Friday night after we won our football game. Technically, Chase Jackson didn't get the messages. The Outlaw was the recipient.

From: napoleon
Date: October 2. 22:05
Subject: (blank)

Dearest Wart,
The future king,
Marc Antony,

Did you know the United States Marine Corp sent two teams of Navy SEALs into Paramount three days ago? It was not publicized. I had them chopped into little pieces and fed to the next batch of tigers.

I see that you are working with my old friend Mitchell. He and I collaborated on some interesting work in the 90s. Not even Carter the Stodgy Chain Smoker knows about it. Pass along my regards. I always enjoyed Mitchell's company, though I wasn't happy he crushed Eve with his truck.

Speaking of Carter, he cannot be pleased that you are 'in cahoots' with the military. I can almost hear the poor man grinding his teeth. Don't let him get to you. He's a control freak, nearly as crazy as me. We're two sides of the same coin, he and I. Control and chaos.

It is nearly time for me to carve out another slice of the city. Last time you fell squarely into my trap. Will it happen again? I hope so. It was so much fun. How is your shoulder? Before your rescue dues ex machina, you were being devoured. I would have prevented your total destruction. I would have saved your arm. Your pain will be necessary, when it happens. You must die, before being reborn.

In the meantime, I imagine you have many questions. Ask away. About anything. About me. About our chat that night. About Carter. About the virus.

In exchange, I have two questions. First. Is your mother dead? Did you ever know her? I've gathered as much information on you as I can, and I think you lack the mother's feminine touch. Mothers worry. Mothers fret, no matter how old their sons grow. If your mother was still alive, I don't think you'd be leaping out of helicopters. She would have built in a higher degree of fear.

My second question is more of an observation. You are lonely. Yes? Insincerity prevents true intimacy. I imagine you haven't revealed your identity to those closest to you. And thus you are cut off from them. My advice is, tell them. You'll sleep better.

Write back, and I'll delay the destruction.

Caesar
Merlin
Atticus

Jeeeeeez. What do I say to all *that*?? The Chemist's letters made my brain hurt.

Lee's message was simpler.

>> OUTLAW!! Heard you jumped out of a helicopter! I have another gift for you. Specifically designed for FLYING, bro!!!

I smiled. I adore Lee.

You are lonely. Yes?

Yes. Yes I am lonely.

I used to spend days at a time at Lee's house. No longer. The mask hid him from me. From everyone. The Outlaw ate up more and more time, banishing me from my former life.

But did it have to be this way?

I was going to tell Katie. About the Outlaw. If Tank truly loved her, he wouldn't hurt her. That had always been my fear, but now…

I was going to tell her. Soon.

Maybe I could tell Lee. But not tonight. I needed to work up the courage. I texted him back.

When can I see it?

>> ARE YOU KIDDING?!?! ANYTIME!!!!!

How about right now? I'd been invited to a party, but I didn't want to go. Samantha and Croc went. They were really enjoying high school life, which was weird because their combined age was around seventy-five. Katie was with Tank at the movies. I'd rather do anything than think about that.

>> YES!!! WOOOOOOOOOOAAAAAAUUUUUGHHHH!!!

At an early age, Lee built a workshop in the basement of his parent's luxurious home. Out of this laboratory of horrors came a regular supply of new inventions, like electroshock weapons, media devices, and Outlaw gear. The workshop opened directly into his spacious backyard, where I waited in darkness, under a thicket of gold medallion trees.

"Check it out, dude," Lee said as he held up a pair of black pants. His voice trembled slightly; he could barely see me. His shirt had a red Japanimation sketch of the Outlaw's mask across the chest.

I growled, "Pants?"

"Yes. But, ah, better. Do you know what a wing-suit is?"

"The wearable parachute that makes jumpers look like a flying squirrel?"

"Exactly, bro! Err, Mister Outlaw. It's a suit that gives parachuters wings.

They can fly!"

"You mean *glide*."

"Well, yes, glide. But glide super fast and super far."

"I've seen those suits." I was keeping my voice to a dark rumble. "They're bulky." I'd look ridiculous flopping around in one of those!

"Yeah they are!" he laughed. "And cumbersome. That's why I designed your wing-suit to be retractable!" His whisper was triumphant.

"How?"

"Look!" He dropped the pants onto the ground and pulled on a pair of black gloves. "Watch."

"I am."

"Watch this."

"I am."

He hooked the gloves onto his own pants and then raised his arms. Swoosh! He had wings. The wingtips attached to his gloves and the material pulled-out through slits from within the baggy pants. He looked...like a flying squirrel.

"Instant wings! The wing-suit is designed to increase your surface area, allowing you to glide. The wind will fill the interior of these wings, giving you a hard surface to sail on!"

I nodded slowly, at a loss for words. "...okay..."

"I'm not done! Check this out." He connected the pants somehow around his shoes and then spread his feet, revealing another black surface, like a webbing between his legs. "For stability!"

"...wow..."

"I'm not done, dude!" He made fists and uses his thumbs to press a button near his knuckles. With a click, the wings immediately released from the gloves and zipped back, disappearing into the interior of the pant legs. The same thing happened to the webbing between his legs when he clicked his heels together. "Strong cords made of strengthened elastic draw the wings back in. Retractable!"

"That's remarkable, kid."

"Wings on!" He pulled the wings out again with a swish. "Wings off!"

He clicked the gloves and the material zipped back. "Wings on!" Swish open. "Wings off!" Zip, gone. Swish, zip. Swish, zip. Wings, no wings. Wings, no wings. Each transformation took about two seconds. I had to admit, that was slick. "There's only one problem…"

I asked, "Which is?"

"…I don't know if it works."

"Ah."

"I have no way of testing it." He sounded self-conscious about his inability to fly.

"That's understandable." I retrieved from the ground the pair of pants he made for me. They were thick, full of material. Probably be hot. I rubbed them between my fingers, thinking. How *would* he test it? Jump off a skyscraper? When would I ever use this invention? I didn't plan on leaping out of any more helicopters. In fact, I never wanted to see one again. "I'll test it out."

"Yes! But if it doesn't work, use your parachute. Right?"

"Right."

"Can I come too??"

But I was already gone.

Natalie North was on her roof. I could see her clearly, despite the night, despite the distance. She sat on a black wrought-iron chair, long brown cardigan wrapped around her slender body, chin in her hands, elbows perched on the table. She sat alone, facing south, towards Compton.

I was reminded that she and I had a lot in common. Both of us had celebrated public personas we hid from as often as possible. We were both quiet, private people, and lonely much of the time.

My sneakers dangled over the city. I was perched on the uppermost ledge of City Hall, 450 feet in the air. I enjoyed the silence up here. Wind whispered through the tower's antennas and tossed Natalie's hair, hundreds of yards away.

I texted her.

You look lost.

A moment later, her posture straightened. She stood up and pirouetted twice, searching in pantomime. I could wave and shout and she'd still never spot me.

My phone buzzed.

>> You can see me?!?! Where are you?? My sneaky superhero
High above you.
>> Come visit. I insist.
Must I?
>> You must.
Are you lonely?
>> Desperately.

I rubbed my heels together, connecting the pants' webbing. In order for the webbing to stretch between my legs, I had to properly connect the hooks. It wasn't easy, and I didn't want to try it mid-air, so I connected them before I jumped.

Jumped. A knot formed in my throat. I was WAY up in the air.

I practiced connecting black gloves to wing-tips. This was easier. The gloves were strong and well-made, presumably to avoid ripping. The wings felt sturdy too, and the pant's ankles and waist had clearly been reinforced.

Lee might be a genius. He was at least an excellent tailor.

My heart pounded a little harder. It was time.

I stood up, wings and webbing extended. A gust caught the fabric and nearly tossed me off the tower before I was ready.

If this didn't work, I told myself, I still had the parachute. How long do I have to decide if the wings are operational? Four or five seconds? If not completely satisfied, I needed to release the wings and open the chute *fast*.

Gulp.

I didn't really *need* to do this. This invention was almost completely useless for the Outlaw.

But I *wanted* to. The disease craved adventure and excitement and I wouldn't sleep a wink tonight if I didn't try. Part of me wanted the wings to fail. To feel the terrible fall, the disorienting tumble, the possibility of death. Infected went insane fighting these longings. To give in would be so easy, so sweet...

I shook my head. Best not to give the virus too much control.

"This is a stupid idea," I whispered as I began to tilt forward, forward, past recall. I bent my knees. I reached a parallel plane with the ground and jumped into the sky.

I plummeted face first. The cold wind snapped at the wings. I started to count. One. Two. The fabric filled. My eyes stung. Three. Four.

The wings hardened, hauling my shoulders up and away. To remain extended I had to fight them forward, but…it worked! I was gliding! My body leveled out the harder I pushed down with my legs. My velocity transferred from vertical to horizontal.

I'd seen dozens of videos, of jumpers sailing through the air wearing wing-suits. What the videos failed to convey was forward speed. I was a missile! I was streaking through night so fast I couldn't catch my breath, and far off glass towers were growing larger at an alarming rate. Updrafts kept twisting me back and forth, gyrating motions impossible to control. I wobbled and shifted and discovered I could bank and change direction by raising and lowering my hands, like a plane.

Where was Natalie's building?? I had no idea! I was adrift and off course.

I made frantic fists and mashed the buttons. Nothing happened. The wings were so tight they resisted release! I dropped my hands to my sides, and pressed again. Click! The wings zipped back into my pants.

And I fell like a rock. Face first.

Oh yeah! Gravity!

I released the parachute. Pow! It filled and nearly jerked the vest clean off. I began drifting towards the ground at a much more acceptable rate, gasping for breath like a fish. The webbing between my legs zipped home when I clicked my heels, and directly beneath my knees I spotted Natalie's building spiraling upwards.

My chute was smaller than average and so I dropped faster. I swung like a drunken pendulum, hauling on harness lines and overcorrecting. Natalie never saw me coming until I almost bowled her over. I slid to a stop on the astroturf, barely keeping my balance and dignity.

"Holy…!" She clapped hands over her mouth. "Where…how…?"

I hauled the chute back into my vest (by pulling on two chords Lee built into the front pockets). It disappeared with a whisper.

She nodded with a big beautiful smile. "That was incredibly shocking. That's why this city has Outlaw fever. Rather I should say, the whole world."

"Hello Natalie."

"Hello Outlaw." She wrapped her arms around me and stayed there. "How I've missed you."

"Why are you up here alone?"

"I was pondering the universe, of course. Debating reasons for our existence. Wondering if other professions are more fulfilling. Examining depression and solitude. The usual."

"This late? It's after midnight."

"That's the best time to be disconsolate." She sighed into my chest.

"Only evil things happen after midnight. At least from my experience. Evil things and lonely thoughts."

"I can't sleep."

"Why not?"

She shrugged. "Nobody can sleep. Haven't you read the articles? We're all too worried. The whole globe is fixated on Hyper Humanity, and the world's first super villain and how he's going to destroy us all."

"Nah. I won't let him."

"I know you won't." She laughed, a cute breathy snicker through her nose.

"Are you still getting calls, asking for me?"

"Deluged. My publicist had to get a new phone. You're a war hero, a tabloid fixture, a religious idol, and our only hope." She was smiling. "Possibly the most fascinating person of all time. Of course people are calling."

I shook my head, disengaging from her. I sat down, suddenly feeling heavy with the weight of her words. "The truth isn't very exciting. It's going to be a tremendous disappointment, if my identity comes out."

She sat opposite me and took one of my gloved hands in both of hers.

"You're wrong, sweetie. I know the Outlaw better than most, and I'm more fascinated than anyone."

I glanced around at the roof. I'd made a lifetime of memories up here. She was the first girl who ever kissed me, and it was a doozy, and it happened right here. "I've always liked this spot. You get to enjoy the city without being touched by it."

"It'll be destroyed soon, if you believe the sensationalist news channels."

I grunted, wishing I could say otherwise. But the message I received from the Chemist wouldn't let me. He was planning on enlarging his territory soon. "Maybe. Maybe not. We can fight. I'm tired of having beautiful things taken from me."

She perked up. "Are you referring to me?"

"I never had you."

"Oh. Yes. Yes you did. A thousand times yes. I was yours forever. In many ways, I still am."

I didn't want to smile, but I couldn't help it. Being adored, even unwarrantedly so, was a hard thing to ignore.

She twittered wickedly and poked my ribs. "Outlaw! Are you blushing under your disguise? Did I embarrass the mighty and fearsome vigilante?"

"The Outlaw does not blush. He doesn't even like saying the word."

"Has your reluctant damsel seen the error of her ways?"

"...my what?"

"The girl you love. Does she return your affection yet?"

I took a deep breath and let it out against the mask. "No. Maybe a little. I think. I hope. But she's very attached to someone else."

"This girl you love, is she an idiot? Do you love a fool, Outlaw?"

I chuckled. "No. Katie is the smartest girl in our...she's one of the smartest people I know."

"Katie." She said the word experimentally, like hearing it for the first time. "Katie."

"Yes. Katie."

"Give me her phone number."

"What?!"

"Now." She held out her hand and snapped her fingers. "I want to talk some sense into this intelligent girl brazen enough to reject the Outlaw."

"She doesn't know I'm the Outlaw."

"You haven't told her??"

I shook my head. "That's going to be a tough conversation."

She stared at me for a long moment, a piercing gaze with churning gears. She opened her mouth to speak, paused, sucked at her teeth briefly, and then said, "The girl you saved last year. Up here on this roof. Her name was Katie, if memory serves."

"Yes."

"Is that the same girl?"

"Yes."

Her mouth curved up in a victorious smile. "I'm getting closer to the truth. I'm tight on your trail, Outlaw. I actually met the girl. In the hospital. Did I tell you?"

"She told me she met you," I lied. It was partially true. I'd been there when they met, lying in a hospital bed as the world swirled around me.

"She's very pretty."

"I think so."

"And she doesn't know you rescued her?"

"No. I couldn't tell her. There were complicating factors."

"Like what?"

"Her captor is still at large. I know who it is, but I can't prove it. And he threatened to kill her if I 'snitched.'"

"Do you believe him?"

"Not anymore."

"I want to tell her."

"Natalie," I growled, and she started and grinned. "I will tell her."

"Okay! I'm just envious and angry at her, that's all."

"Don't be. You found a good man. A great man. Not many guys are worth your affection. But I think Isaac Anderson comes close. He was brave that night, facing down angry gods. He was prepared to die."

"Ugh." She let her head drop onto my shoulder. Somehow during our conversation she'd gotten closer. She was good at that. "Don't remind me. I chewed through three sweaters that awful night, staring at the news, waiting for word. He was the only...normal human that made it out, right? From the gunfight on that college campus?"

I nodded. "As far as I know."

"Why on earth did you let him go into that place?"

"He's not a man that takes orders well, from what I've seen."

She fixed her hair by pushing it all behind her ears, and she issued a deep sigh. "What bizarre and frightening men you two are. I am drawn to the attractive and the foolish, apparently."

Better than the attractive and the evil, I thought. Like Tank. Stupid Tank. He and Katie should have returned from the movies over an hour ago. I hoped he was home by now. Thinking about him staying at her place past midnight made every part of my body hurt. I could ask Puck to locate him. But I'd rather not know, actually.

Natalie North said, "Time Magazine is going to name you and the Chemist both the person of the year."

"Yippee."

She laughed and pushed me. "Don't you care?"

"Not at all. I have bigger things to worry about. I'm barely passing...err, I mean...you know...I'm barely sleeping."

"Do you want to be interviewed?"

"Nope."

She squeezed my hand. "Everyone has a story to tell. Yours is the most fascinating of all time."

"I'll let you know if I change my mind. They should interview Captain FBI instead."

"He can't. He's besieged. By the government and the media. I'm not positive which is worse. We can't communicate, or they'd know immediately. Our secret would be out. And there's no way they'd permit an interview." Somewhere in the midst of her words, her face fell two octaves, from happiness to anxiety.

"He did his job well. What does the government want with him?"

"You. But he's not giving away any information, which has him in hot water. But he's their only link to you, and you've become a hero even to the soldiers."

"Oh yeah?" I grinned, which may or may not have been detectable through the mask. "That's nice to hear. Even the soldiers?"

"The police and the military whole-heartedly support you. They all wear red bandanas around their necks or belts, which is against dress code or whatever, but they all do it." She pointed at a long Outlaw banner festooned across a nearby building. "The Outlaw Fights For Us," she quoted. The words rippled as the banner flapped like a cape.

I grunted, unable to find any words. Gratitude. They were grateful. What a powerful emotion. "I'm glad people know. That I'm trying to help."

"The people love you."

"Maybe too much."

"*Definitely* too much. I know I do."

"Tell them I said thanks?"

"Tell them yourself. It would mean the world to everyone if you'd do that interview." She squeezed my hands and searched my eyes. "You know?"

"Maybe."

Chapter Seventeen
Thursday, October 8. 2018.

I texted Lee and told him the wing-suit worked, and five days later he still talked about it. Our crowd at the lunch table wasn't sure we believed him until Thursday, when Channel Four news released footage from their tower camera. They superimposed a red circle around the Outlaw, highlighting Friday night's harrowing journey across the skyline. The flight was short and hard to see, and the Outlaw quickly dropped out of sight but not before providing Lee enough visual evidence to vault himself into stardom. Lee really HAD made the Outlaw a wing-suit?!

Our lunch table was three chairs deep. The cafeteria monitors shook their heads at us, but eventually shrugged and smiled and left us alone.

"The monitors let all these kids sit here because of you," Katie told me. We were sharing a seat again and her left calf was touching my right calf and I swear she was doing it on purpose. She was a dancer and runner, so her legs were good and I was in heaven.

"What do I have to do with it?"

"You're the most popular boy in school."

I protested, "I don't even know these people. And I don't think I'm that popular. It doesn't feel like it."

The cute blonde girl beside me smiled and said, "Yes you are, silly." I really needed to learn her name. She'd been sitting beside me for weeks, and it was WAY too late to ask now.

"And besides," Katie continued, pointedly ignoring the blonde girl, which made me love her all the more because it hinted at jealousy. "You are a nationally-ranked quarterback. You are being given perks."

"The cafeteria lady is *not* the girl I want to give me perks."

The beautiful skin of her cheeks turned pink and she playfully bumped her leg harder into mine. "You want a perk? Maybe you'll get lucky and my butt will fall completely asleep on this stupid chair and I'll have to sit in your lap."

My heart quickened. "Could be dangerous. You might like it. And I'd certainly never let go."

Lee banged his hand on the table and we all jumped. "You're not even listening!"

"Sorry Lee," Katie apologized. "Please continue."

"See here?" He jabbed a finger at his iPad and glared. The rest of his audience was already silent. On screen, the gliding figure waffled uncertainly on repeat. "The Outlaw's not used to having triple the surface area. He hasn't figured out how to use subtle movements."

I leaned in and scrutinized the screen. "What do you mean subtle movements?"

"Everything is exaggerated, bro, when you're going a hundred miles an hour. He needs to make smaller corrections."

"A hundred?! He was going that fast?"

"Maybe a little faster. It's a wild ride, dude."

Katie sighed deeply. "He's so fantastic. I miss him a lot."

"But he's *not* flying!" Lee scolded us all in turn with fiery gaze. "Don't believe the Outlawyers or the blogs. He can't fly. It's *my* wing-suit."

Samantha Gear, in a loud and irritated voice, asked, "Lee, did you explain to the big *OAF* that he could have died? And that someone with *zero* base jumps shouldn't try a wing-suit?"

"Oh Gear," I groaned, "Don't be such a *mom*. It's not like you're the Outlaw's *parent*. Jeez."

For the longest second of my life, her eyes blazed and she debated between smiling and shoving her apple down my throat. Finally, after an eternity, she decided not to kill me. Instead she smiled dangerously and said, "Not yet."

"I dunno, Samy-girl," Croc was saying. "I think it looks wicked fun. Well done, mate. Next time, Lee, tell the Outlaw I want to tag along."

"Mitch." Lee shook his head with a condescending chuckle. "Dude. This is only for Hyper Humans, bro. I designed the vest and wing-suit specifically for him, and they only work for him because he's a god and he could survive a fall."

Samantha snarled, "No he couldn't and no he's not."

"Either way, mate. I want one. How much?"

Lee asked, "How much what?"

"Hundos, Lee! Crikey! Hundees! Pineapples! Money! How much would it cost for you to make me one?"

"Yeah man," Cory nodded solemnly, briefly looking up from his reuben sandwich. "Make me one too. I'm down."

"You...you idiots aren't even listening..." Lee's exasperation at dealing with mortals was monumental. He pinched the bridge of his nose and took deep breaths. "...I don't know how to explain this to you...You can't have one. You. Would. Die."

"All the same," Croc grinned and all the girls at the table smiled with him. I almost did too. "How much did it cost to make?"

"I don't know, Mitchell." Lee steepled his fingers and closed his eyes. "Off the top of my head, I'd guess...two thousand for materials. Plus thirty hours of work."

"Thirty?!" I yelped. "Thirty hours? That's way too much!"

"Whatever dude!" he thundered, red in the face. "It's a sophisticated piece of aeronautical equipment! They take a long time to make!"

"That's not what I meant." I backtracked quickly. Katie snickered and pinched my leg. "I mean, you shouldn't spend that much time on the Outlaw."

Samantha said, "I agree."

Croc mused, "Two thousand dollars? Your oldies lend you that much credit for your projects?"

"My oldies?"

"Parents, mate."

"Oh. No, the Outlaw left money a couple times. Always straight cash, bro. I think he's loaded."

"He's rich, too?" Katie said. "Of course he is. He's perfect in every way."

Her hand was still on my leg.

When I returned home from practice, Dad's car was in the driveway but he wasn't in the kitchen and he wasn't watching television. I went to his room but it was empty.

He was in my bedroom. Sitting on my bed. Head down. The room was dim in the fading evening. The Outlaw's vest lay between Dad's feet. The Outlaw's black mask was in one of his fists, and the red bandana was in the other. His hands trembled.

All the air rushed out of my body.

He knew.

Dad knew.

He held my secrets in both hands.

I am the Outlaw.

I couldn't breathe. I tried to speak but nothing happened. Dad, I said silently. My pulse was so loud it sounded like the walls were throbbing. Dad.

He wouldn't arrest me. At least, I was pretty sure he wouldn't. He was a detective charged with apprehending the Outlaw and other Hyper Humans, but I knew him; he couldn't do it. And I wouldn't let him, if he tried.

Oh gosh Dad please don't try.

"It's you," he whispered. His voice wavered. "You're him."

"I'm him." My throat was tight. My voice wavered too. "I'm sorry."

He stood up. He was a giant man who looked tired and sad. Tears carved lines down his granite stubbly face. He grasped me by the neck with both hands, a long-range embrace, still holding the mask, and said, "You could have died."

"I wanted to tell you."

"Why didn't you?"

I shrugged and failed to find the words.

"The whole world is looking for you, son. What did…why are you…how? How are you the Outlaw?"

"It's a long story." My voice was strangely loud in my own ears. I couldn't meet his eyes.

"Tell me."

"Dad…first…I need to know you won't tell anyone. You know? This is a pretty big secret."

"Hell, Chase, it's more than that."

"Dad, I'm serious. Only, like, five people know the whole truth." My knees were weak and I was dizzy. Dad *knew*.

"Five others? That squad you're with? The Fearsome Five or whatever crap name the media cooked up?"

"Yes. They're the only ones who know the truth."

"Samantha," he said, and the muscles in his jaw worked. "She's the girl in the pictures."

"…yes."

He sank back onto the bed and I shakily lowered into my desk chair. "Christ. You two are the monsters she suggested sending into Compton." He rubbed his thick hand across his forehead, still visibly trembling.

I nodded.

"I knew," he grunted. "I didn't know what, but I knew she was lying. About something. Mitch too?"

"Mitch too."

"Why are you like this? You are…you are different than the rest of us?"

"Yes. I'm different. So is Samantha and so is Mitch." I was speaking in short phrases until my air came back. He was handling this better than I'd have guessed.

"Why? How?"

"We're sick. A very rare disease. A virus that kills most of its victims in adolescence. We survived. Now the disease just sits inside our body, over-producing muscles and adrenaline, and making us…weird."

He stared hard at me with red eyes while he processed that. "Have you been to a doctor?"

"No. It's nothing medicine can help."

"And the Chemist?"

"He's sick too. Like us. We're trying to stop him."

"Wow," he said and he screwed the heels of his hands into his eyes and took a deep breath. "My son is trying to stop the Chemist. This is a lot to…how long have you been like this?"

"I'm not sure. Around twelve months."

"So it was you on the rooftop last November?" he asked sharply, remembering past Outlaw exploits.

"Yes."

"Of course it was you." He chuckled without humor. "The kidnapper had your Katie."

He still does, I wanted to say.

"And you were in Compton earlier this year? With the bus explosion?"

"Yep." I nodded. "That was me."

"I bet that was an awful night. You saved Katie but couldn't get to Hannah."

"Very awful."

"I'm sorry. That's…that's rough. I didn't know." He paused and studied the vest at his feet. "Where do you get this stuff? Like the mask and the vest."

"Lee makes them. He hasn't realized I'm the Outlaw."

"I'm not surprised. You fooled me too. I can't believe that was you in Compton!" He shouted the words, like trying to force their meaning into his ears. "I thought you were at Cory's house that night. What about the hospital shootout over the summer? That was you? And Samantha?"

"That was us. We barely got home before you woke up."

"You shouldn't take her to gunfights, Chase. Doesn't sound very chivalrous to me."

I barked a laugh. That's hilarious. "Dad, she's a lot older than me. I'm not her boss. And she's one of the most lethal people alive."

"How old is she?"

"Thirty, I think."

"How old is Mitch?"

"Not sure. Maybe…forty-five?"

"My age?" He sat up straighter. "He looks closer to twenty-five."

"The disease slows our aging. The Chemist is over two hundred years old."

"Two hundred?!" he roared. He stood up in a rush. "Two hundred? You're kidding."

"I'm not. Fortunately he's about to die of natural causes. But there are more maniacs waiting to take his place."

"I'm a detective, Chase. My job is to apprehend him. Hell, my job is to apprehend *you*. What am I supposed to do now?"

"I suggest focusing more on him."

"Ha ha, kid."

"Actually, no. Don't focus on him. Don't go anywhere near him. He's a madman. He came very close to feeding me to his tigers. I got bit before escaping."

"You *what*?!" His face turned white and he grabbed my dresser for support.

"Long story. But I'm fine. Mitch ran the tiger over with his truck."

"Okay…we will…I need to lie down." And he did. He dropped heavily onto my bed (it squeaked and protested and nearly broke) and covered his eyes with a beefy forearm. "This…this is a lot for a father to hear. We will continue this discussion in a few minutes. I might be sick."

"I'll get you some water."

He grunted approval.

I hustled downstairs to the kitchen. As I was filling a glass from the refrigerator filter, my phone buzzed. It was Puck. Odd. He usually texted.

"Hey Puck."

"Sup man. That was brutal. Sucks your dad found out that way," he said.

"Yeah, no kidding."

"You probably shouldn't have mentioned the tiger, dummy."

"I agree. In retrospect, it was...hang on, how do you know?"

"I listened on the microphones Carter planted in your room, dummy."

I didn't say anything, just glared vacantly as the cold water overflowed the glass. I had NO privacy!

"...sorry. I *might* be addicted to eavesdropping," he admitted.

"You think??"

"In my defense, all hackers are. We crave access. And your life is extremely entertaining."

"What do you want, Puck?"

"Well, in a magnificent twist of irony, I've been eavesdropping on a few other people and decided to alert you."

"No. I don't like this. It's creepy."

"It's about Tank and Katie."

"......go on."

"Hah! You see? It's addictive! PuckDaddy isn't creepy."

"Puck! Just tell me. What is it?" I set down the glass, Dad momentarily forgotten.

"Well...okay. Here's the deal. So, Tank and Katie have a date tonight-"

"On a Thursday?! I HATE that guy."

"Don't interrupt PuckDaddy. Tank told her it'll be really romantic, right?"

My legs went a little numb so I sat down on one of the wooden chairs at our kitchen table. His words became harder to understand.

"...okay."

"I monitor Tank's text messages, just so you know. Anyway. The date is at his condo downtown, and he sent his parents out for the evening."

"Okay," I said again. Breathing hurt. I was losing sensation in my fingertips. Tank was bringing Katie back to his empty condo tonight...

"That means they'll be at his place alone, dummy."

"I realize that, Puck."

"So Katie has been texting one of her friends. I monitor her texts too, by the way. Wow, PuckDaddy is really nosey. I digress. Katie has picked up on Tank's hints that tonight will be…special, if you know what I mean."

"I *do* know what you mean. What'd she say?"

"I mean, one of those special nights that couples have. Special and romantic. Right?"

"YES Puck. I get it. What did Katie tell her friend?" I was close to hyperventilating. Too much oxygen. My head felt light.

"Katie is conflicted. She's excited about the date, but she doesn't want to have sex until she's married. She's worried Tank will try, and she doesn't know what will happen."

I made a noise that sounded like a whimper.

"She says Tank is intoxicating and sometimes it's hard to think straight."

I didn't respond.

"And she doesn't want you to find out."

I slid off the chair and landed on the floor. The linoleum needed to be swept. I rested my forehead on the sink cabinet and closed my eyes.

"Chase? You there, homie?"

"Yes. I'm here."

"You okay? It's hard to hear you."

"I kinda wish you hadn't told me this. I want to die."

"Don't say that. That's not funny."

"I love her, Puck."

"I know! That's why I'm telling you!"

"What can I do? I told her how I felt. You can't make people love you back." I blinked away hot tears. "I wish I could. But he likes her and…she likes him."

"You're talking like a loser. You're not a loser! You're the freaking Outlaw!"

"So?"

"What do you mean *So*?? What are you doing?"

"Sitting on my kitchen floor."

"Get up!"

"No."

"Get up! Get up Outlaw! I'm so pissed at you, you big idiot!"

"Get up and do what?" I asked, but I obeyed. I stood up.

"Fight! That enormous homicidal maniac declared WAR on the Outlaw, and Katie is the battlefield. Go fight!"

I was quiet. I took deep breaths and tried to remember where I was, and who I was.

I was shamelessly in love with Katie, and I didn't care who knew. But there was a fine line between being in love and being a stalker. I couldn't prevent her from living her life. I was the Outlaw, not a nuisance.

However, this would be different if she'd chosen another guy. Another *good* guy. Then I'd just accept that I'd lost, another guy had won, and I'd try not to meddle. But she'd chosen Tank, a maniac with anger issues. And she didn't know the truth about him.

And no matter which guy she ended up with, I cared about her. And no matter which guy she ended up with...it couldn't be Tank.

"Chase? Hello??"

"Puck."

"What?"

"You're wrong."

"What about?"

"About two things. He didn't declare war on the Outlaw. He declared war on me. This is Chase Jackson's fight."

"And the other thing?"

"Katie is not the battlefield. Katie is the prize." My distorted reflection glared back at me from the stainless steel refrigerator. My laser vision would have burned a hole through our house if I was Superman. I was mad.

"What are you going to do?"

"Fight."

"Yeah baby!!"

I checked my watch. Quarter till seven. "What time is the date?"

"He picked her up fifteen minutes ago."

I called Katie from the motorcycle. It rang a few times and went to voicemail. I accelerated to 95mph, passing cars in the emergency pull-off lane. Los Angeles would be elysian if not for the traffic.

"What are you going to do?" Puck asked me again through the bluetooth headset in my ear.

"Ring the doorbell and punch him in the nose."

"Negative. Abort. Not a good idea, dummy. Carter says he's twice as strong as anyone else. Even you."

"I'm going to do it anyway."

My motorcycle slid to a stop across from Tank's building, leaving a trail of rubber on the street. I parked directly beside the ATM where Natalie North had been mugged over a year ago. I checked my watch. Quarter after seven. I dropped my helmet onto the handle and jogged across the busy street.

"PuckDaddy suggests an alternative strategy."

"Suggest all you want," I said. I pushed into the quiet lobby. The floor was marble and the ceilings were high and the walls were whitewashed. The doorman was busy sorting packages with two different tenants. Tank and I had destroyed part of a house during our last wrestling match; it'd be a shame to damage this place. Plus, it would make Natalie North sad. "Make it quick."

"Pull the fire alarm."

Hm. That wasn't a bad idea. It would save me a fistfight, and interrupt the romance. But...

"Won't their date resume after it's verified as a false alarm?"

"Maybe? I don't know."

"Can you work your computer magic to trigger the alarm?" I was spinning in a circle, looking for the red fire alarm box.

"Negative. It's an old building with a closed system. I can make the fire station *think* the alarm was triggered, but that wouldn't alert people within the building. The date would continue."

"Okay. I see the box. I could go to jail for this, right?"

"Technically. But PuckDaddy is your guardian angel. I'm watching you on the monitors right now, and deleting all the data. When they check the digital tape for a culprit, they'll find nothing."

"I think I'm just going to knock his teeth in. That would feel better. Plus, it might impress Katie."

"No! Chase. He'll murder you. My plan is better. Trust PuckDaddy."

"I dunno." Several other people entered the lobby, and the noise ricocheted around the cavernous room.

"Know what else I can do?" Keyboard clicks were loud in my ear. "PuckDaddy can make the fire department think the alarm originated within Tank's condo *and* at the lobby. He might get in trouble."

"Bingo! Let's do that. Ready?"

"Hell yeah, homie!"

I strode to the red alarm next to the mailboxes and yanked on the small white handle. The safety glass broke and an awful horn began wailing. Above us, a brilliant white light flashed. Pandemonium ensued and the building emptied.

Fifteen minutes later, I was waiting outside with everyone else while firemen checked the building. They parked their giant truck in the middle of the street, diverting traffic and nearly crushing my bike. A small crowd formed to witness the excitement and I hid within it. Nearby, Katie and Tank stood together. Katie was hugging herself and Tank towered over everyone, clearly frustrated, hands shoved into his pockets. Zero romance. Hah! An official-looking man with a badge on his chest began questioning Tank, and soon Tank's parents arrived, and everyone was gesturing in confusion.

After forty-five minutes, Katie was embarrassed and bored, and I caught her eye. She did a double-take. I winked and disappeared into the audience.

"Puck, you are brilliant."

"Thanks, Outlaw."

"You probably just cracked the top five on my Best Friend List."

"…that's the nicest thing anyone's ever said to me."

I caught sight of her from a different angle. She was smiling and shaking her head, searching the crowd. She appeared…pleased.

She knew. And she wasn't angry.

I said, "I want to respond to the Chemist's recent letter."

"Um, okay. Puck thought we were having a moment, but whatever. You might have ADD. What do you want to say?"

"Ask him why Katie was able to block my aneurysms and insanity."

"Huh?"

I peeked around another corner. Her romantic date was over, from the looks of it. Night had fallen and Tank was in trouble with his parents and the fire chief. I continued, "Don't use Katie's name, obviously. But I want to know why Katie relieved my pain and headaches when she touched me. Do you remember? My headaches were so bad I couldn't function, and I was having regular aneurysms. But they went away when she touched me. The Chemist said I could ask him anything. That's what I want to know."

Puck sent the message. And the Chemist replied.

Chapter Eighteen
Saturday, October 10. 2018

My carefree childhood was long gone, but I'll remember Friday and Saturday as golden halcyon days for as long as I live. Which could potentially be hundreds of years.

I was selected for Homecoming Court. I discovered this on Friday, the day of our Homecoming game. (I missed the announcement at school due to a tiger mauling, and everyone assumed I knew.)

"I told you," Katie said, when I expressed my shock, "but you were off in la-la land. It was all over the internet. Don't you check social media anymore?"

I didn't. Who had time? Katie was voted onto the court too. She got the nerd vote, she explained.

I nodded. "And the super-hot vote."

She smiled and laughed, exactly as an angel would.

I continued, "And the dating-a-stupid-moron vote."

She stopped smiling.

To our great shock and delight, Lee was voted in too. His Morning Show hijinks had rocketed him into the upper levels of high school hierarchy.

"Of course I was voted in, bro. I got the math and science vote. Plus, I'm a god in Outlawyer circles. Where you been?"

That night, I forgot all about the coronation ceremony. We were winning 24-7 at half-time and I marched down the tunnel with all the other football players. The pageant coordinator came scurrying to our locker room, squawking and sweating, and she hurried me back onto the field with the other nominees.

I was paired with my old friend Erica. A year ago I anonymously recovered a ruby locket for her, and used the reward to pay for Dad's physical therapy. She'd been friends with Hannah Walker, and had ascended onto the Hidden Spring's throne of popularity after Hannah died.

Katie and Lee were paired, both exuberant, though Lee tried to mask his excitement with Ray-Bans.

We paraded to the middle of the football field as the stadium roared and thundered. Erica and I found our mat and clapped during the proceedings. Her hand returned to rest on my arm and her fingers shook. Katie stood ten feet away, but I could hear her heart beating. Above the trumpets and awards and screaming, her pulse throbbed pleasantly in my ears.

The announcer proclaimed Erica and Lee Homecoming Queen and King. The unlikely couple went to receive their crowns as the band played and the audience cheered, and I abandoned my mat. I grabbed Katie's hand and stood beside her. Neither of us cared about winning. She beamed and her heart quickened and mine did too, and that will forever be my favorite moment under the lights of a football field.

Tank was grounded. How sublime is that?? He'd been scheduled to make a scandalous appearance at our Homecoming Dance, guaranteed to create an uproar, but his parents punished him for having Katie over without approval and for pulling the fire alarm.

I laughed continuously for ten minutes when I heard. So did Puck.

I attended the dance wearing the same vest as last year. Katie wore a new sparkly teal dress that displayed her fantastic legs, and a thin diamond-pendant necklace. We met in the middle of the floor, along with Cory and Lee and Samantha and Croc. We danced, and hopped, and whipped, and cha-cha'ed, and backed it up and laughed the whole night, like best friends should. Samantha danced terribly and glowered at the exits, which she called a tactical nightmare.

Around 10pm, Samantha and Croc vanished, and Cory and Lee were claimed by their admirers, leaving Katie and me alone for the slow dances. Just the two of us in a private universe, our sky full of starlight from the disco ball and camera flashes. No words, just our bodies pressed as close as we could, fingers entwined, her forehead resting against my chin and lips, and we both trembled and held tight.

The romance of the evening dissolved her resistance. We both knew it, and we both surrendered to the magic. She was wild and carefree, and she was mine for the night.

At one in the morning, I drove her home in my dad's car. I burned and ached for her. She leaned against me, expectantly and perfectly during the trip. The planet slowed, the moon froze, the angels held their breath, all watching, all waiting as the night drew to a climax, hot and hopeful. The car ride was deafening with silent communication and longings.

My heart was a hammer as we walked to her front door. My adrenaline seethed and my shoes shrunk, my sleeves grew shorter, and the shirt tightened across my chest. Her door never looked so scary, the welcome mat a land-mine ready to incinerate our platonic friendship. We couldn't look at each other, couldn't speak, couldn't breathe. Her sidewalk kept getting longer, torturing me as I brainstormed for words.

We almost made it to the door.

I loved her. I needed her. I tugged on her hand, halting our stroll. No words. She knew. She flew into my arms, her mouth on mine. I'd wanted to kiss her for months, years, forever, but her lips were better than fantasy. Her face pushed against mine, my arms crushed her waist, her fingers in my hair, and we eagerly forgot everything else.

It was good. It was so good. It was Katie and she was everything and she wanted me too.

Her hands pulled me harder against her, walking us backwards to her apartment, and we bumped against her door. Arms around my neck. Nobody would wake up; we were urgent and eager but we were silent.

Too soon, she placed both hands on my cheeks and pushed me away. "Chase…"

"Katie," I panted.

"I shouldn't." Her eyes pooled immediately. "No..I…I can't…it's just the night, and you look so good, and…I can't…and…I'm so sorry…"

"Katie. I'm in love with you. I'm yours."

She covered my mouth with her fingers, a sob escaped, and she said, "I can't. I can't…I can't, I can't…"

And she disappeared behind the front door.

But she didn't stay long. Fifteen minutes later I crawled into my bed, overwhelmed by an arcane mixture of euphoria and frustration. I had barely settled under the sheet when I heard her familiar footfalls padding up my driveway. My ears perked. She let herself in with our secret key, softly slipped up the stairs, snuck into my bedroom, and then she was kissing me again.

"Yes I can. Yes I can," she moaned against my mouth. She'd changed into her pajamas, and she stretched herself on top of me. Her lips brushed mine with each word. "Yes I can. I want to kiss you, and I will. But not yet. I can't yet."

"Now."

"I'm sorry I missed your birthday," she said and she started drizzling kisses down my cheek and onto my neck.

"My birthday? When?"

"Yesterday, you big oaf."

"Really? Are you sure? What's today?"

Her lips found mine again. "I love you, Chase. I'm so in love with you. I don't know what's wrong with me, or why it's taken so long. I love you so much I can't sleep."

My heart swelled to bursting, and hot tears began scalding down my skin. We both smiled so big that she spoke from the corner of her mouth.

"I respect you more than any man I've ever met, and you're perfect, and I love you and I want you." She was whispering and we were both breathless. I tried to sit up but she wouldn't let me. "You're the only thing I think about all day. I can't yet, though. I can't kiss you yet," she said, even though her lips pulled on mine with each syllable. "I can't kiss you yet. I want to. Oh gosh, how I want to. But I'm not like that. I need to break up with that other guy first, before I kiss you."

"That's a great idea. He's so dumb."

"I can't believe how good this feels," she groaned and then I was kissing her ear and neck and shoulder. I wanted her in every way a person can want another. Her thin silver necklace kept falling into my mouth. "I can't believe how big you are." She was whispering between gasps. "You take up the whole bed. You didn't look this big at my house. And your muscles…"

We were silent for several minutes, enjoying each other, pretending she wasn't kissing me.

"Okay." She sighed and slid away from me. "Okay. I have to go before things get out of hand and we start making out."

"This isn't making out?"

"No."

"That was *definitely* making out."

"Chase, my mom would kill you if we were making out."

"What would she do if she heard you say you *want* me?" I grinned.

"I don't mean sex!"

"Keep your voice down! And it sure sounds like you mean sex."

"No way," she whisper-shouted. "I've never had sex!"

"Me either."

"You and Hannah…never…?"

"Remember when you and I were little? We said not until after marriage."

"But we were little kids then. Our parents told us we *had* to wait."

"Yeah, but I meant it."

She breathed out with her eyes closed. "I don't know why. But that's sooooo hot."

"Then let's Not Make Out more."

"No! I can't. It's not fair to you, not while I'm technically someone else's girlfriend. But I won't be for much longer. Then I'm all yours."

I began rising but she forced me down on my pillow again. She focused all her weight into her hands on my shoulders, directly above me. Her hair cascaded down and tickled my face.

I said, "Then text him. Right now. I'll help you write it."

"He'd be at my house in five minutes."

"Then I'll snap his neck and bury him in your backyard."

Katie shook her head. She was sad, I could tell. And worried. "No. I need to pick the right moment, and the right words so he'll go away quietly. I can't offend his pride or make him suspicious, or he'll make trouble."

"He's going to make trouble, no matter what."

"Maybe not. I'm leaving. You stay here, handsome."

"But-"

"But nothing. I'm in love with you, but I can't tell you that yet. I want to kiss you, but I can't. Not yet." She sat back, straddling me, her knees at my ribs. Her smile was brilliant and seductive, her hair disheveled.

I said, "You're the sexiest crazy person ever. Please let me up."

"No. You want more kisses that don't belong to you. I don't trust you."

"Oh Katie. *Trust* me."

"No! And don't smile at me like that. Something…significant might happen. And it can't. You haven't even asked me out on a *date* yet."

"Please go on a date with me."

"I *can't!*" she laughed. "I'm someone else's girlfriend. What would people think?"

"Who cares?"

"Chase. My love. I'm yours. And I'll tell the world that I'm yours as soon as I'm single. Until then, no more making out. I'm not like that."

"Me neither," I said with as much innocence as I could muster.

"Not if I can help it. But. I'm going. This is the best night of my life-*don't*…" she snapped as I sat up, "…*don't* follow me."

"I'm going to."

"No!"

"Then you better run."

"Chase!" She stifled her laughter, cautiously backing up, and kicking over all my stuff. "Do *not* get out of that bed. I *have* to go. I have not been very ladylike tonight."

"I'm so in love with you."

"I know." She beamed and it nearly powered the lightbulbs. "And I love you too."

And she was gone again, this time for the rest of the night. I laid back down, enjoying the impressions she seared onto my body and mouth.

This was the happiest moment of my life.

My phone buzzed. A text from Samantha. I forgot she was in the adjacent bedroom! Embarrassing.

>> That was the hottest moment of my life.

Then another buzz, another text, from Puck.

>> mine 2…omg…i need a nap…

Chapter Nineteen
Monday, October 11. 2018

Monday, at school, I met Katie at her locker. Her eyes smoldered and she flushed with pleasure, but we maintained a steamy distance that would discourage gossip, although closer than friends should. As the day wore on, however, the distance shrunk. She stole a kiss in English. She rested her head on my shoulder at lunch. Samantha enjoyed this painful charade immensely.

That afternoon before practice I sat in the sunshine, tying my cleats, examining my inner maelstrom of emotions. I'd never had much to lose before. Now I had a taste of how good life could be. And I was afraid. Afraid for Katie. Afraid for her future. Our future. Afraid of the Chemist.

I dialed PuckDaddy.

"I want to speak with Carla."

"What? Who?"

"Come on, Puck. Carla."

"The Infected girl inside Compton? One of the Chemist's henchmen? Errr, hench...women?"

"Yeah, that's her. Tell her we need to talk."

"And how the *hay-yell* do you expect Puck to do that?"

"I thought you were the baddest hacker on the planet."

"Better watch yo'mouth, dummy."

I said, "If you are, get me her number. Or talk to her yourself."

He remained silent, except for a sigh. Practice was about to start.

I asked, "Well?"

"Fine," he grunted. "But I'm not your secretary."

"You already *have* her number. Don't you."

"No! Kinda. Not really. I have a handful of educated guesses I'm monitoring. She's quiet, doesn't communicate much with anyone. I've narrowed her specific phone down to four or five devices, and now I'm waiting on one of the numbers to give away a clue."

"We're out of time. Send a text to your best guess."

"And say what? We better encode your message in case Puck guesses wrong, which, unbelievably, could happen."

"Okay," I thought out loud. "Okay. How about this. 'You told me in that hallway we should be allies. I want to talk.'"

He slurped some kind of drink and said, "You sure? That's pretty...vague."

"Yeah. Try it. I'm tired of the Chemist taking parts of our world. Let's invade *his*."

>> Tank and I are meeting as soon as his parents let us, my love. I will break up with him then. Please don't fall for any other girls until then!! =)

I smiled at the phone until my jaw ached.

There are no other girls.

Ooooooh. That was a good line. I was going to be a dynamite boyfriend.

I reluctantly pulled out my science homework and progressed to the third problem before my phone buzzed.

>> ur old pal the Chemist emailed u back im forwarding it 2 u. ur correspondence w/ him really trips PuckDaddy out this 1 is a doozy

From: napoleon
Date: Oct 11. 21:15
Subject: To Joseph, King of Spain

Good question, son. And it comes at a good time; I'm particularly lucid at this moment. (Yes. The virus causes bouts of temporary insanity, even in me)

So you were saved from the aneurysms by a girl, and you want to know How. She must truly love you, to withstand the emotional swings and irritability and insanity caused by the virus during late adolescence.

To answer your question. Are you familiar with Maslow's Hierarchy of Needs? The levels of needs that humans must have met to survive and function properly? The third and fourth levels are Love and Esteem. These are vital, especially to a blooming Infected. Love, in particular, is hurricane in strength. Easily the strongest force in the universe.

One of the de-humanizing aspects of the virus is that it transforms you into a genuine malcontent. A truly awful and dangerous person, especially during periods of extreme stress. While the virus is attacking your brain, you need love and support more than ever. Unfortunately this is precisely the stage when most people withdraw it, because your behavior has become so appalling.

In other words, most Infected die at age 18 because they need Love and Esteem desperately, and don't receive any. Not even from parents, who suddenly have an adult-aged monster on their hands.

This girl of yours shielded your brain from the onslaught by satiating your basic needs for Love and Esteem, especially through physical touch. She poured water on the fire raging inside of you, and gave your brain a chance to heal itself. She sounds quite special.

And I will kill her in front of you if I have to. Slowly. To make you see reason. To coerce you to join me. I don't want to. But I'm already planning on it.

See you soon.
Martin

My skin crawled. He was threatening Katie. I wanted to vomit, reading his final paragraph. Perhaps this communication had been a bad idea.

But his explanation made sense. It also clarified why I felt a little better at that Catholic church, a place I also experienced love.

Puck called me. "That's an intense email, right?"

I said, "Yes. Extremely. I'm a little queasy."

"We won't let him get her."

"He's going to, Puck. He's too strong and too intelligent. He'll get her eventually. We have to eliminate him."

"Let's get started. Carla wants to meet you tomorrow."

Chapter Twenty
Tuesday, October 12. 2018

Carla requested a rendezvous on top of the Wells Fargo Tower, one of the tallest in the city, over seven hundred feet.

"Wells Fargo," I quietly repeated for the tenth time. Samantha sat beside me at lunch. Katie was across the table and currently playing footsie with me. "Why the Wells Fargo tower?"

"Who cares? It's probably familiar to her, and she's being cautious," Samantha said under her breath. "Besides, that tower is ideal. I'll post up on the BP Plaza and monitor the encounter. If she twitches, I'll eliminate her. If it's a trap, I'll provide support."

"It's not a trap. Puck is monitoring her phone. Well, he monitors everything really. There's no indication she's the bait in some kind of snare."

Samantha glared out of the far cafeteria window, in the direction of downtown. She simmered a minute and said, "I'm going now." She stood up.

"Now?? The meeting isn't for..." I checked my watch. "...ten hours!"

She grumbled, "I should have been there since yesterday," and stormed out of the cafeteria.

Katie asked me, "Where's she going? What meeting?"

"Oh. You know. Football stuff."

"At ten o'clock tonight? That's pretty late."

"Weird tradition," I shrugged. I didn't like lying to her. That was going to end. Soon.

Croc called, "Too right, mate! Weird football tradition." His arm was around Katie, and she didn't seem to mind. I debated pulling his arm off and hitting him with it.

Croc was on the ground, circling the Wells Fargo Plaza in his truck. Gear was in the air, perched behind her sniper rifle on an adjacent tower. PuckDaddy was in the cameras, monitoring everything he could get his hands on.

The Outlaw stood on top of the US Bank Tower, peering across the chasm of sky towards the rendezvous below. Carla wanted to meet on top of a skyscraper. Well, the Outlaw would drop in from above.

"Quiet as a prairie down here," Croc reported in my ear.

I said, "She's late."

"No," Samantha said. "She's already there." All the voices were soft in my ear, hushed in wary anticipation.

"Negative," PuckDaddy retorted. "Puck would have a visual. Got active cameras."

Samantha replied, "You do not yet fully appreciate her. Nor does the Outlaw. She's an Infected. She's there. Trust me. I can feel her."

"I'm going."

"Careful. I hate that stupid wing-suit."

I connected my gloves to the suit's wings, and then locked the webbing between my legs. I was ready to fly.

If I didn't pass out first. This tower was high. So...so high. I felt light-headed at the thought of leaping off. This high up, there was no traffic noise and I could see most of the planet.

Puck whispered, "I can hear your pulse through your microphone."

"Shut up, Puck! I'm nervous!"

"Then don't do it, Outlaw," Samantha said. "I'll be forced to hide from Carter in Antarctica if you die. I hate hate hate this."

I jumped. The swirling vicissitudes caught the fabric and hauled me violently to the north. The earth turned into an unrecognizable smear of lights as I plummeted.

"…oh my god, I hate this, Chase…"

"I lost him. Puck is scared."

I really needed to remember goggles next time. I banked hard to the left. The wind was a thousand waves, all shoving me in disparate directions. I gathered speed breathtakingly fast. Through the tears I saw my landing spot. …I think.

"Chase….you're too close, Chase…" I heard above the sky's roar. I pulled back my arms and mashed the release. The wings disappeared into my pants, and I threw open the parachute. The world returned to order with a brutal jerk and rose up like a screaming elevator. I landed on the Wells Fargo Tower's rooftop tarmac and retrieved the snapping parachute.

Touchdown.

"Damn Outlaw," Carla grumbled, materializing from the penthouse shadows. "Startled me. And that ain't easy."

Puck hollered, "Holy shoot! How'd she get there?"

Samantha snarled, "Told you! She's Infected, so she's a witch. I hate this!"

"The sheila's already there? What a bottler! I bet Samy-girl is ready to stone the crows!"

I'd turn my stupid earpiece off soon if they didn't shut up.

Carla waved a gloved hand at the sky and told me, "I know that sniper bitch of yours is around. Tell her to ease off the trigger. I came alone."

Samantha, in my ear, said, "No."

I told her, in a low growl, "I know you took a risk, coming here. Thank you."

"Damn right I did."

Carla was dressed in similar fashion to Samantha: tight-fitted utility pants and a shooting vest. Her hair was pulled back in corn-rows, and like always she wore sunglasses. Her face could have been carved out of granite.

"Why now, Outlaw? It's been months since I asked for help."

"I'm taking him more seriously."

"You're a fool if you weren't already."

"And I'm getting desperate."

She scoffed. "I been desperate for months. Welcome to reality. What solution you got?"

"We want to take him out."

"Doubt you can." She crossed her arms and tsk'ed her lips. "But I'm riding with whoever is going my way. We going one direction, we in business."

Puck whispered in my ear, "All is quiet. Puck sees nothing. She came alone."

I asked her, "What direction are you going?"

"Out. I want the hell out of here. Too many Chosen. Freaks me out. I want peace."

"Then just leave."

"The Father would find and kill me. And my family. I seen him do it."

"He's really like that?"

"No. Not really. But he will. He's not a violent dude, 'sept when he has to be. He vowed he'd release me, after I keep my end of the bargain."

"Bargain?"

"He took me in, gave me a home, took away the headaches, you know? In return, I gotta work for him."

"You're his servant."

"Slave, more like it."

"So you want to kill him too."

She scowled and stuck a finger in my direction. "Don't want to kill nobody. I'm good at it. Don't mean I like it. I want peace. I want him to let me go, one way or the other."

"I don't see a lot of options here, Carla." My voice was a deep growl, in case she was recording. "He wants to destroy the world, as far as I can tell. We have to stop him. I don't know how, other than elimination."

"Ways to eliminate, other than death. And he don't want destruction. At least, not total. He wants chaos. He wants to topple governments, tear down systems, reboot societies. He's proud, right? He thinks we should be in charge. Or at least, be honored. Not hiding. You know? I heard him tell you once that his ass spent years in prison. Makes a lot of sense to me. He hates authorities, hates anyone more powerful than him, like the government."

"I remember that. He and Carter were in the same prison."

"Carter," she sniffed. "Don't trust that old man. He's no better than the Father, you ask me."

"I agree. But at least he isn't trying to tear down governments."

"You sure 'bout that, Outlaw? What I hear, he does the same thing with different tools. And both old men are trying to control you."

I nodded, temporarily at a loss for words. This frank conversation with the enemy was a lot to absorb. Especially an enemy that might believe in a lot of the same things I did.

"The Father, he's obsessed with you."

"I've noticed," I chuckled without humor.

"He educated us. About you. That your body contains something within it, you know, something like a siren call. Draws us to you. He warned us to be careful. But the Father feels it most of all, even when you ain't around. Drives him crazy. Can't let you go. Needs to either work with you or destroy you."

"Can you feel the siren call right now?" I asked. "I don't totally understand why the virus is reacting this way. Or how."

"Yeah. Yeah I feel it. Weird as hell. I'm usually freaked out by Chosen. Sept the Father. But not you. You don't repulse me. Just the opposite." She took off her glasses and looked me up and down, frowning. She even sniffed the air, and then shook her head. "Dunno, Outlaw. Dunno how to explain it. You're...attractive. To my senses."

Samantha grunted in my ear piece. "Yes. That's it. Exactly how I feel too. I like this chick."

"What about Walter? How does he fit into this picture?"

"Walter." She rubbed her eyes and put her glasses back on. "You best stay away from Walter."

"He doesn't feel the siren call?"

"Don't know. Don't matter. Walter kills. Walter hurts. He's a cold, blood-thirsty mercenary. He likes to cause pain."

"Great." I rolled my eyes. "He'll be fun to deal with. Sounds like a perfect side-kick to the Chemist."

"You're ain't listening, Outlaw. *Listen.* Walter and the Father do not get along. Walter is evil. The Father is only impulse and pride. Walter wants to hurt. The Father only does what he has to. Want to kill someone? Kill Walter. Because the Father can reason. He can think. Not Walter. Walter will burn this world down. He hates."

"What about Blue Eyes?"

"The hell is Blue Eyes?"

"That girl, in the hospital. Really pretty. Has blue eyes. She got into my head."

"Oh she got you?" she cackled. "She got you? We thought she didn't. You in trouble, then."

"Why?"

"Mary a crazy-ass hot girl. Loves control. Loves to control men. She and the Father been together for several years, before Compton. She ain't new. Not as fresh as us. She's like the Father's pet, but she got her own pets too. All dudes. Makes me sick."

Samantha said into my ear, "This is taking too long. Get to the point."

"Our plan is to remove the Chemist," I told Carla. "We think everything will fall apart once he's gone. We want your help. We know he's dying, but we want to speed it up before he causes more problems."

"Dying? Why the hell you think that?"

"Multiple reasons. You disagree?"

"You think that because he looks so ugly? Like a wrinkly old man? That's not age. I mean, it might be. He might be dying. But he looks so old like that because he always bleeds himself dry."

"We figured. His blood's become powerful."

"Got that right."

"Any idea what he's doing with it?"

"Course," she scoffed. "Making his army."

"Infecting a lot of infants?"

"Infants? Hell no. Teenagers. Like, seventeen- or eighteen-years old."

"*What?*" Samantha hissed.

I stammered, "But...but that's not possible."

She put her fists on her hips. "Why not?"

"The virus is too strong. It kills adults."

"Oh Outlaw." She cackled again. "You in a lot more trouble than you know."

"...ooooooh myyyyy gooooooosh," Puck groaned. "This could be bad."

"Crikey," Croc said. "He can make adult Infected out of anyone??"

"Details, Outlaw, get us details!" I could practically hear Samantha's teeth grinding.

I said, "Okay...so... He's making an army. How?"

"Easy. Injects them with his own blood, and puts them to sleep. Comatose. Preserves their mind. He's like a mad scientist. Always talking 'bout genes and DNA crap."

I started pacing. "That explains why he had so many at that Camino College. He had like thirty Infected."

"Thirty?" she laughed, a short angry bark. "Those just the ones he woke up. He got hundreds."

Puck quit typing. Samantha's breath caught.

"...hundreds..."

"*Hundreds!?*"

"About half die," Carla continued. "The survivors are called Twice Chosen."

"And they're just like us?"

"No. Thank God. Not as strong. Not as fast. They didn't grow up with the virus, you know? Longer you got the virus, the more work it does. You had yours since birth. They don't. I mean, they still a handful. But us born with the virus? We superior."

"Good."

"And they be crazy."

"How so?"

"I mean, crazy. Crazy as hell. Brains don't work right. Can't think. Just act on impulses. Like trained monkeys for the Father."

"How does the Chemist do all this?"

"Damn, you ask a lot of questions. The Father is brilliant. Above all else, remember that. A genius. You see why I want out of this mess? We need a solution. We need peace."

"Absolutely. Okay, I have some ideas."

"Me too. You go first."

Just as I opened my mouth, Puck freaked out. "Whoa. What? Whoa! Whoa whoa WHOA!!"

I put my hand to my head, his shouts hurting my ear. "Ouch! What?"

Samantha's voice came urgently over the speaker, "Puck! Explain! What's going on?"

"Okay…" his voice was shaky. "…I'm not sure I'm really seeing this…"

Carla cocked an eyebrow at me and waited. I started turning in a circle, looking everywhere. I could hear Samantha doing something similar. My heart rate increased.

"Puck?! Talk!!"

"I haven't been watching the monitors." His voice still wavered. "Until now. And…"

"…and what??"

Carla asked, "You okay? I need to be worried?"

"I don't know," I replied. "Someone is yelling in my earpiece."

"I think you getting taller."

"…okay…" Puck said again. "Someone is coming up the staircase. But…"

"What? Who?"

"…you better brace yourself…on my gosh…"

I turned to the penthouse door and started backing away across the expansive roof. Carla did the same. She pulled out a pistol and thumbed back the heavy hammer. "What the hell, Outlaw."

"Dunno," I growled. "Someone is here."

Puck said, "I think I'm going to pass out…"

The penthouse door swung open. Someone stood there. A silhouette with blonde hair. Carla sucked in air between her teeth.

A girl walked out.

It looked like-

It was-

Hannah Walker.

Hannah Walker.

"Hannah Walker," I breathed.

"What's going on?!" Samantha roared. "Use words! I can't see!"

Hannah Walker had been my girlfriend. We broke up in February. She'd been a popular and attractive cheerleader who attended my high school until six months ago, when her body was incinerated in an explosion. I was there. When she died. In Compton.

She's dead.

But she's stepping out of the stairwell. Right now, wearing a tight red cheerleader outfit and white Nikes. Staring at me. Holding a heavy package in her hands. All the hairs on my body stood on end.

"*You?*" Carla recognized her and scowled, holstering her weapon. "You followed me here?"

"It's…Hannah Walker." My voice was a wheeze.

"*What??*" Samantha cried. "Hannah Walker, the dead Hannah Walker? I don't understand. That blonde girl coming out of the stairs?"

Was it her? She didn't look right. No. It was her, but…different. Changed. Like her skin was stretched. Or rivers had worn down her features over time. Her eyes bigger, her fingers thinner. She stopped and placed the wrapped bundle at my feet. Her hair was shorter than Samantha's.

"I don't get it," I breathed. "Hannah. You died."

Hannah watched me emotionlessly. I couldn't stop shivering.

I said, "I went to your funeral."

Carla shot me a sharp look. "You did? You were there?"

"She died."

"Walker," Carla said loudly, and she snapped her fingers. The dead cheerleader turned her big blue eyes away from me and watched Carla. Her eyelids were abnormal. Or missing. "Walker. Hey kid. You follow me?"

I sputtered, "Carla. What's going on? How could she..."

Carla waved her hand at Hannah. No response. She sniffed, and said, "The Father rescued her, still on fire. Pumped her full of his blood. Like a full blood exchange, instead of the usual small dose. Made her strong as us, maybe. The virus saved her body, to some degree. Only woke up a few weeks ago."

I collapsed. I landed on my knees and slumped forward onto my fists. A million emotions were drowning me. Fear. Pain. Sadness. Loneliness. Heartbreak. Confusion. So dizzy. My stomach threatened to empty itself.

Hannah patted me on the head. I groaned.

"She crazy as hell. More than most," Carla continued. "Operating on animal instincts. She's obsessed with some kid. Former boyfriend, we think. High school sweetheart. Keeps trying to escape and go see him."

Me, probably. Chase Jackson, I mean. Not the Outlaw. She didn't know.

Hot tears splashed on the tarmac below me. I let them fall. I failed Hannah. Couldn't reach her before the eruption. Now she lived, a shell of herself, playing with my hair. I was feeling too much to identify, to control.

"She can't speak. Breathed in too much fire."

I looked up in time to see Hannah swallow and flex the muscles in her throat. She winced in pain and said, "I. Speak." It came out as a whisper, low and harsh, almost masculine. That wasn't her voice. That was a wrecked and ruined voice.

Carla's brows rose and she nodded, impressed. "Aight, kid. Good for you."

In my ear, "This is insane."

I asked, "Her skin is different. Everything is. Because of the fire?"

"Yep. The virus over-produces our body, right? Did the same for her skin. But it's not the same. Real thick, like pliable metal. Her eyes wrinkled from the heat, but those partially healed too. She the Father's greatest creation. So he said."

"She has a scent," I said. "A little like..."

"Gasoline. Dunno what will happen when she around fire. She a big science experiment."

"I. Am. Gift," Hannah rasped. Each word was a forceful burst of air, shaped into syllables. The effort clearly caused suffering.

"You are gift?" Carla said. "How'd you get out? Can't tell nobody. Okay kid? This trip a secret. For both of us."

I pointed at the package. It was long and thin, like a wrapped table leg. "What's this?"

"Dunno. Like I said. She crazy. Can't believe she followed me. That ain't easy."

"There's a card," I noticed. "Addressed to me."

That got Carla's attention. She shut up and squatted next to me.

Outlaw,

I present you with two gifts. Am I not magnanimous?

One, the girl. You couldn't save her. So I did. She is yours to enjoy. She's quite beautiful. I lavished resources on her to salvage the body. Unfortunately the virus dismantled her sanity in the process. Oh well.

Two, this package. Open it now. You will like it. I spent two months making it.

By the way, please reassure Carla. She is, no doubt, in hysterics at this point, wondering if she'll be fed to tigers. Unbeknownst to her, I knew about this clandestine rendezvous and I allowed it. I do not begrudge her exploring her options.

But she must return home.
Now.
- Martin.

Now it was Carla's turn to collapse. She landed on her butt, her face turning several shades lighter. My eyes might be deceiving me, but Hannah appeared to smirk.

"I'm dead." Carla said simply. I barely heard her.

"He told me to reassure you," I pointed out, unwrapping the bundle. "Which means you'll be okay, right?"

"You don't get it, Outlaw. The Father can't abide desertion. Else it be rampant. I'm dead."

I discovered and hefted the Chemist's gift. It was a rod, made like his staff, heavy beyond belief, black and deep blue in color, about as long as a baseball bat. One end was tapered, like a handle. There was another note.

Just like mine.

Constructed with man-made nano materials, nitrates, lonsdaleites, osmium, managing steel....I won't bore you with details. (Indulge this one fact: I purchase the material from meteorite impacts. Essentially graphite from outer space)

In layman's terms, it's a metal alloy. I molecularly combined the hardest and strongest and densest substances on earth. Seven gigapascals, which is impossible.

It's indestructible.
You could sell it for millions.
Please don't.
You need a weapon.

- Martin

PS. Carla is considering suicide. Convince her otherwise. She will get to pick from several mild punishments.

Carla's pistol was in her fist. She was pulling back the hammer and then carefully releasing it, with shaking fingers. Over and over. Her lips were pursed in thought.

"Carla-"

"Shouldn't have come." She shook her head, her voice high and tight in her throat. "Knew it. Bad idea. Shouldn't'a come."

"You said he's not evil. He doesn't hurt people."

223

"Does when he has to. Damn."

"Stay with me. With us. We'll help. We'll provide shelter."

"Kill my family." One big tear fell off her sharp cheek. "Kill my mom. Kill my brothers."

"Not if we stop him."

"You still don't get it, Outlaw." She stood up, returned the pistol to the holster, removed her glasses, and wiped her eyes. "You have to kill the man without me. I'm dead. Probably tomorrow."

"Then don't go back!" I stood up and grabbed her shoulder. She sagged against me. I glanced around. "Hey. Where'd Hannah go?"

Samantha replied through the bluetooth headset, "She left. While you two read the note."

I repeated, "Don't go back, Carla."

"I go back, my family lives. Maybe. I don't, they die. Definitely." She began walking purposefully towards the door. "I'll trade my life for theirs. All day. Every day. So long, Outlaw."

She left.

I was alone on the roof, powerless and foolish.

Samantha crackled, "That is a lot to digest."

"In summary," PuckDaddy said, "The Chemist's body is producing a communicable form of the virus. He has Infected hundreds of adults. He is able to keep them alive, which provides him an army of hyper freaks. Walter is a blood-thirsty maniac who clashes with his boss. Blue Eyes is a witch who likes to control men. And Hannah Walker is alive, Infected, and obsessed with Chase Jackson. We're screwed. So so screwed."

"Puck, where is Hannah going?"

"No idea. She vanished into some utility elevator. Puck'll try to pick her up later."

"I got a bad feeling," I said. "She's going to be trouble."

Chapter Twenty-One
Friday, October 15. 2018

Friday was the Hidden Spring Eagle's final home game of the year. Our team remained undefeated, and that wasn't likely to change tonight; we would roll over the Burbank Bears, a young team trying to rebuild. With over ninety minutes to go before kickoff, much of the team was still tailgating in the parking lot, enjoying celebrity status while they could; their football career was almost over. Four Eagles had received college scholarships thus far. Cory signed his commitment letter earlier this week. Next year he'd be playing for the UCLA Bruins! We were so proud of him we could pop. He made the decision based on their culinary program, obviously.

I wasn't joining the parking-lot revelry. I was hiding in the coaches' conference room. Like a coward.

Coach Keith stuck his head in. "Hey bud. Everything okay?"

"Peachy." I stuck up my thumb to show just how peachy I was. I wasn't peachy, though. I was grumpy. And annoyed. Annoyed at the many things I couldn't control. Katie couldn't meet with Tank, because the big dumb moron was still grounded. So technically she still had a boyfriend. Hannah Walker disappeared, and who knew where she was. The fate of Carla weighed heavily on my mind. Samantha Gear and Dad had been giving each other lingering looks recently. AND I had a D in Science.

Coach Keith said, "The ESPN crew is still here. The interview wouldn't take five minutes."

"No thanks."

Despite my best efforts, college scouts were rating me as one of the best quarterbacks in the nation. A Blue Chip recruit, one of the top three guys every coach wanted. But news about me refusing college scholarships spread like wildfire, catching the attention of ESPN, who would be televising a short documentary on me whether I liked it or not.

Coach Keith pulled out the grey metal folding chair across the table and sat down. "I've never seen such a beloved and successful quarterback look so bummed. If you went into the parking lot right now, the fans would probably parade you around the field on their shoulders."

"Conditional love, Coach," I said, and he nodded with understanding. "That's all that is. Performance-based adoration is...tiresome."

"I sometimes forget that you are wise beyond your years, Chase."

"No. I've just experienced the power of *un*conditional love. There's no contest."

"How'd your dad take the news? That you won't play in college?"

Hah! He handled that news better than the Outlaw discovery. "He understands some things are more important than football. I wish more people got that."

"What do you mean?"

"Our country is facing its biggest threat since World War Two, in my opinion. There's a terrorist-occupied city *down the street*. And yet football still dominates our culture. How can people still be so obsessed with sports?"

"I agree. Our priorities are skewed." He drummed his fingertips on the table. The gold ring on his finger had some special Catholic significance. "But don't judge us too harshly. We need happy things to cling to, in dark times. Sometimes the best we can do is eat, drink, and be merry."

"That's *not* the best we can do. We can fight. Fight the darkness."

"Ah, but you see, eating and drinking and being merry *is* fighting the darkness. Just not with violence."

"How on earth is that fighting?"

"Well. Take the evil in Los Angeles. What is that guy after?"

"The Chemist? He's after chaos. He wants to topple our society, our way of life."

"Notice, Chase, that the Chemist conquered one of the most segregated and unhappy parts of our state. Maybe the country."

"Okay. You're probably right. So?"

"Evil cannot win where there is unity, where there is community, where there is happiness and love. The Chemist is still in Compton because the people haven't kicked him out. The people there were already divided, already full of anger and divided into gangs. It's hard for us to fight evil together when we hate each other."

I nodded and said, "A house divided against itself..."

"Precisely. If Compton had been a happy place, with healthy levels of communal eating and drinking and merriment, the Chemist would have been forced to pick another location to land."

"So it's partially the people's fault?"

"Didn't say that. Assigning blame is narrow-minded and accomplishes almost nothing. Society's ills are never black and white."

"I forget...what does this have to do with football?"

"One of the reasons you'd be carried on your fans' shoulders is because you're good at football. Another reason is that they love you. You draw people. You create community. I've seen your lunch table in the cafeteria. Fifty people sit there. I've seen the way our football team obeys you. They would die for you. You love unconditionally, Chase, and people respond. You create community naturally. You're a safe place. A sanctuary for people who need it. Love is powerful. It drives out evil more effectively than violence."

That's wildly ironic. Coach Keith and the Chemist telling me the exact same thing about love within a week of each other. Love is a hurricane, the Chemist said.

"I get how community can help a football team," I said. "And even a school. But I'm not sure how it defeats evil and violence."

"Who knows," Keith shrugged with a grim expression. "Maybe, before it's all over, the people of Compton will surprise us."

"You're a priest," I said. "Or something like it. Do you ever wonder where God is in all of this?"

"I know exactly where He is. God is in Compton. He hurts when His people hurt. He cries when we do. If there is pain, that is where God goes."

One of the linebackers in the other room was howling and pounding on the lockers, either letting off steam or trying to generate some. To be good at football required a certain abandonment and mania.

I said, "Sure would be nice if God would deal with the Chemist, instead of the hurting."

He chuckled. I loved Coach Keith; nothing I ever said was ridiculous to him. He took it all seriously, even when I displayed my ignorance. "Our God does not carry a sniper rifle. Or launch nuclear missiles. Because where would He draw the line, between those who get executed and those who don't?"

"Good point. That line could get awfully blurry. He'd be a busy guy midnight after Homecoming."

"Hah!" he laughed. "Good one. Our God heals. He doesn't destroy."

"Well. Compton needs some healing. So does all LA."

"Which is why we need to eat, drink and be merry. Together. In love."

I grinned and pointed at him. "I see what you did there. You brought it all back around. Very clever."

"Thanks." He stood up. "I'll go tell ESPN there will be no interviews with you."

"I appreciate it."

"By the way, bud. I think you're making a very brave and courageous decision. About college football."

That was nice to hear. He and Katie were the only two people supporting me. Although neither of them totally understood the reasons, they believed in me and my judgement. "Thanks, Coach. Everyone else seems to think I'm wasting the opportunity of a lifetime."

"They're wrong. Football is a terrible place to invest talent. You're too valuable to waste on this game."

Former Hidden Spring quarterback Andy Babington returned home from college to watch tonight's game. He was Glendale nobility, and still beloved here because he was playing well as a rookie at Fresno State.

He didn't like me. And I didn't like him. I supplanted him at quarterback last year after he broke his hand, and he resented my success. This year he had loudly campaigned for his younger brother to start, instead of me. Now he sat with his buddies in the stands, an arm around the beautiful girl he brought. His voice separated itself from the caterwauling crowd, rattling around in my brain no matter the distance.

I picked a terrible game to throw my first interception. The center hiked me the ball. I stood in the pocket of protection, slow-motion defenders scrambling in vain, and lazily surveyed the field. Bright lights gleamed off dirty helmets. Steam snorted from facemasks. The linemen growled and barked. In the distance, Katie cheered. The trick was to throw a good pass, but not a perfect one. I wanted my receivers to put up good stats and our team to win, but I needed to play within the boundaries of human limitations. Josh Magee separated from his defender, slashing across the field, so I tossed the ball ahead of him. That gave him room to run after the catch. He'd be the star, not me.

But it was a bad pass! Careless mistake. The safety jumped in front of him and snatched the ball. The crowd groaned.

I was so stunned that I forgot to chase the guy with the ball. We needed to tackle him. Instead, a Burbank linebacker put his shoulder into my stomach and drove me into the dirt. It didn't hurt, but I was humiliated. He came up wincing in pain and holding his arm.

I dusted myself off and trotted to the sidelines, and Coach Garrett grinned the way he did when his players make a mistake and learn a valuable lesson.

Andy Babington roared in laughter. "What'd I tell ya??! Over-rated!!"

After the game, I texted the prettiest girl on earth.

I'm coming over.
>> No you can't!
>> But come over anyway =) =)
I am.
>> Okay! I've missed you!
>> No. No no no. Not yet.
>> I haven't broken up with Tank yet.
>> I will soon.
I'll just come over and not touch you.
>> Good idea!
>> Except I'm going to touch you.
>> A lot.
>> So hurry.
>> No. No don't! AHH!
>> I'm very conflicted.
I'm not. I'm confident enough for both of us. ;)
>> My scruples are causing me intense grief.

I grinned at the phone and slipped on my shoes. I was going to visit Katie. At eleven at night. Woohoo! Maybe I should pop a breath mint.

My phone buzzed again. From Puck.

>> bad news
>> chemist hijacked another plane this 1 from central america
>> nothing we can do just wanted to alert u

I sighed. Oh yeah. The Chemist. Until he was eliminated, I couldn't be fully happy. Maybe I'd take Coach Keith's advice and just go love him. Doubtful. He had threatened Katie.

I will kill her in front of you. Slowly.

I couldn't go to Katie's and pretend everything was okay. It wasn't. She was in danger. It felt like she was always in danger, because of me. But what could I do? I couldn't find the guy. And he kept getting stronger, because of these stupid airplanes.

Nothing we can do.

Right?

A wild idea popped into my brain. Insane. Crazy. Ludicrous.

Hey Puck. What time will that plane get to Los Angeles?

Fifteen minutes later I was at Lee's backdoor. I could hear him inside yelling, probably playing video games. The motion sensor activated the porch sconce, casting the backyard into harsh light.

"Oh man. You sure this is a good idea?" Puck asked.

I said, "No."

"Puck is nervous."

"*You're* nervous?? He's *my* best friend!"

"So what, jerk? I'm allowed to be nervous too!"

I turned the knob and pushed into Lee's workshop. Electronic stuff lay everywhere. I carefully stepped around expensive messes on the floor and found Lee on his recliner, learning forward, his face nearly touching the big television, playing a first-person shooter. His fingers were flying over the controller.

"Hey Lee."

"Sup Chase," he said, without turning around. Then he yelled at the screen, "Hah! Die Newb! Ridiculous weapon choice for this map. Can't snipe around corners, bro!"

"How'd you know it was me?

"Saw you on the monitor. Duh." He pointed at the small screen next to him. A black and white live picture of the backyard. "You tripped the laser, and my new Apple Watch warned me. I'm trying to capture footage of the Outlaw on his next visit."

"Oh," I laughed nervously. "That's really funny. And ironic." I was soooooooo anxious. Butterflies ROARED around my stomach. "So. I need your help with something."

He hit pause and instantly stood up. "Boom. I'm in! Whatever it is, dude, let's do it. What's up?"

"Okay, wow. Thanks. So…here's the deal." I took a deep breath. "I need help using your wing-suit."

He rolled his eyes. "Pass. No way, bro. You and Croc are idiots. You need dozens of parachute drops before you're qualified to base jump off a mountain with a wing-suit. Heck, dude, I *made* the suit and I would never try it."

"Well. I don't want to jump off a mountain. I want to jump out of a helicopter."

"It's like you guys don't have ears! No! Noooooooooooo! It's not a toy, bro. Besides no helicopter in the world would take you up and let you jump off." He shook his head with a huff, shaggy mop of black hair sliding into his eyes.

"I already secured a ride. Tonight. You want to go?"

"What?!" he shouted and he actually shoved me. "Dude! What?? You. Are. In. Sane! You can't jump at night, bro! That's suicide!"

"Nah. I've done it before."

He blinked twice, and then held up a forefinger and waved it back in forth in front of my face. He had to reach up. "Chase. Follow my finger, dude. You high, man? Doing drugs?"

"Actually, you shouldn't go, now that I think about it. It's an FBI helicopter and I don't want them to know who you are."

"Uh huh. Alcohol?" He sniffed my shirt. "Been drinking? I can't smell anything." Sniff sniff.

"I just need to know how fast you think your suit can go. And anything else you know about vertical versus horizontal speed. I'm going to try and land on a moving plane. It'll be tricky."

"Okay, man. Why don't you lie down on my couch? Before you hurt yourself. Cause you sound crazy weird."

Another deep breath. "And if you have any idea how to enter a plane while it's in flight, I'd like to hear it."

"This is the strangest conversation ever, dude. I think I'm going to record it, and show you tomorrow." He began hunting through the junk collection beside his chair, looking for his phone. "That way, you'll hear how stu-pid you sound, and you'll never smoke crack again."

I grinned. This was kind of fun. "I'm ready to go, Lee. I'm already wearing the suit."

"You're *what*?!" He glared at my pants. "What the heck, man?! You go through my room?"

"No. You gave-"

"You're wearing the gloves too!" he hooted in anger. "That's so messed up! You can NOT try this. If it doesn't work, you'll *die*!"

"No way. Your parachute works great!"

"You're wearing my *vest* too??"

Puck said into my ear piece, "This is hilarious."

I told Lee, "Of course I'm wearing the vest. You made it for me. I love it."

"No I didn't! You big dumb white American, always think stuff belongs to you, take my suit off!"

"Okay," I laughed. "I think it's time I show you something."

"No! Just take my suit off. It cost a lot of money and I'm a lot smaller than you, and you're probably ripping it!"

I pulled out the mask. My hands trembled. "Just try not to freak out."

"Too late!"

I tied on the red bandana, Rambo style. He rolled his eyes. The black sleeve was already around my neck, so I tugged it up until it covered my mouth and nose. Lastly, I unzipped and removed the jacket. I was now in full Outlaw regalia.

"What...dude, what are..." he stopped and started, his eyes peering at me as if from a distance. "I don't...this is weird..."

I lowered my voice to the Outlaw growl and said, "Lee! I need help retaking the Chemist's plane. Tonight!"

"WHOA!" he yelped, and he actually fell backwards over his chair. "Whoa whoa WHOA! DUDE WHAT??"

"Hah!" Puck laughed.

"Lee!" I snarled. "Now, Lee!"

"No!" He cried, stumbling up again. "What! No! You? You? YOU?" He climbed into the chair and started hopping. "You? You? What! You! You're the Outlaw?? Chase Jackson is the OUTLAW?!"

I yanked the mask down and said, "Shhhh. Lee. Hush. Your parents."

"You! You! No! Really? Really dude? No. You're messing with. Aren't you. This is a joke." His face was flushed with pleasure and doubt.

"Lee, I'm sorry. I should have told you. This thing just got out of hand, and dangerous people have threatened my friends. I feel bad about deceiving you."

He leapt off the chair and landed on me, like a squirrel jumping trees. He started yelling in my ear, "It's you! It's you! It's yooooouuuuuuuu!!"

The door at the top of the staircase opened and Lee's mom called, "Lee, please! It's the middle of the night!"

"Sorry mom," he said. "Just having a good time. Everything is okay. I'll be quiet."

"Thank you," she said curtly and she closed the door again.

"THIS IS AWESOOOOOOOOME!!"

Chapter Twenty-Two
Late Friday/Early Saturday, October 15/16. 2018

"Okay, Lee." I placed him onto the floor. "Now I need your help. The plane flies overhead in sixty-five minutes."

"Ohmygoshohmygoshohmygoshohmygosh this is really happening, my best friend is the Outlaw, ohmygosh ohmygosh." He marched in place and chewed on all ten fingers at once.

"Lee, focus."

"Dude. Dude. I have so many questions, dude."

"Later."

"Okay. Later. But how high can you jump?"

I set my phone flat on the table. "I'm going to put a friend on speaker. You two should really get along." I pushed a button on the phone and the sounds in my ear began pumping out of the phone's speaker instead. "Puck? You still there?"

"Yeah dummy. I'm here," the speaker replied.

Lee frowned at the phone and asked, "Puck? Puck who?"

"He's a friend that-"

"PuckDADDY?!"

I said, "Well, yes, actually."

"Oh man! PuckDaddy, I'm a huge fan, bro!"

The speaker said, "Ah my adoring public. You are clearly a man of sophisticated taste."

"PuckDaddy, I know all about you. Your takeover of the Swiss Banking Interfaces was Hacktivism at its best!!" Lee was hopping from one foot to the other, shouting at the phone.

"Thank you, thank you. A mere dalliance, really."

"I read that article about how you used their own cameras to identify the keystrokes which…" His reminiscences stopped mid-sentence. His face went blank. "…huh."

I said, "What?"

Lee stomped over to his computer and yanked out the power cord. The computer, as well as several other devices, blinked off.

"What the…" Puck grumbled. "What just happened? Hey! I was using that!"

"You mean you were snooping through my files, dude," Lee retorted.

"Obviously."

"And you were spying through my camera."

"Duh. Have been for months."

"Guys," I cried. "This is a super weird. We need to focus."

Lee rubbed his lower lip in thought. "I'll need to purchase a better firewall."

"Hah! Good luck, little man. I break those to kill time. I don't need your stupid camera anyway."

I sighed, "Okay. You guys done? Now, here's-"

Lee's face went blank again. He stomped over to his X-Box.

Puck shouted, "No no no! Not the X-Box! No! Getaway!"

Lee shut down his game console, including the attached Kinnect camera. "Suck on that, computer nerd."

"Dang it," Puck groaned through the phone. "This sucks. It's like I'm blind."

Lee shoved a big pile of stuff off a table. It landed with a crash, revealing a clean workspace and whiteboard underneath. "That cargo plane is a Grumman Greyhound, a twin-prop almost solely operated by the United States Navy. The Chemist found one of the very few not on a carrier. This one is probably a decommissioned model sold and overhauled for private use." He leaned over the table on his elbows and started sketching lines on the whiteboard with a dry-erase marker.

"How do you know all that?" I asked.

"I looked it up as soon as the news broke. Duh. You have three immediate problems. The Greyhound has a cruising speed of 250 miles per hour. Your suit won't go that fast. You'll fly forward at hundred miles per hour, and fall vertically around twenty-five." He was drawing red and blue lines and numbers, the markers squeaking. "This means you can't catch up to the Grumman Greyhound. It's faster. Make sense?"

"Yes. This is super cool."

"The second problem is altitude. The cargo plane is almost certainly cruising above 20,000 feet. Maybe over 30,000. Far too high for you. Your helicopter turbines will start to complain around 10,000." He drew the earth with dotted lines to represent altitude. "Your suit won't let you fly upwards to reach the Greyhound. It'll be far above you. Making sense?"

"Yes."

"Your only chance is to capture it during approach. The plane will descend and reduce speed as it nears the runway. But even then, it'll be flying around 150 miles per hour. Fifty miles per hour faster than you."

"No sweat," I grinned.

Puck said, "Oh my gosh, Shooter's going to kill me." He used Samantha's codename to preserve her identity.

Lee asked, "Who is Shooter? How strong are you? Like, could you pick up my house?"

"What? No. No way. That's insane."

"Does Katie know?"

"No," I groaned. "I've been waiting to tell her."

"She's going to freak, bro."

"I know. I want to wait until we're dating, so she'll have to forgive me."

"But seriously, dude. Are you joking? Is this a prank?"

"No," I grumbled. "Get back to your numbers."

"The third problem is those big propellers. They'll mess you up, even if you *are* Superman."

"Which I'm not."

"But kinda."

"Nope.

"You'll be forced to let the plane slide underneath you, and then land on it. Like jumping from a bridge onto a speeding train. But a train with big metal propellers of death."

"Sounds fun."

Puck said, "I've decided this is a bad idea." We ignored him.

Lee continued, "If you think there's even a remote chance those rotors are messing with your wind, then you should bank out of there, dude. Live to fight another day. You follow? I've got it!" He snapped his fingers. "When you're in position, and the plane is almost underneath you, close the wings! You'll still be moving forward at the same speed, but the wind won't be able to manipulate your wings. You'll be a rock, instead of a leaf. Make sense? Might be easier to land that way."

"Good idea," I nodded.

"Wow." He pulled at his lip in thought, one of his constant habits. "You're definitely going to die."

"No I'm not!"

Puck said, "Yes you are."

"I have no idea how you'll get *into* the plane." Lee shook his head and dropped the marker onto the board.

"We're hoping he won't have to," Puck said. "Five years ago this plane was outfitted with advanced autopilot. I can access it remotely."

"That's so cool!!"

"Agreed. Puck rules," the speaker rattled. "We're hoping Chase landing on the plane will spook the pilot. He'll parachute out, and I'll engage the autopilot and chart a different destination."

"This is the best night of my life. What if it doesn't spook the pilot?"

I said, "Then I'll improvise."

"How?"

"No idea. But I need to go. I'm low on time. Can you figure out the numbers on helicopter altitude, when I need to jump in relationship to the plane's approach, and all that stuff?"

"Sure, bro. I can get close. But no promises."

"Check this out." I handed Lee my new rod, the gift from the Chemist. He immediately dropped it, and I was forced to catch the rod before it made a crater on his hardwood floor.

"Dude!" he gaped. "How is that so heavy?? Like a baseball bat made out of lead."

"Not sure. It's a gift from the Chemist."

"........." he said. "...say that again?"

"I'll explain later." I had to laugh. My life sounded so weird when I tried explaining it. "In the meantime, maybe I can beat open the plane's door with it."

"You're capturing the Chemist's plane with the gift he gave you. You should call it the Rod of Karma. Or the Betrayal Stick."

Puck offered, "Stick of Treachery."

At 12:30am, Isaac Anderson and I were in the rear passenger cabin of an FBI A-Star, whose rotors were screaming and pulling us higher over Newport Beach. The sky was black and so was the Pacific Ocean to the west.

"This is a terrible idea!" Anderson yelled. His usually handsome face was stony and lined with worry. The bay doors were open and the wind threatened to suck us out.

"Those are my favorite kind!"

"You're definitely going to die!"

I was wearing my motorcycle helmet to provide eye-protection from the wind and so Puck and I could still communicate. The phone was in my pocket, connected via bluetooth to the helmet. If I ended up in the ocean (which I almost certainly would) then both would short-circuit.

"Remember!" Anderson called. "Once you hit the water, we won't be able to see you. You must activate the beacon!"

"Got it!"

Puck was monitoring the cargo plane via the FAA's radar, and he had Lee's calculations. "The Greyhound has shifted westward," Puck reported. "You need to be farther out to sea. It's descended to 15,000 feet."

I relayed the instructions to the pilot and we changed heading, soaring away from the coast. The pilot called back, "We're at 10,000 feet. The air's too thin to go higher! We're barely hovering!"

Isaac barked, "Roger that! Hold position!"

I grabbed the handhold beside the door. The metal vibrated and complained with effort. Below us was nothing.

Puck spoke into my ear again, and I said, "Ten miles out! Altitude 13,000. Speed one hundred seventy-five!"

"Special Agent Anderson!" the pilot called. He was a silhouette, surrounded by incomprehensible lights. "We can get this helicopter up to one-fifty! Why don't I fly above the Greyhound and match his speed? The Outlaw could just hop off?"

"Negative! We don't want to alert the Greyhound pilot. He'd identify us too far in advance!"

We heard the pilot say, "I'm going to get fired for this."

"You and me both," Anderson mumbled.

I asked, "Did you get clearance for this operation?"

"Hell no. You think they'd authorize this?"

A thought occurred to me. Whoops!!! I forgot to tell Katie I wasn't coming over! I texted her.

Sorry. Something came up. I can't come over.
>> =(=(=(
>> Maybe for the best. I was feeling...deviant.

"Darn it," I said. That could have been fun.

"What?"

"Nothing."

Puck said, "Three miles. 10,000 feet."

"Bingo! I got a visual!"

Anderson ordered, "Lights out! We're flying dark. Converge with the Greyhound's course, but keep your distance!"

"Roger, wilco!" The pilot dipped the helicopter's nose and we surged forward. My heart's RPMs sped up too. Isaac's phone lit up in his shirt pocket.

"That's PuckDaddy calling you," I said. "He wants to be on a three-way call."

"Understood." He answered it.

"Outlaw," Puck said. I could tell through the headset he was anxious. "Prepare to jump. Going by the numbers, you've got thirty seconds.

Through our wide door we saw the big cargo plane lumbering down through the sky to the south. Jeez it was big. And loud. And fast. A winking behemoth swaying out of the heavens.

Puck said, "In roughly twenty seconds, the Greyhound will drop below 10,000 feet. Tell the pilot we need to match his speed, as closely as possible, and remain roughly five hundred yards above him."

I did. The helicopter banked and roared.

Anderson shook my hand grimly and said, "Good luck, Outlaw."

Soon we were half a mile ahead of the cargo plane, but we turned and it disappeared behind our tail. I'd be jumping blind.

"In position!" the pilot called. Our helicopter was really moving now, overtaxing the engines to keep up with the decelerating Grumman Greyhound.

"If you're in position, then you're free to jump," Puck said. He was breathing heavily. "Wow this is nuts."

I hooked the gloves onto my wings and connected the leg-webbing. Anderson watched without comment. I hadn't really thought much about the actual jump, because I would chicken out.

Don't think.

Don't think.

I began counting to three, but I jumped on two. Out into the empty cosmos. The air was a painful wall which hurled me away from the invisible helicopter. The swirling gales snatched and pulled on the wings and I was instantly lost, tumbling in circles. The helmet rattled around my ears, the visor buzzing, my exhalations hot and loud. The distant city lights spun into my vision over and over again. I felt like a marble in a dryer.

I forced my arms forward and my legs wide. The effects of the wind increased and I was tossed like scrap paper in a storm. But I didn't release the position. I ground my teeth and held. I found the glowing electric horizon and made small corrections until the twisting leveled. Finally! A quasi-stable surface of air to ride.

I was panting. Where?? Where was the plane?

There! I was hurtling straight at it!

I rotated my shoulders, arms shifting like wheel-spokes, and executed a rapid 180-degree course correction, a dramatic turn that displaced my blood and made me light-headed, until the lights of the city settled to my right. Now the plane was behind me and I fled before it. I hunched over, head bent down, hunting for the Greyhound between my legs. The visor was foggy, but I located the flashing collision lights approaching fast.

Instantly I could tell this wouldn't work. Despite our best efforts, there were just too many variables that could and did go wrong. I was too far away and I would shoot under the plane's flight path before it passed by.

"Status report," Puck wheezed. He might have been holding his breath the whole time.

"Shut up! I'm thinking!" I was a rocket, and I didn't have time to talk.

I was definitely too far away and too low. I needed to slow down. I unfettered the wings and launched the parachute. The jarring change in speed nearly pulled my arms out of socket. I swung wildly below the chute, like one of those toy army guys whose parachute never worked exactly right. I hauled on the ropes, trying to correct the ferocious undulations.

The roar of the wind tunnel died. I could have been floating in outer space. The world was wintery and silent and lonely. I hung from blackness in the middle of nothing, slowly drifting into a void. Just me and, to the north, the white moon.

"This is kind of creepy," I panted. The air was thin.

"What?"

"Nothing. Shut up again. I'm trying to think."

By pure chance, I was floating in my target's path. The Greyhound was plunging, shedding altitude quickly, and would dive directly below me in just a few seconds. It was closing the distance in a mad rush!

This wasn't going to work either! I had lost all forward momentum, now only moving downward, and the plane was traveling at 150mph! It would be like getting hit by a truck speeding on a Nascar track. I needed velocity.

I eyeballed the flashing lights barreling in my direction, judging the distance. The plane was enormous, with gargantuan blades slicing the air on either wing. I took a deep breath, heaved the parachute back into it's backpack, began free-fall, and snapped the wings open again. Instantly I started picking up speed, both forwards and downwards. Faster. Faster.

I was being overtaken as we raced in close proximity. Craning my neck downwards, I could see the lighted cockpit and movement inside.

The Greyhound's raucous engines decreased an octave and the plane visually slowed, casting off speed and altitude. I inched nearer, joining the cacophony.

I was in position and as close as I dared. Even from this distance, parallel ten meters above the fuselage, the wind was acting wonky.

"Here we go," I whispered.

"What??"

Zip! My wings retracted and I fell like a stone.

I was too far forward. I had planned on skipping along the plane's surface and using one of the many protrusions as a hand-hold. No such luck. I flew straight at the cockpit windshield.

Painfully I smacked like a bug onto the nose of the Grumman Greyhound. The wind forcibly compressed me into the metal sheeting, and prevented me from slipping off.

It worked! I was on the aircraft!

The cockpit had four separate windshield panes, giving the pilot a wide field of vision. Through the two foremost windows, I peered into the brilliantly lit cockpit and witnessed the pilot pass out. The man was probably already stressed, tired, maybe high, and the sight of me falling from the heavens, landing on his nose and staring back at him was simply too much. His eyes rolled up and he slumped forward, head temporarily resting on the control yoke.

Well. That works.

Time to improvise. I pulled out the rod, the Stick of Treachery, and struck the closest pane with as much force as I could bring to bear. The heavy tip punched a hole through the multiple layers of glass. The change in cabin pressure blew the pieces straight out and up into the night. The airflow also caused the pilot to lean farther towards me, pressing the control yoke forward.

Uh oh.

The Grumman's nose dipped as the plane changed pitch and began a more aggressive descent towards the earth.

That's not good.

I smashed the glass again and again to create a sharp hole big enough for me to slither through. I grasped the metal windshield housing and hauled myself into the relative quiet and warmth of the cockpit. It was tiny and militant, not built for comfort, and I couldn't even sit down.

"Believe it or not, Puck," I grinned, "we did-"

The cockpit door opened and a gunman ducked in. He took one look at me, his eyes widened and he screamed, "Aiieeeee! El diablo!!"

I dove at him as best I could, awkwardly launching over the co-pilot seat. My foot brushed the unconscious pilot, and the plane shuddered. I landed on the surprised terrorist, and we both hit the ground. His head connected solidly with the deck and he moved no further.

The airplane began rolling to its left, westward. Freight in the cargo area shifted and strained against restraints. Two gun-wielding terrorists came staggering forward to investigate the disturbance. Both cried in alarm and fumbled with their weapons.

I flung the cockpit door closed, the heavy metal barrier blistering from bullet impacts.

We were diving towards the Pacific Ocean at an alarming rate now. I hauled the pilot's limp body off the stick, but I had no idea how to fly a plane!

"Puck, take over! We got a problem! Get this thing's autopilot working!"

"I'm trying! It's unresponsive!"

"Do it anyway!"

I waited until the gunfire stopped, then kicked open the door and threw my heavy metal bat at the nearest assailant, shoving it like a chest pass in the close confines. He caught it full in his stomach and fell.

With a thunderous SNAP, the restraints broke and tons of freight collapsed sideways, swallowing and crushing both men.

That works too.

The Grumman's forward pitch was so steep I fell backwards into the cockpit. The cargo jumble began inching closer, threatening to fall down the sloping deck and plow through the cockpit bulkhead, killing us all.

"Puck, fix this thing!"

"I can't! Outlaw, you're below three thousand feet! Pull up!"

"How?!"

Isaac's voice blurted into my ear piece, "The control you need sticks straight up between the pilot's knees. Usually has two handholds, like prongs. Pull back on it, towards your body."

Nothing was visible through the windshield except rippling moon reflections. We were diving straight towards the water, pitched so far forward I couldn't sit down. As best I could, I stood in the co-pilot seat and hauled backwards on the yoke. The mechanism actively fought me. One of the terrorists crashed into our seats, still unconscious.

"I'm pulling! Now what?!"

"Two thousand feet!"

Isaac said calmly, "Keep pulling. That's the only thing you can do."

I pulled until the metal began to bend. Sweat leaked from my red bandana in rivers, soaking into the black mask.

I could jump out. My body wouldn't survive a plane crash, but could withstand the water impact if I abandoned ship. Pull!! I couldn't leave. Everyone aboard was dead if I did. C'mon you stupid old bucket, pull up!!

City lights reappeared from the top of the cockpit, indicating we were dragging out of the dive. At least I hoped so; I had no idea how to read airplane dials.

"How we doing, Puck??"

"Leveling out at four hundred feet. I can't feel my fingertips."

"Keep pulling, Outlaw. You're too low. You need altitude, especially before you hit the coast."

"Hah! Never in doubt!" I laughed in delirium. I wanted to wipe the sweat out of my eyes but I didn't dare release the controls. "I'm flying a plane! Woohoooooo!"

Puck never got the autopilot to engage remotely, but he taught me how to activate it within the cockpit. The engines surged and the controls commenced independent operation and I was finally able to take a deep breath. The FAA was howling about airspace, squawking through the pilot's headphones. I let Isaac Anderson handle all communication as we cruised over the incandescent city, level with familiar skyscrapers

The plane even landed on autopilot, as if by magic, at Bob Hope Airport, a small airstrip in Northern Los Angeles. Word of the airplane mid-air hijacking had reached the media, and news vans ringed the airstrip, pressed to the security fence.

As soon as the Greyhound braked to a full stop, Anderson's FBI helicopter landed alongside. Emergency vehicles came screaming in, shading the night red, blue, and loud. Airport personnel poured from hiding spots, cheering with raised hands, racing to the Grumman.

I waved to them from the nose of the cargo plane, squinting against blinding lights. They whooped even louder. I jumped down. Anderson waved me into the rear passenger bay of the FBI A-Star, and we took off as police cars, ambulances, SWAT vehicles, and firetrucks made a solid ring around the Greyhound.

The helicopter dipped forward and we left the madness in our wake. Anderson and I shook hands and congratulated each other on being lionhearted morons. The pilot yelled, "I'm being ordered to take both of you back to base!"

"Negative!" Anderson laughed. "Tell them I've got a gun to your head!"

"No need, sir! I'm with you. You and the Outlaw! We can all burn together! What's our heading?"

"Second star to the right!"

"What??"

"Just get us out of here!"

Chapter Twenty-Three
Wednesday, October 20. 2018.

The Grumman Greyhound had been hauling several tons of illegal weapons, ammunition, and narcotics. The three terrorists were all on South American Most Wanted lists, but the pilot was just a local flyboy living near an airport in Panama, unlucky enough to get kidnapped and forced to fly the plane north.

The sensational story dominated the news, and the Outlawyers were stirred into such a frenzy that Natalie North temporarily moved into a hotel. The Outlaw worshippers set up camp surrounding her apartment building, which was senseless but the building had become a shrine, the only known frequented haunt of the Outlaw. Dozens of Outlawyers were being arrested daily for loitering and disturbing the peace. A new Outlaw Support Compound was established near Glenoaks Canyon, providing refuge for Outlaw pilgrims and even an Outlaw prayer chapel, all within an abandoned Boy Scout campground and shelter, bought by a wealthy patron calling himself The Priest.

I debated burning it down, to relieve the worshipers of their ridiculous religion. Soon I'd probably be forced to come clean with the media and discuss the illness, if only so people would stop leaping to absurd conclusions.

>> You need to do the interview with Time Magazine, Natalie told me.

But I don't waaaaaaaaant to.
>> I insist. Please?
Why not with Teresa Triplett? She's always been very helpful.
>> Why not with Time? You're being labeled the Person of the Year!!
Booooooooring. But I didn't tell her that.

The Chemist wrote me a curt email. It said,

> Bravo.
> Now witness my retribution.
> - Martin

His revenge was swift and terrible. Tuesday night at 11:30pm, Chemist forces swarmed over security fences at every major military base within two hundred miles. Armed with firearms and explosives and superhuman quickness, the attackers caught the bases completely off guard and ravaged the facilities.

Chain-reaction explosions at Los Angeles Air Force Base in El Segundo destroyed or damaged 100% of the attack aircraft, and their airstrips were spiked with bombs and rendered unusable. (To make matters worse, this was the primary airstrip used for military ingress. No reinforcements could arrive via this location until crucial repairs were completed.)

The detonation of munitions at the Naval Weapons Station on the coast was heard as far as thirty-five miles away. Vast warehouses and underground bunkers went up like volcanoes.

Los Alamitos, the joint forces facility, was left without a single helicopter or transport jeep.

The reports issuing from the bases were all the same: the enemies came to destroy, not to kill, and they were too fast to be shot. The United States suffered relatively few casualties compared to the billions lost in equipment. The attack was aimed at vehicles, not personnel, and the result was staggering: for the time being, much of the world's most powerful military was immobile and stranded on the West Coast.

The attack was especially effective because a larger-than-usual military contingent had gathered around Los Angeles, prepping to invade the occupied territories. The Chemist hadn't just destroyed vacant outposts; he'd gone after the biggest and most heavily-armed assemblage on American soil in decades.

The special forces at Los Alamitos had the most success in repelling invaders. That's another way of saying, they managed to kill a few.

Wednesday morning, after the sun came up and the smoke cleared and the damages tallied, the awful truth was realized: the military was missing twelve fully-armed attack helicopters, four vertical take-off Harriers, and three cargo choppers. The Chemist had robbed the United States of America, stealing hundreds of millions worth of equipment, and he could open fire whenever he wanted. Strategists suggested the cargo helicopters were probably filled with weapons and ammunitions, maybe even fuel, for the vehicles.

It wouldn't be difficult for recon satellites and drones to locate the stolen vehicles, once the armed forces regrouped. But chances were the Chemist would have his new toys well protected with civilians, preventing recapture or destruction. However, it would be days or weeks before such an operation was even possible due to the sudden lack of mobility.

The in-fighting among the military branches revved up, humiliation rife over the catastrophe. It was a global embarrassment. The media screamed for answers, and politicians screamed for heads to roll. The Pentagon and Joint Chiefs of Staff and Generals and the Admirals all deflected responsibility. So who was to blame?

"I'll tell ya who's to blame," Carter said, chewing on an unlit cigarette. He dropped a fresh set of large photographs onto his truck's hood. "She is."

Croc, Samantha and I were meeting with Carter and Russia that night in our usual spot, the lonely, gravel parking lot behind a construction depot.

After my meeting with Carla, we had immediately reported the disastrous news to Carter, that the Chemist could Infect adults with a high rate of success and his army was already hundreds strong. Much to our surprise, Carter hadn't been angry with us. He praised our bold counter-insurgence strategy and called the intel 'priceless.' As much as I hated to admit it, being praised by Carter felt awesome, like pleasing an angry father.

Now, at 10pm, we huddled around his truck, staring at pictures of Blue Eyes, the witch. Even in still photographs, she was shockingly attractive. Carter continued, "She's seduced at least a dozen of the most powerful men in Washington, both on Capitol Hill and the Pentagon. With her in their ear, and Martin influencing the politicians in California, it's no wonder the military just got their pants yanked down."

"She's a looka," Croc nodded. "I'm glad we haven't been properly introduced."

Carter said, "I agree, Mitchell. I'm rethinking Gear's suggestion, that she go *eliminate* Mary, otherwise known as Blue Eyes."

Samantha's jaw was set. "Just say the word."

I asked, "What's she doing that's causing problems?"

"She's whispering in their ears, hero," he responded, an edge to his voice. "Planting suggestions. Those jackasses do whatever she says. She's the reason the U.S. hasn't retaliated against the Chemist yet. He's been sitting there with impunity for months, because the Blue-Eyed Witch has the Defense Committee stalling and fighting in congress."

"And when a decision is finally reached, certain high-ranking generals will dissent," Samantha growled.

"Exactly. Martin has paid or blackmailed them to break ranks." He struck a match and lit the cigarette, and offered the smokes to Russia. Russia lit up, too. They looked cool. Maybe I should give it a shot. "The whole thing is a mess."

I said, "I want to give names of the saboteurs to the FBI."

"Tough."

"You have a better idea?"

"I do. We need to alter our strategy. Samantha and I came here to recruit you, and keep an eye on Martin. But things have drastically changed since January. Martin is no longer just a nuisance that should be disposed of within the Infected community. He's become a global menace."

"Too right. A bloody maniac."

"My goal has always been to prevent our discovery." He was frustrated and animated, his deep breaths inhaling and spewing the same smoke over and over. "The last thing we needed was media attention. But now...thanks to the bloody maniac, and to pajamas here, the whole damn planet is after us."

Samantha said, "Don't blame Chase. He's always done what he thinks is best for Los Angeles."

"I *do* blame him." His eyes were fiery. Carter at night was especially scary; larger, angrier, and his shadow appeared to give him black wings. "If he had, just once, followed my instructions, this whole ordeal could be finished."

I scoffed. "Give me one reason why I should follow your instructions."

"Because you're a child! An arrogant and ignorant toddler playing games with grown-ups, and you've cost us *everything*." His voice was a whip, snapping with accusation. Samantha casually moved her body to stand between Carter and me.

I shouted at him over her shoulder. "You and I have never been playing the same *game*, Carter! I don't need your instructions, because we're not going in the same direction."

"Think about this, little boy." He simmered and smoked and boiled. "There's not an Infected alive today who didn't need my help. Even Martin, in the past. Every Infected for the past thirty years only survived because of ME! They *all* accepted my help."

"Because you forced them! You brought a GUN to our first meeting, because you were going to kill me if I didn't play by your rules! Are you sure you're any better than the Chemist??"

The final straw. I pushed him too far.

It happened in the blink of an eye. Maybe even faster...

Croc saw what was happening first, and he reached for Samantha protectively.

Carter produced a pistol, like a murderous magician.

He shot at me over Samantha's shoulder.

I yanked the Stick of Treachery free from my vest, and slashed it across my body.

I got lucky; the rod connected with the bullet, which ricocheted harmlessly into the lumber yard.

No one moved. The Stick rang in my hand, like a siren masking the gunshot echo.

Carter lowered the heavy weapon in disbelief. I didn't blame him. That was cool. It happened on instinct.

Russia spoke for the first time, a deep, blubbery voice. He woofed in surprise and said, "Kiddie has new toy."

"...what..." Carter sputtered. "Where the hell did you get that?!"

"We're not friends, Carter," I said with a lot more steel in my voice than I felt. The Stick was pointed at him, my arm straight like a fencer. "But that doesn't mean we have to be enemies."

Russia laughed again, a dark humorless noise, and I couldn't tell if he had a new appreciation for me or a new hatred. I was surprised to see Samantha's two guns out and pointed at Carter, a fact I hoped he overlooked.

"Very well," Carter said stiffly. He shoved his gun back into a leather holster. "I wash my hands of you, ungrateful little boy. Enjoy your independence. You will die alone."

Samantha was glaring at both of us. But behind the anger, I saw fear. At least she'd put the pistols away.

Croc shifted awkwardly and chuckled, "Well...now what?"

Carter stared hard at me for an uncomfortable ten seconds, then snapped, "We're leaving."

"Leaving?"

"Leaving Los Angeles."

The furrows in Gear's forehead deepened. "But the Chemist is still here."

Carter began packing up and throwing things into his truck. "Martin just effectively declared war on the United States, and America doesn't lose wars. The George Washington, a Nimitz Class nuclear-powered aircraft carrier, has been diverted from off the coast of Asia. The entire carrier group will arrive within a few days, prepared to bomb his fortress and launch a full invasion. Martin will strike first, or be long gone by then. Along with most of his Infected. Either way, our work in Los Angeles is at an end."

"You can't just abandon the city!" I shouted. "You helped *start* this mess!"

"What *we* do is not your concern. We're leaving. You...actually, kid, I don't care what you do."

"Los Angeles needs our help!"

Carter shoved a finger at Gear and Croc. "You two. We're flying out in less than a week. I want to lay low and locate Martin's next landing spot. Once I do, we leave immediately."

"Righto, boss," Croc said grimly.

Samantha didn't respond, her eyes distant, arms crossed over her chest.

Carter and Russia roared off into the black night. Croc coaxed a silent Samantha into his truck, and they left. I remained in the parking lot, lonely and miserable and confused, holding the Stick of Treachery.

Chapter Twenty-Four
Thursday, October 21. 2018.

Tank's long punishment would finally come to an end on Monday, only four days away.

"I'm meeting him Monday night," Katie purred into my ear during English class. "And then I'm coming straight to your house."

"Whatever shall we do?" I asked.

"I'll be a single girl," she winked. "You'll think of something."

I was growing more and more worried about that break up. Tank was born an angry giant, and now he was infested with a virus that thrived on adrenaline and emotion, crippling his feeble brain even further. I might tag along in the shadows, for her safety.

Croc and Samantha attended school and football practice, which surprised me. I figured they'd keep their distance.

"Carter doesn't control our personal lives," Samantha snapped, when I asked.

"Besides, mate," Croc grinned. "If the Chemist attacks, that right bastard, we've been ordered to kill you instead of protect you."

"Which we'd never do." She was fuming, obviously battling her emotions and the virus's inflammatory responses. "And we have a football championship to win before we leave."

Dad was in the kitchen when I came home from practice. He'd been watching me warily the past few weeks, like I could implode any minute. Today he looked especially troubled.

He asked, "How you doin, kid?"

"Better than you. You look rough."

"Haven't slept in a while. The military lost their rides, so police have been scrambling to pick up the slack."

I started devouring chocolate cookies and pulling homework out of my backpack.

He proceeded slowly. "I know we don't talk about this much. But. How is your...other profession?"

"The whole masked-vigilante gig?" I grinned. "For a part-time job, it's surprisingly troublesome."

"I've debated grounding you for the cargo-jet stunt you pulled."

"Dad! Come on," I laughed. "That was brilliant. You should be proud."

He lowered into a chair with a grunt. "I am. After all this is over, and I don't have to worry anymore, you can tell me about it."

"I heard a carrier group is going to park off Los Angeles."

He looked surprised. "How the hell do you know that? That's top secret stuff."

"Dad, do you think the Outlaw should do an interview? I'm being pressured to."

Anytime I called myself the Outlaw, we both flinched. This was still new territory for us. "Who is pressuring you?"

"Natalie North."

"Natal...*the* Natalie North? You and she communicate?"

"That's kinda weird, huh," I nodded, opening my math book and starting on an apple.

"Tell me about it later. Why would you do an interview?"

I shrugged. "I don't know. She thinks it'd be good for Los Angeles. Give them hope."

"She's probably right."

"Plus, I feel I should warn them, you know? If the people knew everything I do, they'd leave town. In fact, I'd advise them to."

He thought quietly for a minute. He was a big man, stoic and rough after years of working Homicide, grilling witnesses, and wrestling perpetrators. He looked years older than he did a few months ago. And maybe...years lonelier. Finally he said, "I think that's a good idea. If the chiefs weren't bitching at each other so much, we would have called for an evacuation already. Maybe the Outlaw could do it for us."

"Okay." I checked my watch. "I'll do it right after homework."

I called Puck from my motorcycle.

"Hey man," he said. His voice was somber and lacking the usual moxie. "Why are you driving downtown?"

"I need a favor. Call Teresa Triplett and tell her I want to do a live interview. In like...thirty minutes. On her roof, in total darkness."

"Chase...I've been ordered not to help you anymore."

"Oh, come on! Carter sucks! Forget that guy."

"You still don't get it. He'll kill me."

"Fine, fine," I sighed, which partially fogged my helmet visor. "But I hope you break free from his reign of terror. For your own sake."

"Yeah, okay, whatever."

"In the meantime, would you at least connect me with Teresa's personal cell phone?"

I leapt easily onto the roof of the Channel Four News building, and by sheer happenstance I almost landed on Teresa Triplett. She was early.

The first Teresa Triplett/Outlaw interview was considered one of the most widely-circulated news articles of all time. The paper sold out four times, and the website crashed due to heavy traffic. The notoriety launched her into the upper stratosphere of celebrity reporters, and since our conversation in March she'd also interviewed the President, Academy Award winners, Nobel Peace Prize recipients, and even the Pope.

She was wealthy now; that was obvious, even in the dark. Her clothes had gone from professional and trendy to tailored and lavish. Her hair and makeup were flawless, though I'd given her no warning. She even smelled rich.

She gasped and nearly fell over, but I caught her. She giggled nervously, and then wrapped me up into an unexpected hug. I took the opportunity to scan the rooftop. My night-vision was improving; darkness had become several shades less black, for lack of better phrasing. We were alone.

I reduced my voice to a low growl. "What's this for?"

Her voice was muffled. "I decided if I touched you immediately, I wouldn't be scared of you."

"Oh."

She released and said, "Also it was a quick moment of indulgence." She regained her composure, brushing hair back into formation. "Because of you, I have the career I always wanted. I'm very grateful you chose me for your interviews."

"This will be a short one."

"Speaking of…you don't look quite as big."

"My body can swell, like a muscle after exercise. Plus, I think people view me differently, depending on their fear level."

A cameraman stumbled onto the roof, hauling equipment. He saw me and dropped a bag. "It's him. Holy lord, it's really him."

"Rick," she said, like reassuring a child that's seen a ghost. "We're professionals. And he's nice. Get set up."

I asked, "Just the one camera?"

"As you requested. I'd do this interview in a clown suit if you asked."

Soon Rick was ready, Teresa got the cue from her producer, and we were rolling.

"This is Teresa Triplett, reporting with Channel Four News from Los Angeles. Please forgive the poor lighting, but it was a prerequisite for this interview, at the behest of the Outlaw himself, making a welcomed appearance at last. Outlaw, these are dark and scary times for us Los Angelenos. Since your warning earlier this year, our world has erupted. We're desperate to know: who *are* you, and how did you know trouble was on the horizon?"

Her question caught me off guard, and I stammered, "I'm a friend of Los Angeles. But that's not why I'm here."

"The Chemist appeared soon after our last interview, and America still doesn't know what to do about him and his terror group. What involvement do you have with him?"

"I am his enemy. Just like you. But while-"

"We have footage of you and the Chemist and others doing things that defy normal human limitation. Who are these people?"

"Teresa," I said, and I took her fist and microphone in both my hands. She tried to pull away, but my fingers were iron. Her hand shuddered and she tried suppressing fear. "You want to have a rapid-fire question and answer session. But we're not."

"The people of Los Angeles-"

I spoke over her words. "I am here for the people. And I want to speak to them." I looked into the camera, which I hoped conveyed the gravity of my careful word selection. "I bring a warning. The evil you face is stronger than you realize. Stronger than I realized. Their sinister influence has even reached members of our government and military, preventing decisive action. But the darkness will not prevail. Not if forces of good band together. I will not rely on the government, and neither should you. Good men and women must cast evil out where they find it.

"But this battle will not be won overnight. And in the meantime, you are in danger. I suggest, if you have children and you have the means to leave Los Angeles, you should."

Teresa couldn't mask her astonishment. "Evacuate? Which areas?"

"All areas. We're not just fighting the Chemist. His strength has grown, and so have his weapons. We're battling hatred and arrogance and disease and our own biases. We'll not win with brute force alone."

"Then how...how will we..."

"Leave, if you can. Otherwise, stay here with me and together we'll drive out the darkness. Together. The Outlaw doesn't fight *for* you. The Outlaw fights *with* you."

Dad gave me a high-five. "Best one yet, kiddo. I'm inspired."

Puck texted me, **>> dang Outlaw nice 1**

Lee texted me, **>> OUTLAW!!! CHASE!!! AAAAAAAAAA THAT WAS AWSOME!!!!**

Katie texted me, **>> Did you see the Outlaw interview? I love him so much.**

Natalie North texted me, **>> Goosebumps, my superhero. I have goosebumps. If I didn't have a boyfriend, you'd be in trouble tonight. =) (By the way, that was still too short. You MUST do the Time interview)**

The Chemist emailed me.

> So you are a true believer. How disappointing.
> I will enjoy breaking you.
> And Los Angeles.
> And your girlfriend.
> I'm coming for you, Brutus.
> I will discover your real name.
> I will find out where you live.
> I will knock on your door.
> I will tear down your high places.
> -Martin

His notes had become shorter. That was a bad sign, I bet.

I trudged upstairs, tired and eager for bed. Before entering, some preternatural awareness, some sensory receptor I didn't even know was active, detected movement within my room. I had a visitor.

Katie! My day just got a lot better.

A girl was under the sheets.

260

But. No. It wasn't Katie…

Like a sensual phoenix molded imperfectly and scandalously from worn clay, Hannah Walker was reclining in my bed, smiling and resting on her elbow. In the light of my lamp, her injuries appeared more severe. The virus had prevented her destruction, but her skin was thick and twisted, like a burn victim. Her smile was stretched and her eyelids didn't close properly, unable to hide the madness therein. She wasn't wearing anything other than the sheet.

"Hello quarterback."

Facts and memories began bursting like fireworks in my mind.

She doesn't know Chase Jackson is the Outlaw.

Carla said Hannah was obsessed.

And insane.

The world thinks she's dead.

She's Infected, powerful enough to bring the house down.

Dad is downstairs.

I can't call Puck or Carter for help.

The police wouldn't be able to handle her.

What on earth should I do…????

"Hello…Hannah."

"You don't seem surprised to see me." Her voice was still a painful rasp, though perhaps stronger now. I bet the virus was healing her, still.

"I'm very surprised! Just a little stunned." I sat cautiously at the head of the bed. She laid down fully, head on my pillow, looking upwards at me through lashes and short blond hair. "How are you…alive?"

"A man saved me. An amazing man. The Father."

What would Carter do? Probably kill her. What would Croc do? Or Samantha Gear? I had no idea.

She smiled, "Have you missed me?"

I answered truthfully. "I'm very *very* glad you didn't die. I cried. A lot. Are you living with your parents?"

"I just visited them."

"Good. Did they…I bet they were…how did it go?"

"Now they are dead."

Her eyes remained on mine, unblinking, shallow blue pools, clean and free from human emotion. In the air I smelled the tang of gasoline. "Is that a joke?"

"I only need one Father."

"Hannah, your parents, did you-"

"I will take you to him. To the Father."

"Have you been to a doctor? Maybe we should go see one."

"I don't need a doctor." She yawned and stretched indolently, pressing arms over her head and touching my skin with her fingers, remarkably warm. "The Father said I am Twice Chosen, doubly blessed, and I will live forever."

"The gift that will keep on giving," I mumbled.

"I slept for years and years," she sighed, "and dreamed only of you. Loving you. Marrying you. Killing you. Burning you. Kissing you. Your cheerleader. My quarterback. My future."

I had no words. My mouth moved futilely.

"Now we can be together, while all the world burns. And burns. And screams." Her eyes were mostly closed, her voice softer.

"Hannah…"

"You're not in love with anyone," she said, a trace of malice in her syllables. "I know you waited. For me."

Katie.

Did Hannah really kill her own parents? I wouldn't doubt it.

Katie.

Does Hannah remember? After we broke up, I admitted to her I loved Katie. Dear God, please let Hannah forget.

"Hannah, who knows you're still alive? Any of your old friends? Or family?"

"No," she cooed. "The Father says it is not time." She suddenly sat up, facing me. The sheet fell from her shoulders. "I cannot stay awake long, not yet. The Father told me that will change. Eventually. But you can have me. While I sleep. My quarterback."

I snatched my comforter from the floor and threw it around her. Despite the injuries, she maintained a very eye-catching physique. I pulled both sides of the comforter closed, like a robe, and she leaned against me, her head nestled under my chin, my arms around her shoulders.

"I am happy," she said. Her breath caressed my neck, and again I smelled gasoline.

"Hannah-"

"For the first time, I am happy. Please, Chase. Please don't leave me? Not again? The dreams, Chase. The fire. Please?"

I couldn't help it; tears sprang into my eyes. Hannah Walker had been a bizarre and brutal girlfriend, and gotten even worse after we broke up. And she died at least partly because of her prejudices and arrogance. And now she was insane and possibly a murderer. But...she also sounded like a frightened little girl, desperately needing to be loved.

I'm not Carter. I don't use people, don't require things of them, don't abandon them in times of need. I will be the opposite of Carter.

"I won't leave you," I said. "I will help. As best I can."

Her head nodded but she was already asleep.

A short time later, the Outlaw carried Hannah's sleeping body into Gateway, a local mental health center. She slept like a baby. The sliding doors slid open for us and the tired receptionist gaped.

I announced, "I need to speak with the doctor on duty. And we'll probably need a straightjacket."

Chapter Twenty-Five
Friday, October 22. 2018

The news broke the following day; Mr. and Mrs. Walker had been murdered in their sleep. Police had no suspects.

What do I dooooooooooo?!?! Hello, police? Yeah, the murderer is their daughter, who's been dead the past six months. She's insane and freakishly strong and will probably kill you if you wake her up.

The staff at Gateway had been very helpful, and took in Hannah based solely upon my request. I'd probably been granted extra favors due to being the Outlaw. As Katie put it, I was being given perks.

But what else could I do with her? I didn't know yet. I couldn't just ship her back to the Chemist. Hey! Keep track of your stuff!

I left a long note for her, explaining I would come visit soon, and I wasn't abandoning her, and I was so glad she was alive. I hadn't signed it, so no one would connect Chase Jackson to the Outlaw.

Speaking of the Outlaw, I was telling Katie the truth about him. About the Outlaw. Monday night, right after she broke up with Tank. Whether she freaked out or not, it was time.

Besides, she'd be fine with it. Right?

The other big news story of the day: the Los Angeles exodus began. Apparently some of the city's embattled citizens believed me, and they left. City officials estimated thirty thousand residents packed up and fled by supper time. A drop in the bucket compared to the fifteen million living in greater Los Angeles, but more would follow. City planners and politicians publicly decried the migration, labeling me a doomsayer and warning about disruptions to the local economy.

That night, we won our final football game before playing the Patrick Henry Dragons. It was an effortless affair, an easy victory, so I threw an interception to help the other team out. And to make my stats look more human.

I drove Katie home afterwards. She nibbled on my neck the whole way. "This doesn't count as kissing," she said. At her door, I returned the favor. She gasped and laughed and told me to stop and then we were kissing. Her mouth was warm and eager to please. Too soon her mom burst through the door and pushed us apart.

"No!" she scolded us. "You two wait! It is not time!"

I snuck around to the rear sliding doors, but her mom met me there too, glaring at me from the curtains like a specter. "You!" she said, stifling a smile. "I thought Chase was a gentleman! You should not sneak into young girls' bedrooms!"

"Yes ma'am," I said sheepishly. Katie was inside, giggling. "I love her. So much!"

Her face melted, and I thought she miiiiight let me in…but her resolve stiffened at the last moment, and she slammed the door closed.

The military finally retaliated at midnight, launching a full invasion. The Chemist's stronghold was assailed on three different fronts: 1) Navy SEALs and the FBI's HRT and Army Rangers all HALO jumped into Paramount; 2) the army's infantry pushed into Compton from Downtown, overwhelming forces moving en masse; and 3) the carrier strike group, parked ten miles off the California coast, launched strategic missile strikes to support the efforts.

In future history books, military experts will credit the Chemist's deeply embedded moles and spies for the disaster. The attack was anything but a surprise to the Chemist.

The army's infantry was slaughtered, a true national tragedy. Twenty thousand soldiers forced their way south without significant resistance, until the trap was fully set. Only after retreat became impossible did Walter give the signal; kill them all. Bombs and gunfire and carnage, ten city blocks wide and ten city blocks deep. The few tanks and aircraft providing support were easy prey for Walter's unending supply of rockets. After the initial massacre, Infected roamed the killing-fields like Death with his scythe, too fast to be resisted with any efficiency. The soldiers fought and died bravely, taking with them as many enemies as possible. Afterwards, in the burnt wasteland that used to be Northern Compton, fifteen thousand soldiers and two thousand terrorists lay dead, and the Chemist chuckled darkly on his throne undisturbed.

The paratroopers in Paramount fared much better, but only because the enemy willingly surrendered the territory. Paramount was retaken by America, but the price was far too high.

The media loudly wondered where the Outlaw and the Fearsome Four were during the battle. I really hated that nickname. The Outlawyer's frontman, the increasingly troublesome Priest, released a YouTube video denouncing the bloodbath as just retribution for casting aside the Outlaw.

The other question on everyone's lips - How would the Chemist respond? Surely it would be cataclysmic.

I watched the news alone the following morning, crying tears of frustration. Dad was downtown, but alive. He hadn't woken me in the middle of the night. Neither had Puck. Samantha was gone.

I texted Isaac Anderson. **WHY?? Why didn't you tell me?? We could HELP!! You need monsters to fight these monsters!!**

He replied quickly. **>> I had no idea. The government is divided, and many of us were never even notified this was coming. Impossible, but true. We haven't been this divided since Vietnam, or maybe the Civil War. Besides, despite our victories and public accolades, I'm not trusted. I'm very unpopular right now.**

That makes two of us.

Chapter Twenty-Six
Friday, October 29. 2018

Monday was supposed to be the best day of my life. In fact, I penciled that on my calendar. Katie would break up with Tank. I'd drive straight to her door and ask her out on a real date, for that very night. During the most romantic date of all time, I'd confess I was the Outlaw. She would understand and marry me on the spot.

But. Nothing goes as planned.

My intention was to trail them to Tank's condo, in case he got violent, but Katie departed during football practice without telling me. Katie's mom drove her downtown, and she was waiting for Tank when he returned from his own football practice. She dumped him in the lobby, while her mom watched from the car.

"I told him I wanted to do it in person, because I respected him so much," she told me, through her tears.

"What'd he say?"

"Nothing! He was silent. That was the creepy part."

Without word, Tank got into the elevator and left. Katie and her mom drove off, not knowing whether to laugh or cry.

Halfway home, as they exited the Five, an unmarked car side-swiped them, forcing their Camry off the road and into a cluster of palm trees. It was a hit-and-run and the perpetrator got clean away. Ms. Lopez's driver-side door caved in, breaking her shoulder. She also suffered severe seat-belt burns and a concussion. Katie was scared but unscathed.

I visited them in the hospital that night, and Katie cried while telling me the whole story. On Tuesday, Ms. Lopez came home from the hospital. On Wednesday, Katie stayed home from school.

The identity of the attacker remained a mystery. I had an educated guess, but no way to prove it.

Croc and Gear only attended classes once that week, just enough so they could play Friday night against Patrick Henry. Samantha nodded grimly when she heard the news about Katie, but she didn't respond. Croc didn't speak the whole day. Neither looked well, like they weren't sleeping. Our lunch table was a somber vacuum of joy.

Finally, Friday.

In the sports world, our showdown became national news thanks to Tank's freakish and historic season (and partly thanks to mine, despite my best efforts). The Dragons were the number one ranked 5A team, with ten players receiving full scholarships to division-one college teams. My team, the Eagles, were ranked number five. The winner would move on to state play-offs as the heavy favorite.

Rumors circulated that after the game, assuming the Dragons won, during the pageants and celebrations and confetti, Tank would officially sign a letter-of-intent to play at USC.

I wanted to rain on that parade.

Our school bus lumbered into the city, traveling against the outbound congestion. Another ten thousand were taking to their heels, families leaving Los Angeles behind, heading for greener pastures. With dour satisfaction I watched the traffic, much of which had luggage strapped to the roof, through the bus window.

Samantha spoke up from the adjacent seat. "I think it was a good idea."

Her voice startled me; she hadn't spoken since Wednesday. Croc sat beside her, eyes closed, listening to music through headphones. "What was?"

"Telling people to abandon the city."

"What did Carter think?"

"Didn't care. He's moved on. Cat's out of the bag, so to speak."

I glanced at Cory, sitting next to the window. He was absorbed in a game on his phone, not paying attention.

I asked her, "Is Carter still planning on leaving?"

"This weekend. Maybe Monday."

"Why are you talking now? Are you no longer mad at me?"

"*Mad* at you?" To my absolute astonishment, her eyes welled up. An actual tear! I didn't know Samantha could cry. "Wow. Sometimes I forget that you know nothing."

Our bus plunged into the shadow of downtown canyons. Soon, Dragon banners began adorning the storefronts. Green and black bedecked fans streamed in increasing numbers towards the stadium. We lurched into the parking lot and police were forced to push back Dragon fanatics, booing and screaming at us. The coaches and players scampered off the bus and hurried into the visiting team's tunnel as rotten fruit rained down, splattering the pavement with pulp gore. Samantha cackled and taunted them, pirouetting and side-stepping the aerial bombardment.

The stadium was massive. A fitting home for Tank. I felt like a human sacrifice being led into the temple bowels. In the locker room, the team stared at the ceiling, envisioning the over-whelming assemblage it would take to make these walls shake. We dressed silently.

Coach addressed us, reviewed the game plan, and we marched out for warm-ups, greeted with swirling jeers. The early fans laughed and caterwauled. The grass was painted in sick shades of green and black, and seats rose to the sky, preventing direct sunlight. Soon, Hidden Spring Eagle fans began populating the visitor section.

My ears pricked when Katie arrived. She came with friends who sheltered and escorted her to safe seats. News broke yesterday about her breakup with Tank, and she'd been ripped apart on social media for twenty-four hours straight, by both the Dragon fans and wanna-be celebrity gossip blogs. For her safety, I wish she hadn't come.

There were two fights before the game started, both requiring security intervention. Croc and Samantha stood at my shoulders, watching the tussle in the seats.

"These people are idiots," Samantha grumbled.

Croc grinned. "Chockers with dills and dogs."

I had no idea what that meant, and I didn't ask. The crowd roared with delight as Tank finally made his appearance.

He looked like an NBA player standing among middle-schoolers, almost comical. The size differential would be funny if he hadn't injured multiple players in every game so far, some of them severely. He wasn't nineteen yet, but he would already be the biggest kid on his *college* football team.

Tank! Tank! Tank! Tank! Tank! Tank!

Samantha noted, "Carter says he's pretty much indestructible once his adrenaline is flowing. Strongest person on earth."

Croc winked. "Maybe we can drown the drungo."

"That'd work. Too bad we're in a drought."

The National Anthem was sung. The crowd belted the song too, one big happy American family. Or not. Soon the referees would call for team captains, but Tank was already there, standing alone at mid-field. Just like last year.

I'd been dreading this.

The crowd screamed and began calling for me. Me! By name! *Jack-son! Jack-son! Jack-son! Jack-son!*

Croc had to shout, "What's going on, mate?"

"He did this last year too," I grunted, grabbing my helmet. "Sort of like a challenge."

The fever was already burning in Croc's eyes. "I don't like this."

"Just a game." My mouth twisted into a lopsided and unhappy grin. "Right?"

I left the sidelines and teammates behind, and trotted out to meet Tank. I tried to ignore the forty-thousand-person mob stacked over my head going bonkers.

"I know you took her!" he shouted before I got to him. His eyes were red, his face strained, and his muscles appeared to be constantly flexing and relaxing and flexing. He was...insane. "I know you took her from me!"

"And I know you ran her off the road!" I shot back.

"Did not."

"Then you paid someone who did!!"

"I know you stole her. On purpose!" Spittle flew from his mouth. Tank was usually a very handsome kid, but not right now.

"Katie can make up her own mind. She doesn't need my help."

"I told you I loved her!" The crowd was quieting, probably hoping to hear our conversation, and they would if he kept shouting. "I wasn't ever going to hurt her!"

"You already did! That's one of the differences between us."

"No difference," he snarled. "We the same."

"No. You had to possess her. Own her. But I don't. I love her, no matter what. We're *not* the same."

Tears were flowing freely down his cheeks. He placed a big gloved hand over his left ear and pressed, wincing, like he was ignoring a siren. "We the same."

"You're in pain. Aren't you. Your mind. You need help, Tank. Talk to me after the game, and I'll do what I can."

"The game. Just a game." He chuckled, shook his head, and then pulled his helmet on. "Kids die during football games all the time. Just a game."

Finally the referees approached and called for captains. All the players slapped hands, except Tank and I. We faced off, fuming and hating.

The Eagles won the coin-toss and elected to receive. The Dragons kicked but our returner, a kid named Gavin, couldn't field it properly. He was pelted with single-A batteries from the stands. The game suspended temporarily as the batteries were retrieved and police investigated.

Then we got the ball and the game began, at last.

Our whole plan was based around Tank. Stay away from the beast. If he lined up to our right, we would run or pass left, and vise-versa. No one could block him, not even Cory, so we wouldn't even try. Last year, Coach Garrett told us, "Keep Tank away from Chase!" This year, he told us, "Don't worry about Tank! Beat your man and Chase will keep the ball away from him."

It worked for a few plays. We didn't need to change the plan at the line of scrimmage; we all knew. Tank lined up to our *left*, so I hiked the ball, the players crashed into one another, our running back sprinted to the *right*. He gained seven yards before Tank and the Dragon linebackers wrestled him down. Tank lined up to our right, so I passed to Josh Magee on the left. Thirteen yards. Again and again, up the field, automatically moving away from Tank, who bellowed like a bull, enraged and impotent.

The Dragon coach sent in new orders: Tank, line up in the middle!

"Hike!" I called, and Tank vaulted *over* my offensive line. He easily chased down Gavin and knocked the wind out of him. Next play, new running back, same result. Pow! Just like that, we were going backwards. Next play, we had to pass, but Tank gave me no time. He came howling like a freight train; pass or die. I threw it early, and he shoved me down anyway. Incomplete.

Samantha kicked an absurdly easy fifty-yard field goal and the Eagles took a 3-0 lead. Eagle fans yelled and cheerleaders danced. Our team congratulated each other, all except Coach, me, Samantha and Croc.

"How we gonna stop *that*?" I asked. My jersey was already dirty, which hadn't happened much this year.

Coach Garrett chomped ardently on his gum. "Working on it, kid."

"I got ideas, if yours don't work."

Croc and the defense took the field. So did Tank. Unlike last year, Tank now played both offense and defense. He was the state's leading defender *and* rusher, an absurd fact.

Tripping him was the only option opponents had, and it usually required the whole team. Photos in newspapers captured Tank running with six defenders clinging on. But those teams didn't have Croc.

Croc prowled the field, using intuition to delve the run's direction and then attacking. He was no match for Tank physically, but time and again he dove at Tank's shoes, wrapped them up and spun him down while other Eagles piled on.

"Learned it Down Under," he would pant later. "Gotta hogtie cattle!"

Despite Croc's best efforts, the Dragons moved down the field. Tank's rushes were reduced from fifteen yards per carry (against other teams) down to four (against Croc). But still. That was a lot of yards, and Croc's vaunted pass-defense was completely absent, so focused was he on Tank.

Tank rumbled and stumbled into the end zone six minutes later. Touchdown Dragons. The fanatics frothed and roared and threw debris onto the field in celebration.

Touchdoooooooooown Dragons!

"He's a battler! That's bloody hard business!" Croc laughed, limping off the field. "And it didn't even work!"

"It worked, buddy," Garrett said. "That lasted almost seven minutes. Usually takes them ninety seconds. Keep it up, kid, and we got a chance. He'll fumble eventually."

"God, I don't want to lose," Samantha muttered.

We took the field again. Coach put a running back to either side of me and kept the three receivers split wide. "You can toss or throw it either way, just don't get killed, kiddo!"

I had about one second each play. One second to evaluate what Tank would do and then respond. One second to decide and throw. One second to decide and toss. One second before Tank could murder me legally within the rulebook.

We inch-wormed down the field. Our plan wasn't elegant or particularly effective. In fact it was exhausting. But it worked well enough to get within field goal range, and we only suffered one injury: Rawls, the back-up running back (Tank wrenched his leg out of socket, which I didn't know was possible). Between plays, Tank pounded through his helmet at his left ear. He was in pain, or hearing voices. Samantha kicked another field goal, narrowly missing Tank's fingers as he leapt to block it.

The Dragons got the ball and ended the half by scoring another touchdown. 14-6, Dragons were winning. Each team only got the ball twice, a shockingly low number, because the drives took so long.

In the locker room, Coach Garrett clapped and railed and encouraged the troops. The three of us freaks sat in the back and put our heads together.

"This isn't fair," Samantha sighed. "This is a game for teenagers, being decided by monsters."

"Too right."

I whispered, "But if the three of us don't play, all the normal teenagers will get killed by Tank."

"We're going to lose anyway," she grouched.

I said, "I got an idea."

"Which is?"

"I'm going to play defense."

Both teams stormed back onto the field, red and green armies invading the same territory. The crowd raved and heaved. The Dragons got the ball first.

I grabbed Caleb by the arm. He was a safety but he was terrified of Tank and reluctant to tackle him. I barked, "Caleb, sit this one out. I'm going in."

He was so startled and relieved that he made no objection. Croc and I jogged onto the field and into position. It was such an unexpected move that Coach Garrett didn't even notice. Nor the crowd. Nor Tank.

"Ready brother?" Croc called.

"I'm going to enjoy this."

The alignments looked odd from this side. But at least I finally got to hit someone.

The Dragons hiked the ball and shoved it into Tank's arms. He leapt forward, a 375-pound sprinter. From experience, he was ready for Croc. But he wasn't ready for me.

Boom! I put my shoulder into his ribs like a battering ram and sent him stumbling backwards. His arms flew upwards in surprise.

The ball! The ball came free!

Fumble!

Nothing is as dehumanizing as the animal-pile on top of a loose football, all claws and gouging and screaming. Relatively sane kids turn into werewolves and zombies, bloodthirsty and desperate.

The Eagles recovered and the stadium groaned in disbelief. Tank had fumbled?! He wanted to come after me and tear my head off, but couldn't; the refs were watching and he'd be ejected. Instead he issued a Jurassic Park roar that sent Croc and I scampering back to our sidelines.

Garrett yapped at me, "The hell you think you're doing??!"

"Helping, Coach!" I grinned. "You're welcome."

"You're too valuable! You can't play defense. We need you for the next game."

"Won't be a next game if we lose! By the way, I'm installing Croc as my fullback. You call the plays, but I need him." Before he could sputter a reply, Croc and I joined the huddle on the field. Our offensive players cheered and pounded him on the back.

Tiny little 195-pound Croc couldn't stop Tank, but he slowed him down. On the first play, Tank came barreling over our line and Croc met him midair; the collision sounded like boulders breaking. Instead of having one second, now I had two. Maybe three. An eternity to throw or run. We started gaining more yards. After each play I pulled Croc out of the dirt. He rose gingerly but with a smile on his face.

"Most fun I ever had, mate!"

Four plays later, Gavin ducked his head and shoved across the goal line.

Touchdown Eagles...

14-13, Dragons still winning. Our contingent of fans was delirious.

Croc looked like he'd been wrestling a tornado. His jersey was torn and unrecognizable from dirt, and his hands and face were bleeding. I knew the vast host of cameras were enjoying his embattled figure; he'd always been photogenic, and now he was a sports hero too.

Samantha told him pointedly, "You keep this up, Mitch, and I might be tempted to rub ointment all over your body later."

"Only on our honeymoon, sheila!"

Dragons' ball again. This time Tank was ready. He stomped on Croc and went through me like a Peterbuilt diesel truck. Our impact was so violent I thought he crushed my soul. I tripped him from the ground, and the Eagles piled on but Tank still fell for the first down.

I could *hear* Katie holding her breath. Not possible, but I could.

Croc and I got back on our feet and did it again. Again he crushed us, almost breaking free for a touchdown. Our combined weight wasn't much more than his. Another Eagle defender limped to the sidelines, this one holding his shoulder.

Croc grinned wearily. "A corker, ain't he."

Coach Garrett paced the sidelines, fists in his hair, watching his quarterback get steamrolled play after play. Samantha clapped and cried encouragement. There's no way she could help; it would arouse too much suspicion.

We battled to a stalemate and the Dragons kicked a field goal. 17-13, Dragons.

Samantha helped shove chocolate granola bars and apples into our mouths during a pause in the action. "Doing good, boys! Keep it up!"

I gasped, "Why isn't Tank getting tired??"

"Samantha, love," Croc said and placed his hand into hers. "Pop my finger back into place, yeah? I get a little squeamish."

Back onto the field. We bashed and crashed and exchanged punts, moving deep into the fourth quarter. Time wound down and so did our energy, even Tank's. He moved like a tired lion with a limp. Neither team could score, and Samantha kept booming punts far into the night.

The Eagles got the ball back with two minutes left.

"Do or die, boys," I croaked in the huddle, all of us bloody and broken. Cory's eye was swollen shut from an illegal punch.

"Let's go!" Brad Atkinson yelled. "I want to live forever!"

"Meh," Croc panted. "S'not that great."

The final drive was a legendary contest of wills, two minutes of valiant blocking, tackling and running for our lives. Katie would tell me later that, during the last quarter of the game, a mounting sense of apprehension settled over the stadium, an awareness that maybe something else was happening other than a mere football championship. The crowd no longer watched Tank, entranced and entertained, like they once had. Instead, the colossus on the turf, flinging around healthy young men, caused a sense of dread and sick apprehension. Perhaps he was more than just a genetically gifted giant. Something wasn't *right*.

"Last play of the game," Coach Garrett chomped and grinned anxiously. "Ten yards from a touchdown. Ten yards from victory. Want to run it in?

You haven't done that yet."

I took a deep breath and said, "No. I want to throw it to Josh, in the end zone. Let the normal kids decide the outcome."

"Normal kids?"

I nodded, still trying to catch my breath. "I'll throw it up. Whichever team catches it deserves the victory."

"Hell, son, just make it a good throw."

"You got it."

The stadium bawled and thundered, with the players at the base of a massive noise funnel. The world shook beyond my facemask. Katie was whispering prayers and chewing on her thin silver necklace.

Tank dug in like a bull. He wanted to decide this game, to beat me himself. I wasn't going to let him.

"Hike!" I cried.

Tank and Croc crunched in midair again, fighting and shoving, all kicks, claws and wrath.

The two lines smacked together.

Linebackers howled and raced to cover the running backs.

Josh Magee zipped towards the far corner of the end zone. I lofted the pass towards him, a full half-second before Tank reached me.

He hit me anyway, a tsunami washing over a hill, and we both toppled.

Time expired.

The ball floated forever, arcing over intrusive fingers.

Josh Magee wanted it more. He out-jumped the Dragon defender, hauled the ball in, and landed on his back for a touchdown.

Game over. 19-14, Eagles victory.

We won!

The Dragon band stayed quiet. The prepped fireworks were doused. No eruption of confetti.

And no time for celebration. Tank released a peal of frustrated rage, grabbed me by the facemask, and Threw me. I mean, *Threw* me! My neck popped painfully and I soared. The stadium spun end over end, ground sky ground sky ground sky, until I landed forty yards away at midfield with an awkward, "*Oof!*" My impact shoveled up a thick divot in the ground.

The stadium rang in stunned horror. That wasn't possible. Not even close. Not even human.

Tank grabbed Croc's limp body by the ankle and hurled him like a discus into the Eagle bench, scattering coaches and players, defying human limitations.

He can't do that! He shouldn't be able to do that!

A monster among us!

Madness! The crowd panicked. Dragon coaches timidly tried calming Tank. The loud-speaker announcer stumbled through his post-game rituals. Police came stomping down the stadium steps.

"No no no," I groaned, watching the world's reaction; pure fear. "Tank, no!"

He raised a terrified referee by the throat and started to squeeze, but that's when Samantha Gear arrived. She carried a football helmet by the facemask in each fist, and she cracked one against Tank's skull. The impact sounded like a gunshot. He dropped the referee as the second helmet shattered against his temple, black and red Eagle colors. He hit her, a sucker punch, and she tumbled backwards into the Dragon coaching staff, who now slowly retreated.

I finally got to my feet. Croc was still trying. This was a disaster. A nightmare. Tank was revealed, unmasked, Infected. And he made us all look like aggressive barbarians. Fiendish demons. The cameras still rolled and thousands watched, but we had to stop him. No other choice.

We police ourselves, Carter once told me.

Tank's quasi-normal life was over. He was a Hyper Human. Thousands knew it. Soon millions. No college scholarships. No professional football.

I had no energy. No more muscle power. But Tank had to be running low, too. I hoped.

Before I could move, an eerie high-pitched scream throttled through the nearest tunnel, a piercing siren that silenced all other sounds. The echo bounced around like ghosts in the bleachers.

What the heck?? What was *that*?

Through the tunnel came a little girl. No, regular-sized girl. She just looked little. It was one of our cheerleaders. Soaking wet, like she'd walked through a waterfall.

She came onto the field, this streaming, angry girl. We all watched warily, even Tank. Something about her.

Uh oh. Oh no.

Hannah Walker's chest was heaving, her baleful eyes fixed solidly on Tank. "Stay. Away. From him," she whispered, spitting water with each word.

How'd she get out of the hospital?!

She had a lighter. What was she…

That wasn't water.

"Hannah no!" I cried. Too late. She flicked the flint. The spark caught, and the gasoline lit. Whoosh! She blazed to life. An immediate conflagration, an inferno-shaped cheerleader.

The crowd screamed again, but not louder than Hannah's angry ear-splitting cry. She Moved, a comet streaking across the field, a banshee trailing ash and vapors, far too fast to be human.

Tank was too agitated to dodge. The fireball launched herself and grabbed onto his upper body. Bright coils of fire splashed off the struggling pair. She held fast, like napalm, as Tank bellowed and pried uselessly at the slippery figure clinging and biting him.

"Showers!" I cried, hurrying closer. "Tank, get to the showers!" Hannah was protecting me!!?

He couldn't hear. He and Hannah were both making too much noise. An Infected once told me our hardened bodies could be burned to death. It was happening right before my eyes!

Police and coaches tried to tackle them with jackets but Tank bolted. No way he'd be stopped or caught, speeding like a smoldering torch from the field. I was too exhausted to chase. They disappeared into the stadium bowels but his screaming remained long after.

Chapter Twenty-Seven
Sunday, October 31. 2018

Samantha Gear

The whole freaking world was talking about the football fiasco. Puck sent me a constant stream of news updates that I didn't bother reading. The planet, apparently, was coming apart at the seams with this new fresh devil. Now we had to hear about the Chemist's terror group of mutants, the Outlaw and his band of merry mutants, and the football mutant.

Ugh. No thanks.

Tank was missing. So was Hannah. No one knew where they went, not even Puck. The city's over-taxed law enforcement offices launched a massive manhunt for the enormous Kid Who Defied Physics. The acrid smell of burnt flesh was almost potent enough to track. But I didn't want to try. I wanted to get out of here.

And that was the plan. Tomorrow. We'd fly out of Van Nuys, a private airport on a private jet.

If I can get Chase to come. And that's a big If. Otherwise I'm not sure what I'll do.

I drove to Chase's house that evening. First time since the big fall-out with Carter; I couldn't bear to face the piercing truthfulness of the Outlaw. His innate trust in me, his innocent belief, flayed me alive and stripped my professional defenses.

It was Halloween and half the kids in Los Angeles dressed like the Outlaw. I carefully wove around the late Trick-or-Treaters and parked in his driveway. Chase sat on his front porch with a bag of candy, staring southwest toward towers in the dying light. Of COURSE he'd be giving candy to kids.

"Come to say goodbye?" he called.

I slammed the heavy truck door and said, "We don't leave until tomorrow afternoon."

"Ah."

"And you're handing out candy."

"Yep," he nodded and took a long unsteady breath. "And working up the courage to tell Katie. About the Outlaw. About everything."

"Tonight?"

"Yes. Finally."

Wow. This would be huge. I kinda wanted to tag along. Maybe PuckDaddy would record it for me. Although I'm not sure why I cared. But I did.

"I'm nervous."

I laughed. "I don't blame you."

"She didn't handle the news well, about Tank being Infected. Pretty disturbed."

"That's different. Katie loves you, and she's a smart girl. You've always fought for her. She'll see that."

He changed the subject. "Whither shall you travel?"

"Whither?"

"Yes. It means, 'to where.' I've been working on English homework. Whither shall you and Carter's consortium travel?"

"We're flying to Houston." I sat beside him, wincing. My facial fractures needed a few more hours of knitting. Tank threw a mean left hook.

"Houston?"

"I want you to come with us."

He chuckled and presented candy bars to two approaching little kids, one ghost and one Outlaw. He said, "I like your costumes!" They waved and walked off with their father. Chase mumbled, "That's what I've seen tonight. Vampires and zombies and skeletons and Darth Vader and the Outlaw. All monsters."

"Think about it, Chase. Carter would welcome you back. I know he would. Give you a job. An identity. A team."

"I don't need Carter to provide those things."

"Chase-"

His voice was urgent, full of concern. "You don't need him either. You're stronger than him. He's just mystery and shadow and money. Nothing real."

"You said it yourself. You're a kid in high school. But I'm not. This is my life."

"Waiting around for Carter to beckon so you can go murder another kid isn't a life, Samantha."

His words were like a slap. I recoiled away from him and my eyes stung.

"Besides," he continued, "do you want to work for a maniac? A maniac that terrifies you?"

"Better to work with him than against him. What would you suggest I do?"

"Stay here. Los Angeles needs you."

I shook my head. "Los Angeles is lost, Chase."

"I disagree."

"The Chemist will attack in the next day or two and destroy as much as he can. He has the firepower and manpower and there's nothing we can do about it. Then he'll withdraw before the might of the American military can fully focus against him, and he'll relocate to Houston."

"How do you know this?" He was alarmed. He ground his teeth and his muscles swelled.

"Carter has sources. The Chemist is going to Houston next, the biggest port in southern America. We think he's planning on leveling Los Angeles as an example, and then declaring Houston an independent province where Infected can roam free, instead of hide. He's going to bully his way into a new kingdom. That's our best guess."

"Impossible." He picked a piece of fuzz from his pants and threw it into the grass. The muscles in his arms bunched and coiled, like thick knotty ropes. "The people of Houston won't let him. They'll kick him out."

"The people of Los Angeles haven't."

"We're not done yet!" he snapped at me. "Samantha, I'm not leaving until I know the city is safe. Understand? This is my home. And it's yours, too."

"No it's not," I scoffed. "I've lived here less than a year."

"Oh yeah? Then where is your home?"

"I told you. I have two. One in Atlanta-"

"And one in Germany, I know. But I didn't ask where you keep your stuff. I didn't ask where you have houses or apartments. Where is your *home?*"

"I don't...I mean, I'm not..."

"Our home is wherever our family is." He tapped himself on the chest, just below the hollow of his throat. "I'm your family, Samantha. Me and Puck. And Katie and Lee. And Dad. We're your home."

"Jeez, Chase," I grumbled, and I pressed the heels of my hands into my eyes as they began to burn. Something deep inside me ached. I didn't want to leave.

"Carter is no better than the Chemist. He wants to use you up, advancing his agenda. You belong with me. Not with him."

"Carter is a hard man. But he's not an evil one."

He chuckled but his eyes remained flat. "That's what the Chemist's henchmen say about their boss, too."

"What would I even do here? After this is all over? I'd need a job."

"Are you kidding? You'd be the best cop on earth."

I grinned. "I'd be pretty good at that."

"Holy crap, yes. Two months flat, crime would stop cold. Besides, I think the Chemist is right about one thing; we shouldn't be hiding. You were born with traits that others don't have. You could use them to make money. Probably a lot of money. Legally."

I shook my head. We were getting side-tracked. "But Chase, in the meantime. There's a megalomaniac out there. And he's dying. And he wants you to be the face of his new empire. And our best chance of getting him is in Houston. Then life can go back to normal."

Before he could argue, the breeze shifted and tossed strands of his hair. He froze. His eyes sharpened and he stood up. I felt it too. The falling dusk air carried something new. The hairs on my neck rose in alarm. There was…something…

"Do you feel that?" he whispered.

"Yeah. One of us. An Infected."

He closed his eyes, tilting his head and inhaling deeply. He held it a long moment, let it out, and said, "Tank."

I can move fast, but nothing compared to Chase.

We Moved, bolting toward Katie's. I'm not sure Chase touched the ground. Tank's distinct odor, mixed with seared flesh, became stronger as we neared. Most trick-or-treaters had gone home, thankfully.

Tank was behind Katie's, about to leave. He had a struggling bundle of sheets hefted over one shoulder. His appearance was gruesome. Second and third degree burns coated his shoulders and face, some leaking puss, discolored and swollen. Much of his hair was missing.

The crosshairs of my .45 Beretta locked onto his left eye-socket. Our only chance. The other eye was caked shut, a coagulated mess. He backed defensively into the bricks, growling.

Chase asked, "Kidnapping again? Didn't you already try that?"

The pile of sheets squeaked, "Chase?!"

Tank spoke in a rattle, "Not kidnapping. Just want to talk without that bitch of a mother screaming at me."

"Fine," I said, and I thumbed the hammer back. Unnecessary but effective. The clicking sound is so sexy. "Put her down and let's talk."

"Did you hurt her mom?"

"Ain't hurt nobody, pajamas. And I won't. This between me and her."

"No chance, Tank." Chase was furious, his voice a low and dangerous whisper. "You can't have her. Not again."

"Ain't like last time," Tank woofed. He was getting angrier too. Could be a problem. "Don't want to fight. Just talk."

Katie's muffled voice, "*Last* time??! What last time??"

"You two little people sure you want to do this? You can't win. I know that now." His voice caught, and he closed his one good eye in pain and frustration. "Not even sure I *can* die."

"I'll think of something. Put her down."

I kept my gun trained on him, but I needed to call for reinforcements. We couldn't beat him, not just the two of us. There'd never been an Infected like him before.

"Tank," Chase said, "You need a doctor. Like, serious medical care. I will help you. I swear I will."

To my relief, he dropped Katie onto the grass, against the wall. The sheets fell away from her head. There she was, a cocoon with a beautiful face. I hated Katie for making me love her.

"This wasn't your business," Tank said. "Just wanted to talk, hero. Didn't want to fight. Now, no choice."

"Chase, Samantha," Katie panted, tears pooling in her eyes. "Call the police! Please! He's too strong."

"Police?" Tank chuckled, giving Chase a long, penetrating glance. "She still ain't know the awful truth about you?"

"I will tell her. Not you."

"Let's tell her together," he grinned. Once handsome, his face was now twisted and splotchy. I almost pulled the trigger then. Almost.

Katie asked, "Tell me what?"

"Lover Boy here is a liar," Tank said. "A secret keeper."

"Tank," Chase groaned, raking nails through his hair. He appeared wildly anxious, and kept glancing at Katie. "Please. Maybe this could be the one area of my life you don't try to ruin?"

"Can't trust him, Katie." Tank shook his head. "Not who he says he is. He's a fraud and a coward. Lies to you. Constantly."

"Chase, what-"

"Katie." Chase took a big breath. Let it out. Then he took another one. Oh wow. Now *I* was nervous. "I returned your phone that night."

285

"My phone?"

"A year ago. When it was stolen? I got it back. It was me on that video. Wearing a stupid mask."

She didn't speak. Just stared.

"It's been me all along. I didn't know how to tell you. And then the whole charade got bigger and out of hand. I took you jumping on rooftops. That was me." He was crouching now, fixing her hair, pushing it behind her ears. His fingers trembled. "I almost kissed you then, but Samantha shot me."

"Oh yeah!" I laughed at the sudden memory. "Forgot about that. ...sorry."

"Samantha shot...how did...Chase, what?"

He continued. "I visited you. With the mask. We sat behind those pine trees and talked and you rested your head on my shoulder."

She glanced at the pines, nodding, stunned.

"It's me." He pulled out the bandana and mask. "I was born weird. My abnormalities cause me to do weird stuff. Like put on masks. I'm the Outlaw."

Katie's eyes were large pools, capturing and holding Chase and all the galaxy within. As always when she truly looked at Chase, a rosy patina settled into her cheeks. Finally, at last, the truth was open between them. Their faces were close and the sheets rose and fell with her deep breathing. Her lips slowly turned up into the most magnificent smile I've ever seen. She was so beautiful it hurt.

"Really?"

He nodded. "Really."

"Both of the men I love are found within the same man?"

"If you'll still have me, we're both yours."

"This is the hottest thing ever. Why did you not tell me?"

The moment was forcibly wrenched from them. I made a mistake. I was distracted. I cared too much. I let my guard down. And Tank took advantage. Before I knew it, he had my pistol and my fist in his huge hand. His other hand was around my neck, easily raising me off the ground, squeezing. No air! I hit and kicked but it was useless. He was a statue made out of tempered steel.

Katie cried, "Samantha!"

Chase spun. Tank crushed the pistol until my fingers popped out of socket.

"You took everything from me!" Tank roared. "An eye for an eye!"

A new voice interrupted us. Lee!? Cute little Lee ran around the corner, wearing an Outlaw vest, and cried, "Not while I'm around, bitch! Bam!" He shut one eye, raised something that looked like a pistol, and fired.

In his surprise, Tank released me just as the electroshock projectile connected with his chest. Lee's handheld device transferred a high-voltage current through the wire and into Tank's body, an instantaneous bolt of lightning. A bright pop of blue energy, and it was over.

It was too much for Tank. The distress, the football championship, the injuries, the heartbreak, and now the electricity. He was felled like a mighty tree, unconscious.

"Oh crap. I killed him, dude."

"No, you didn't," I coughed and gagged. "He'll live. And I need one of your toys."

Katie wondered, "Samantha, where'd you get a gun?"

Lee cried, "She's the Los Angeles Sniper, baby! And I'm the Outlaw's sidekick! Waaahoooo!!" He pumped his fist and started dancing around Tank's prone body. "In your face! In your face!"

Chase picked up Katie, cocoon and all, and held her close, her face in the crook of his neck. No more distractions. No more lies. A union of souls. I pretended I wasn't jealous of her beauty. I pretended I wasn't jealous of their white hot happiness.

I flexed my fist, realigning bones and joints, and used my other hand to make a phone call. A familiar voice answered and I rasped, "Richard. Come to Katie's apartment. We've got Tank. He needs to be restrained. Bring…bring everything you got."

"And a doctor," Chase called. "He's hurt."

I sighed, "And I suppose a doctor. But seriously, you'll need every elasticuff you have. And chains. And tranquilizers. And the biggest straightjacket on the planet. I'm not joking, Richard. Chains."

Richard and two squad cars arrived. The four grown men worked quickly. They bound Tank's wrists together, behind his back. And, because I demanded it, his forearms. Then they pinned Tank's arms tightly against his torso. Six elasticuffs so far. Next, his ankles. And finally, two cuffs connected his ankles and wrists.

He was trussed like a chicken. And it wasn't enough.

He woke, flexed, and snapped one of the forearm locks.

The cops panicked. Richard calmly drew his X26 stun-gun, but I got there first. I pressed the big barrel of a shotgun into the soft flesh under Tank's jaw and switched the safety off. He froze.

("Whoa! How'd she get my shotgun?" the cop yelped. Richard lied, "I gave it to her. Now shut up.")

"Tank," I said reasonably, "I pull this trigger and your brain turns to jelly. It'll be noisy and messy. And you'll be dead."

He made a soft noise.

"You've lost this round. You understand that. Right? I'd rather not kill you."

Another quiet sound.

Chase knelt by him. "You need help. I promise I'll come explain things as soon as I can. Our fight is over."

Another noise. It was a whimper. He was crying. This mountain was leaking tears.

"Hurts," he said. "Everything. All of it. Hurts."

"Tank," I said. "Did you kill that cheerleader? The girl on fire?"

"Told me," he spoke between great shuddering sobs, "burning me to help Chase. Screaming. Fire. To protect him. Burning. Hurts."

"Is she dead?"

"Don't know. Hope so."

Richard spoke. "I don't want to transfer him in a squad car."

"Smart move," I said. "He could tear it apart."

Richard ordered a flatbed truck. Six men hefted Tank and laid him on the cold, hard slab. A heavy chain was crisscrossed five times over his inert figure and cranked tight. The eighteen-year-old kid was being treated like Godzilla. Made sense though; he was the only living Infected the government had. Richard was part of the Hyper Human apprehension team, and this capture would surely bolster his career.

One of the uniformed cops called, "Detective, the office just radioed. News chopper inbound."

"Fantastic," he grumbled. "Load up. I don't want our caravan escorted the whole way with a spotlight. Ryan, you're riding in back with a taser."

The cops jumped into action, and Richard walked our way. He eyeballed all of us in turn. I tried not to preen.

"Nice job...kids." He put a thick hand on my shoulder and squeezed. It was warm and strong, and I wondered how long it'd been since I was touched like that.

"Thanks Dad," Chase grinned.

"I zapped him, Mr. J! Zap Pow, baby!" Lee demonstrated.

"Well done, Lee. Saved the day." Richard looked at me then. I fidgeted. "I'm in over my head. I know it. You know it. You'll let me know how I can keep him locked up?"

I nodded, thrilled he wanted my help. "I'll call you later."

"Or swing by. I have a lot of questions."

"Okay...I'll swing by. Still have stuff in your guest bedroom anyway."

Chase groaned under his breath.

Chapter Twenty-Eight
Monday, November 1. 2018

Katie and I stayed up late talking. And kissing. Lots of kissing. That night, her perfume, her soft neck and shoulders, her lips, was pure magic.

She had questions about everything. I answered them all honestly, anything to prolong the enchantment. We talked about the Infected, and Tank, and Samantha, and the Chemist, and my headaches, and my mask, and the future. She insisted on strapping the mask to my face, which quickly led to another bout of intense making out.

After all the years. After all the longing. After all the lies. Finally we belonged to each other. Every second that our lips weren't touching felt wasted.

Her mother had not been hurt, just knocked unconscious. She recovered, iced the back of her head for several hours, and then shooed me out the backdoor at two in the morning.

I barely slept, and then shattered my alarm clock on accident when it blared to life at six.

Puck texted me as I dressed for school.

>> hey dummy Carter is on his way
On his way to my house??
>> yes he wants u to know he comes in peace. no fighting
Thanks for the heads-up.
>> hey man. just so u know. Ive decided whatever happens,
PuckDaddy will keep in touch with u. my allegiance is 2 both u and

carter he will just hafta be pissd. But. i might need 2 live with u if he gets mad. need protection

That'd be AWESOME! Definitely. Come live with me.

>> was just a joke. PuckDaddy is a loner

Carter arrived four minutes later. Dad wasn't home yet. I met Carter in the yard; no way that creep was coming into my home again. The early morning was foggy and crisp, and my grass was damp with dew.

He greeted me by saying, "I'm withdrawing my protection from Los Angeles."

I shrugged. "Wasn't doing a lot of good anyway."

He ignored the insult. Usually he dressed in simple black tactical clothes. Today he wore a duster, similar to the Chemist's trench coat. His hands were shoved into the pockets. His truck was idling. "You pack your stuff now, you can come with us. Jet goes wheels-up in ninety minutes."

"Not leaving until the job is done. This is my home."

"Job here is finished. He's going to ruin as much as he can in the next twenty-four hours, and then he's gone. Activity is ramping up in Houston. We'll be ready."

The next twenty-four hours?? Felt like I'd been kicked in the stomach. Today. He was attacking today.

I asked, "Ruin as much as he can? What's his plan?"

"Don't know. Don't care. Couldn't stop him if we wanted. Got his hands on too much firepower."

"Can't we-"

"We're not public defenders, boy. There's six of us. And he's got hundreds. Can't play defense. We'll go offensive in Houston. Plan hasn't changed. Cut the head off the dragon."

"We need a better plan."

He shook his head, and his fists flexed in his pockets. "Not open for debate."

"Because you're the boss?"

"Because I'm the boss."

"The boss of what, Carter?" I snapped. "You're the boss of nothing. Your team barely knows each other. And collectively you accomplish zilch. Tell

291

me one good thing you guys have done in the past ten years."

"We take care of our own-"

"No you don't! You bully them into doing what you want. Else you kill them. You recruit new members into a disjointed team used to further your personal shadowy operations."

He did not like being interrupted. He boiled quietly for a moment, and I made a note to let him finish next time. No reason to get my teeth kicked in.

"You know nothing about me, hero," he spoke through a clenched jaw. "Or how I use the Infected."

"Shouldn't use them at all."

He grinned, a wicked twist of his bloodless lips. "If Martin gets his hands on you, you'll develop a new understanding of *being used*. You'll be used to kill thousands. Maybe millions."

"No chance." I spoke confidently while shivering on the insides. Millions.

"His biochemists and DNA scientists have made incredible leaps in DNA transference. You'll have new mental processes *implanted*. And all will be lost. Which is why you need to be with us."

"I agree. Stay with me. Here. And help."

"You have one hour. Then we're gone. And Shooter is coming with us." He turned and stalked back to his truck.

"She's staying here," I called.

"Nope. She changed her mind." He slammed the passenger door and the truck rolled away. I was tired of watching his tail-lights.

Puck texted me.

>> Puck was listening. It's true. samantha is already at the airport. she decided 2 leave
Why???
>> dunno
And Croc?
>> he's there 2. every1 is leaving
Well...........not me.

I called Dad on the way to school, to warn him about the eminent attack. He already knew. Thermal imaging picked up increased heat signatures within the Chemist's aircraft hangar. He estimated the attack would begin tonight.

Great. That gave me just enough time to finish my homework before getting killed. A great empty chasm replaced my stomach.

Today. It was all happening today.

In Science, the two seats behind me remained empty. No Croc. No Samantha. Like most of last week.

I couldn't focus in English, not even on Katie. She was watching me with renewed interested, enjoying the Outlaw secret. I twisted and shifted in my chair, wondering if Katie was safe out here in Glendale. Probably. Hopefully.

At 10:15 am, Puck texted me. It was a doozy.

>> **attack beginning now**
>> **all chemists attack vehicles spinning up**
>> **america can't launch missile strike tho.**
>> **still protected by innocent civilians**
>> **navy will scramble fighters soon**
>> **this will b bad**

Craaaaaaaap. Already?? Not even lunch time. Ugh.

>> **carters plane taking off soon cant reach him they r all gone**

I grabbed Katie by the hand and pulled her out of class. The startled teacher watched us go, gaping as her prize pupil stumbled after the class dummy.

In the hall, I whispered, "I have to go. The Chemist is attacking."

"Where?" she asked. She was a goddess. Her hair was up today, with a pencil stuck into the stylish pile of perfect brown twists. Her green shirt turned her eyes hazel, and everything about her was bright and golden.

"No one knows what he'll do. I probably can't help. But. I'm going just in case."

"I understand." She pulled down the zipper of my hoodie a few inches, enough to reveal the red thread of my Outlaw vest. "Come home with your shield, handsome. Or upon it."

I blinked. Huh?

She said, "Spartan women used to tell their lovers that. Before battle."

"Pretty gruesome."

She wrinkled up her cute nose and mouth in thought. "Then how about...come home in one piece and I'll give you extra kisses?"

"That's a deal."

"Could you be hurt doing this?"

"I *could* be. But I'll try *not* to be."

She kissed me lightly on the lips and said, "I'm in love with a maniac. I guess this is part of the job. But please come back to me. You've been mine for only twelve hours. And I require much more than that."

The Outlaw flew down the 5 on his silent motorcycle. Traffic was already backing up. Awful days always start this way.

Puck related the news to me. It wasn't good.

Once again, the Chemist struck first. Twenty minutes ago, as the George Washington aircraft carrier prepared to scramble its F/A-18 Hornet fighter jets, a lone AV-8B Harrier Jump Jet lifted off from the Chemist's hangar and raced towards the aircraft carrier parked ten miles offshore. Radar identified the threat, and the carrier's Combat Air Patrol immediately swooped in and neutralized the enemy Harrier. However, before being blasted apart by interceptors, the Harrier released four air-to-surface AGM-65 Maverick missiles. The missiles were inexpertly launched; two of them splashed harmlessly into the water. But two of the Maverick missiles struck the massive carrier, detonating against the hull and damaging millions worth of equipment, including (among other things) the elevators and catapults. It would be hours, if not days, before another fighter jet could launch.

In other words, the Navy could only provide the two patrolling F-18 Hornets as protection for Los Angeles. Not good enough.

By sheer luck, I found my dad. His car was parked at Exit 3A of Interstate 101, barricading the downtown entrance, hopefully outside the killing fields. He and a handful of cops were glaring south and west, into the towering glass canyon. A mandatory evacuation had been dictated, and the Los Angelenos fled, but not fast enough. Dad and his crew helped orchestrate the stampede.

"Whoa…holy hell, it's the Outlaw," one of the cops blurted. The crowd of motorists noticed and began to cheer.

Dad glanced sharply at me. "What are *you* doing here?"

I parked my bike and jumped on top of his car for a better view. "What?! Is this not Santa's parade route??"

"Hey Richard," one of the guys laughed nervously. "Aren't you supposed to arrest this guy?"

"I'm thinking about it," he barked.

It was one of those days where the blue sky rose forever. The distant clouds piled high and deep, like the surface of another planet just out of orbit. Clear skies except for the grey birds-of-prey screaming overhead. The two remaining Hornets, sixty million dollars of ugly steel death, were encircling the city and ravaging our ear drums. Those two fighter jets were temporarily the only thing keeping Chemist aircraft grounded.

While police officers watched the air show, Dad tapped my foot and whispered, "You need to go home."

"I cannot, Detective Jackson," I replied.

"Why not?"

I crouched so we could speak. "A wise man once told me that we need to stand between the world and the monsters."

He glowered, not enjoying his words used against him. "That's my job! Not yours."

"*Our* job. I live here too."

"Please, son. Don't do this."

One of the onlookers blurted, "Here comes the cavalry! Those are Air Force Pave Hawks!"

A small squadron of six green helicopters thundered in from the north, moving ridiculously slow compared to the Hornets. State-of-the-art Pave Hawks, bulky and powerful utility choppers. It was the best America could muster on short notice; all other nearby vehicles, *hundreds* of them, had been destroyed, captured, or couldn't lift off. Perhaps America's most humiliating moment…ever?

The Chemist had twelve helicopters, at least. And several Harrier jets.

Dad took my shoulders in his beefy fists and held tight. "This is too big. He's too strong. He'll kill you."

"I would die to keep you safe, Dad."

"No!" He was shaking me and blinking back tears. "You're the only good part of my life. You're my *child*."

"How many people are downtown, Dad? A million? How many in those towers? I'd guess a hundred thousand. I figured it out on the way here; the Chemist bought himself a few hours of destruction. That's what he'll do. Destroy the towers. He told me he was going to tear down our high places."

"Let the military handle it. Please."

As if on cue, the Chemist struck again.

Sinister hisses and bright streams of fire erupted from three Los Angeles skyscrapers, including the US Bank Tower and the Aon Center. Like firework launches. Dozens of vapor trails snaked off into the sky.

The gathering crowd of stranded motorists gasped and aah'ed. *What's going on??!*

"He's clearing the way for his attack," I growled.

The two Hornets had no chance. One or two surface-to-air missiles could be out-maneuvered by modern fighter jets, but not dozens. The Hornets evaded desperately, curving and ducking across the sky, but the SAMs were numerous and dogged. The fighters were bucked by near misses, the pilots tossed sideways, disoriented, and then, contact.

I closed my eyes. The sound of detonations reached us soon after the bright flashes. Hornets breaking apart. The sounds of war.

The nearby helicopters, new Pave Hawks, had been hovering two hundred feet in the air over Korea Town, a half mile from the towers. They responded to the new threat, their noses pointing skywards and climbing, closing the distance. They were going to engage the enemy on the towers.

Their shadows fell across Natalie North's building.

Natalie! I hope she's out. No time to text her.

I said, "Those choppers are toast. I'd bet my allowance he's got Infected waiting for them. I gotta go. Get on the radio and get the people out from the towers. Those are his targets."

I saluted him. He finally let go and I Jumped.

But it was already too late. In order to reach the taller peaks, the Pave Hawks first had to pass above smaller ones, like the Century Plaza Towers. The Chemist's men were there and ready.

His monsters lifted off into the sky. Dozens. Maybe more, Jumping from the lower roofs, aiming for the helicopters as they flew past. Their leaps carried them farther and higher than humanly possible, bodies slamming into the unprepared Pave Hawks. Like swarming parasites, the Infected climbed aboard, easy ingress provided by the open gunner doors. All six helicopters were boarded in less than twenty seconds. The furious battle between crew and Infected caused one Pave Hawk to spiral out of the sky and crash into Pershing Square Park. Two others collided mid-air, metal shrieking, blades breaking. They plummeted out of our sight.

Downtown Los Angeles is not very big in comparison to other cities like New York or Tokyo. Most of LA is flat, not tall. City planners built the city horizontally instead of vertically, and arranged the few high-rises in a relatively tight cluster. Other cities have a hundred skyscrapers stretching to the sky; Los Angeles holds only twenty within its downtown area.

During periods of high stress and adrenaline, I could jump between many of them.

As I moved, the institutions in my mind broke down and gave way to the virus, to anarchy, to the unimaginable. I went up the twin California Plaza towers, leaping between them using both arms and legs, like a panther scrambling up boulders. My shoes squeaked like trumpets on the glass. I'd marvel at the feat later; right now, the swelling urgency was too great.

Puck's voice came into my trusty bluetooth headset. "Oooooooh no, Outlaw. Where're you going, dummy? You're making me nervous."

ALAN JANNEY

"Get'cha war paint, Puck!" I cried, throwing myself up and across the airy void between the two glass-sided vertical mountains. I was out of breath already. "We got work to do!"

On top of Two California Plaza, I landed in the midst of three men dressed in faux Outlaw masks. They weren't Infected; their bodies were thin and flimsy, and they struggled to rearm two shoulder-mounted rocket launchers. I took a well-deserved deep breath, and then incapacitated all three with one swoop of the heavy rod, their skulls clunking like pumpkins. Their faces were dusted with a thin coating of the Chemist's super drug.

"Chase," Puck scolded me. "You can't win this."

"Neither can the Chemist," I panted. "He knows he's got only a short timeframe to get these towers down. We just need to stall until help arrives. WOW I'm up really high."

"How do we do stall?" His voice was sad, already resigned to my fate, my march towards death.

"No idea! But I need every eye you got!"

I leapfrogged buildings, moving southwest and surprising henchmen at each landing spot. I broke weapons and tried not to permanently damage feeble bodies. The earth was only a distant concern far below.

Puck said, "Evacuations are ramping up. Apparently the explosions in the sky were unsettling."

"I bet!" I called, landing on the City National Tower.

All three remaining Pave Hawk helicopters were now piloted by the enemy. One of them hovered just off the tower on which I landed. The attack began with a roar. Both miniguns blazed to life, rattling the edifice and pouring .308 shells into City National Tower windows. The surface exploded, filling the sky with thick glass fragments. Anyone inside would be killed within seconds.

This was happening too fast.

I dove off the ledge of the tower, headfirst. Not my brightest move, but I had abandoned reason. Some deep surging madness craved near-death adventure.

The Pave Hawk was ten floors below me, enough time to regret the free fall towards spinning razors. With both hands I brought the heavy rod down in a tomahawk chop that connected with rotor blades just milliseconds before my face did.

In that instant, two things happened.

The aluminum-composite blades were spinning so fast that all four connected against the impossibly-strong Stick of Treachery, and all four shattered. The noise hurt as much as the impact.

Also, the resulting crash hurled me through a gaping hole and onto the 41st floor. I went *through* office walls, skidded along a carpeted hallway, and came to a stop inside the women's restroom.

My arms weren't broken, but they were completely numb.

"Well," Puck mumbled, "that didn't last long."

"I'm alive," I coughed, spitting particleboard.

"Nope. Not possible."

From without came the noise of a helicopter crunching heavily and noisily onto streets below. I staggered back to the destroyed ledge of the 41st floor and gazed at the city. My arms began to tingle. Painfully.

"But seriously," he said. "How'd you do that?"

"Luck."

"Maybe. But I prayed. So I helped too."

Swinging and shaking my arms. "One helicopter down. Ten to go."

"More like fifteen, dummy. The Chemist's strike group has lifted off. Heading your way. Four minutes out."

The City National Tower was geometrically all right angles. Everything square, including window sills. Climbing back to the top was simple, other than my leaden arms. I made it seven floors before Puck warned me, "You've been spotted! Second chopper, coming in fast!"

Pave Hawks have front-mounted miniguns operated by the pilot, and bigger .50 machine guns handled by gunners on the side. Fortunately I wasn't facing trained war veterans. This pilot opened fire with his front-mounted weapon instead of allowing his gunner to mow me down.

I shoved off the tower, floated over the six-hundred-foot abyss, and grabbed onto a refueling probe protruding from the helicopter's nose.

"I can't see you. I hate this! Where are you??"

Dangling, one hand on the gear, the other holding the heavy rod, I hacked at the belly of the cockpit, burrowing deep inside machinery and mechanics. Sparks and oil sputtered in my face and the aircraft started to whine. Bingo!

I swung off the extended probe like Tarzan and landed hard against tower windows with an "Ooff!" as the Pave Hawk lost control and altitude. It was going to land hard.

"Two down!" I called. "I bet Dad is *freaked*."

I climbed and Puck kept updating. "Chemist forces have arrived on foot, swarming over the Ten and moving into the Fashion District. Both Beale and Edwards Air Force bases have scrambled F-35 Lightning fighters that should arrive within the hour."

"The *hour*?! Not good enough! This thing will be over in fifteen minutes!"

"The Army is inbound with surface-to-air launchers, but they might not have enough. They're being transported on civilian vehicles and encountering heavy traffic."

I reached the crest and collapsed on the lip of the roof. I let my feet dangle while sucking wind. In the distant southern haze, I could see a large force of aircraft advancing. They'd reach the Aon Tower soon, and Apaches would release Stinger and Sidewinder rockets. That many helicopters could collapse multiple towers.

Tiny trails of cars and pedestrians were retreating from the metropolis. I was still out of breath but I climbed to my feet anyway. "Any good news?"

"There is a Destroyer in the Pacific battle group that can intermittently lock-on to targets with guided anti-air missiles, but the helicopters are too low to the ground. Plus they could accidentally hit civilian structures."

"Puck, how do you know all this?"

"I'm filtering a dozen military and police frequencies. I can absorb and parse a lot of information. But all cameras are pointed your way."

I stood quietly for a moment, watching the world move in slow motion, summoning energy for round two. For this instant in time, all was quiet. A calm before the storm.

"That was super legit, by the way. Can't believe you destroyed two helicopters."

"I just interfered. Gravity did most the work."

"Still. You're the coolest. I'm so sad you're about to die."

"Thanks bud. I'm glad you're here. At the end of all things."

He sniffed. "I think I saw that in a movie once."

"Or a book. Katie would be proud of me."

"Whoa! You've got company! Rising straight up from below."

Another helicopter. I was SICK of them. Although this machine was civilian. Below my feet and rising fast.

"I can't tell," Puck grumbled. In my mind's eye, PuckDaddy was sitting in a computer lab somewhere and squinting at a monitor, watching the live feed, nose inches from the screen. "Looks like a news helicopter?"

"Yep," I confirmed. "But it's not being flown by a news team."

The helicopter was white with a blue television logo painted on the tail. The passenger-bay door was slid back, and the Chemist himself stood there, holding onto the bulkhead with one hand and his staff in the other, a madman grinning crazily at me across the thirty-foot gap.

A young girl about my age was aiming the vehicle's television camera at me. I found out later the news channel was streaming video live around the world.

But what caught my attention was Carla. She was strapped to the outside, a gruesome and haunting sight. Her arms were pulled backwards by chains, pinning her against the fuselage, the vehicle's nose pressing painfully into her back. Her mouth was gagged, and her feet dangled freely into space.

"Welcome, son," the Chemist hailed me. He appeared unnaturally gaunt, a walking corpse. "To my shock and awe campaign!"

"Stop this, Martin!!"

"Soon we shall have the planet's full and undivided attention, my boy. And our wishes will be law!"

"Let Carla go!"

"Oh!" he cackled. "She is there of her own free will. This was the punishment she chose!"

I pulled the stick free from my vest. If I hit those chains hard enough, they'd break and release Carla. But I'd only get one chance...

"Carter is gone," he called, sounding disappointed. "Told me himself. It's just you now. All alone, on the wrong side of this war."

"I think it's always been that way! Carter's as screwed up as you are."

He roared in delight. "YES! Finally, after decades! One of his minions sees the truth. I welcome you with open arms!"

"Very well," I growled, crouching.

"Don't miss, dear child! You make life worth living!"

I Jumped. A powerful leap, straight and true. Carla's eyes widened.

The pilot was ready. He pulled up sharply and banked out of reach. I streeeeeetched and missed the landing gear by inches.

"No!" Puck cried.

There was nothing below me.

Nothing. For nine hundred feet.

As quickly as I could in the buffeting zephyrs, I squirmed my gloves into wing grommets, shot arms forward and SNAP! My wing-suit filled with a crack, hardening into solid surfaces and thrusting me forwards. I also connected leg-webbing to provide stability.

"Ohmygosh," Puck sucked in air. I did too. "I can't take this."

I couldn't locate the Chemist's chopper. High above me...somewhere.

I was aimed south, sailing away from the towers and directly into the teeth of the enemy armored regiment pushing north, bristling with weapons and bringing death. My altitude was nine hundred feet and falling. Theirs was three hundred feet and climbing. Fast.

Puck said, "Chase, you have to fly straight at those attack helicopters."

"I do?? Why?"

"Right now you're a tiny bullseye. They probably can't even see you. If you turn, you'll be a much bigger target. They'll kill you for sure if you expose your profile."

"That's nuts."

"Fly straight at them. Like stealth mode. Hopefully you'll sail past and they won't shoot you."

"Probably going to happen anyway. But. May fortune favor the foolish, right?"

We'd intersect beyond the Downtown boundary, outside the cluster of high-rises and in the open air somewhere above Santee.

Below me, an eternal distance away, gunfights raged between terrorists and police.

The world was mad.

"I can barely see you," Puck called. It was difficult to hear him over the wind. "You're just a speck inside an infinite sky."

"That's kind of beautiful, Puck. And sad."

I plunged straight at the oncoming might of the Chemist's armada. Just a fool floating without armor or weapons, a lonely moth fluttering into the volcano.

"You'll tell Katie I love her?"

"I will. I promise."

Our plan didn't work. The first gunship fired. Others followed. Angry whining invaded my airspace as I flew into the broadside.

Chapter Twenty-Nine
Monday, November 1. 2018

Samantha Gear

Carter's black Toyota ground to a halt on gravel just off the tarmac. He and the Shadow climbed out.

"Well?" I called. I was standing beside the rolling stairway which led onto the privately chartered Lear Jet. Carter spared no expense on travel. I still wore my backpack, but I wasn't climbing aboard until I knew Chase would too.

"He's coming," Carter said.

Oh thank god. Relief flooded my body. Chase would be safe.

And also…something else. My relief was tinged with disappointment. Deep down, I think I wanted Chase to stay. And I wanted to stay with him.

I wanted Chase to be strong enough to resist Carter, to do the right thing, to ignore the odds, glare at Death and not blink. There *should* be someone in the world brave enough to face the Chemist and defy him. I wanted to follow that person into battle. Our dark world would be better for it.

I wasn't disillusioned with Chase. That wasn't fair; he was only a nineteen-year-old kid. Too young to be a savior.

But our future looked bleak. If Chase wasn't strong enough to resist, who was?

Carter pushed past me and mounted the steps. "He'll arrive at takeoff. Has to say goodbye to the girl."

I nodded and followed him. "That sounds like Chase."

The jet's storage compartments were crammed with our gear. Enough firepower to make the FAA's eyes pop out. I sat in the rear of the lush passenger cabin with Croc. There were only ten wide chairs and a few tables. Plenty of room for standing and moving.

Carter and Russia were in the front, speaking in hushed tones. I couldn't hear them due to the hissing air vents. No idea where the Shadow went; he's like that. The door was still ajar, permitting the hubbub of airstrip activities to fill our cabin.

"Where's the kid?" Croc asked.

"On his way."

A long silence. I tried settling into the plush cushions. Our departure wasn't for thirty-five more minutes.

Why was I so agitated? That's easy. Because I'm a hypocrite. Because I was flying away while brave men and women fought for what they believed in. Men like Richard.

"We shouldn't be leaving," I said finally, chewing on my nails. I was feeling punchy, ready to fight. Just the virus talking. And my anxiety.

"Hows'at?"

"This city needs our help. We shouldn't just…retreat."

"Say the word, love. I'll follow you anywhere."

I smiled. "Thanks Croc. You're sweet. But say something helpful instead."

"The kid's tagging along, right?"

"That's what Carter told me."

"Stick to the plan, I say. No reason to kick a hornet nest."

"Yeah," I nodded, forcing myself to relax.

"Live to fight another day."

"Right."

Ten more long minutes. Croc was reading an article about cattle insemination, of all things. His beautiful face, for the moment, looked slack and tired.

"Croc, I've never asked. How old are you?"

"Dunno. Lost track. Guess fifty-five?"

"Do you have a guess about Carter's age?"

"Dunno that either. He's an old cracker, though. One-fifty, maybe? One seventy-five?"

"Do you miss your ranch?"

Finally he put the magazine down and scrutinized me. "You're a chatty Kathy. What's got you ruffled?"

I shrugged and peered out the window beyond him. "We don't get to have friends in this business. Just thought I'd ask."

"Nah. Don't miss the ranch. Gets lonely. Might not go back."

"You're kidding. It's worth millions."

"Yeh," he nodded. "Rooms full of the stuff. But nothing to do with it."

"Chase thinks we should stay with him. Stop hiding. Come clean about our illness, and make our lives that way."

"Hah. And a child shall lead us."

The lone stewardess pulled the swinging door shut and the jet taxied forward.

"Hey!" I called. "We're not leaving yet."

The stewardess glanced at Carter and replied, "No ma'am. Traffic control requested we remove to a different tarmac."

I didn't like it. I stared angrily at the small airport sliding by.

Croc's preternatural instincts picked up the deception first. He saw through the lies in Carter's posture, the stewardess's anxiety, the tone of her voice.

"Samantha, my love," he said quietly. "He's told you a corker."

"What?"

"Lied. Carter lied. The Outlaw isn't coming."

My blood ran cold. That sounded like something Carter would do. From my backpack, I retrieved a nasty surprise and hung it on the chair, within easy reach but out of Carter's line of sight. Croc's eyes widened. I stood up. Immediately so did Carter. Our stares crackled along the aisle.

"Where's Chase?"

"He'll catch the next flight," the evil bald man barked.

"Then I will too."

"You'll sit back down." He half-turned to the flight attendant. "Get us in the air. Now."

"Yes sir."

"Carter, stop this plane. I'll wait here for him."

"He'll meet us there. We stay together."

Croc stood up, glancing unhappily between the two of us. "Carter, my old mate. Open the hatch. I'll keep her company until the Outlaw shows."

"No deal, Mitch."

"Why not?"

"You'll have to trust me."

Russia stood up too. His pudgy hand rested on the seat-back, gripping a pistol. His wintery eyes were empty; he'd kill us without hesitation.

The four of us glared at each other, an uneasy stalemate, as the jet advanced to the runway.

"He never said he was coming," I spit in fury. "You lied."

"I lied. You do not possess the ability to contend with his influence. It's clouded your judgement. I made the choice for you."

We all swayed as the engines surged. The jet was taking off.

"Chase will try to stop the Chemist. By *himself*."

"I know."

"You're leaving him here to die!"

"I am."

"Carter," I seethed, "I'm going to kill you."

Russia's pistol came up without him moving a muscle. "Pretty little girl should try."

Carter and I shouted over each other as our wheels left the runway. We were airborne in this floating palace.

Enough.

I grabbed my nasty surprise. A grenade.

With a flick of my finger, I sent the safety pin clattering onto the jet's cushioned aisle. Carter stopped shouting. Russia blinked and his pistol wavered.

"I'm getting off this damn plane, Carter. One way or the other."

"Samantha," Carter stammered. His complexion turned two shades lighter, and he held up his palms. "What are you doing?"

"I'm going to blow a hole in the fuselage and force an emergency landing if I have to."

"Mitch, old friend, reason with her. It'll take over an hour to turn this plane around and land, if we even get clearance."

"Got a better idea, mate. Samantha and I are leaving. Right now," Croc said.

"How's that?"

"I'm wearing a parachute. We'll leave and you go on your merry way."

I glanced at him, stunned. He *was* wearing a parachute backpack. When had he...?

"We can leave one of two ways, Carter. She can release the safety lever, toss the tarter your way, and then Sammy-girl and I'll go out the gigantic hole in the side of aeroplane."

Russia looked terrified. Wonder if he was afraid of heights? If he fired his gun, I'd release the lever and we'd all almost certainly die.

"Or," Croc continued, "she and I can go through the emergency hatch."

I glanced out the window. We were gaining altitude quickly. I shrugged into my backpack and announced, "Croc, open the hatch. I'll release the safety if they move."

"Right-o, love!"

"Samantha," Carter shouted. His voice was stern and frantic. "Don't do this. You do this and our association is permanently over!"

"The hell with you, Carter."

"You need me! And I need you."

"You're fired."

Croc hauled up the emergency release below the rear window. The heavy door pried open at the bottom, and our pressurized air began howling through the thin opening. This was nuts! Deep breath. Croc kicked the door. Hard.

The door popped into the atmosphere like a champagne cork. Croc and I were sucked out.

We spun far from the thundering jet, which would have to make an emergency landing somewhere south. I was disoriented and sick immediately. Why did Chase enjoy this??

I threw the grenade into the brilliant blue sky. No idea where, and I barely heard it pop. The wind was too loud.

I spread my arms wide, maximizing surface area and slowing as much as possible. Croc pinned his arms back, like a rocket, and sped up. He put a shoulder into my stomach and I wrapped arms around his neck.

"Most fun I ever had!" he called into my ear.

"Release the chute, you stupid Aussie!"

His pack sprang open and the chute deployed. I clung tight and we dangled over Beverly Hills, fifteen hundred yards high.

"Where'd you get a parachute??" Our faces were pressed together, my mouth practically in his ear.

"That little black fella! The Shadow. Pushed it into me hands when nobody saw."

"Where'd he come from?!"

"Dunno. Slippery bloke. Must be an Outlaw fan, like me."

I stared at the dizzy ground below us. "Find the phone in my backpack. I need to make a call. Now."

As we drifted softly back to earth, two F/A-18 Fighters screamed by, too close for comfort. We even felt vague heat waves thrown by their after-burn.

Special Agent Isaac Anderson finally answered his phone and informed me the FBI had only two remaining helicopters, and neither was equipped with an armament.

I had to shout over a nearby squadron of Pave Hawks churning towards Downtown. Los Angeles was preparing for war. "Get me one! I need to be airborne *now*!"

Before he could reply, an unbelievably large salvo of anti-aircraft rockets launched from the downtown spires.

Croc mumbled, "Bloody hell. There's trouble."

The Hornets scrambled, barrel-rolling and accelerating, but the sudden artillery overwhelmed them. One of the Hornets erupted in our vicinity, an ear-splitting pandemonium. The radiating heat caught and violently jostled our canopy.

"You watching this, Anderson??"

"I am. We're being crushed."

"Get me a helicopter!"

"What else do you need?"

"Parachutes. And rifles. All of them."

Four minutes later, Croc landed us on the swanky Los Angeles Country Club, hole sixteen near an astonished foursome. They were watching the fleet of Pave Hawks get ambushed by mutants.

My god, what a nightmare.

Was Chase up there somewhere?

My phone was full of recent text messages from Puck.

>> attack beginning

>> u probably wont get this message

>> ur plane is taking off

>> u guys r assholes 4 leaving chase alone

>> hes going up the towers by himself

>> to die

No. No no no no no.

This was all happening too fast. Just the way the Chemist planned it. Anderson called me again.

"Your chopper is inbound," he shouted into the receiver. "Figure I might as well give you a chance to stop the world from ending. Give me your coordinates and I'll pass them along!"

After an anxious five minutes, the FBI's Little Bird landed on the fairway. It was a tiny, bug-like helicopter used primarily to shuttle VIPs.

"Special delivery from Agent Anderson!" the pilot cried.

Croc hauled the surprised kid out of the cockpit. "Sorry mate! You want no part of this biff! This is a one-way trip! No coming back!" He climbed into the pilot's seat and strapped in. I did the same in the small passenger bay. Croc threw us into the sky and aimed toward the city skyline.

I busily checked the ordnance provided by Anderson. A Remington sniper rifle and two M4 carbines. Boxes of ammunitions and empty cartridges. It'd have to suffice. I pounded rounds into magazines, fingers flying.

"Christ almighty," Croc said. His voice came into my headset. "A chopper just crashed. Not far from the basketball stadium."

"Go go GO! Get me closer!"

"Moving faster than a 'roo crossing hot sand, love!"

"Scan those rooftops! I need to take out any launchers!"

"I bet Chase already has, the rascal!"

I finished loading magazines. Hopefully I had enough. I tore my eyes away and finally looked out into the Los Angeles sky. There was a squadron of attack helicopters moving in from the south, half a mile from the towers, each fully armed.

I called PuckDaddy.

"Samantha!" Puck cried into my earpiece. "Where are you?"

"Coming in fast! Is he alive??"

"For a few more seconds!"

"WHAT?!" I roared. "Put us through to Chase! We're in a small chopper heading his way, just west of Downtown! Where is he?"

"South of the towers! He's flying straight at that strike force!"

"NO! Why?? Damn it, damn it, damn it!"

"I see him," Croc groaned. "Kid's a maniac!"

Our transport screeched and shook. I raised the sniper rifle's powerful scope. The distant speck leapt closer. Chase, waffling and alone on the bright blue horizon, was braving a murderous hail of bullets.

I leaned way out into space, trusting the harness not to snap and drop me five hundred feet. I pushed the safety free on the rifle. This was not ideal; I'd need to fire four times to hit a target once.

"Keep us level, Croc!"

"No promises!"

"Okay," Puck said, "I'm connecting you to Chase."

The line clicked. A new static greeted my ears.

"CHASE!" I yelled. "Bank hard to the right! NOW!"

I squeezed the trigger.

Chapter Thirty

Monday, November 1. 2018.

The Chemist had stolen three different types of helicopters, I noted.

The smallest was a McDonald Douglass 500 Defender. Looks kind of like a gnat. With guns.

He also got his hands on some heavy Black Hawks, the same helicopter Samantha and I fly into Compton. Elite and state-of-the-art.

Perhaps most significantly, he captured multiple Apaches. Apaches are black and green and menacing, dragonfly in appearance. They were built for one purpose: destruction.

The strike force wasn't flying in formation. In fact, it was a mess. The Chemist's pilots were clearly not military trained. Otherwise I'd be dead already.

I couldn't hear them yet. Other than the wind, everything was quiet. And bright. And calm.

Maybe I *am* dead?

One of the incoming bullets got so close it actually nicked my shoulder.

Nope. Not dead. Yet.

My earpiece burst to life. "Chase! Bank hard to the right! Now!"

What??! Samantha??

I twisted my shoulders and curled off to the north, presenting a full-body target to the gunners. But I trusted her. Turning at this speed was a harrowing punishment that compressed my lungs.

A starburst splintered the windshield of the nearest Apache. An armor-piercing round had punched clean through! The sinister helicopter pitched up and began cork-screwing, out of control. The pilot had been shot! The Apache slammed into a smaller, gnat-like Defender. Blades gouged great holes into both aircraft and deafening explosions sent the attack force scattering, like a swarm of fireflies.

"Nice shot!" I called.

Debris and bright trails of fire arced across the cathedral of infinite blue. I twisted away from the radiating junkyard and glanced over my shoulder. Samantha was behind me, hovering near the massive cluster of Downtown towers and shooting over my shoulder at the oncoming attack squadron.

A Black Hawk ahead, just off my flight path. He rotated enough to allow the gunner a firing angle, and the enemy released the awesome power of a .50 caliber machine gun, heavy devastating rounds. But he wasn't firing at me. He was firing at Croc and Samantha!

I minutely altered course. This Black Hawk had all doors removed, even the cockpit's. I howled straight for it, moving so quickly the air stung my eyes, tearing blurring my vision.

At the last second, I snapped my arms back and streaked *through* the cockpit, like an arrow threading a needle. I entered through the port hatch and exited the starboard at a hundred miles per hour, my rock-hard shoulder clipping the pilot's exposed skull. Instant death.

The Black Hawk and I plummeted. I snapped wings out and curved back towards the city, smoldering hulk dropping in my wake. Now I was traveling *behind* the Chemist's strike force, pursuing them, all of us aimed downtown. I'd never seen Los Angeles from this southern angle during the day. The mammoth San Gabriel mountain dominated the eastern horizon, already tipped with snow.

"Chase, I saw that! Holy SMOKES dude!" Puck cried.

Samantha landed a second miraculous sniper shot, lancing the pilot of another MD 500 Defender, but now she and Croc had to fly for their lives. Two deadly Apaches broke away from the group and attacked them, both with infinitely superior firepower. Croc led them on a wild chase though, and I doubted the Apaches would ever get clean shots. He flew like a professional stunt pilot compared to amateurs.

"The Chemist is up here somewhere!" I shouted. "In a news chopper!"

"Roger that." Samantha's voice.

Puck alerted us, "Warning! Enemies have begun assault on city!"

The remaining attack helicopters quickly and efficiently demolished the stately 777 Tower, the southernmost high-rise located on the fringe of the tower cluster. All six unleashed anti-armor Hellfire missiles at close range, hammering the south face. The attack was so powerful it hurt my eyes.

The tower's inner structure only withstood three salvos. The gunners concentrated their attack, pounding marks until steel relented, essentially cutting out two of the tower's legs. Seven hundred feet tall, weighing two hundred thousand tons, the majestic skyscraper began a slow collapse. The helicopters scattered before rising dust clouds.

It was an awful sight. Monstrous and impossible, like a mountain decaying in seconds.

"Oh my goooooooooosh," Puck groaned.

I asked, "Was everyone out?" My voice sounded hollow and small, like my heart was in my throat.

"No idea. I doubt it. Also be advised, it's about to get worse. Three enemy Harriers inbound."

Samantha shouted, "I'm abandoning ship! Croc, fly over the new Wilshire and I'll jump."

"Negative, my love." His grin came clearly over the headset. "Wilshire is not on our bloody flight pattern. Can I talk you into the City National?"

"Whatever, Croc! Just put me over a stable firing surface. You can't fly straight and I can't hit these jackasses chasing us!"

Attack choppers were now inside Downtown proper, still on the fringe of the tower cluster. They reformed near the Aon Center, a building resembling a tall dark mirror. I aimed straight for them.

Our adversaries could probably knock down two or three more towers. Their aircraft was outfitted with stub-wings to hold extra ammunition. But then the Chemist's Harrier Jump Jets would arrive, bearing more rockets.

We couldn't stop them all.

Something caught my eye. The world was *caving* in! The street below disappeared, followed by an eruption of fire.

"The roads are collapsing!" I yelped. "How?? What??"

"Yeah. Chemist is destroying the red and purple underground metro lines." Puck sounded sad and exhausted. "He has suicide bombers carrying explosives through the tunnels. National Guard and Army forces are on their way. I didn't tell you because there's nothing you can do."

More and more streets buckled and collapsed, releasing plumes of airborne dirt. The luxurious and beautiful City of Angels was devolving into hell.

Samantha called, "Great. Just frickin' great. Anything else you're not telling us, Puck?"

"Just one more thing.

"Which is?"

"Tigers. At least four tigers spotted prowling the Skid Row area."

Samantha said, "This is a nightmare."

I agreed. "I hate those things."

Puck said, "We can't stop him. We've lost."

"We can try!" I shouted. I was still playing catch-up, trailing the faster helicopters, streaking towards Downtown. "He brought enough firepower to take down almost every tower. We can limit him to one or two. We've already destroyed four helicopters-"

"Six," Puck interrupted. "Don't forget the two Pave Hawks you dropped."

"Whatever! Point is, we've already reduced the destruction, and we're not done. He wants to level the city. We're not going to let him!"

"Outlaw, MOVE!" Samantha screamed.

One of her pursuing Apaches broke off and came at me, guns blazing.

No time! I unfettered the wings, which zipped back into my pant-legs, and I dropped like a stone underneath shredding gunfire.

Wings re-engaged! They caught the air with a Snap and thrust me forward. The Apache and I crossed paths, me twenty feet under, slashing through rotor wash.

At my initial jump, I was nine hundred feet high. Now I was at four hundred. Running out of sky!

I flew serpentine patterns, desperate turns, toward the Aon tower. The Apache pursued, firing wildly, the lion chasing a gazelle.

"There he is!" I cried. "The Chemist's helicopter, next to Aon! He's watching the attack."

Samantha replied, "I'm dropping now! He's my primary target!" Her chute opened directly above the nearby City National tower, the same building I'd been on when I first jumped after the Chemist's helicopter. From there she'd be able to fire directly at the other attackers.

"Geronimo, Samy-girl!" Croc laughed.

Bullets ripped through my leg webbing. The Apache was too close behind me! I immediately lost stability.

"This is a bad idea," I mumbled, but I did it anyway.

Zip! I released the wings.

Pop! I launched the parachute and was jerked to a painful and jarring stand-still, swinging crazily in the sky, earth off its axis.

The Apache bore down at a trillion miles per hour. He was going to slice my canopy lines with his blades.

"Whoa!" Puck cried. "What??! What are-"

At the very last instant, I hauled the chute back in with a mighty yank. It disappeared into my vest with a hiss.

The Apache crushed me. I hit his windshield like a bug on a semi-truck, just like the Grumman Greyhound cargo plane so long ago. Shoulders, hips and ribs all popped.

But I held on. My face was twelve inches from the astonished gunner's. I saw him through my reflection in the glass.

I shoved the canopy assembly upwards. Metal locks and clasps squealed, bent, and broke. That wasn't humanly possible but I was mad.

"I'm NOT happy with you!" I yelled. The gunner squawked as I stepped onto his lap, reached over the tandem cockpit bulkhead, and ripped *out* the pilot's control stick. "Have fun with *that*."

I abandoned ship as the Apache began plunging.

"Well," Puck mumbled, "more than one way to skin a cat, I guess."

I opened the wing-suit, which caught air with a sharp crack, and I darted toward the Aon Center, the nearest and southernmost tower in the cluster. I was sailing two hundred feet in the air.

The attack choppers released their first bombardment on the Aon. The western glass face shattered, filling the skyline with deadly confetti.

"I don't have a shot on the Chemist," Samantha snarled.

"Take out those choppers!" I yelled. "They'll have that tower down in less than a minute!"

No time! They were ready to fire again.

I remember the next fifteen seconds only through a series of mental snapshots.

The attack choppers were gathered at the tower base like yellow jackets fighting for pollen.

I rocketed into the cloud of fragmented glass at a hundred miles per hour.

The airborne glass cut my wings to ribbons.

I flew at the tower without control.

Out of options, I threw the Rod like a hatchet into the nearest chopper, a heavy Black Hawk.

The Rod entered the Black Hawk's cockpit like a wrecking ball.

I entered the Aon Tower's seventeenth floor like…well, a wrecking ball.

Samantha told me later what happened. The Black Hawk's pilot was either killed or injured by the Rod. The Black Hawk reeled sharply to the left and banked into the next helicopter. The two aircraft ruined each other and erupted, slamming the third chopper into the fourth, a deadly domino effect. Another thunderous detonation, and the entire sky was set on fire. The fifth chopper corkscrewed away from the high-rise, smoking and whining. The brilliant red billows of flame and fury stormed against the teetering tower, but the steel held.

Samantha disintegrated the sixth and final attack chopper's windshield with multiple rifle rounds as it fled the mushroom blast, forcing it to spin aground in a shower of sparks, near the Dignity Health Hospital.

Echoes of eruptions. A ceiling of rising filth and particles. But the heavens were temporarily clear of aircraft. For the moment, the Aon and all persons inside were safe.

Samantha radioed, "Where?? Where is the Chemist?"

"Dunno, love," Croc called. "I've lost the bloody Apache that was chasing me, too. That rascal's 'round here somewhere."

PuckDaddy said, "Too much smoke, too many hiding places. I'm scanning."

"Outlaw, you alive?" Samantha called. "I need you up here."

I pulled myself out of a supply closet, covered in buckets and mops and spray bottles. "Okay," I groaned. "Gimme a sec." The thin carpet glistened with sharp flecks. This floor appeared to be empty. At least offices in this engineering firm were. A good sign. I staggered out.

"Harrier jets approaching," Puck warned. "Coming in from the west, instead of south."

"Croc, you need to find a hiding spot," Samantha called. "Those jets might have air-to-air missiles." I could hear noises of her reloading. "And I'm not sure how much help I'll be. Outlaw, where are you?"

"I'm coming," I grumbled.

"The Chemist is broadcasting live from his helicopter," Puck announced. "But the camera is out of focus on his face. I can't tell where..."

I asked, "What's that maniac saying to the camera?"

"He's describing the future. A new age, ruled by his Chosen. Earlier he recited a poem about the Outlaw."

Four minutes later, I laid down at Samantha's feet, on the hot tarred rooftop, gasping. "That's...a long...climb..."

She wrinkled her nose. "You're all gross and dusty. Get up, wimp."

"Shut up," I wheezed. "Just need...a quick nap..."

"Bad place for a nap. We're exposed and we've got enemies inbound."

Puck said, "I have bad news and good news."

"Bad news."

"America sent reinforcement fighters, but they're still thirty minutes away. Won't get here in time."

"Good news?"

"*Two* pieces of good news, actually!" Puck chirped. "First, the final Apache just crash landed to the north. It was forced down by police with assault rifles."

"There you go, Los Angeles," Samantha nodded grimly. "Good work." She was scanning the western horizon with her scope.

"Woohoo," I offered weakly.

"Secondly, I have Isaac Anderson on the line."

"Anderson," I yelled into the mic with all the air I had. It wasn't much. "We need to stop the inbound Harrier jets. Or at least stall."

"I'm here," Anderson called. My ear piece was getting crowded with voices. "I'm in the FBI's last helicopter, a Little Bird. I've got a launcher and two rockets. That's all we could find on short notice. The army won't get here in time."

"You'll only get one shot off before those Harriers blow you out of the sky," Samantha warned.

"I know. But we have to try."

"And here they come."

I stood beside Samantha and peered west. The Harrier Jump Jets were fifty feet off the ground, skimming houses. They were *fast*. We couldn't stop them. Helicopters were one thing, but fighter jets moving at three hundred miles per hour were another.

"I see them. Preparing to launch," Anderson said.

"He's going to fire the rocket launcher from inside that tiny chopper's backseat," Samantha chuckled. "Going to be loud. And hot."

"Damn right it is," he radioed, and he fired. We couldn't see his vehicle, but a missile flared from the downtown maze and arced towards the Harriers.

These pilots were good. They scrambled and climbed into the atmosphere, and the rocket missed by a mile. We watched them thunder overhead, turbines hurting our ears. The Jump Jet wings were freighted with deadly Maverick missiles.

"I'm never going to hit those bastards," Samantha snarled, tracing jets through the air from behind her scope. I watched. Nothing else I could do.

All three Harriers loosed a Maverick missile on their first pass above Downtown. The missiles dove into the city bowels and connected with three different structures. The earth shook. Fire plumed east of us.

The Harriers executed sharp turns and came roaring back, prepared for another bombing run. They could strafe with impunity until exhausting missile supplies. Samantha fired her whole magazine to no effect. Three more Mavericks fell and the city was rocked to its foundations. Los Angeles was a city in torment.

The Harriers were just past us when one erupted. A lance of fire pierced the turbines and the Jump Jet loudly broke apart. The pilot ejected.

"Got one!" Anderson announced. "But now I'm out of rockets."

Puck laughed, "But the Navy isn't! Way to go, USS Gravely! Watch this!"

Two massive eruptions shattered the sky, larger and more violent than Isaac's rocket impact.

The Harriers had flown high enough in the sky to be fired upon from ten miles away. The naval destroyer, USS Gravely, had launched three guided missiles at the Harriers during their first staffing run. The missiles arrived and connected with the final two Jump Jets as they banked over Korea Town. Instant destruction.

Reverberations caromed off remaining downtown windows. Burning gasoline and debris filtered down to earth.

Samantha and I watched the show, our hearts heavy with loss and massacre.

But we'd forgotten about our real enemy. He attacked from behind.

Puck cried, "Sammy, move!"

The Chemist's television chopper rose straight up from the eastern face of our tower. We turned in time to see his aircraft plunge, poor Carla's eyes scared and angry. He was ramming the tower's helipad, kamikaze-style.

In that instant, I saw how it would happen.

He was too close. We couldn't reach the open air before his machine detonated. We'd be engulfed in fire. Even if we could jump, Samantha was dead. She wore no parachute. And she was too far from me.

We would die.

So would he.

So would Carla. And the pilot, and the girl operating the camera.

I could see the Chemist. I could hear him screaming.

I was almost too tired to care.

But I didn't want to disappoint Katie.

I bolted for Samantha. Maybe I could reach her. Maybe the explosion would throw us out of harm's way. Maybe we could land before we burned to death. Maybe a miracle.

"Not today, ya tosser!" Croc laughed.

Croc's FBI Little Bird materialized out of nowhere and plowed into the Chemist's television chopper. The two machines tangled, a riot of twisted metal, and glanced off the edge of the City National, swaying the entire high-rise.

Croc rammed him! Sacrificed himself to save us! Above the screaming steel, the Chemist howled in rage.

The wreckage plunged in slow motion. Nine hundred feet is a long way to fall. An eternity.

"Croc!" Samantha cried. She slid to the edge, an inch from falling, and watched in horror. "NO!"

Crackles of static reached our ears.

"...now, Sammy-girl...all my love, the rest of your long gorgeous life...my pretty sheila..."

Spilled gasoline caught fire. The ruined vehicles touched down. 5th Street became an inferno, instantly destroying the beautiful street and the beautiful life of our dear friend Mitchell.

Samantha and I remained on the tower another hour. Too exhausted and heartbroken to evacuate.

Downtown Los Angeles still stood. But it was being rapidly overrun by hundreds of Infected and twenty thousand drugged gunmen.

As the dust settled and reports began coming in, we learned the Chemist had attacked multiple locations. Multiple BIG locations.

Houston was being invaded, evidently by Infected in substantial numbers. Videos also showed assailants dressed like the Outlaw.

Seattle was under attack too.

Plus, additional California military bases were being ambushed, and their vehicles immobilized.

Every report was the same: the enemy's goal wasn't death, but destruction of property and vehicles. He wasn't after lives; he was after structures and systems. He was disabling the country, piece by piece.

"Think Martin died?" I asked Samantha after we stared at the azure infinity for forty-five minutes.

"Doubt it." Her face, like mine, was a mask of caked dirt and tears. "The older we get, the stronger. The harder. The faster."

"Carter was right," I sighed. "Los Angeles was already lost."

"No. No, we saved thousands of lives today. Those lives weren't lost. The Chemist didn't get them. We did the right thing."

Puck spoke up. "Meanwhile stupid 'ol Carter is just circling New Mexico, looking for a place to land. All airstrips are closed. Even if he made it to Houston, George Bush International is locked down tight."

I grabbed Samantha's hand and squeezed it. She squeezed back, uncharacteristic of her. She must've been as stressed and overwhelmed as me. "Thanks for coming back," I said.

"We're a team. That's what we do."

"Yeah," Puck said. "We *are* a team."

Anderson arrived in his small FBI chopper and plucked us off the helipad. We were too tired to fight the gunmen that Puck reported were about to arrive.

We flew north, away from Downtown, away from towers and smoke and fires and sirens. Away from mayhem.

And towards Katie.

Chapter Thirty-One
Thursday, November 25. 2018

Samantha Gear

Katie and her mother came over to Chase's house for Thanksgiving. So did Lee. (His parents approved of, but did not celebrate, Thanksgiving. Cory's parents, on the other hand, invited their whole extended family, so he couldn't come.)

I do not cook. So my contribution was a new table that would hold us all. The Jackson tribe had grown in size considerably since their last Thanksgiving.

It was an extravagant feast, especially for me because I hadn't attended a Thanksgiving meal since I was eighteen. Chase is weird like that; he invites everyone into his life, including the lost and lonely, like me. He even asked Carter, but never received a response.

Like many families in America, we ate and drank and laughed to intentionally spite the Chemist. There were signs that people were uniting against him. Right after he seized downtown Los Angeles, the Compton community finally united and heaved out the remnants of his forces. The citizens banded together and took back their city.

But there could be no such rebellion downtown. The people had fled and they weren't returning. Downtown was not a besieged American city; it was an empty shell, occupied by terrorists with captives. It was a fortress pure and simple, brazenly defying the world. The hostages were not allowed to roam free; they were locked away in the towers. Several national figures were missing, including television personality Teresa Triplett and movie star Natalie North. Chase was especially upset over those two.

The Chemist was alive. He made a brief appearance after the helicopter crash. But now? No idea. Maybe here. Maybe Houston. Maybe Antarctica.

I snuck back to the wreckage to confirm Croc's death, but I already knew the truth. I found his remains within the mangled cockpit. Carla's body was still strapped to the burnt fuselage. She'd been brave; wish we could have helped her. I salvaged and buried Croc's charred cowboy boots, and I wept. Sweet Croc deserved better. He was one of the few Infected with a clean and untainted soul.

I also discovered and returned Chase's new Thunder Stick. At least that's what I call it. It was unscathed, lodged inside a Black Hawk's burnt carcass. Might be useful in upcoming battles.

Houston and Seattle still smoldered, their power grids and public services all decimated. The Chemist's forces retreated after the initial attack, blending back into the population, waiting to strike again.

He had also destroyed key sections of oil pipelines coming out of Canada and Houston. Much of the country would soon experience crippling oil shortages.

Despite all the gloom, hope still rose. The world had watched his forces fail in Los Angeles. The towers still stood in direct defiance of his plans. They were enemy territory now, but they hadn't fallen. Nor would we.

The media, the military, and the citizenry all cried out for the Outlaw and his team. Now was the time for unity. Now was the time to stand together.

And we would. Chase had decided to meet with Isaac Anderson's select group of loyal government officials soon. No more hiding. No more secrets. No more masks.

He was going to change the world.

Anderson's team had taken custody of Tank and several other incarcerated Infected. They also located several large stores of the super drug, and soon they'd understand what was in the mixture.

We still had a job to do, but today was for family and love. Chase and Katie glowed like twin suns orbiting each other, generating irrepressible heat and shining despite the darkness. Beauty and the beautiful beast, unable to keep hands off each other.

We had just started on chocolate pies when the doorbell rang.

"I'll get it," I said. I rose from my place next to Richard and squeezed his thick shoulder before walking to the front door.

An unfamiliar man was there. A black man, about my age, with a buzzcut, sitting in an electrified wheelchair. A very impressive RV was parked on the street. Looked more like a space shuttle.

He smiled sheepishly and said, "Hey dummy. Can I come in? Chase said I was invited."

I didn't know the face, but I knew that voice!

"Puck!!"

The End

Epilogue.

The Chronicles of Martin Patterson
Emperor of the New Age
January 4. Year Two (2019).

As recorded by Teresa Triplett

We are woken in the middle of the night. The Father calls, so I dress quickly at gunpoint. My new roommate, Natalie North (perhaps the most famous hostage of all time?), is not allowed to accompany us.

I am taken into the basement of the Ritz, the hotel where I've been living. The Father has use of an underground labyrinth that connects him with many of the city's more important structures; part of the maze passes below the Ritz apparently. I'm taken down corridors until I'm hopelessly lost, and then left with him.

His mania has grown. He sings and quotes poems incessantly. We hear him laughing at all hours of the night.

This chamber is dark. Only a lamp in the corner. The air reeks of metal, iron in particular. He's gathered a macabre collection of medical equipment and technology, but I know this is not one of his fabled laboratories.

A tube connects his arm to a blood bag. He is being drained of blood every moment of the day. Bags of the stuff lay on tables, waiting to be stored or used immediately. Nearby, raw meat and fresh spinach await ingestion. One of his attendants once explained that the Father consumes over seven pounds of meat and vegetables per day, and drinks a comparable volume of water and juice. And yet he still looks like a shrunken cadaver.

The old man is shaking and sweating. His eyes are huge, unblinking. His pallor is pale, partly from the glow of the computer monitor. He giggles and whispers at the screen.

He's looking at two digital photographs. One is a newspaper photo taken at a funeral service, zoomed in on the mourners. I know that funeral. I covered it for Channel Four News, the funeral of Hannah Walker, the beautiful blonde girl killed in Compton.

The other photo is from a local football game, with an inset profile of star quarterback Chase Jackson.

He is whispering, "…I found him…I found you, dear boy…"

From the Author

The most commonly asked question I get is…
How many books will there be in the Outlaw series?

Here's your answer:
Chase's entire adventure will last eight books. (Maybe nine. But I think I can wrap it up in eight.) However, after Book Four the story will look dramatically different. The first four books are a mini-series within the overall story. Books Five and Six will be a miniseries. And Seven and Eight will be a miniseries. I might even label them differently.

That sounds confusing. Think of the Star Wars movies. There will be nine total movies in the Star Wars story arc, but there are three distinct trilogies within those nine.

Same with the Outlaw series.
The Outlaw is the star of the show. But it's going to be a wild ride.

I will try to deliver two books a year until the story is done (and maybe even a few tangential short stories). Waiting a decade on one series is the worst.

Thanks for reading.

Text me and let me know what you think.
(260) 673-5450
Leave a review where you bought it. Pleeeeeeease.

Find The Outlaw on Facebook
Find me on Twitter or Instagram

Many thanks to everyone involved
    - artists (Anne Pierson, Mike Corley, Jeff Brown, Nimesh Niyomal)
    - test readers (Sarah, Liz, Becky, Will, Anne, and Debbie [twice!])
    - formatting (Polgarus Studio)

49432759R00208

Made in the USA
San Bernardino, CA
25 May 2017